Praise for Valerie Bowman and

Secrets of a Runaway Bride

"A sexy, quirky, altogether fun read, Valerie Bowman's *Secrets of a Runaway Bride* is everything a romance should be. Block out a few hours for this one . . . once you start reading, you won't be able to stop!"
—*New York Times* bestselling author Sarah MacLean

"Valerie Bowman pens fabulous, sexy tales—it's no secret she's a Regency author to watch!"
—*USA Today* bestselling author Kieran Kramer

Secrets of a Wedding Night

"The most charming and clever debut I've read in years! With her sparkling dialogue, vivid characters, and self-assured writing style, Valerie Bowman has instantly established herself as a romance author with widespread appeal. This engaging and sweetly romantic story is just too delightful to miss."
—*New York Times* bestselling author Lisa Kleypas

"Clever, fun, and fantastic!"
—*New York Times* bestselling author Suzanne Enoch

"Ms. Bowman is quite the tease. How I love a good society scandal. The hero is absolutely yummy!"
—Donna MacMeans

MORE . . .

ALSO BY VALERIE BOWMAN

Secrets of a Wedding Night

Secrets of a Runaway Bride

VALERIE BOWMAN

St. Martin's Paperbacks

This is a work of fiction. All of the characters, organizations, and events portrayed in this novel are either products of the author's imagination or are used fictitiously.

SECRETS OF A RUNAWAY BRIDE

For information address St. Martin's Press, 175 Fifth Avenue, New York, NY 10010.

ISBN: 978-1-250-00896-1

Printed in the United States of America

St. Martin's Paperbacks edition / April 2013

St. Martin's Paperbacks are published by St. Martin's Press, 175 Fifth Avenue, New York, NY 10010.

10 9 8 7 6 5 4 3 2 1

For Marcus,
for being the one.
With all my love.

CHAPTER 1

London, Late September 1816

Annie Andrews was halfway up the side of Arthur Eggleston's town house—scaling an oh-so-convenient and strong ivy vine—when the telltale clip-clop of a horse's hooves stopped her. She squeezed her eyes shut. Oh, this was *not* good.

Despite the fact that she was in the alley at the back of the house and it was dark as pitch, she'd just been discovered. She knew it.

Please let it be a servant.

But even as she wished it, she knew it couldn't be. A servant in the alley on horseback? No.

And the odds of it being Aunt Clarissa were decidedly low as well. Annie had ensured that lady had been well into her cups and asleep before she'd even attempted tonight's little escapade. Besides, Aunt Clarissa was horribly frightened of horses.

Annie bit her lip. Then she slowly turned her head.

She gulped.

It was worse than a servant. Much worse.

"Lost?" The arrogant male voice pierced the cool night air.

Jordan Holloway, the Earl of Ashbourne, swung his leg over his saddle and dismounted.

Oh, drat. There was absolutely no plausible way to explain this. Annie lifted her chin in an attempt to retain her dignity. As much as one could when one was clinging precariously to a vine.

The moon peeked from behind the clouds, casting a bit of its glow upon the scene as Lord Ashbourne strode up the steps and stood regarding her, his arms crossed over his chest. He leaned back against the stone balustrade, crossed his booted feet negligently at the ankles, and watched her with a mocking look on his oh-so-handsome—too handsome if you asked her—face. The man was easily two inches over six feet tall, possessed broad shoulders, narrow hips, a straight nose, dark slashes for brows, dark, ruffled hair, and the most unusual knowing gray eyes.

"If it isn't the runaway bride." He grinned. "What are you up to this time, Miss Andrews?"

Annie gritted her teeth. She hated it when Lord Ashbourne called her by that ridiculous name. The runaway bride. Hrmph. As the closest friend of her new brother-in-law, Lord Ashbourne had just so happened to have been involved in coming after her following an unfortunate incident in which she'd run away to Gretna Green with Arthur last spring. But that had been months ago and things were different now. Ahem, present circumstances notwithstanding. And it was so like Lord Ashbourne to mock her while she wasn't in a position to kick him or at the very least give him a condemning glare. It was exceedingly difficult to conjure condemnation while perched on a plant.

Her palms sweaty, Annie tightened her hold on the vine and summoned what indignation she could muster. "I don't see how it's any of your business." But even as she said the words she knew how ludicrous they were. "How did you even know I was here?"

"Let's say I made an educated guess. But, before I assist you in removing yourself from this ridiculous . . . situation," he drawled. "I insist you tell me why, exactly, you're doing this."

Annie blew an errant leaf away from her mouth. "I don't require your help, Lord Ashbourne. I'm quite capable—" She glanced down. It was at least a five-foot drop to the porch below. She'd just have to jump. She tugged away from the vine, but discovered, to her dismay, that the hem of her gown was snagged upon the brambles.

Lord Ashbourne shook his head. "Seriously, Miss Andrews, why?"

She expelled her breath, still trying to retain a modicum of dignity. Oh very well. Some explanation was obviously in order. "It's not as bad as it looks. I merely wanted to get Arthur's attention. I planned to toss a rock at his window and—"

"A note sent round to his door would not suffice?" Lord Ashbourne's mocking tone did not waver.

Annie clenched her jaw. Why, oh, why was she always at her very worst when Lord Ashbourne appeared? It was quite a phenomenon, actually.

"And Aunt Clarissa?" Lord Ashbourne continued. "She's asleep, is she not? After imbibing a good bit of port?"

Annie bit her lip. "Sherry." As companions went, Aunt Clarissa was a great deal of fun, but an apt chaperone she was not. The woman was overly fond of spirits, in a variety of forms.

"As I suspected. Very well, there's no help for it." Lord Ashbourne uncrossed his ankles and took a step toward her, lifting his arms to pluck her from the vine like a foolish little grape.

Just then, the back door opened. A ray of candlelight splashed across the porch. Annie's eyes flashed wide. Pure terror pounded in her chest.

She held her breath. Who had discovered her? Please don't let it be—

Lord Ashbourne didn't wait. He quickly grabbed her by the waist and pulled. She gave a small yelp before tumbling into his arms and sliding down the front of him, her body pressed to his.

And that's how Annie came to be completely tangled in Lord Ashbourne's arms when Arthur Eggleston, the man Annie loved, the man Annie intended to marry, strode onto his back stoop.

Jordan's first instinct was to set Miss Andrews's delicate form on the porch and break their contact.

She was a nineteen-year-old troublemaker with a penchant for putting her reputation at risk. The little baggage had proven to be nothing but trouble since her sister, Lily, and his closest friend, Devon, had left for the Continent on their honeymoon trip. They'd both begged Jordan to keep an eye on the chit. Miss Andrews, it seemed, required more than one chaperone, especially since their closest female relative and only suitable companion, Devon's eccentric aunt Clarissa, was overly fond of the bottle.

Jordan had spent the past sennight following Miss Andrews around and ensuring she was not making a fool of herself in her dogged pursuit of that sop Arthur Eggleston. But it seemed the closer Jordan watched her, the more outrageous her antics became, culminating in this particularly egregious bit of madness here this evening.

She was about five feet four, with a mass of wide brown curls, an impertinent nose, warm dark eyes, and a penchant for trouble. "Spitfire" was the word that readily came to mind. And while Jordan was mentally counting the days until Lily and Devon returned to properly see to the girl themselves, he had to admit to a sort of reluctant admiration for Annie. Things were never dull when Miss Andrews was involved. That much he would allow.

At the moment, her lithe body pressed against his was making him feel things he shouldn't, however. He needed to disentangle her from his arms. Immediately.

Eggleston cleared his throat and sanity returned to Jordan's mind with a vengeance. He quickly plucked Miss Andrews's arms from around his neck and let her slide down the length of him until she was standing on the porch next to him, a chagrined look on her pretty face.

Arms crossed over his chest, Eggleston glanced between them, a mildly perturbed expression on his face. "Miss Andrews, Lord Ashbourne. What is the meaning of this?"

Annie backed away from Jordan quickly, her breath coming in short pants. She snatched her arms behind her back and didn't meet his eyes. "Arthur. We were just . . ." Annie bit her lip. That was her tell. Jordan had played enough hands of cards to learn a person's give-away and the past week spent in Miss Andrews's company had informed him that when she was up to no good, she nibbled her pink lips with her perfect white teeth. It was a bit endearing, actually. And extremely convenient for him.

She glanced away. Her other tell. "That is to say . . . I'd come over to . . ." She stopped, words obviously failing her.

"Anne," Eggleston said, giving her a stern stare. "For your sake and the sake of your reputation, I shall pretend I didn't see this."

Jordan fought the urge to roll his eyes. First of all, this was the same man who'd nearly destroyed Annie's reputation last spring. His concern now was a bit too little too late for Jordan's taste. Secondly, if Annie had been Jordan's potential fiancée and he'd just caught her in the arms of another man, he'd be pounding the bloke into a pulp about now. But this dolt obviously wasn't jealous enough even to take a swing at him. Probably better for Eggleston's sake, of course, but leave it to Arthur Eggleston to be little more than inquisitive.

Annie swallowed. "Yes, Arthur. Quite right. It won't happen again."

"I'm glad to hear it. Now, may I escort you home?" Eggleston asked Annie, giving Jordan a once-over.

"No need. I was just about to escort her myself, Eggleston," Jordan replied with a smirk.

Annie nodded. "Yes, I'll be quite fine."

"Very well," Eggleston continued, looking down his nose at the both of them. "Then I shall call upon you tomorrow, Anne, for our usual afternoon ride in the park."

Annie bit her lip. "Yes. I should like that very much."

"Good evening." Arthur turned on his heel, reentered the house, and shut the door with a resounding crack.

The whoosh of air from the door tousled Annie's curls. She plunked her hands on her hips and glared at the door, completely ignoring Jordan. "He didn't seem a bit jealous, did he? Next time I shall just have to kiss you."

CHAPTER 2

Lord Ashbourne nearly dragged Annie down the street to her own back porch. He'd return for his mount later. Thankfully, Colton's town house wasn't far. He jerked open the back door, yanked her into the darkened kitchens, and spun her away from him.

Annie wrapped her arms around her middle. Now that she was alone with Lord Ashbourne again, she wanted to sink through the floor. That comment about kissing him had merely flown from her mouth. As things often did. But she hadn't meant it . . . really. Though making Arthur jealous was an idea worth exploring. She glanced up hesitantly at Lord Ashbourne.

She was always an idiot in the earl's presence. Always. And to make matters worse, he seemed to be present a great deal more often of late.

"Just what the hell do you think you're doing?" Lord Ashbourne demanded, brushing the dust from the sleeves of his midnight-blue topcoat. "Have you any idea what that incident could have done to your reputation?"

Annie straightened her shoulders and lifted her chin.

Two actions she often seemed compelled to do in Lord Ashbourne's company. "Not that I expect you to believe me, but I really hadn't any intention of actually climbing inside Arthur's window."

Lord Ashbourne gave her a dubious look. "I'm glad to hear that."

"That would be *much* too scandalous," she continued. "And despite my sister's insistence, I *do* have a care for my reputation."

Lord Ashbourne narrowed his eyes on her. "Let me see if I have this right. You believe climbing up the side of a house in the middle of the night consists of having a care for your reputation?"

She tossed her hands in the air. "I didn't expect to get caught, obviously."

"I see. But that hardly explains why you were climbing up the shrubbery in the first place."

Annie folded her hands serenely. "As you know, Arthur and I are courting and—"

Lord Ashbourne put up his palm to stop her. "Courting? Is that what you call it? What I know is that you have been making a spectacle of yourself chasing Eggleston around while he demonstrates remarkably little interest."

Annie swallowed. That hurt. But she wasn't about to allow the arrogant Lord Ashbourne to see it. "I don't expect you to understand, Lord Ashbourne, but Arthur and I are in love."

"Forgive me for pointing it out, Miss Andrews, but I daresay if Mr. Eggleston returned your affections, you wouldn't be forced to attract his attention by climbing up the side of his house. You're not Romeo. And if anyone should be doing insane things like scaling the side of a town house, it's him, not you. If anyone other than Eggleston had been the one to see that, you'd be an outcast by now."

Annie winced. Why did Lord Ashbourne have to make so many good points? "I admit, it was poorly done. I should have thought about it more, before I . . ." She glanced down at the tips of her slippers, convinced her face was an outrageous shade of pink by now. "It's just that Arthur hasn't quite come up to scratch the way I'd hoped he would and . . ." Oh, this explanation was hopelessly inadequate. She might as well just stop talking.

Lord Ashbourne leaned a hand against the countertop and regarded her as if he were speaking to an idiot. "You don't see anything wrong with that? If Eggleston loves you, why would you need to make a fool of yourself over him?"

The "fool" part hurt too. Annie clenched her jaw. Last spring, Arthur had been eager to marry her. Yes, it was true that the bit about her having no dowry had become public knowledge and his affections had cooled temporarily. But that had been because of his father's misgivings, not Arthur's. They'd found each other again and run off to Gretna Green unsuccessfully.

Now, months later, she had an indecently large dowry settled upon her, thanks to her new brother-in-law, but Arthur appeared to be taking his time. He escorted her on a ride through the park every afternoon and called upon her, but he'd made no move to offer for her formally. Annie was convinced it was a combination of his fear of Lord Colton, who obviously disapproved of him, and his desire to please his own father, who obviously disapproved of her. And it didn't help matters that Arthur spent an inordinate amount of time escorting his spinster sister to Society events. Sigh.

The problem was, Arthur tended to listen to whomever he was with at the moment, and whenever Annie had convinced him that they should marry, he'd return home and speak with his father, and his father would convince him to keep his options open. Arthur was only two and twenty, after all, and didn't need to settle down so quickly. It was all Annie could do to dissuade Arthur from listening to his father.

But despite all of that, Arthur loved her. She knew it. He'd told her so. He was the only man who'd ever paid her so much attention, ever told her she was lovely, ever thought of her as something more than just a good friend. And she wasn't about to let go of him.

Besides, Lord Ashbourne couldn't possibly understand. The man could get any woman in the country— well, any woman but *her*—with a crook of his handsome finger. He knew nothing about the rigors of the marriage mart or her relationship with Arthur.

Very well. That was not *entirely* true. In addition to tonight's unfortunate incident, Lord Ashbourne did know *one* thing about her relationship with Mr. Eggleston. The one thing she desperately wished he didn't know. That she'd run away with him. Another sigh. Again, always an idiot in Lord Ashbourne's presence. With. Out. Fail.

Annie squeezed her hands together. "I'm very sorry for any inconvenience I've caused you, Lord Ashbourne, but you should know better than anyone that Mr. Eggleston is indeed interested."

He reached out and plucked a leaf from her hair. "If you're referring to your ill-advised trip to Gretna Green last spring, yes, I remember."

Annie cringed. Oh, now she was sure her face was bright pink. As pink as the trim on her favorite bonnet.

Lord Ashbourne pushed his hat firmly atop his head. "I'm leaving now. No damage was done, thank God, but if something like this happens again, I'll be forced to inform Aunt Clarissa."

Annie hid her smile. Aunt Clarissa could barely ensure her shoes were on the correct feet, let alone keep Annie from doing exactly as she pleased.

Lord Ashbourne pulled open the back door and tossed over his shoulder, "Miss Andrews, please. Have a care for your reputation. If not for your own sake, for your sister's."

"I will consider everything you've said, my lord," Annie replied. No, she wouldn't. But she nodded as she watched him go. Then she shut the door behind him, locked it, and pressed her back against it. She let out a long breath. Just like Lily, Lord Ashbourne didn't understand. It wasn't that Annie didn't have a care for her reputation. She simply prized following her heart over silly things like Society rules and strictures.

She peeped out the window to see Lord Ashbourne swing up onto his mount. She narrowed her eyes and tapped a finger against her cheek. Perhaps it was no coincidence that Lord Ashbourne happened to be wherever she was of late. She might just have to take a bit more care to not be such a ninny in his company. The man was . . . imposing. She touched her fingertips to her waist where his strong hands had lingered minutes earlier. A shudder coursed through her.

Lord Ashbourne was a famous rakehell, a dashing rogue, a confirmed bachelor, and her brother-in-law's oldest and closest friend. He ran with a fast set and did as he pleased. He was handsome, charming, and completely the opposite of what Annie was looking for in a mate.

But, oh my, being pressed against him when he'd pulled her from the vine had been . . . delicious.

CHAPTER 3

"Arthur! Stop the coach!"

Arthur's handsome blond head swiveled around. Obligingly, he pulled on the reins, braced his booted feet against the wooden slabs, and yelled, "Whoa!"

The phaeton jerked to a skidding halt, bumping along the gravel path in Hyde Park and coming to a rest with a solid thud.

"Why did we stop?" he asked, breathing a bit heavily.

One hand fixed atop her bonnet, Annie gestured frantically with the other toward the bushes they'd just passed on their afternoon ride through the park. "I saw a fox."

"A fox?" Arthur's eyes were wide. He shook his head. "I hardly think a fox is something we ought to—"

"Shh." Annie pressed a finger to her lips. "We mustn't scare the poor creature."

Sitting up straight, she pulled her kid gloves tight. Thankfully, Arthur hadn't mentioned her episode with Lord Ashbourne last night. He seemed quite content to pretend it had never happened, and for that she was immensely thankful. She'd spent the better part of the hour they'd been out riding attempting to get Arthur to kiss her. Having failed miserably, she had let her attention wander and she'd caught a glimpse of bright red fur peeking from the bushes as they'd dashed past.

Craning her neck, Annie kept her eyes trained on the little fox she'd seen crouched in the hedges several paces away. A cluster of berries marked the small animal's spot.

Annie began to climb down the side of the coach.

Arthur placed a hand on her shoulder to stop her. "Here, now. Do you really think you ought to—"

Annie slipped out from under his hand and hopped to the ground. "He may be hurt, Arthur. I must see to him."

Looking chagrined, Arthur snapped his mouth shut and watched as Annie tiptoed through the grass toward the hedgerow. He clucked to the horses, who, no doubt alert to the scent of the fox, twitched their ears and flared their nostrils.

When she was close enough, Annie bent down, flicked up her skirts, and crawled on her hands and knees on the grass toward the fox. Its little whiskered head peeped out from behind the berries and tilted inquisitively to the side.

Annie eyed the fox carefully. She'd rescued enough strays in her time to know when one was particularly sick or rabid, and this animal looked perfectly healthy. And he was just a baby too. Her brow wrinkled. A baby who didn't seem to be frightened by a human. Odd.

Just then, a glint of sunlight glanced off a bit of metal and the fox limped forward, dragging a small trap that was secured to his tiny paw. Annie sucked in her breath and turned her head back toward the coach. "Oh, Arthur, just as I suspected. He is hurt."

Facing the tiny animal again, she slowly tugged off

her glove, cupped her palm, and presented it to the fox to show him she meant no harm. "You poor little thing. Let me help you, darling."

She eyed the trap carefully. It was somewhat rusty. Perhaps merely prying the prongs apart would do the trick. She bent low, her hands braced on the soft earth to get a good look at the contraption.

On the other hand, forcing the jaws open might only serve to hurt the little fox's paw even more. She snapped her fingers. "A hairpin. Of course." She plucked a pin from the back of her coiffure, little caring that one unruly dark curl bounced free, and carefully inserted the pin into the hinge on the side of the trap. Her brow furrowed, she poked out her tongue, intent on her work.

She pushed the pin into the hinge as far as it would go, then slowly twisted it back and forth.

Sweat beaded on her forehead. The fox stared at her dolefully, his little sherry-colored eyes blinking. "Don't worry, dear. I'll get it. I'll get—"

The hinge popped open with a click. The fox leaped backward, then froze, staring at her. His ears perked and his whiskers twitched. He licked his paw.

Annie edged closer. The fox eyed her.

She edged forward again. The fox's eyes darted back and forth.

She reached out a hand. Slowly. Slowly.

The fox sniffed at her.

Finally, Annie scooted close enough to scoop the tiny fox into her arms, careful not to touch his sore paw. At first he tried to dart away, but she petted him softly and cooed to him. Finally, he settled into her arms, allowing her to hold him.

She stood up and turned back toward the coach. "I have him," she called cheerfully to Arthur. "But the poor thing's paw was caught in a trap. Who would do such a thing? And in a public park, where children might stumble upon it and get hurt too."

"Who indeed?" Arthur shook his head, an inscrutable look on his face.

She made her way back to the coach with the fox cradled in her arms.

Arthur had descended from the coach and stood ready to help her back up. "You don't intend to keep that thing, do you?"

Annie blinked at him. "I intend to take him home and treat his paw. I have a recipe for a poultice for just such occasions. That and a bandage will help it to heal much more quickly."

Arthur frowned. "Do you really think that wise?"

"What do you mean?"

Arthur plunked a hand on his hip. "Taking a wild animal into your home is hardly something propriety dictates."

Annie glanced down at the fox. "But he"—she turned the animal over carefully and glanced down—"yes, *he* needs help."

Arthur gave her a doubtful look. He assisted her back into her seat, the fox cradled in her arms. "I don't know that I recommend it. Not to mention a fox like that should be on the run from a pack of hounds, not having his paw wrapped in a London town house."

Annie's mouth fell open. "Hunted? You cannot be serious, Arthur. Please tell me you don't condone that awful sport."

Arthur settled back into the seat next to her and shifted his eyes away uncomfortably. "Very well. Take him home if you will."

Annie straightened her shoulders and nodded. "Thank you. That's exactly what I intend to do." She cuddled the baby fox, trying to get a better look at his sore paw.

Arthur laughed. "Now that you've got the fox to worry about, at least you won't be so intent upon asking me for a chance to take the reins."

He clucked to the horses again and headed for the park's entrance, while Annie contemplated the afternoon's turn of events. It was true. After the kissing bit had failed, Annie had turned her attentions to convincing Arthur to allow her to drive his father's phaeton. He'd said no. Again. Annie sighed. Arthur was under the mistaken impression that she didn't know how to drive. The fact was, the groomsmen at her family's country house had spent hours teaching her when she was a girl. Her parents had always been much more concerned with Lily and her schooling, her beauty, her future prospects. They'd left their younger daughter to become a complete tomboy. And that's exactly what she'd done. Every boy she'd ever met treated her like an unruly friend. That's why she loved Arthur so. He'd been the first man who'd ever paid a compliment to her beauty. The first man to ever treat her like a *girl*. But that meant Arthur didn't realize what she was capable of, either. If she were only given a chance to drive, their afternoon outings wouldn't be a *complete* waste. Though today, at least, she'd saved a fox.

"Since you brought it up, Arthur, won't you allow me to drive when we go riding tomorrow? I'm really quite—"

He puffed up his chest. "We've discussed this, Anne.

A team like this is hardly something just anyone can handle."

Annie smiled wanly and glanced away. Arthur was perfectly right; it *wasn't* something just anyone could handle. Arthur wasn't doing a particularly good job of it at the moment. She winced. In fact, the placement of his hands on the reins was all wrong. But it would hardly be polite of her to point it out. The second son of a baron, Arthur was tall, blond, and had the blue eyes of an angel. It wasn't his fault that driving wasn't quite his forte.

"Besides," Arthur added, "I'd hate to see you get hurt."

Annie smiled at that. There was no point in arguing with him and he'd just said the sweetest thing. "I'm sure you're right, Arthur. This has been such a lovely afternoon." Annie glanced up and the smile drained from her face. "Oh, confound it. Not him *again*."

Arthur's head snapped up. "Not *who* again?"

Annie wrinkled her nose and shook her head, her curls bouncing along her cheeks. "Lord Ashbourne." She nodded to the lone horseman who approached. "He's coming this way."

Drat. She wanted to disappear. After last night's incident, she'd been hoping she wouldn't see Lord Ashbourne again for . . . ever. But just as he had been the last three afternoons, Lord Ashbourne was in the park, crossing her path.

"Tomorrow we must take a different route," she mumbled.

Arthur gave her a skeptical glance. "What's your quarrel with the Earl of Ashbourne? I hate to be indelicate but you didn't seem that interested in eluding him last night."

Annie pressed her lips together. She supposed she deserved that last bit. "Last night I came over to your house to see you and he just . . . appeared. And now here he is. I'm beginning to think he's following me."

"Following you?" Arthur chuckled. "Anne, with all due respect, half of London drives through the park in the afternoon. Lord Ashbourne is no different."

"You don't think it more than mere coincidence that he just happened to encounter us each day this week?"

Arthur shook his head. "I daresay we've seen Miss Abshire and the Coxes each day too."

Annie sighed. Arthur could be so naïve. Miss Abshire and the Coxes weren't following her; Lord Ashbourne was.

"Do you dislike him?" Arthur asked.

Annie contemplated the question for a moment. Ashbourne was a bit arrogant, a little judgmental, and he'd been keeping far too close an eye on her since Lily and Devon had been away. Not to mention she usually found herself completely embarrassed in the earl's illustrious presence. But she wasn't about to expound on that part to Arthur. Perhaps she might like Lord Ashbourne a bit more too if he were to stop referring to her as "the runaway bride," she thought with a smirk. "I wouldn't say I dislike him . . . exactly," she hedged.

She glanced down at her lap. Oh bother. How would she ever explain her fox to the earl? Just perfect. Something else for Lord Debonair to mock.

"There must be something redeeming about him if Lord Colton chooses to be his friend," Arthur was saying.

"If you say so. Look lively." Annie pasted a smile on her face as Ashbourne's black gelding clipped to a stop beside them. Lord Ashbourne tipped his hat. "Miss Andrews. Mr. Eggleston. Good afternoon." He eyed Annie closely. "I trust you survived your climbing adventure last night?"

Oh, of course the man would have to mention her humiliation. No doubt a "runaway bride" comment was not far behind. She braced herself. "It *was* a good afternoon," she replied brightly, settling the fox on her lap. Ooh, perhaps she should inform Lord Ashbourne that the fox might be rabid. That might make him leave.

Ashbourne's smile widened. He flashed his perfect white teeth. "What have you there?" He nodded toward her fox.

As usual, Annie lifted her chin and straightened her shoulders. "We just found this poor boy in the bushes. His paw was caught in a trap."

Lord Ashbourne's face turned into a scowl. "What idiot set a trap? He'll need a poultice and a bandage. May I help you procure those items?"

Annie eyed him cautiously. How did Lord Ashbourne know so much about it? And very well, he'd surprised her with his concern. It was nice of him to offer, but it didn't change the fact that the man seemed determined to thwart her ambitions of late. In addition to his appearance last night, he'd interrupted her potential trysts with Arthur Eggleston all week long. The least he could do was be understanding about her fox.

"No, thank you, Lord Ashbourne. I have everything I need at home . . . which is where Arthur and I were just going." She nodded to Arthur, hoping he'd read her thoughts and set the coach into motion again.

He did not.

Sigh.

Lord Ashbourne inclined his head. "I'm disappointed

to see, Miss Andrews, that you are not driving the coach today. Did I mistake my guess or have you not been intent upon asking Mr. Eggleston if you could take the reins?"

Was he was eavesdropping now too? "Indeed that's true, Lord Ashbourne. But Arthur wasn't up to it today."

Lord Ashbourne flashed her a smile that her friend Frances—who was completely smitten with the earl—would say made her weak in the knees. Very well, the rogue was *very* handsome. She would give him that. As handsome as he was troublesome.

"A shame, really," Lord Ashbourne said. "I should very much like to witness your skill at driving."

Annie nodded. "It's impressive to be sure, my lord." Oh, what naughtiness had made her say such a thing? She usually wasn't such a braggart but there was something about Lord Ashbourne that brought out her competitive side.

Lord Ashbourne's eyebrows rose. Was that an impressed look upon his face? "I shall take your word for it," he said. "I do hope my arrival hasn't ruined your day, Miss Andrews."

Annie pinned her most inauthentic smile to her face. "Not at all, Lord Ashbourne. Indeed, I look forward to your visit *every* day. I was just telling Arthur, it's a wonder we hadn't run into you before now."

Their eyes met. Neither smile faltered.

Eggleston cleared his throat and shifted in his seat. "Yes. Well. What are you up to today, Ashbourne?"

Lord Ashbourne inclined his head toward Annie. "Actually, I've come to ask you if you'll be so kind as to accompany me to the Lindworths' ball tonight, Miss Andrews."

Annie snapped her mouth shut. Despite the fact that

the London Season had been over for months, the Lindworths were hosting an autumn ball. Annie had spent the better part of three days trying to get Arthur to invite her to the grand affair. Tried and failed.

"That is, unless you already have an invitation," Lord Ashbourne continued, blinking at her innocently. A man shouldn't be allowed to have such long, lovely eyelashes.

"Well, I . . ." Of course this moment would be the ideal opportunity for Arthur to invite her to the ball. She turned her head and looked at Arthur expectantly. Waiting. She briefly considered elbowing him but thought better of it. She stroked the fox.

Arthur turned to her, a bright smile on his face. "Why, yes, yes of course." Annie's heart stopped beating. Oh, finally she would have her invitation in only a matter of seconds.

Five. Four. Three. Two. One.

"Yes," Arthur repeated. "You should attend the ball with Lord Ashbourne. I am escorting my sister there and would so enjoy seeing you both."

Annie's heart sank. "Oh, I—" She scrunched up her nose and dared a glance at Lord Ashbourne. He was wearing his most mocking expression. It was one she knew well. Blast it.

Annie cuddled the fox and contemplated the matter. She had two choices. She could either turn Lord Ashbourne down, a slight he richly deserved, and stay home tonight curled upon the settee with her fox, wondering which young ladies were dancing with Arthur, or she could accept Ashbourne's blasted invitation and gain entry into one of the most talked-about events of the year.

Annie straightened her shoulders again. The Annie Andrews of six months ago would have asked Arthur to take her with him, would have begged him possibly, but this Annie—no, Anne—the older, more mature Miss Andrews, was forcing herself to behave with a bit more dignity, the incident of clinging to the vine on the side of his house last night notwithstanding.

Her jaw hurt from keeping her smile tight. She gave a curt nod. She couldn't, just couldn't, allow Arthur to be at the Lindworths' ball without her. "Yes, thank you very much, Lord Ashbourne. I should love to attend the ball with you this evening."

CHAPTER 4

The poultice and the bandage worked wonders for the baby fox's paw. Though seeing to her little patient hadn't left Annie much time to prepare herself for the Lindworths' ball. No matter. It wasn't as if she were a great beauty. Annie wasn't like her sister. Men didn't stop and stare when she walked past. She didn't have a bevy of suitors lined up at the door waiting to court her or a constant supply of fresh flowers, sweets, and original poems.

Annie would simply toss on one of her new gowns and make do. Perhaps Arthur wouldn't notice that her hair was a mess of loosely bound curls and she smelled a bit like fox-paw poultice.

She laughed to herself at the thought and shook her head. Then she pulled a blanket over the sleeping fox. His bandaged paw stuck out like a bright white beacon from the pile of blankets she'd wrapped him in. She'd tucked him in a small basket and the tired little thing had fallen asleep almost immediately.

"There you are, you dear," she cooed. "You'll be back dashing through the woods in no time." She wagged her finger. "In fact, I think that's the perfect name for you. . . . Dash."

Mary, her maid, her old friend, came scurrying into the room, pushing the door shut behind her to a chorus of barks. "I swear Leo and Bandit have been circling outside this room all evening," she said, referring to Lily's two dogs, strays her sister had adopted through quite different circumstances. "Once they realize you've got a fox in here, I don't know what they'll do."

"No doubt they can smell him already," Annie replied. "They'll be fine." She glanced at Dash again to make sure the barking hadn't wakened him. "I just wanted to keep them away until Dash has a chance to rest. That poultice should help his paw right away."

Mary shook her head. "Miss Lily is going to return to quite a sight. A 'ouse with a dog, a raccoon, and a fox."

Annie laughed. Leo was a scruffy brown terrier. Bandit was a dog, of course, but they'd joked plenty of times that the little black, gray, and white animal looked just like the interesting animal the Americans called a raccoon. "Lily will understand. I couldn't let the poor thing fend for himself in the park with a sore paw."

Mary smiled and slowly shook her head. "Ye've always been a nurturer, Miss Annie, ever since ye was a little girl."

Annie sighed. Mary was one of the only people she allowed to call her Annie. Everyone else had been informed in no uncertain terms that Anne was her name now that she was old enough to have a come-out and be married.

And Mary was right. Annie was a nurturer. She'd always taken care of little animals that needed care. But her real dream, to become a wife and a mother, to nurture her own babies, was still only that, a dream, until she could get Arthur Eggleston to come up to scratch and convince Lord Colton to accept him, that was.

Ever since Annie and Lily's parents had died, Annie had lived with her sister, Lily, who'd been a widow. Their male cousin who'd taken over the estate and inherited their father's title was supposed to be her guardian, but he'd been more than happy to see Annie leave for the city to live with her sister. After Lily had married Lord Colton, he'd immediately seen to it that he took over her guardianship.

Annie had enjoyed her time with her sister. She looked up to Lily and adored her. But Annie wasn't a child anymore and Lily was a newlywed with a husband, a five-year-old stepson named Justin, and a new life of her own. She didn't need Annie lingering around any longer. Lily had more than done her duty to her sister and Annie wanted more than anything to marry, have a family, and allow Lily to relax and enjoy her new life. No longer worrying about her pesky younger sibling. The problem was, Lord Colton and Lily didn't seem particularly keen on Arthur. Partially, Annie knew, because they hadn't forgiven him for running off with her to Gretna Green, but there was more to it than that and Annie knew that these final weeks while Lily and Devon were off on their honeymoon trip would be crucial in getting Arthur to finally commit to her.

Annie stood up and shook out her skirts. She crossed over to the washbasin and scrubbed her hands with soap and water. Then she glanced at the clock on the mantel. "We must act quickly, Mary. Help me into a ball gown. Any one will do. Lord Ashbourne will be here any moment."

Mary's eyebrows shot up straight. "Lord Ashbourne?" She whistled. "Now that is a change o' pace. Since when does Lord Ashbourne escort you anywhere? Does Aunt Clarissa know about this?"

Annie turned to Mary. "Oh, don't look so curious," she said with a laugh. "I was out riding in the park today and Lord Ashbourne arrived, as usual, and invited me to the Lindworths'. And Aunt Clarissa is coming with us, of course."

Mary had scurried over to the wardrobe and was busily sorting through the gowns. "I take it yer Mr. Eggleston didn't ask ye first."

Annie let out a long sigh. "If he had, do you think I'd be attending with Lord Ashbourne?"

Mary emerged from the wardrobe with a pretty pink gown draped across her arm. "I don't know. Lord Ashbourne *is* one of the most eligible bachelors in London." She waggled her eyebrows.

With a smile, Annie tossed the towel she'd been using to dry her hands at Mary. The maid snatched it up with her free hand and laughed.

"Oh, just help me on with the gown," Annie said.

Mary bowed. "As ye wish, me lady."

The two had a jest about what a fine lady Annie was now. She'd come up in the world, to be sure, since her sister had married Lord Colton. Just a few short months ago, she'd been wearing the same three gowns repeatedly and had no accessories to speak of. The home of her brother-in-law, Devon Morgan, the Marquis of Colton, was luxuriously furnished and perfect in every particular. And Annie had been given carte blanche to purchase a new wardrobe. Her generous brother-in-law had spared no expense.

Mary helped Annie into the soft pink gown and tied the wide white sash around her back. New white kid slippers, matching gloves, and an adorable bonnet with a bit of pink velvet trim completed her ensemble. Of course, the entire effect would go completely to waste on Jordan Holloway. Why, the man might as well be her brother. Her exceedingly annoying older brother. Her exceedingly annoying older brother . . . whose hard muscles she had felt a bit too closely last night. She shook her head.

"Is it getting hot in here of a sudden, Mary?"

Mary's brow furrowed. "Not that I've noticed, me lady."

"No matter." Annie waved her hand in the air. She glanced down at her clothing and wrinkled her nose. Even wearing such fine clothes, she was still just Annie. Her dark brown eyes were perfectly fine, but they were just plain brown. Her dark brown curls were a mess and had only recently begun to show some promise. She'd spent a lifetime being an unimportant younger daughter and a great friend. She was not one to make a man's head turn. No one's but Arthur's, that is.

Annie moved toward the windows and glanced down from her second-story bedroom. The street below was empty. "Lord Ashbourne's not here yet."

Attempting to secure a jeweled comb in Annie's coiffure, Mary nodded toward the clock on the mantelpiece across the room. "'Tis not yet the hour. He isn't late."

Annie expectantly looked out the window again, willing Lord Ashbourne's coach to appear. "I must be the only young lady in history who is ready *before* her escort arrives. I can't help it. Primping and preening simply don't interest me."

"Let me worry about that, me lady," Mary said, fastening a string of pearls around Annie's neck.

Mary shuffled into the wardrobe humming to herself, and Annie watched her go. The maid was always happy lately. While she still suffered from an unfortunate memory problem, Mary too had come up in the world. She was now a servant in a grand town house of a marquis. She and Evans, the sisters' former butler, were now ensconced in the magnificent home. They had smart uniforms and they both were quite proud of themselves. Though the butler actually was more of an esteemed overseer, an assistant to the marquis's fine butler. But with Evans's penchant for nodding off at the most inconvenient of times, he was happy to have the pressure of perfection removed. He was content to spend his days scurrying about after Devon's butler, Nicholls, agreeing with him on nearly every count, and taking naps whenever possible.

"I do hope Lord Ashbourne arrives soon," Annie called.

Mary's singsong voice floated from the wardrobe. "Seems ye're in quite the 'urry tonight."

Annie traced the violet coverlet atop her bed with her fingertip. "I do not want to leave Arthur alone at the ball."

Mary stuck her head out of the wardrobe. "Ye don't trust 'im? I mean, him." Since arriving at Lord Colton's home, Mary had been doing her best to pronounce her *h*'s. "It wouldn't do," she often said, "for a marquis to employ such a common maid in his home." "His home," of course, was pronounced with much care.

"I trust Arthur," Annie said, picking a bit of lint from her skirts. "It's the other young ladies whom I don't trust."

"Now don't ye think there is something wrong with that?" Mary asked. "It seems to me that yer Mr. Eggleston isn't—"

Annie gave the maid a pleading look. "Oh, not you too, Mary. Since Lily's been on holiday, I thought I'd have a reprieve from the daily speech about how I ought to stop pining after Arthur. I thought you were on my side. Besides, I don't have a choice. I must act quickly. As soon as Lily and Devon return from the Continent, they intend to remove us all to the country until Christmas. With Justin being tutored at Colton House, they'll be eager to see him. We'll be in Surrey for months. I won't even see Arthur until then unless I can convince him to offer for me first."

Of course Annie had studiously avoided mentioning last night's escapade to Mary. The less the maid knew, and would be tempted to repeat to Lily, the better. If she remembered it, that was.

"But ye can't blame yer sister for being worried about the match," Mary replied. "Seems ta me yer Mr. Eggleston should 'ave offered for ye long before now."

"Arthur's just waiting for the perfect time," Annie explained. "His father was very aggrieved with him when he found out we went to Gretna. He promised his father he'd wait and think about things sensibly."

"It's been six months," Mary pointed out.

"Don't I know it," Annie mumbled.

In the past few weeks, she had become positively determined to bring Arthur up to scratch quickly. Hence her unfortunate little incident last night. Tonight she just might be forced to do something even more outrageous to garner his attention.

The rattle of carriage wheels snapped Annie from her

reverie, and she spun around to face the window. There it was, the grand coach with the deep blue crest and gold lettering of the Earl of Ashbourne. Four finely matched black horses pulled the conveyance. His lordship had arrived.

Annie bit her lip. Lord Ashbourne's coach was much more elegant than the little one Arthur's father allowed him to borrow. She'd feel positively out of place in such a magnificent vehicle. Why, it was as fine as Lord Colton's, and she hadn't become used to riding in that one yet.

Annie checked her reflection in the looking glass, pushed a stray curl into place as best she could, and tugged on her gloves more tightly. "Good night, Mary," she called, hurrying out of the bedchamber. She'd only gotten a few paces away before she hastily recalled her reticule and flew back into her room to snatch it from the dressing table.

Mary plunked her hands on her hips. "Aren't you the same young lady who recently told me you mustn't appear too eager when a man comes to call?"

Annie slipped the reticule's strap over her wrist. "Oh, but this isn't a man," she said, patting the maid on the cheek. "This is Lord Ashbourne."

"The most eligible bachelor in London," Mary called in a singsong voice.

"The most aggravating bachelor in London," Annie sang back. She stopped for a moment and a small laugh escaped her lips. "Besides, a bachelor he may be, but he's about as eligible as the Prince Regent. Lord Ashbourne has said a hundred times he never plans to marry. Now keep an eye on Dash and don't wait up." Annie blew a kiss to Mary and rushed from the room.

Hoisting her skirts with one hand, Annie clutched the

balustrade with the other to keep from falling. As she rounded the landing, however, she forced herself to take a deep breath and count to five. She was nineteen now, after all. She must act with grace and decorum. She was Anne now, no longer Annie, no matter how many times she had to correct everyone. No matter how often she reminded them to use her new name. No matter how often she had to correct herself, even.

Ashbourne's booming voice addressed the exceedingly staid Nicholls. Annie willed herself to push her shoulders back and descend the last several stairs more slowly.

As soon as she came into view, Ashbourne's head snapped up to look at her and a grin spread across his face.

"You were running, weren't you?" he asked.

She bit her lip to stifle her horrified laugh. "What? No!"

"Yes you were." He slapped his leather gloves against his thigh. "I can tell. Your cheeks are bright pink. And you aren't known as the runaway bride for nothing." He grinned at her.

Annie's free hand flew to her cheeks. Ooh, how she wished she could will away the telltale pink that spread across her face whenever she was anxious. Her hand moved to her hair. Only lately had the crazy ringlets of her youth been replaced by wide, luxurious dark curls that flowed down her shoulders and back. Hair that had always been scattered was now enviable. Arthur had remarked upon its beauty on more than one occasion. Of course she had her hair up tonight. But she always let a few loose curls out to frame her face.

Her cheeks might be slightly pink, but her hair was

perfectly in place. Lord Ashbourne was just teasing her. As usual. It seemed to be his favorite sport of late.

"If I was running," she said, lightly tugging on the delicate edges of her gloves, "and I'm not saying I was, mind you, it is only because I am eager to get to the ball."

He gave her a mock-sad look. "You mean it's not because you're eager to spend time in *my* company?"

She came to stand by his side with a long-suffering sigh. "You cannot blame me. You've done nothing but cause me trouble at every turn ever since Lily and Devon left town."

Oh, perhaps she shouldn't have said that, given the events of last night. Why was she forever saying and doing things without thinking about them first? Particularly in Lord Ashbourne's presence?

Thankfully, the stately butler appeared with her pelisse over his arm. Annie turned her back to allow Nicholls to drape it across her shoulders. But Lord Ashbourne stepped forward and pulled it from the older man's grasp. "Allow me," he intoned.

The earl's strong hands made quick work of it, pushing the coat over her shoulders and . . .

Annie shuddered. A lustful thought sprang to mind. An unexpected rush of something foreign and hot where his breath had touched her neck. Though she quickly brushed the uncomfortable feeling aside.

This was Lord Ashbourne. *Jordan*. He was handsome, yes, but he didn't make *her* head turn. No. No. Certainly not. Ludicrous notion. Why, the man was thirty-one years old, for heaven's sake, old enough to be her . . . older brother.

She turned around and glanced up at him. She needed to take another look. He was well over six feet tall with broad shoulders, an athletic build, and short, cropped, dark brown hair. But his eyes were the real appeal. Dark silver, they glinted like ice or steel depending on his mood.

Oh. Very well. He was unmercifully handsome. Every woman in the *ton* thought so. But it took a great deal more than a pretty face to garner Annie's attention, and Jordan Holloway was nothing but . . . troublesome.

Besides, men like Jordan Holloway never looked twice at girls like Annie Andrews.

She cleared her throat and tugged out of his reach. But it didn't keep her from trembling a bit at his touch. Drat it all.

She shouldn't be thinking such thoughts about Lord Ashbourne.

"How is your fox?" he asked.

Yes. Small talk. Just the thing. "Resting comfortably, thank you," she replied.

"And Aunt Clarissa?" he asked, glancing around.

"Should be here any moment now," Annie replied, and as if on cue, Aunt Clarissa appeared, rounding the bend in the hallway. Her suite was on the first floor as the poor woman had difficulty maneuvering stairs. Her cheeks were rosy, a sure sign she'd already been into the sherry this evening.

"I'm here, dears. I'm here," she said, scurrying as quickly as a woman of her age and girth was able.

"Good evening, Aunt Clarissa," Jordan said, bowing.

"Ah, Lord Ashbourne, when Anne told me you'd be escorting us to the ball tonight, I told her she was certain to have gotten the name wrong. But I daresay, I'm pleased to see she did not."

Lord Ashbourne looked as if he were having considerable difficulty swallowing his laughter. "It's a pleasure to escort both of you fine ladies," he replied in his most debonair tone, and Annie couldn't help but smile at the little wink he gave the older woman.

"If I were forty years younger and four stone lighter . . ." Aunt Clarissa winked at Lord Ashbourne and this time Annie covered her mouth with her hand. Good heavens, the lady was positively shocking. Annie smiled wide behind her hand. She actually couldn't have asked for a better chaperone.

Annie dropped her hand and turned to Lord Ashbourne, the smile still pinned to her face. "Shall we?"

Lord Ashbourne's grin widened. "I believe you just stole my line."

Jordan escorted Annie Andrews and Aunt Clarissa down the steps and out to his waiting coach.

"Oh, those horses," Aunt Clarissa exclaimed. "They looked positively beastly."

"It'll be all right," Annie replied, allowing Aunt Clarissa to clutch at her sleeve while she patted the woman's hand reassuringly.

Jordan watched the rigid way Annie held her small shoulders erect and the slight jut of her stubborn little jaw as she did her best to ignore him.

His closest friend, Devon, had fallen for this slip of a girl's sister, Lily, five years ago. Devon and Lily had been reunited in the most unexpected of ways in the past year. Lily had authored a scandalous pamphlet entitled *Secrets of a Wedding Night* that had sold among the young ladies of the *ton* as quickly as it was printed. When Devon's fiancée had cried off after reading it, Devon had been angry enough to go looking for the young widow.

He'd issued her a challenge: write a retraction or prepare to be seduced to find out just how good a wedding night could be.

Of course Lily being Lily never had any intention of writing a retraction and the two had led each other on a merry chase before finally admitting to themselves that they were still in love after all those years.

Now, Jordan stared at Annie. After assisting Aunt Clarissa, he helped Annie into his coach, pulled himself up behind her, and slid into the seat across from her. She was slight but spirited. Whereas her sister, Lily, looked as if she'd been carved into porcelain, Annie had a simple beauty. But one, Jordan thought uneasily, that was somehow even more compelling. More compelling, still, given his reaction to her being in his arms last night.

With her dark hair and eyes, she looked like a Gypsy. And she'd somehow managed to grow even more beautiful in the past several months. He hadn't had occasion to look at her so closely before, but now, in the coach with her, he realized that her hair, which had been passably pretty, was now a deep, luxurious knot of silk on top of her head. Her skin was fair and smooth, accentuating the dark slashes of her brows and her long black eyelashes.

Miss Andrews was a deuced beauty, if one were interested in innocents, which Jordan assuredly was *not*. Good God. The close confines of the coach were playing with his head. She was Devon's sister-in-law. Completely unsuitable for him. Devon would lay him out flat if he knew Jordan had had as much as one inappropriate thought about Annie, let alone the several that had come to mind in the last twenty-four hours. Jordan shook his head to clear it of such unsettling ideas. Very well. The chit was a beauty. Why she insisted upon throwing herself at that fool Eggleston was anyone's guess.

Jordan relaxed against the seat and glanced out the window. Aside from last night, he already knew, first-hand, how much trouble the girl could get herself into.

Now, months after her ill-fated attempt to marry in Gretna Green, it seemed she was still convinced Eggleston was the right man for her. Absurd, of course, but that was none of Jordan's affair. Young ladies making their debuts and their choice of husbands was not something he concerned himself with. He was tasked only with ensuring Miss Andrews stayed out of trouble on his watch, and that, he assumed, meant that she stayed innocent, unmarried, and came through with her reputation intact. Easy enough, he supposed. There were three weeks left before Devon and Lily returned and then he'd be finished with this unwelcome chaperonage.

However, Jordan had a gut feeling the girl was not about to make the next few weeks easy on him. He'd spent the last week chasing her about the park while she attempted to convince Eggleston to invite her to the ball tonight. It had all been easy enough, but now, despite the fact that the Season had been over for an age, there were a few actual events coming up. And events, like the Lindworths' affair tonight, meant trouble.

Annie, it seemed, was every bit as stubborn and impudent as her sister. More so, if the dire warning Lily had issued to him before she'd left was to be believed. Yes, as much as he didn't relish the idea of playing chaperone to an unruly young woman, he was sure he had quite the time in store for him keeping an eye on Miss

Andrews. The end of the next three weeks couldn't come soon enough for him.

"Do explain your earlier comments," Jordan said to her. "How exactly is it that you believe I'm causing *you* trouble?"

Annie's mouth fell open. She glanced at Aunt Clarissa, who was already nodding off in the corner. Drinking made the woman sleepy. "You cannot possibly be serious."

He gave her an unaffected stare. "Humor me."

She tossed one delicate little hand in the air and began counting off his transgressions on her fingertips. "You've dogged my every step. Whenever I go riding in the park with Arthur, you're there. Whenever I go out to pay my afternoon calls, I eventually see you. When I go shopping on Bond Street, whom should I encounter? It's like having an unwanted overseer everywhere I go."

Jordan reclined against his seat and crossed his legs at the ankles, regarding her. "You haven't considered the fact that it may very well just be pure coincidence that I am at these places you list?"

"Hmm. What sort of business did you have at Miss Moneyham's milliners? Did you need a new ribbon for your best bonnet?" She batted her eyelashes at him.

Arching a brow, Jordan leaned to the left and settled his weight on his elbow. "How do you know I'm not following Eggleston?"

Annie snapped her mouth shut. He could tell by the slight wrinkling of her brow that she had not considered such a possibility.

He'd stumped her.

Good.

"You're not following Arthur, are you?" she asked, leaning forward a bit, a disbelieving look on her face.

Jordan whistled. "Arthur? Really? Let's talk about that. I noticed you've been using his Christian name. Hardly seems appropriate, now, does it?" He nodded toward Aunt Clarissa.

Annie glanced at the older woman. Her little snores were shaking the gray curls on the top of her head. "Hardly seems any of your affair," she said sweetly to Lord Ashbourne. "And you've yet to answer my question."

Lord Ashbourne shrugged. "What if I told you your sister asked me to keep an eye on you?"

Annie blinked at him. "Why would she do that? I've got Aunt Clarissa."

Jordan gave her a look dripping with sarcasm as he nodded again to the chaperone's sleeping form. "Must I really provide you with an explanation?"

Annie shrugged. "Oh, you know how dramatic Lily can be. Why, she caused a complete scandal last year with her pamphlet. I love her dearly, of course, but she relishes histrionics." Annie leaned forward even farther and gave him a conspiratorial whisper. "Just between the two of us, you cannot take everything Lily says entirely literally."

Jordan struggled to keep the smile from his face. "Is that so?"

Annie nodded. "Yes, yes, of course." She looked quite pleased with herself, obviously sure she had convinced him.

"It sounds as if there has been a misunderstanding," he continued.

Annie nodded even more emphatically. "Yes, yes. A

misunderstanding." She sat up straight, a happy smile on her pretty face.

Jordan cocked his head to the side. "Seems there's been *quite* a misunderstanding," he said. "Because I distinctly remember you being the selfsame young woman whom I assisted Devon and Lily in chasing up to Gretna Green when you took off with Eggleston last spring, the runaway bride. And your sister was quite clear with me that she very much did not want history to repeat itself."

The smile dropped from Annie's face, and she audibly gulped.

"Am I mistaken?" Jordan prodded, blinking innocently. "Do I misunderstand the matter?"

Annie busied herself with plucking at the strings of her reticule. "Arthur and I—"

"Please, for your sister's sake, call the man Mr. Eggleston, at least in my presence."

She narrowed her eyes. "*Mr. Eggleston* and I did not go to Gretna Green."

He gave her a long-suffering stare. "You mean you did not *make it* to Gretna Green."

"Oh, what does any of that matter now? That was months ago. I'm much older and wiser now. Besides, Arthur . . ." She cleared her throat. "Mr. Eggleston and I did not marry in Scotland and that's the only concern, isn't it? We shall be married, however, properly."

Jordan steepled his fingers together and regarded her. He was actually enjoying the repartee more than he'd expected. Playing de facto chaperone to Miss Andrews was hardly at the top of his list of pleasant activities, but her company was proving somewhat amusing tonight after all.

"It was only a few months ago, wasn't it?" he asked. "I'll leave alone your claim to be older and wiser, but the fact is you attempted to run off to Scotland with Eggleston, and if Lily and Devon hadn't tracked you down and dragged you back to London, you might well be married to the bloke now and living a life of shame, mightn't you?"

The only sound from across the seats was a vague harrumph. And then, "No one ever found out. We all managed quite well to keep that a secret and my reputation didn't suffer. I'd rather you didn't mention it. It's entirely unchivalrous of you. Not to mention that your calling me the runaway bride drives me mad."

Lord Ashbourne shook his head. "No one ever found out only because Devon and your sister told everyone it was *they* who married."

Annie pointed an accusing finger at him. "A situation you admit to helping to bring about."

"Yes." He grinned. "I did my part in pushing them together, but it doesn't change the fact that you did something infinitely foolish."

She glanced away and Jordan momentarily regretted bringing about the light blush that stained her cheeks. He'd embarrassed her.

But when she turned back to face him, her eyes crackled with dark fire. "Oh, I suppose you would never have done anything like that, would you?" she snapped. "That's my problem with the lot of you telling me what to do. Lily and Devon had attempted to run off to Gretna Green together when they were young, and you're famous for your blackened reputation, but I'm taken to task for my every misstep."

Jordan arched a brow. Well. Well. Well. In addition to

being a bit of trouble, it seemed the chit wasn't one to accept accusations without fighting back. Blast it all if he didn't like that about her. "It's true, Miss Andrews. I was doing things that would shock you before you were out of pinafores. But perhaps that merely proves I know whereof I speak."

Annie turned her head away and crossed her arms over her chest.

Jordan continued. "Your sister, at least, seems to believe you might be disposed to try your hand at matrimony again. My own encounters with you prove your penchant for spending time in Eggleston's company. So, frankly, I'd have to say I agree with your sister. You are a risk."

"A risk?" Annie's head swiveled back around and she blinked. "What exactly do you mean by *that*?"

He shrugged. "I'll be honest. I asked you to come with me tonight because I happen to be tired of following you around in false secret. I don't relish this task any more than you relish my presence."

She opened her mouth as if to retort but Jordan put up his hand to silence her. She snapped her lips closed again.

"You agreed to suffer my company for one reason and one reason only, and that reason is because your beloved Eggleston didn't invite you himself and you cannot stand to be without his company for one evening," Jordan continued while Annie positively glowered at him.

"And the fact is I *have* been following you for the past sennight. I'm following you *and* Eggleston because I've been assigned by your new brother-in-law and your sister to watch over you while they are away. I'm paying attention not because I give a toss whom you marry, but because I blasted well care how you go about it. Devon and

Lily made it my affair to care and I intend to fulfill my promise to my friends. So let's get one thing clear between us, *my dear Miss Andrews*. When we get to the ball, I intend to make it known to every breathing male on the premises that no one—but no one—is going to dance with you without my explicit approval. And that approval does not extend to Arthur Eggleston."

CHAPTER 5

After rousing Aunt Clarissa from her sleep, Annie and Lord Ashbourne helped the older woman up the steps to the Lindworths' second-story ballroom. The grand affair was ablaze with the light of a thousand candles. After leaning a bit too long on Lord Ashbourne's arm and giving him a score of inappropriate winks, Aunt Clarissa took herself off to find the nearest glass of wine and the company of the other older ladies while Annie quickly excused herself from the detestable Lord Ashbourne.

Annie scoured the ballroom in search of her closest friend, Frances. As much as she tried to banish it, the conversation in the coach with Lord Ashbourne replayed in her head, making her angry all over again. She counted to ten. How dare that man lecture her? And then have the nerve to issue a decree? He would not *allow* her to dance with Arthur? Who did Jordan Holloway think he was? Why, he was as overbearing and controlling as Lily could be. And Annie was even less likely to listen to *him*.

Frances was standing in a corner, humming along with the music, a pleasant yet slightly bored look on her face. She held a glass of questionable punch in one hand and was tapping her slippered foot in time to the tune.

She jumped when she glanced up to see Annie barreling toward her.

"Anne, there you are. I've been waiting an age."

Annie glanced over her shoulder to ensure they wouldn't be overheard. "Tell me," she asked breathlessly. "Have you seen Arthur tonight?"

Frances discarded her glass on a nearby table. "Yes, yes, of course. He's here with his sister. Now you tell me something. Did you arrive with Lord Ashbourne?"

Annie rolled her eyes. "Ugh. Yes."

Frances looked as if she might swoon. "And what, pray tell, were you doing with him?"

"You'll never believe. It appears Lily and Devon have asked Lord Ashbourne to watch me while they're gone."

Frances's mouth dropped open. "You *must* be joking."

Annie leaned against the wall, her hands behind her back. "No, I'm afraid I'm not. He's been following me around for days. Now it all makes perfect sense."

Frances clutched her throat. "Oh, Anne. You have all the fun!"

Annie blinked at her friend. "Fun? What in heaven's name are you talking about? The man has been insufferable. He won't give me a moment's peace." She wasn't about to tell Frances about her unfortunate encounter with Lord Ashbourne last night.

Frances had extricated her fan from her reticule and was busily flapping it in front of her face. "I should hope not. If I had Jordan Holloway following me around, I wouldn't want a moment's peace. The man is positively gorgeous."

Annie shook her head. Frances had had an ill-concealed infatuation with Lord Ashbourne for months. It was quite provoking, actually. Especially now that Lord Ashbourne was the equivalent of Annie's gaoler.

Annie glanced across the ballroom to where Lord Ashbourne stood. He was a few inches taller than the other men in his company. And he cut a striking figure in his black evening attire and perfectly starched white cravat. "All I see is a towering know-it-all who refuses to leave me alone."

The fan still hovered in front of Frances's face. "Now I know you're joking. Why, the man is one of the most sought-after bachelors in the realm. It's just not possible that you don't find him handsome."

Annie scrunched up her nose. "Oh, he's handsome, I'll allow. But he's only sought after because he's rich and titled." She plucked her arms out from behind her and crossed them over her chest.

"Hmm. Let's just see. He's tall." Frances snapped her fan closed and tapped it against her palm.

Annie glanced over at Lord Ashbourne again. "Yes. He is that."

"And he's dark." Another tap of the fan to her palm.

Annie dared another surreptitious glance. "Admittedly."

"And Lord above, those eyes!" Frances snapped the fan open again and rapidly waved it in front of her face.

Annie shrugged. "I haven't even noticed his eyes."

"You are positively daft," Frances declared. "Everyone knows the Earl of Ashbourne has London's most beautiful gray eyes."

Annie squinted. "Whatever his eye color, he's nothing but the Earl of Meddlesomeness as far as I'm concerned. Besides, he's a little *too* good-looking if you ask me. Like he's not real. And men who look like that only have the incomparable beauties on their arms. Not young ladies like us who are pretty at best."

She refused to think about the little shiver that went through her earlier in the coach when he had called her "my dear Miss Andrews." And very well, she *had* noticed those eyes. Even in the dark of the coach, they shone like silver.

Frances shook her head. "No, Anne. *I'm* pretty at best. You're absolutely gorgeous, only you don't know it because your sister just happens to be one of the most beautiful women in the country. Compared to me, however, you are a goddess."

Annie squeezed her friend's hand. Frances was such a dear. The two of them had had this conversation scores of times and it always ended the same way. Annie knew— *knew*—it wasn't true, but it was exceedingly kind of her friend to try to tell her how beautiful she was.

"I'm no goddess," she whispered. She was catapulted back in time to being fourteen years old again at her parents' country estate. "You'll just have to be witty, Annie," her father had said, "because you won't catch a husband with *your* looks." It was one of many careless statements her father had made through the years and Lily, like Frances, had spent hours trying to tell her how untrue it was, but Annie knew they had merely been trying to make her feel better. She wasn't pretty. That was a fact. All the more reason that Arthur was the right man for her. Arthur saw something in her other men didn't, couldn't.

Frances snapped open her fan again, shaking Annie from her reverie. "Before you argue with me," Frances continued, "I would simply like to point out that Lord

Ashbourne came here with you tonight, didn't he? And if you're *normal-looking,* then perhaps there's hope for me." Laughing, Frances dropped her fan back inside her reticule. "Besides, careful what you say about Lord Ashbourne, Miss Andrews. Your sister wouldn't approve."

Annie smoothed her pink skirts. "That's just it. I thought I was going to a have a reprieve from Lily's meddling while she was gone on her honeymoon. Instead, she's left her stand-in in the form of the meddlesome Lord Ashbourne."

"The charming and dashing Lord Ashbourne," Frances corrected, clearing her throat.

Annie tucked a wayward curl behind her ear. "If you had heard how rude he was to me in the coach, you wouldn't think he was nearly so charming or dashing. Besides, Arthur is a man who looks real. Lord Ashbourne looks like he's been chiseled from stone."

Frances bit her lip and averted her eyes. "Ah yes, dear, of course Mr. Eggleston is a fine-looking man."

Annie nodded approvingly.

"But he's no Lord Ashbourne," Frances finished, causing Annie to narrow her eyes at her friend.

"I don't expect you to understand, Frances. But my affections for Arthur go much deeper than mere looks."

"As do my affections for Lord Ashbourne," Frances insisted. "He's witty, rich, intelligent, immensely popular, a gifted horseman, bowman, and shot. There are many things to like about him. The fact that he looks like Adonis has very little to do with it, really."

Annie rolled her eyes. "So what? Arthur went to Oxford."

"Ashbourne went to Cambridge."

"Arthur stands to inherit a decent income when he turns twenty-five."

"Ashbourne is already an earl, for heaven's sake, and one of the wealthiest men in London."

Annie tossed up her hands. "What is your point, Frances? They are two very different men."

"My point is merely that Mr. Eggleston is a perfectly respectable chap. But oh, my dear, he doesn't make one want to swoon the way Lord Ashbourne does."

Annie pushed up her chin. "Swooning is quite overrated."

"Have you tried it?"

Annie gasped. "I have not. And I have no intention of it. Now let's desist in this silly conversation and discuss more important matters. Like how shall I make Arthur stop talking to his sister and ask me to dance? I only have three weeks left to get him to ask me to marry him." She nodded across the ballroom to where she had spied Arthur standing in a small group of people, including his older sister.

"It's a shame his sister hasn't married yet," Frances whispered. "I think it's her nose, poor thing. Though it may very well be the chin . . ." Frances rubbed her own chin and shook her head.

Annie stifled a horrified laugh. "That is just ridiculous. No doubt she hasn't found the right chap yet. That is all. I'm sure she's a lovely young woman. I've yet to make her acquaintance but—"

Frances clutched at Annie's arm. "He hasn't introduced you to his sister?"

"No. Not yet. Perhaps tonight—"

"May I ask you something?" Frances said, reaching for her discarded glass of punch.

"Yes?"

"If I find a way to get Mr. Eggleston to ask you to dance, will you introduce me to Lord Ashbourne?" She winked at Annie.

"Oh, Frances, no. I just can't stand it. I don't want you to meet Lord Ashbourne. I can barely tolerate him myself. Now, come with me."

Frances in tow, Annie took off across the ballroom, headed toward the group in which Arthur stood.

She and Frances waited on the outskirts a bit too long, hoping to be included. Annie glanced over and briefly made eye contact with Lord Ashbourne, who stood in the midst of a giggling group of overly anxious young women, a mocking grin on his perfect face. She longed to slap it off. He held up his glass in a silent salute to her and Annie suddenly felt like a fool waiting for Arthur's attention as if she were standing in a queue.

She glanced away from Lord Ashbourne and swallowed, nearly ready to turn and leave, when Arthur's timid sister, a pale, yellow-haired girl with the most unfortunate (ahem, Frances was right) nose and chin Annie had ever seen, cleared her throat and tugged on her brother's sleeve.

Arthur looked up at his sister's urging and glanced at Annie. A surprised smile lit his face. "Ah, Miss Andrews, so good to see you. And Miss Birmingham," he said, bowing to Frances, "always a pleasure."

Annie and Frances murmured their greetings and Arthur turned to introduce them to his sister. "My sister, Miss Theodosia Eggleston. Theodosia, Miss Anne Andrews and Miss Frances Birmingham."

Ah, he'd finally introduced her to his sister. Annie gave Frances a triumphant smile and greeted Miss Eggleston, who murmured something pleasant. They lingered for a bit, talking about inconsequential matters, before Miss Eggleston declared that she was in need of some air. Wouldn't Arthur take her nearer to a window in order to obtain it?

Soon after the two siblings left, the rest of the group dispersed, and Annie and Frances were left standing alone again.

"I cannot believe he didn't ask you to dance," Frances said. "Especially when you so obviously wanted him to."

Annie shook her head. "It's his sister. I know it. He feels such an obligation to see to her. She's not well. I have no idea how I'll ever get him to come up to scratch if she continues to remain unattached."

"It certainly seems to be a problem, doesn't it?" Frances replied, biting her lip. "What can we do?"

A flash of black slid past, and Annie glanced up to see Jordan Holloway making his way across the room. Frances clutched at Annie's arm like a crab frantically snapping its pincer.

"Seems you've lost your Mr. Eggleston," Lord Ashbourne drawled, not breaking his stride.

CHAPTER 6

It was nearly two hours and four glasses of tepid punch later before Annie was finally able to locate Arthur without his sister at his side. Apparently Miss Eggleston had gone to the ladies' retiring room.

"It's about time," Annie breathed, handing her glass to Frances. "Please hold this while I go speak with him."

"What do you intend to say?" Frances called after her.

Annie tossed a quick wink in her friend's direction. "I'll think of something."

She made her way over to Arthur, who stood alone near the sidelines of the dancing, a pleasant look on his face. "Arthur, there you are."

Arthur glanced up; his smile did not falter. "Anne. How have you been enjoying the evening? Where is Lord Ashbourne?"

Ugh. Why did Arthur have to mention that man's name? "He's here . . . somewhere." She kept the smile pinned to her face. "And I've been enjoying the evening very well but would like it ever so much more if I were dancing."

Arthur's face turned into a scowl. "Won't Lord Ashbourne ask you to dance?"

Annie ground her teeth. She leaned in closer. "Arthur," she whispered. "I was hoping *you* would ask me to dance."

A brief flash of surprise registered on Arthur's smooth face before he replied, "Anne, you know I should like that very much, but I don't think it would be very prudent."

Instinctively, she took a step back. "Why not?"

He cleared his throat, then lowered his voice. "I had words with Lord Ashbourne earlier and he . . . he rather implied that you and I shouldn't . . . that I . . ."

Annie's face heated. She clenched her teeth. "Arthur," she whispered, her voice shaking. "Lord Ashbourne does not choose my dance partners and I—" Annie caught sight of Miss Eggleston making her way back toward her brother from the retiring room. She didn't have much time. Only a matter of seconds. "Arthur," she whispered. "I must speak with you, alone. Meet me downstairs in the gardens. In ten minutes."

Arthur started to shake his head but Annie wouldn't allow him to speak. "I'll be waiting, please," she said, just before she flew away. She nodded to Miss Eggleston on her way out the door.

Fifteen long minutes passed while Annie waited outside in the gardens. It was easy enough to elude Aunt Clarissa. The woman could barely see beyond five paces in front of her face. If Annie insisted she was off dancing, Aunt Clarissa smiled and nodded and raised another glass of wine.

Annie wrung her hands. But where was Arthur? She'd nearly convinced herself that he wasn't coming when the French doors finally opened. Through a shaft of moonlight she could see his handsome face, blond hair, and sky-blue eyes.

"Anne," he called softly from the terrace. "Anne."

"Over here, Arthur," she called back from her refuge behind a large, flowering bush.

Arthur strode toward her and captured her hands when he found her. "I'm sorry I'm late. It was difficult to get away."

Annie nodded. "I understand."

"I cannot stay long, Anne. What if someone sees us? And I must be getting back to my sister."

Annie resisted the urge to shake him. "Arthur, I've barely spoken to you all evening. You cannot spare a few moments for me?"

"Yes, of course," he said, covering her hand again with his. "I'm here."

Annie took a deep breath. She'd carefully considered what she would say. Desperate times called for desperate measures and all that. She would come right out with it. "Do you want to marry me, Arthur?"

Arthur squeezed her hand again and gulped. He looked genuinely shocked. "Of course I do, Anne."

"Then why have you not offered for me?"

Arthur turned away and shoved his fingers through his hair. "Ever since we tried to run off to Gretna Green, my father's been very disappointed in me. He says I should take time to consider my behavior carefully and I tend to agree. There's no rush, is there?"

Annie's throat tightened "But you said your father had got over his doubts about me."

Arthur faced her again. "He was worried about your lack of dowry before, that's true. But he knows you have a large dowry now that your sister has married Lord

Colton. Now that everyone knows Lord Colton is so wealthy."

Annie scanned Arthur's face. "Then what's the problem?"

He nodded. "Father doesn't think it's a good idea to rush into anything. A marriage, that is. And you know as well as I, it's not just my father who stands between us. After what happened on the road to Gretna, I know Lord Colton has his doubts about me. Then there's the matter of my sister. She needs me right now. I must look after her."

Annie took two steps toward him. She wanted to reach for him but checked the impulse. She threaded her fingers together instead. "Don't you love me, Arthur?"

"Of course I do, Anne, but if we're to marry, what does it matter if it's this year or next?"

Annie shook her head. "What does it matter?" she repeated brokenly. "I want a marriage, children. Those are the most important things to me, Arthur. I thought you wanted those same things too." She put her hand on his shoulder, and when he looked down, she searched his face.

Arthur must have heard the pain in her voice. He reached over and squeezed the hand that rested on his shoulder. "Oh, Anne, it is. And I do. I promise. I'll speak to my father again. I'll convince him. Don't worry."

"And I'll see to Lord Colton," she promised with a nod.

"It will be all right, Anne. You'll see." Arthur pulled her into his arms. "Besides, it seems I may have some competition in Lord Ashbourne."

Annie couldn't help her unladylike snort. "Lord Ashbourne?"

"Yes. First I find you in his arms on my back porch

and tonight he told me in no uncertain terms to stay away from you."

"Oh, that, it's just that—" Annie stopped herself. A slow smile dawned across her face. She could tell Arthur that Lord Ashbourne was merely carrying out a favor to her sister and Lord Colton, or she could let him think he did indeed have competition. Just what he might need, in fact. What was the harm?

"Are you jealous?" she asked, a catlike smile pinned to her face.

"Should I be?" Arthur pulled her even closer and a shot of happiness spread through her limbs. Oh, he *was* jealous. Perfect.

Annie tilted up her chin to look into his eyes. She searched his face. This was it. The perfect opportunity. Finally. "Oh, Arthur, kiss me, please."

Arthur gulped, his Adam's apple bobbing in his throat. Looking very earnest, he blinked several times.

Annie closed her eyes and leaned up on her tiptoes. He was going to do it. Arthur Eggleston was going to kiss her. She sucked in her breath. She tilted her chin. She puckered her lips. Oh yes, this would be her very first kiss from her one true love.

"Now *this* I do hate to interrupt," a cocky male voice intruded. "But I'd hardly be doing my duty as a chaperone if I did not."

CHAPTER 7

Jordan Holloway emerged from the shadowy side of the house, his eyes fixed on his unruly charge.

Eggleston's hands fell away from Annie's arms. He cleared his throat multiple times and moved several paces away from her as quickly as possible.

"Uh, good evening, Lord Ashbourne," Arthur said. "Thank you very— Good evening!" Arthur nodded toward Jordan, nodded toward Annie, and without meeting their eyes, dashed past both of them back toward the house like a hare scared by a hound.

Laughing softly, Jordan stepped into the moonlit nook.

Annie crossed her arms over her chest. "Of course you would have to pick that precise moment to insert yourself into my affairs again. Proud of yourself?"

"Immensely," Jordan answered with a nod.

"You are a detestable eavesdropper."

Jordan cracked a smile. "I take offense to that, actually. I am a very skilled eavesdropper. But I came out here to enjoy a perfectly good cheroot. One that I've been forced to snub out since you arrived."

"You had no right to—"

His hand went up to stop her. "I'm sure Lily and Devon would see things quite differently. No doubt they'd thank me."

Her cheeks flushed the loveliest shade of pink.

"My sister and Devon don't understand and, apparently, neither do you. But it is absolutely none of your affair!" She turned her back on him.

"It is my affair, actually. I am your chaperone. Not to mention, if you intend to use me to make Eggleston jealous, then it's even more my affair." He crossed his arms over his chest and arched a brow at her.

She turned an even brighter shade of pink and bit her lip. The tell.

Jordan eyed her. "I've done you a great service this evening and this is how you repay me? Outrage and ingratitude?"

Annie's jaw dropped open. "A great service? Are you mad? How do you think you've done me a great service?"

"Trust me. You wouldn't have wanted to kiss Eggleston."

Annie squeezed her reticule, and Jordan could only guess she was imagining it was his throat. "Really? How would you know? Have *you* kissed him?"

Jordan shrugged. "It's just a sense I get about the chap. The way he sits a horse, refuses to drink, mentions his *father* four times in one conversation. To be honest, I've been convinced the man isn't interested in women at all." Jordan shook his head. "I'm sorry to tell you, none of it bodes well for your marital bed."

Annie's cheeks flamed. Her voice shook with outrage. "First of all, you should not have been eavesdropping. It's unspeakably rude, and second, what would you know about a marital bed? You're not married!"

As soon as the words left her mouth, she clapped her hand over it. "Oh, good heavens, I want to sink through the grass," she murmured, pulling her hand away.

Jordan arched a brow. "Guessed, did you, how I might know such a thing?"

She closed her eyes, reopened them slowly, and cleared her throat. "Frances says you're a rakehell. I assume that's how you know."

"A rakehell? Really? I suppose that's fair." At the moment, all he could think about was wrapping up this little matter with the unhappy Miss Andrews and making his way to his mistress Nicoletta's town house.

Annie's eyes shot dark sparks at him. "Very well. If you're a rakehell, you must be quite experienced, then."

Jordan coughed. "Experienced?"

"Yes. At kissing."

He shook his head. "I've had no complaints."

Annie tapped her slipper on the grass. "Will you kiss me then?"

Jordan's head snapped up and he gave her a look as if he were convinced she'd lost her mind. "Pardon?"

"Will you kiss me?"

He arched a brow. "Under no circumstances."

She gave him a smug smile. "Afraid?"

Jordan took two steps toward her and towered over her. "Miss Andrews, you should learn not to play games with vastly superior players."

Annie stared straight up at him. "Vastly superior? My. My. Arrogant, aren't we?"

"Merely confident. And I'm not about to play into your little game of trying to make Eggleston jealous, which I assume is the reason for your request."

She didn't look away. Impressive.

She glanced about, holding out her hands. "Arthur isn't here now to see, is he? If you're heaven's gift to the fairer sex, why don't you prove it?"

Oh, now she was challenging his skills. Taunting him. Foolish woman. But doubt flickered in Jordan's mind. He eyed the appealing Miss Andrews. For some deuced inexplicable reason, he was actually tempted. She was beautiful, she was lively, and she was luring him with her know-it-all attitude. But she was also Devon's sister-in-law, blast it. Kissing her would be a phenomenally bad idea. Phenomenally bad.

"Given that you're Devon's sister-in-law—"

"Oh, I'm sorry. It must not have been you who said you were doing shocking things before I was out of pinafores."

Jordan narrowed his eyes on her. The smug look on her face made him shake the doubt away. The chit was a bit too sure of herself. She'd only get into more trouble with an attitude like that. She needed to learn a lesson and the sooner the better.

"You do not know what you're getting yourself into," he warned.

"Don't I?" she countered. She'd pulled off one glove and was contemplating her fingernails as if she hadn't a care in the world.

That did it.

Jordan narrowed his eyes on her. This girl *definitely* needed to be taught a lesson. He remembered a night several months ago when Devon had forced him to ask Annie to dance at the Atkinsons' house party. He'd done it, all right, and she'd ever so reluctantly agreed, but it'd been clear the entire time that she'd been scouring the ballroom for a glimpse of Arthur Eggleston.

Arthur Eggleston of all people. That little episode had left a bad taste in Jordan's mouth. The next morning, Annie and Arthur had run off to Gretna Green and Devon had enlisted Jordan's help in tracking them down.

Jordan was used to the giggling attentions of young ladies and the smooth flirtations of more experienced women. He was a man who was rarely without the company of a beautiful woman and he was accustomed to being the center of attention. Here was this girl with her know-it-all attitude positively mocking him. He wouldn't stand for it. He'd have Miss Andrews quaking in her tiny little slippers in five seconds flat.

And he knew *just* how to accomplish it.

Sucking in a deep breath through his nostrils, he reached out and softly ran a bare finger along the arch of her jaw. Annie glanced up. A flicker of doubt flashed in her eyes. Good. He'd already shaken her. His thumb glanced against her temple, traced along her cheekbone, and tilted up her chin.

She wet her lips nervously with her adorable little pink tongue. Her dark eyes were wide. Also good.

He leaned down and whispered in her ear, allowing his rough cheek to brush her soft one. She smelled like spring flowers and optimism. "You want me to kiss you, Miss Andrews? Really kiss you?"

"Y . . . yes." But her breaths were coming in short little gasps and her heart was fluttering like a hummingbird's wings in her pretty throat.

He slid the fingers of one hand under her chin. He ran the fingers of his other down the length of her velvet neck. Then, slowly, so slowly, his mouth descended toward hers. Her eyes squeezed shut at the last second, and Jordan let his lips lightly brush hers.

He only meant to teach her a lesson. Only meant to touch her lips, once, twice, and then he would end it. His point would be made.

But the sweetness of her mouth surprised him. He brushed against her a third time and when her hands came up to snake around his neck and she fitted herself to his full length, that was Jordan's undoing. He hadn't expected such passion in the little miss. Hadn't expected it, but was helpless not to respond to it.

The hand that had been caressing her neck moved down behind her back to tug her tightly against him. When her tongue tentatively touched his, that was it. He turned her in his arms and pushed her up against the side of the house. He braced his hands on either side of her head, his mouth slanted against hers, her lips parted, and his tongue brushed inside. Annie's entire delectable little body shook. She moaned and Jordan went rock hard. Oh God, how exactly had this happened? He needed to stop. Now. It was insane for him to be kissing Annie on the side of the house. He hadn't meant for this, hadn't meant it at all. She was responding to him like a wanton, and oh God, he liked it.

He liked it too much.

Lord Ashbourne pulled his mouth away from hers, and her hands fell away from his neck. Annie's eyes fluttered open. She trembled. Did she imagine it or was his breathing ragged too? She couldn't look at him. Could only stare at the shadowy ground while she pressed her hand against her stomach, willing the butterflies to stop flying and for her breathing to return to normal.

She braced a hand against the cold stone wall to right herself. What in God's name had that been?

A kiss. Yes, but so much more. She'd never experienced anything like it.

Without saying a word, Lord Ashbourne turned on his heel and stalked back inside the house. Thank goodness he hadn't made a mocking comment. She couldn't have stood it.

Annie counted to ten and willed her breathing back to normal. Lord Ashbourne had been right, she admitted to herself with a wry smile. She *had* been playing a game with a vastly superior player. What had she been thinking to taunt him like that in the first place? She just couldn't stand his smugness. How he ordered her about, told her whom she could and could not dance with, pretended to know everything about rakishness and kissing. It was all too much. She had meant to call his bluff. Only now that he'd gone and kissed her, she was quite convinced Lord Ashbourne *did,* in fact, know everything about rakishness and kissing.

She bit her lip, watching his retreating form against the light shining from the house.

She knew instinctively. That kiss had been dangerous. And even more dangerous, she would be forced to be in his company for the next three weeks.

CHAPTER 8

The ride home from the Lindworths' ball was, in a word, awkward. With Aunt Clarissa propped unceremoniously (and drunkenly) in the corner of the coach, Annie smoothed her skirts, cleared her throat from time to time, and stared out the window of Lord Ashbourne's fine coach. She chewed her bottom lip, opened and closed her reticule for no reason whatsoever, and generally did whatever she could to forget the kiss she'd shared with the smolderingly handsome man who sat across from her.

And it certainly didn't help matters that she was seeing him in a different light now. Confound it all. He was *extremely* handsome. Startlingly so at a close range, like sitting here across from him in his own well-appointed coach. And Frances had been right about his eyes. Those mesmerizing gray eyes. They were startling, amazing. They seemed to pull you into their depths and lose you in their silver pools.

Men like him had always intimidated Annie. He ran with a fast set populated with other perfect, beautiful people who amused themselves with wicked pursuits and scandalous affairs. Annie wanted no part of that life. She wanted one man. Just one man who would love her forever, give her his children, and stay by her side no matter what gorgeous temptation might entice him. She wanted a man who was steadfast and true. Not a handsome rake like Jordan Holloway.

She asked herself for the hundredth time what madness had prompted her to ask him to kiss her? She'd never been one for being bullied, and his eavesdropping and running Arthur off had incensed her. Lord Ashbourne thought he could do whatever he wanted with no impunity. His smug boldness had infuriated her.

He was so used to being adored by women, she'd meant to throw his kiss in his face and mock him. Knock him from his pedestal. Instead, she'd been kissed by a man who obviously knew exactly what he was doing. So much so that she'd felt it to the very tips of her toes. If he could kiss her like that, what else . . . ? She shook her head. Very well. No more kisses with Lord Ashbourne. Point taken.

She glanced over at him and quickly looked away. He was cloaked in shadow. A particularly deep dark one crossed his face, obscuring his expression. She had the uncanny feeling that he was studying her, but she steadfastly avoided looking back at him. Instead she kept her gaze pinned out the window. But she couldn't remember even one landmark they'd passed.

Thank goodness it would be over soon. Just three more weeks before Lily and Devon returned. Why did she have the feeling they would be the longest three weeks of her life?

Her mind drifted uneasily to Arthur. Her chest ached. Why hadn't Arthur asked her to dance? Yes, Lord Ashbourne had apparently warned him not to, but still. If he'd really wanted to, wouldn't he have asked her regardless? Tears gathered in the backs of her eyes. She shook her head and glanced at Lord Ashbourne. He gave her a knowing look, one with a trace of pity. She wanted to hate him for it.

And what would Arthur think if he knew she'd kissed Lord Ashbourne in the garden? The same garden she'd been standing in with him only moments earlier? The same garden where she'd asked *him* to kiss her? She winced. Bad form. But she'd only been trying to prove a point to Lord Ashbourne for being such a know-it-all, so arrogant, so . . . now she had absolutely no idea what point she'd been trying to make. How and when did things become so confusing?

The truth was, she'd really only asked him to kiss her because she didn't think he'd do it. Frances said he was a rakehell, and apparently, a rakehell would kiss anyone. The fact that he'd kissed her just proved it. She'd managed to learn one thing at least. Rakehells did know how to kiss. Yes, they did. It had been an idiotic request, she realized now, but it was too late for recriminations. Besides, Annie didn't believe in recriminations. Recriminations had kept her sister from happiness for five years and had nearly turned Lily into a widowed spinster. Yes, if such a thing *could* exist, Lily would have been one. Recriminations were for people who didn't follow their hearts, and Annie would *never* make that mistake.

She and Lily were so different. Lily had always followed predictable rules and had had no fun. Lily had had no intention of marrying again until Lord Colton came back into her life—and thank goodness he had—but Annie had always wanted to marry. Marriage and family, children and a husband to truly love, those had been her dreams for as long as she could remember. And she'd known the moment she'd laid eyes on Arthur Eggleston the afternoon they'd met that he was her future husband.

If the last six months had taught her anything, it was that husband hunting was quite a tricky business. What had Arthur been thinking saying it didn't matter when they got married? Of course it mattered. It mattered a great deal. She'd handle Devon and Lily. She'd made that clear to him. So why wasn't Arthur coming up to scratch? Was his blasted sister really to blame?

The only sound in the coach was Aunt Clarissa's intermittent snores. Annie shook her head. Poor Aunt Clarissa really was the *worst* chaperone in existence. Which had suited Annie just fine, until she'd realized Lord Ashbourne was her second, *unofficial* chaperone.

She dared a glance into the shadows at Lord Ashbourne. She cleared her throat, wanting to die of embarrassment. "You won't tell Arthur that we—" she whispered. Oh, she simply could *not* bring herself to say it.

"Kissed? No, don't worry. He might actually send his father to fight me. And while I'm quite sure I would trounce the old buzzard, I don't relish spilling the blood of a man so much older than myself."

Annie regarded him coolly. "You don't have to be so sarcastic, you know? A simple no would have sufficed."

She could *hear* his smile in the darkness. "Just tell me one thing," Lord Ashbourne replied. "What is it exactly that you see in Eggleston?"

Annie crossed her arms over her middle and glared into the shadows. "As if you really care."

"I do, actually. I'm fascinated. Why a woman with

your obvious good looks and connections is so set on marrying that fool—"

Annie let out a short laugh. "A woman with my obvious good looks and connections? Why, now I know where you got your reputation for being charming." She shook her head. "But I'll tell you, on one condition."

"What condition?"

"If you promise to stop insulting him."

He snorted. "I cannot make that promise."

"Why not?"

"It's hardly my fault. The man is named after something that drops from a chicken's arse."

Annie pressed her lips together. "Oh, how exceedingly mature of you."

Lord Ashbourne's crack of laughter bounced off the coach's interior and Aunt Clarissa stirred. He glanced at her and lowered his voice. "It's true. It's too easy not to mention it. What if I promise to *do my best* not to insult him? Then will you tell me?"

Annie leaned forward a bit and so did Lord Ashbourne. A shaft of moonlight illuminated his chiseled cheekbones and fell across his firm lips, highlighting just one of his bright gray eyes. She sucked in her breath, then glanced down at her hands folded in her lap. Very well, Frances was entirely right. She would not quibble. The man was swoon-over handsome.

She shook her head to clear it of such thoughts and concentrated on his question. Why was she interested in Arthur?

"Let's see. He's kind and generous. He's handsome and intelligent. He's clever and he's an excellent brother and son."

Jordan rolled his eyes. "The man sounds like a positive saint. How dull."

"But most importantly, he loves me." She nodded.

His eyes narrowed on her. "Love? Is that it?" He sounded incredulous.

"Yes." She nodded again but with a bit less confidence this time.

"Seems to me, when a man is in love he doesn't make excuses for postponing a wedding."

Annie gritted her teeth. She refused to allow him to mock her. "What would you know about it? Aren't you famous for not wanting to marry?"

He shrugged. "Yes, but that doesn't mean I've never been in love."

Annie snapped her mouth shut. She sat back against the seat, silently contemplating his words for a moment She could not be more astonished. "You have? Been in love, I mean?"

"I once *thought* I was in love." His voice was solemn, quiet.

"What happened?" She eyed him carefully. She couldn't fathom, couldn't imagine the arrogant and dashing Lord Debonair in love.

"Suffice it to say things didn't work out. It turns out love is a silly notion invented by poets and fools."

He seemed ready to change the subject and Annie dared a glance at him. "May I ask you another question?"

He nodded.

"Why do you insist upon insulting Arthur? I do not flatter myself and think it has anything to do with me."

Lord Ashbourne arched a brow. "It does, actually. Are you surprised to know it? I didn't give two whits about Eggleston before I met you. I barely knew he existed, really. I mean, he is the second son of a baron, not exactly someone I rub elbows with, but when Devon pointed out to me that the cad refused to dance with you at your come-out, and then he did so wrong by you, carting you off to Gretna Green—I've had it in for the bloke ever since. I just don't particularly like the fellow."

Annie tried to ignore the little shudder of happiness that passed through her body at his words. "Ah, so you're chivalrous now, are you?"

Lord Ashbourne flashed her a charming smile. "Of course not," he scoffed. "I wouldn't want to ruin my black reputation."

Annie bit her lip to keep from smiling. It was nice of him, actually, to be so concerned about her. And the way he said it in that smooth steady voice made her believe he really meant it. But the fact was it was her life to do with what she would. She didn't need Lily or Devon and certainly not Lord Ashbourne telling her what to do. They didn't know how she felt.

"I'll admit it was bad of Arthur not to dance with me at my come-out, but he had a very good reason."

Jordan gave her a skeptical look. "Really? What's that?"

"He had just been informed by his father that he shouldn't be allowed to dance with me. You see, I had no dowry at the time."

Jordan shook his head. "That brings me to my next quarrel with the lad."

"He's not a lad, he's—"

"He's a lad to me, and you should let me finish. If there was a young lady with whom I wanted to dance, you can bet a blasted fortune I wouldn't let my *father* keep me from it." His voice held a savage note.

A bell went off in Annie's brain. Those words he'd just uttered held more pain than he probably meant them to. Despite herself, she was intrigued. First a secret past love and now this? Perhaps Lord Ashbourne wasn't just a devil-may-care rogue after all. Fascinating, really. But she forced herself to remain focused on the matter at hand. "That's easy for you to say; your father is no longer living."

He arched a brow. "Believe me. I didn't listen to my father even when he was alive."

She played with the strings to her reticule. "Be that as it may, Arthur and I"—she stopped at his raised brow—"Mr. Eggleston and I have put that little incident behind us. It's all in the past."

"And the elopement?"

Annie's cheeks burned. She glanced at Aunt Clarissa. Still asleep, thank heavens. Annie was also thankful for the darkness in the coach, for she was certain her face was bright pink. "It was entirely my idea. Arthur was just doing as I asked," she whispered.

"He shouldn't have," Lord Ashbourne said with surprising vehemence in his voice. "That's the problem. He should have known your reputation would have been shattered had you two succeeded. He should have talked you out of it."

Annie expelled her breath harshly. "There's no winning with you."

Lord Ashbourne shrugged. "I'm not trying to win."

Annie took a deep breath and attempted to start again. "Arthur and I both want the same things. Children, marriage, a family."

"Are you *sure* that's what he wants?"

"Doesn't everyone?"

Lord Ashbourne snorted. "No, they don't. I am one, actually, who wants no part of such societal trappings. And I'd venture to guess your precious Mr. Eggleston doesn't either or he would have married you by now."

Annie jerked her head to the side as if he'd slapped her. She sucked in her breath. His words stung. More than they should have. But she quickly shook it off. Regardless of the other nice things he'd said, *this* was exactly why she was not about to let her guard down and befriend Lord Ashbourne. And she wasn't about to let him get the upper hand either.

"You don't know anything about Arthur and me. Besides, you are an earl, are you not? If you don't marry and have heirs, your title will pass out of your direct line."

His perfect white smile flashed in the darkness and he settled back against his seat so Annie could no longer see his face. Good. It was much easier to fight with him when she wasn't aware of how handsome he was.

"Ah, I have the perfect plan," he answered.

There was that smugness in his tone again. "Which is?" She crossed her arms over her chest.

"I happen to have three younger brothers, all of whom are perfectly healthy and strapping. My first nephew shall be my heir."

"Lily told me your brothers aren't married either."

"Not yet. But they don't have an aversion to the institution the way I do. They'll come up to scratch eventually, and I'll have an heir without the tediousness of it all."

"Tediousness?" Annie scoffed. "That's a horrible way to put it. We're talking about love and marriage."

"No, we're talking about false emotions, an ungodly institution, and what amounts to a business arrangement between two people who couldn't care less about one another."

Annie's mouth fell open and she stared at him, aghast. "So that's it? You were in love once and never want to repeat the experience?"

"Something like that."

"What if I told you I believe we all only have one true love in a lifetime?"

His voice was tight. "All the more reason for me to remain a bachelor if that's the case."

She crossed her arms over her chest. "You are positively mad."

His tone remained mocking, jovial. "No. I'm merely attempting to get you to think twice about chasing after Arthur Eggleston. The man isn't worth it."

She clenched her fist in her skirts. "I am *not* chasing after Mr. Eggleston."

"Aren't you?" She couldn't see in the darkness, but she just knew that cocky brow was arched.

"Arthur loves me, and we plan to marry as soon as possible. That's what we were discussing in the garden before you rudely interrupted."

"And as you pointed out earlier, I shouldn't have been eavesdropping, but I was and I happen to know you were trying to convince Eggleston to marry you."

She clenched her teeth. "Then you also heard him say he would convince his father. Or weren't you paying attention to that part?"

"Yes, I heard it and it's most of what I'm basing my opinion upon. A real man doesn't ask for permission from his father."

"And I suppose you're a real man?"

He leaned forward again and flashed that blasted knee-weakening smile again. "I'm sure of it."

Despite the rush of heat his words brought to places she didn't want to contemplate at the moment, Annie shook her head angrily. "I don't care to discuss this topic with you any longer, Lord Ashbourne. In addition to your astounding arrogance, it's clear you're stuck in your ways and convinced you're always right. Far be it from me to try to convince you otherwise. Your heart is obviously made of stone."

He settled back into his seat. "I cannot blame you for wanting to change the subject, Miss Andrews. And I would be happy to do so, but I will not desist in my chaperonage. I don't relish it any more than you do. But Arthur Eggleston is not the right man for you. I'm sorry to be the one to say this. But has it ever occurred to you that Eggleston just doesn't seem that interested?"

Annie slapped her palm against the thick coach cushion. "Of *all* the nerve!"

Aunt Clarissa started awake. "Yes, dear. I'll have another glass of wine. Don't mind if I do. Thank you." She settled back into the cushion and promptly resumed her snores.

Despite Aunt Clarissa's outburst, Lord Ashbourne's haughty expression did not change.

Annie was breathing so hard, her nostrils flared. She put a hand to her chest to still the staccato beating of her heart. She glared out the window. She had nothing, absolutely nothing, left to say to Lord Ashbourne.

Eggleston just doesn't seem that interested.

What did Jordan Holloway know about it? He may have overheard one small conversation between herself and Arthur, but he had no idea why she loved him so.

Annie clenched her jaw. She knew two things for certain: first, she would marry Arthur Eggleston, and second, she would prove the cocky Lord Ashbourne wrong. If it was the very last thing she did.

CHAPTER 9

After seeing Annie and Aunt Clarissa safely inside Devon's town house, Jordan returned to his coach and threw himself inside, slamming the blasted door behind him.

He'd handled the entire evening atrociously. Why did he allow that pixie of a girl to get under his skin? *When* had he allowed it? He had no idea. But she was there. Blast it. Firmly implanted like a pebble in a horse's hoof. Jordan had always prided himself on being devil-may-care. But tonight, he'd cared. A lot. Enough to get into an argument with an innocent, of all people. Enough to show his temper. A temper many people didn't even know he possessed. How could that woman spark his emotions so easily?

Frankly, Jordan also prided himself on not giving a damn. He'd not given a damn in a great many years, actually, and he'd enjoyed it. If only Devon hadn't roped him into this confounded errand, chasing around a silly young miss who thought she was in love with the wrong person. And didn't the young *always* think they were in love? Not that love existed. He'd leave love (or at least marriage) up to his dutiful brothers, thank you very much.

Miss Andrews, that know-it-all, would see the folly of her ways, in time. It was unfortunate, really. She was setting herself up for failure . . . and pain.

Jordan clenched his jaw. That was it. Something about Annie reminded him of his own foolishness years ago. That was why her situation affected him so greatly. For some inexplicable reason he was determined to keep her from making the same mistake he had.

Jordan leaned against the coach cushions and scrubbed a hand across his face. His mind drifted back to a time over five years ago, a time when he'd been just as foolhardy as Annie. He'd fallen for a young lady. A young lady who had managed to convince him that she loved him. Him. Not his bloody title and his bloody fortune or his bloody looks, but *him*. And hadn't he played the fool as if he'd invented the role? Bringing her flowers, telling her he loved her, asking her to marry him . . .

He shook his head. He'd found out soon enough that it had all been a game to her. A game involving money and titles. Nothing more. Thank God he'd found out before it had been too late. Yes, he'd been saved. And he would never make that mistake again. His brothers didn't have to worry about a woman wanting them for their titles alone. They were not the heirs to the earldom. And while each of them had a sizable income, they would fare much better on the marriage mart. It was a risk Jordan had vowed never to take again.

He expelled his breath in a rush, bringing his attention back to the coach and his frustrating night with Annie Andrews. Damn it, he couldn't see Nicoletta now. That infernal kiss with Little Miss Mischief earlier had left him more aroused than he realized. And he couldn't get the confounded chit from his mind. Somehow the idea of losing himself in Nicoletta's lush exoticness didn't entice him the way it usually did. Nicoletta was all cynical and worldly and Annie was . . . the exact opposite. Since when did he find himself aroused by innocents, anyway? Good God, she was messing with his bloody head.

Very well, he'd go to the club and have a drink. There was always an amusement of some sort at the club and it was happily lacking in females.

He rapped on the door to the coachman. "The club, John," he commanded, and the conveyance started down the street with a jolt.

Jordan was two hands into a mildly entertaining card game when James Bancroft, Viscount Medford, appeared at his side. Jordan and Colton were old friends—well, enemies really—with Medford. The three had attended both Eton and Cambridge together. Devon and Jordan had been devil-may-care rogues. Medford was an impeccably starched perfectionist who made stellar marks and was the darling of the schoolmasters . . . and now the *ton*. His nickname was Lord Perfect.

In short, the man was . . . nauseating. *Perfectly* nauseating. But Lily was friendly with the man and that meant he and Colton had to be civil.

Medford pulled up a chair next to him and sat. "Fancy seeing you here, Ashbourne."

Jordan groaned. "Oh, excellent. The ideal end to this hideous evening."

Medford flashed a smile. "Ah, do I mistake my guess or do you mean you are not happy to see me?"

Jordan eyed Medford with a look of excruciating distaste. "When have I ever been happy to see you, Medford?"

The viscount straightened his already straight shoulders. "There is a first time for everything, Ashbourne. A first time for everything."

Jordan tossed his cards on the table, the end of the hand. "Are you going to play cards or bore me with meaningless witticisms all evening?"

Medford nodded to the dealer. "I'm in."

"Very well. Now leave me alone."

Medford cleared his throat. "I heard you'd escorted Miss Andrews to the Lindworths' this evening." He scooped up the cards he'd just been dealt.

Jordan groaned and ran his palm over his face. "Of course you did. Nothing in this town is unknown for long. But cut to the chase, Medford. What exactly do you want to know?"

Medford shuffled the cards in his hand. "Know? Nothing. I merely wanted to remind you that Annie is like a sister to me."

Jordan inclined his head toward Medford. "I'm happy to relinquish my chaperone duties into your perfectionistic hands, Medford. Just say the word."

"No, no, that's not necessary. I intend to enjoy watching you squirm."

Jordan rolled his eyes. "Oh, perfect."

Medford tossed a card on the table. "Lily did ask me to keep an eye on the two of you though. Perhaps she didn't trust you completely, although I can't imagine why."

Jordan narrowed his eyes on the other man. "As I said, I'm happy to relinquish my duties. It surprises me, in fact, that as close as you and Lily are, she didn't ask *you* to chaperone her sister. Says something, doesn't it?"

Medford's smile was tight. "Don't think I didn't volunteer, but Lily's sensitive to the fact that she asked a lot of me this year and didn't want to bother me with more. You'll do, Ashbourne. I daresay I prefer to see Annie in your company as opposed to Arthur Eggleston's. The man is named after a breakfast food, after all."

Jordan pressed his lips together to squash his smile. "Your point, Medford?"

Medford stood and tossed his cards on the table. "I'm out. I'm not much for gambling, as you know."

Jordan inclined his head. "Don't let me keep you."

Medford stared down his perfect nose. "My point is, Ashbourne, you're keeping an eye on Annie, and I'm keeping an eye on you."

CHAPTER 10

Jordan paced the salon at Devon's town house, waiting for Annie Andrews to grace him with her elusive presence. When she finally deigned to arrive, Jordan did his best not to notice she was wearing a yellow day dress that hugged her curves and brought out the sparkle in her dark eyes.

He rose to greet her and bowed over her dainty hand. She looked bright and fresh and pretty, with a smile that should lead many greater men than Arthur Eggleston on a merry chase. Jordan cleared his throat. "I thought I'd save us both a lot of unnecessary time and trouble and invite you to the Roths' this evening."

Annie pulled her hand away and snorted. "My, but you turn my head with your pretty invitations."

Jordan shrugged. "I've discovered that Lord Medford is watching my association with you, and with Lord Perfect taking note, I dare not make any mistakes. Besides, I am tasked with keeping an eye on you, and I've decided to do so with your cooperation rather than your petty unhappiness."

Annie laughed. "And now I'm petty? Honestly, I do

not know how you've remained a bachelor this long, my lord. I also don't know why Frances finds you so attractive," she mumbled.

"Is this the same Frances who called me a rakehell?" He grinned. "She said I was attractive too?"

Annie shook her head. "Oh, never mind, I daren't inflate your ego any further."

Jordan slapped his gloves against his thigh. "Look. You've been keeping me from my pastimes too, m'dear. Believe me, attending balls is hardly the way I prefer to spend my evenings."

Annie glanced away. "I'm sorry, truly I am, for being such a bother. But you're not exactly making my life easy, either. Can't we just agree to be pleasant acquaintances at these affairs?"

He eyed her skeptically. "Pleasant acquaintances?"

Annie nodded. "The truth is, Lord Ashbourne, I am feeling a bit churlish. Despite the fact that you were *exceedingly* rude to me last night"—she paused and gave him a brief, disapproving stare—"you don't deserve to have your schedule interrupted by seeing to me. I very much want to give you your freedom." She smiled at him.

Jordan narrowed his eyes on her. "My freedom? How would we manage that?"

Annie took a deep breath. "Aunt Clarissa is, ahem, a bit under the weather today. I can attend the Roths' dinner party this evening with my friend Frances and her mother. You can arrive late, make sure I'm minding my manners, and then leave. Go off on your usual . . . pursuits."

Jordan contemplated the matter. He liked the sound of it. He might make it to Nicoletta's house tonight after all. The lady had been more than peeved when he'd failed to pay her a call last night. He'd had to send a virtual hothouse of flowers to make up for it this morning. No doubt jewelry would be in order if he missed another visit.

Yes, he did like the sound of Miss Andrews's offer, *if* he could trust her. But what if she were just trying to trick him? The girl seemed honest enough, if completely misguided, but there was always the possibility . . .

He crossed his arms over his chest. "Do you promise not to take off into the gardens again with that sop Eggleston?"

Annie rubbed her temples. "*Must* you insult him?"

"Believe me, I'm doing the best I can. 'Sop' is the least offensive thing I have to say about him."

"Very well." Annie nodded. "I promise."

He eyed her suspiciously.

She smoothed her skirts "You don't believe me, do you?"

"On the contrary, Miss Andrews, I am merely considering your spotted past, including such endeavors as running off to Gretna Green."

Annie pressed her lips together. "That was a long time ago."

"That was six months ago." His arms remained crossed.

She pressed the palm of her hand to her forehead. "Be that as it may, I have no intention of—as you say—chasing after Mr. Eggleston."

"You'll excuse me if I say I find that difficult to believe?"

Annie tossed her hands in the air. She paced over to the sideboard and rang for tea, then she turned back to face Lord Ashbourne. "You have no reason not to trust me."

"I am a student of history, Miss Andrews. And as such, I've learned that history *always* repeats itself."

Annie was glad she was not facing him at present so he couldn't see her roll her eyes. The man thought he knew absolutely everything. About everything. Specifically, about her. But he didn't know her at all. It was true, she had been feeling churlish, and she had hoped they might declare a truce, but here he was acting arrogant again. Apparently, there was no reasoning with him.

Evans soon arrived with tea and Annie made a show of sitting down and pouring. "Don't let me keep you, Lord Ashbourne, if you're too busy for tea."

Jordan took a seat. "I'm not much for tea, to be honest, but I don't think we've concluded our discussion yet."

She gave him her most fake smile and pushed his teacup and saucer toward him. "Very well. What else do you intend to lecture me upon?"

"Lecture you? Bah." He swiped a hand through the air. "If you weren't so deuced sure of yourself, you might actually listen to what I have to say."

She batted her eyelashes at him and raised her teacup to her lips. "I'm listening. On tenterhooks, actually."

The silver of his eyes glinted through slits, but the hint of a smile rested in his perfectly molded lips. "Don't you think that just perhaps I've seen a bit more of the world than you have? Know a few things that you do not?"

She took a sip and set the delicate cup back on its saucer. "It's clear you think you know more but I've yet to hear anything I've found particularly wise."

He smiled then and shook his head. "You, Miss Andrews, are incorrigible. You were this way as a child, were you not? I can tell."

She straightened her shoulders. "I can only imagine

you as a child. A short dictator. Ordering your brothers about?"

He leaned back in his chair. "Something like that. But I was never short." He flashed her a grin.

Annie settled back into her chair. "I know how you older siblings are. Completely sure of yourselves and used to everyone falling into step behind you. You have very little concept of being wrong. But I assure you, it's possible."

Jordan watched her through grudgingly admiring eyes. He liked the young lady's confidence. He would allow her that. Of course she was entirely misguided, but give him a misguided confident person any day over a vacillating sort. Like Arthur Eggleston, for instance.

"I am not wrong about this, Miss Andrews. I stand by what I said last night. Eggleston is not the man for you."

"And I cannot fathom how you could possibly know that."

Jordan groaned. "Let's go about this in a different manner, shall we?"

She shrugged. "Very well."

"Why do you think he is the *right* man for you?"

Annie took a sip of tea. "When I met Arthur, I just knew."

Jordan had to fight to keep his expression blank. She was right. He *had* been exceedingly rude to her last night, and he was doing his deuced best to make up for it today, but she certainly wasn't making it easy for him. "How did you know?'

She got a downright dreamlike look in her eye. "I was coming back from the market with Mary one day. I'd dropped one of my parcels. Arthur picked it up for me. He smiled at me. He said, 'I thought the weather today was the most beautiful thing I'd ever seen until I saw you.'"

Jordan couldn't stop the eye roll this time. "Really? That's it? That's the entire reason you think you fell in love with him?"

"I don't think, I know. Besides." Annie glanced down at her hands then but not before Jordan saw a flash of pain in her eyes. "I don't expect anyone as beautiful as you to understand what it feels like when someone admires you for the first time in your life."

Jordan couldn't stop the jolt of masculine pride that shot through him. Annie apparently found him attractive. But her other words made Jordan frown. Admire her for the first time in her life? That couldn't possibly be true. Why, the girl was an undeniable beauty. What the deuce was she talking about? "No, Miss Andrews, but I do know the feeling when people falsely pretend to like you for who you are when really all they care about are your looks, or your connections, or your money."

Annie's brow wrinkled. "I'd never considered that, but it hardly applies to Arthur's feelings toward me. I had barely any connections when we met and no money at all."

Jordan shook his head. He shouldn't have said so much. And Annie was right. It had nothing to do with her. Besides, he was wasting his breath trying to convince her that she was not in love with Arthur Eggleston. He'd do well to keep his nose out of it for the next three weeks. Convincing her he was right was not part of being a chaperone. It was time to change the subject. "By the by, how is your fox?"

Annie gave him a wary look, no doubt suspicious about his quick shift in topic. "Dash is healing quickly and should be perfectly right in no time."

"I'm glad to hear it." Jordan stood and bowed to her. "I'll see you tonight."

Annie smiled then, no doubt relieved that he was going. "Leaving so soon? Aren't you going to drink your tea?"

"I'm more of the brandy sort."

Her smile was tight. "Not a surprise."

He made his way to the door. "Just to be clear, do you promise not to abscond to the gardens with Eggleston?"

She wore a decidedly impish look on her face. "Yes. Do you promise not to kiss me again, Lord Ashbourne?"

Apparently, she thought she was being funny. He turned to face her, an eyebrow quirked. He doffed his hat. Some devil on his shoulder prompted his answer. "Miss Andrews, I never make promises I cannot keep."

CHAPTER 11

The Roths' affair turned out to be much more diverting than Annie expected. Most likely due to the fact that Lord Ashbourne was noticeably absent. It had worked, her earnest attempt to appeal to his selfish side. When she'd offered to save him from his chaperone duties by requiring that he appear only later in the evening, she truly hadn't expected the rogue to agree. But here it was, halfway through the evening, and her bothersome chaperone had yet to appear. She didn't even have to watch for him. Frances had eagerly taken on that particular task.

Unfortunately, Frances would have liked nothing more than to actually find him, while Annie desperately hoped he would not arrive. She'd spent the evening pleasantly preoccupied with Arthur, who showed her a markedly higher level of interest since his sister had stayed at home with a head cold. It was true, Annie had to suffer through nearly constant sighs from Frances as that young lady held vigil for Lord Ashbourne, but Annie had danced twice with Arthur, he'd offered her a glass of punch, and he kept her laughing with his stories. Yes, all in all, the evening was a smashing success. So much so, that Annie had decided to be especially daring.

Her kiss from Lord Ashbourne replayed in her mind like a traitorous tune. It had distracted her all day. While she'd been receiving calls, walking in the park, and even when she and Mary had gone shopping on Bond Street, which was normally one of her favorite activities now that there was money with which to actually purchase items. But the shopping spree had turned into a nightmare of memories and Annie couldn't shake the image of Lord Ashbourne swooping in and kissing her. And when the man had pushed her up against the side of the house . . . Why, he'd nearly singed off her brows.

And what had he been about, teasing her? Saying he wouldn't promise never to kiss her again. Why, the very idea made her . . . Oh, she didn't want to think about what the idea made her.

She'd spent the entire day contemplating the matter, and she'd come to a most logical conclusion. If her kiss with Lord Ashbourne had been unforgettable and he meant nothing to her, then her kiss with Arthur, who meant everything to her, would be one for the history books.

Annie was extremely eager to prove her theory correct. But Arthur wouldn't like the idea of sneaking off alone with her two nights in a row. He'd been reluctant enough last night. They might not have such a fortuitous evening again, nor such a perfect opportunity. His sister's absence was rare, of course, but even more promising, that spy Ashbourne was blissfully inattentive for one night. Yes, she must act quickly.

"What are you planning to do?" Frances asked when

Arthur had gone off to speak with some of his mother's acquaintances across the room.

"What makes you think I'm planning something?" Annie did her best to replicate her sister Lily's infamous innocent face. It had been their mother's invention and Lily had managed to *perfect* it.

Frances crossed her arms over her middle and twisted back and forth at the waist. Annie eyed her. She could not get away with pretending in front of Frances. Her friend knew her too well.

"Very well, if you must know . . ."

"You know I must," Frances replied with a conspiratorial grin.

Annie lowered her voice to a whisper and glanced back and forth over both shoulders to ensure they wouldn't be overheard.

"I intend to ask Arthur to kiss me."

Frances's eyes went wide. She clutched at Annie's hands. "You're jesting. Oh, please tell me you're jesting."

"Have you ever known me to jest about such a thing?" She gave her friend a devilish grin.

"No," Frances whimpered. "And that is what frightens me."

Annie winked at her. "There is no time like the present, don't you know?"

"Why don't you ask Lord Ashbourne to kiss you? Now *that* would be a kiss."

Annie bit her lip. She'd studiously avoided telling Frances about her interlude with Lord Ashbourne. For one, it was completely irrelevant. It would certainly never be repeated. And two, she just might have to face poor Frances's envy. Why upset her friend over something so insignificant? She skipped over Frances's comment.

"I think tonight's perfect. Don't you? Miss Eggleston and Aunt Clarissa aren't here, and Lord Ashbourne apparently found something better to do this evening than dog my steps."

"No doubt he's off with his mistress," Frances said with a doleful sigh. "I heard she's very beautiful. They say she's an opera singer from Venice. He met her one night at La Fenice."

Annie's head snapped up. "Mistress?" An unfamiliar tightness crept into her chest. It couldn't be jealousy. Could it? But Lord Ashbourne had a mistress? And not just a mistress, but a very beautiful Italian opera singer mistress? Oh, of course he did. No doubt his mistress was an ethereal beauty. A man like Ashbourne would only be seen with the most gorgeous woman on earth.

"Yes, mistress," Frances repeated, dropping her voice even lower. "You know? A woman of ill repute."

Annie scowled. "I know exactly what a mistress is, Frances. I'm not a baby. I just had no idea Lord Ashbourne had one. Besides, how do you know so much about it?"

Frances slapped at her with her fan. "I happen to be excellent at eavesdropping," she announced. "And of course Lord Ashbourne has a mistress, silly. All the noblemen do. Except for Lord Colton and a handful of others who are truly in love with their wives, that is. But the unattached good-looking ones like Lord Ashbourne get their pick of the lot. He may have more than one, as rich and handsome and dashing as he is."

Annie blinked. Since when did Frances know more about scandalous things than she did? She was the sister of the author of *Secrets of a Wedding Night*, for goodness' sake.

"A mistress?" Annie repeated in a daze as if the concept would seem more real to her if she continued to say it out loud.

"I told you Lord Ashbourne is a rakehell. Keeping a mistress is probably the least of his sins." Frances winked at her.

Annie bit her lip. She refused to consider the tightening in her chest when she thought of Lord Ashbourne with a mistress, but there was something else on her mind. Something that made her throat close and her breathing hitch.

"You don't think Arthur has a mistress, do you?"

Frances clapped her hand over her mouth and it took Annie a few moments to realize her friend was . . . laughing. Giggling, actually. Apparently the idea of Arthur with a mistress was comical to her.

"What?" Annie asked, giving Frances a condemning glare. "Arthur might have a mistress."

"I don't think either his mother or his sister would allow it." The giggling continued.

This time, Annie crossed her arms over her chest and glared at Frances. The laughing subsided.

"Oh, Anne, don't take this amiss, but Mr. Eggleston's not . . . He's just not . . . the type of man to have a mistress."

Annie shrugged and pushed up her chin. "Why should I take it amiss? I should think it a sign of great character to not employ a mistress."

"Yes, well, there is that, but I rather meant he doesn't quite have the . . . er . . . situation a mistress requires."

Annie sighed. "You mean because he isn't rich or titled?"

Frances nodded. "Yes, precisely, in addition to being of the highest character, of course."

Annie sniffed. "If being wealthy and titled leads to debauchery, it's just as well Arthur is neither of those things."

"Ahem, speaking of debauchery," Frances replied, "how do you intend to get Mr. Eggleston to kiss you?"

Annie gave her friend a sly smile. "I'm going to *ask* him. And there's nothing debauched about it. I intend to be happily married to Arthur in the very near future and one kiss is nothing compared to that."

"One kiss is nothing *after* you're married," Frances corrected. "Before you're married it is quite a bit of something."

Annie waved her hand in the air, dismissing the subject and trying not to remember the kiss she'd shared with Lord Debauchery himself last night.

"Where exactly do you intend to have this kiss? I thought you said you promised Lord Ashbourne you wouldn't take off alone with Mr. Eggleston?"

The innocent look again. "I promised Lord Ashbourne I wouldn't take off into the *gardens* with Arthur and I have no intention of doing so. Besides, the Roths' gardens aren't much to visit, to be honest." She shook her head.

Frances gave her a warning look. "Anne, are you quite certain you want to defy Lord Ashbourne?"

Annie fought the urge to grind her slipper into the marble floor. "I'm not defying him. I just explained it all to you. But even if I were defying him, who is he to tell me what to do? He's neither my guardian, my relative, nor my husband."

"Oh, how I wish he were *my* husband." Frances sighed.

Annie shook her head. "Look, I must be quick. Arthur will be returning soon. When he asks where I've gone, tell him you're not sure."

She turned to leave, but Frances's hand on her sleeve stopped her. "Wait. Where are you going?"

"Why, to the library, of course." Annie winked at Frances and left in a flash, skittering out the door to ensure her exit before she encountered Arthur.

She made her way down the shadowy corridors of the Roths' town house until she came to the door she remembered as the entrance to the library. She'd been to the house several times before, once for an impromptu musicale that was held in this cozy room. In fact, if she remembered correctly, there was a large green velvet sofa that would be just perfect for a first kiss. Well, a second kiss . . . No, that other kiss hadn't counted. It had been a mistake, one she was about to rectify.

She spent a few minutes nervously waiting in the hallway before a footman happened by.

"May I bother you for a quill and some parchment?" she asked the young man who smiled from ear to ear and hurriedly ushered her into the room, sat her down at the desk, and waited while she penned a note to Arthur asking him to meet her in the library posthaste. When she finished, she folded the sheet, wrote Arthur's name on the outside, and delivered it into the footman's hands.

"For Mr. Eggleston," she said, watching as the servant pulled a silver tray from a nearby divan and deposited her note atop it.

"Right away, miss," he replied, hurrying from the room.

Annie watched him go and sucked in her breath. Her elbow braced on the desktop, she rested her chin in her hand and drummed the fingers of her opposite hand along a leather-bound tome sitting in front of her. Next, she stood and paced across the plush carpets. She found a looking glass on the wall and glanced at her reflection. She'd always looked her best with her hair in a chignon. She pulled one wide curl down to hang against her temple. She pinched her cheeks to pinken them, then puckered her lips at the mirror. Oh, she was hardly as beautiful as Jordan Holloway's seductive mistress no doubt was, but it would just have to do.

"Kiss me, Arthur. Kiss me," she whispered. Then she laughed at her own silliness. She turned back to face the room and hurried over to the green sofa. She had remembered it correctly, and it was even more soft and inviting than she recalled. She settled herself into a corner of the furniture, her back to the door, and spread her violet skirts around her. She pulled down her décolletage, ensuring that she presented the most fetching picture. When Arthur saw her he wouldn't be able to resist. Would he?

A slight knock sounded at the door and Annie's breath caught in her throat.

"Come in," she called, her voice shaking ever so slightly.

The knob turned and the door creaked open. It was shut soon after and the telltale clip-clop of boots on the floor told Annie he was coming toward her.

She squeezed her eyes shut. This was it. Now or never.

"Oh, Arthur, don't say anything. Just kiss me," she breathed.

"The best-laid schemes of mice and men do often go awry."

Annie's eyes snapped open. She knew the line to the Robert Burns poem. She'd read it a dozen times.

But it was not Arthur's voice quoting it.

Slowly, she turned her head.

Just as she'd thought.

Towering over her, a mocking smile on his lips, was none other than Jordan Holloway.

CHAPTER 12

Annie scrambled up from the sofa and whirled to face Jordan with her hands on her hips and an accusing gleam in her eye. "What are you doing here? Why must you forever be nosing around in my affairs?"

"Might I remind you that you agreed to behave yourself tonight?" he drawled.

Annie tapped her slipper on the carpet. "If you were the smallest bit agreeable you would look the other way and we might be friends rather than adversaries."

Jordan ran a hand across the back of his neck. He'd tried. He really had, to keep his nose and his opinion out of her affairs, but the chit didn't make it easy on him. He'd arrived at the Roths' intent upon nodding and smiling at her, before taking her up on her offer and getting on with his own . . . pursuits. But the moment he'd arrived, unable to locate Annie, he'd intercepted a footman who was carrying a note from her to Arthur Eggleston. Apparently, she'd decided it was a good idea to have a clandestine meeting with the bloke in the library. Of all the . . . The girl seemed intent upon ruining her reputation. Which would be perfectly fine with him *if* Jordan weren't currently responsible for protecting it. Annie Andrews needed to see reason and she needed it now.

Jordan slapped his gloves against his thigh with a loud snap. "Allow me to explain something to you. Men aren't that complicated. If they're interested, they show their interest."

Annie sucked in her breath. "Frances says he only has eyes for me when I'm not looking."

Jordan let some of the frustration drain from his voice. He could tell by the way she'd sucked in her breath that his remark had hurt her. "Frances is your friend. She may merely be telling you what she knows you want to hear. "Besides, I've been hearing increasing amounts of gossip about you lately. Lady Cranberry said some things I won't repeat in polite conversation. Your reputation is in danger whether you know it or not."

Annie expelled her breath and wrapped her arms around her middle. Was it possible Lord Ashbourne was right? She didn't want to believe it but she had to admit it was possible. Did Frances only tell her these things to make her happy? Was she being a fool? Was the entire *ton* gossiping about her?

She looked him square in the eye. "Is that what you really think?" she asked him quietly. "That Fran is just saying what I want to hear?"

Lord Ashbourne's countenance softened. "I think whatever his true feelings for you, Eggleston doesn't treat you half as well as you should be treated."

Annie's heart flipped in her chest, then it pounded rapidly.

Lord Ashbourne didn't stop to take a breath. "You should have a young man chasing you about, *not* the other way around. I've seen this before. It's incredibly frustrating. Women love a challenge. They always want what they cannot have. Bah. That's what is ridiculous. The fact is that you're chasing around a man who doesn't care whether you catch him. You deserve better than that, Annie."

It was the use of her Christian name that brought the unexpected tears to Annie's eyes. She swallowed hard and looked up at him; their gazes met. A spark leaped between them.

But just as quickly, the mood was shattered. "You're making a spectacle of yourself," he said. "And I'm attempting to do you a favor. If you weren't so stubborn and sure of yourself, you'd realize that."

Making a spectacle of herself? Annie splayed a hand across her middle. An awful sinking feeling had begun in the pit of her stomach. An awful sinking feeling that Lord Ashbourne was actually right. But she couldn't let go of her argument so easily. Lord Ashbourne was perfectly right. She'd always been stubborn. "You *are* just like Lily," she threw at him. "Completely predictable. Every time one of you meddlers tries to control another person, you use the same old excuse that you're doing it for my own good. Of course you know better. You know best. You know everything!" She stalked past him, intent on leaving him alone in the library.

Lord Ashbourne's hand shot out. He grabbed her arm and swung her around to face him. "Damn it. Why do you refuse to listen to me? You're making me insane. By God, you're more sure of yourself than . . . I am." A muscle ticked in his jaw. "How can I make you see reason? You make me want to yell. You make me want to pound my fist through the wall. You make me want to . . ."

"What?" she asked breathlessly, her eyes still shooting fire at him. "I make you want to what?"

He scrubbed a hand through his hair. "If you weren't so damn stubborn you'd have let me finish what I was trying to say earlier. I know a spectacle when I see one because the exact same thing happened to me, an age ago. I made a complete fool of myself, if you must know. If I could do it over again, I wouldn't hesitate. I'm older than you and I've seen more than you, so in this case, yes, I do know better and I do know best. As for being predictable—"

He tugged her into his arms and kissed her.

It was *anything* but predictable. Annie's hair nearly caught fire. His lips swooped down to capture hers. His tongue invaded her mouth. Her head tilted back and her eyes closed of their own volition. She clung to him. His mouth, which had begun demanding, softened into an insistent invasion. His thumb brushed across her cheek. His fingertips skimmed her hairline. The taste of him, like heat and hazelnuts and spice, flooded her senses. She never wanted it to stop.

She'd made him angry, she knew. Angry enough to . . . kiss her? It made no sense, but at the moment she didn't care. His hot, insistent mouth probed at her lips and she opened to him, allowing his tongue to brush inside, own her, possess her. The man had a way of making her feel all melty. Like molasses and caramel and chocolate. She shuddered. He shouldn't be doing this but neither should she. If she could summon just an ounce of resistance, she would push him away, but the strong, hard heat of him was intoxicating and all she wanted to do was keep kissing him forever.

Endless moments later, Lord Ashbourne shuddered and pulled away. Annie breathed heavily, her chest rising and falling in a rhythm that made her feel as if her heart might beat out of her chest. His face was harsh and handsome in the glow of the candles. If she didn't know any better, she would think he was breathing heavily too.

He set her away from himself. His eyes shone like molten silver. "Now, if you'd stop acting like a brat, you might just realize what is good for you. And that is to take my advice."

He turned on his heel and stalked out of the room. Annie turned her head away and pressed her fingertips to her burning lips.

The Earl of Ashbourne had just called her a brat.

But even more shockingly he'd just kissed her again for no good reason.

No good reason whatsoever.

CHAPTER 13

Annie tapped her finger against her cheek. She and Frances stood in the corner of the Roths' ballroom. Annie had just finished telling her friend the details of her encounter with Lord Ashbourne in the library, minus the small matter of their (ahem, second) kiss.

"I'm telling you," Annie said. "It simply makes no sense. The man is like the statue of David. Made of stone. I just cannot imagine him ever deigning to grace a mere mortal with his earthly presence. I cannot fathom who he would make a fool of himself over."

Frances sighed. "Whoever the woman from Lord Ashbourne's past was, she had to be a complete idiot. Only a fool would turn down David . . . or Jordan Holloway."

Annie snorted. "Perhaps it was because he's rude, arrogant, controlling—" But even as she said the words, her mind was betraying her with thoughts of their kiss in the library. She couldn't even summon anger at his having called her a brat.

She hated to admit it but he was right. She had been behaving like one.

Frances shook her head. "Tall, dark, and handsome," she added.

"Oh, who cares?"

"I do."

Annie grimaced at her friend. It was true, the earl's perfect veneer had cracked just a touch when he'd admitted to her that he'd made a fool of himself over someone years ago, but it still didn't change the fact that he was overbearing—Frances was right about his being tall, dark, and handsome, but overbearing trumped all three of those pesky truths.

So she'd seen a crack in his armor, one that made him seem the faintest bit human for a few moments. She bit her lip. Was Lord Ashbourne right? Was Arthur really completely wrong for her?

True, it was absolutely none of Lord Ashbourne's affair. Just as his past was none of hers. But she couldn't help but be intrigued by the thought that some woman had caused him to make a fool of himself. Lord Ashbourne, more than Lord Colton even, had a reputation for being completely untouchable. The man had three younger brothers all nearly as handsome as he, and he'd famously declared he would never marry and produce an heir. But it caused one to wonder, did it not? Had Lord Ashbourne always been so staunchly against the institution of marriage? Or was the woman he'd made himself a fool over responsible for his feelings on the subject?

And why, oh why, had he kissed her like that?

Annie turned to her friend. She bit her lip. "Frances, may I ask you something?"

Frances stopped and placed her hand over Annie's. "Of course. Anything."

"Do you tell me things you think I want to hear?"

Frances's brow furrowed. "What do you mean, Anne?"

"I mean about Arthur. Do you truly think . . . he cares for me?"

Frances squeezed her hand. "Why, of course he does, Anne. He told you he loves you, didn't he?"

Annie nodded.

"And he said he wants to marry you?"

Another nod.

"He cares for you. I'm sure of it."

Annie gave her friend a small smile. "Thank you, Fran. I love you."

"I love you too." She smiled back, then clapped her hands. "Now, how can we learn the story about Lord Ashbourne's past?"

Annie glanced about. "There must be someone we can ask."

Frances's face held a bit of a pout. "I know no one of an age who is in a position to know what happened. My sisters are both too young and I just asked Mother and she said she had no earthly idea what I was talking about."

Annie shook her head. "Of course Lily and Devon probably know, but they are gone."

"What we need to do is find a gossip, someone who is older than we are and who isn't above sharing the details."

"Good idea. Let's scan the ballroom. We'll meet back here at half past."

"Good plan," Frances replied with a wink.

They took off in opposite directions. Annie made her way around the perimeter of the ballroom, her eyes scanning the crowd for the biggest gossip she could find.

"Anne, there you are."

She turned toward the voice of her old friend.

"Lord Medford, good to see you."

James Bancroft was tall and lean with sandy brown hair and penetrating hazel eyes, a sharp nose, and a straight brow. The man was undeniably handsome and was as rich as anyone save the king himself, but Annie had always known him as her sister's good friend. He was like an older brother to her. And they remained friends, despite Lord Colton's obvious antagonism toward the viscount.

"What are you up to?" Lord Medford asked, a conspiratorial grin on his face.

She shot him her innocent look. "Up to? I don't know what you mean."

His grin widened and he shook his head. "Just like your sister, and let's just say I can always tell when she is up to something as well."

Annie bit her lip. "I'm not up to anything."

"Out with it, miss."

Annie scowled. Lord Medford had always been too smart by half. "Very well, come with me." She pulled him behind a potted palm and glanced about to ensure no one was watching them. She lowered her voice to a whisper. "What do you know about Lord Ashbourne making a fool of himself over some young woman years ago?"

Medford scratched his head. "Is *that* what you're up to? Investigating Ashbourne?"

She shrugged. "He mentioned it. I'm merely curious."

Medford crossed his arms over his chest. "But he didn't see fit to tell you the details, did he?"

Annie scowled at him. "Do you know what happened?"

Medford shrugged. "Actually, I'm quite happy to say

I do not. Not that I would share the gossip if I knew it. Ashbourne's been a confirmed bachelor for a great many years."

"Don't play coy with me, Lord Medford. I happen to know about your printing press. You're not above gossip."

He winked at her. "Believe me, I'd love to have something I could hold over Ashbourne's head. But I don't know anything about it."

Annie tapped her finger against her cheek. "Whom could I ask?"

"You could always ask Colton when he returns," Medford offered with another grin.

"I cannot possibly wait nearly three weeks."

Medford he shook his head. "How did I know you would say that?" He didn't wait for her answer. "Do you know what I find interesting about this, Anne?"

Annie eyed him carefully. "What?"

"I came here tonight expecting to find you hovering about Arthur Eggleston. Instead I find you attempting to ferret out gossip about Ashbourne."

She raised her chin. "First of all, I do not ferret. And secondly, I don't hover."

He gave her a look that implied he didn't believe either claim.

Annie straightened her shoulders. "Truly. I expect Arthur to ask me to dance at any moment and I . . ." She paused and bit her lip. "Lord Medford. May I ask you a question?"

"Of course," he answered gamely. "Anything."

"Do you think Arthur is the right man for me?"

Medford flashed a smile. "Don't worry, Anne. I think you will end up with the exact right man for you."

Annie had no time to contemplate that vague answer

before a footman approached, interrupting them. "Miss Andrews?"

Annie glanced up. "Yes?"

"Lord Ashbourne requests that you gather your cloak and meet him in the foyer. He intends to escort you home immediately."

CHAPTER 14

Annie allowed Lord Ashbourne to help her up into the carriage before jerking her arm from his grasp. She plopped into her seat and stared at him, her lips tightly pressed together, as he settled in across from her. Thankfully, her irritation with him made it easier to forget about their kiss in the library.

"Now who was making a spectacle?" She crossed her arms over her chest. "You embarrassed me back there."

Lord Ashbourne watched her through half-lidded eyes. "It was hardly a spectacle. But the fact is, you've proven yourself to be untrustworthy. I'm taking you home."

She narrowed her eyes on him. "Untrustworthy? How?"

Lord Ashbourne relaxed back in the seat as if he didn't have a care in the world. "You promised me you'd stop cavorting with Mr. Eggshell and act appropriately."

Annie folded her hands in her lap. "I promised no such thing. I merely agreed not to meet Mr. *Eggleston* out in the gardens. And I did nothing of the sort."

Lord Ashbourne groaned. "Even worse than I thought,

a woman who cavils over details. Now I'm going to have to watch you twice as closely."

Annie ground her teeth. "Twice as closely? Are you mad? Besides, I have Aunt Clarissa to watch over me."

His brow shot up. "I think we both know the audacity of that claim." He let out a long breath. "Besides, can't you consider making my task easier and just wait nicely until your sister returns before you act inappropriately?"

"It's highly ironic for you to be mentioning inappropriateness, or wasn't that you who kissed me in the library earlier?"

Jordan cracked a smile and inclined his head. "Guilty."

That was it. Annie clamped her lips together and stared out the window. There was no reasoning with this man. He was convinced he was completely right. And he wouldn't stop. She realized that now. He intended to hunt her down on a daily basis like a hound chasing a fox. And there was nothing she could do to stop it.

She tapped her fingertips along her elbows. If only Arthur would get on with it and ask her to marry him. If she were engaged, she would have no cause to act inappropriately. Why, she could be as proper as anyone.

She settled back into her seat and tried to think through things calmly, rationally. Why wasn't Arthur coming up to scratch? Was Lord Ashbourne right after all? Was Arthur wrong for her? Lily thought so, but Lily of course was biased and Lord Ashbourne agreed with his friends. Annie trusted Lord Medford completely but he'd been maddeningly vague when she'd asked his opinion.

Oh, she didn't know what to believe anymore.

When the coach pulled up in front of Devon's town house, Annie reluctantly allowed Lord Ashbourne to help her down. She gathered her reticule in one hand and her skirts in the other and hopped to the ground.

Lord Ashbourne escorted her to the front door. "Miss Andrews," he said while Annie searched for the key in her reticule. She'd learned to take a key with her. Evans was often asleep by the time she came home. "You might consider acting a bit less . . . rambunctious."

Annie gave him a tight smile. "You would know about acting rambunctious, Lord Ashbourne."

He returned her smile. "Yes. I would. Quite a bit, actually. And I know how much trouble can accompany it."

She slipped the key from her reticule and jammed it into the lock. "Don't let me keep you from your pastimes, my lord. I'm sure there's some sort of dissolution going on somewhere that is missing you." She couldn't bring herself to mention his mistress, but a lump formed in her throat at the thought.

Her key clicked in the lock just then, and Annie pushed the door wide, marched inside, and shut it in his face.

Staring at the closed door, Jordan let out his pent-up breath. Two weeks and five days couldn't come soon enough to rid himself of that hoyden. No doubt it would be the longest fortnight of his life. Dissolution indeed. She knew nothing of dissolution.

He shook his head. It had become clear to him tonight that Annie Andrews was not about to change her ways and make things a bit easier on him. She intended to make a fool of herself over Arthur Eggleston and it was Jordan's nightmare to stop her. He'd tried reasoning with her and he'd tried logic. Now, all he could do was track her like a hound. And that's exactly what he intended to do. The *ton* was gossiping about her and he had to make that stop. The chit thought she could outsmart him, but she was sorely mistaken.

Bloody hell. Why exactly had he agreed to this impossible task in the first place? Colton had better be having a damned good time on his honeymoon trip.

And why the deuce Jordan had kissed her again was anybody's guess. Something about the way she'd said the word "predictable," turning it into a taunt, a challenge. For some blasted reason she brought out his competitive side.

Returning to the street, Jordan hoisted himself into the coach and rapped on the door that separated the interior from the coachman.

"Miss Nicoletta's house, milord?" the coachman asked.

Jordan paused a moment. Damn it, Annie Andrews was responsible for more than just turning him into a preoccupied chaperone. Now she was ruining his sex life. "No, John. Not tonight. Take me to the club."

He sat back against his seat and the coach jolted into motion.

Jordan expelled his breath. Blast it. Tomorrow he'd have to go shopping on Bond Street. For jewelry.

CHAPTER 15

Ah, the theater. Annie had only been there one other time, but she adored the theater. Tonight she'd managed to somehow elude the Earl of Ashbourne when he'd called on her earlier to inquire after her plans for the evening. She'd sent Mary down with a note informing him that she wasn't feeling well and would be spending the evening in her room, resting. Of course, Mary was known for her forgetfulness, so when Lord Ashbourne had pressed the maid for details, she was able to honestly answer that she wasn't entirely sure of her mistress's symptoms. But the note indicated she was ill and that was clear enough.

In fact, it was Evans, hovering outside the drawing room door, who had to tell Annie exactly what the earl had said as Mary was unable to recall those details either. But in the end, the earl had left, apparently slapping his leather gloves against his thigh as if he were perturbed. Annie, when informed of his departure, breathed a sigh of relief, then picked up Bandit and Leo in each arm and kissed the little furry babies upon their heads. Dash rested in his basket under the dressing table. The little fox's paw had steadily healed and he now favored it only occasionally.

After the baffling night at the Roths', Annie had decided that she needed to stay away from Lord Ashbourne for a different reason altogether. As far away as possible. He'd confused her with his kiss. And she'd been thinking about that kiss more and more often lately. Too often. What was that about? It made no sense. No, she needed to stay far away from the man and evading him was the only way she could think of to do so. She'd managed to elude him these last days since the incident at the Roths'. They had two weeks and two days remaining until Lily returned. It couldn't be that difficult to continue to keep her distance, could it?

Yes. She was quite proud of herself for having slipped away from Jordan Holloway tonight. Aunt Clarissa was enjoying an evening of cards with some friends. Annie had come to the theater with Frances and her mother. And she was intent on thinking of neither man this evening, Lord Ashbourne or Arthur Eggleston.

They'd both been causing her nothing but trouble lately.

Lord Ashbourne had nearly convinced her the other night that Arthur felt nothing for her. Unfortunately, the earl had a point. Arthur was maddeningly evasive. One moment he was more than happy to leave with her for Gretna Green and the next he was declaring that they should be in no rush to marry.

And Annie was sick of it. She refused to be the fool chasing around a man who had little concern for her. She'd die a childless spinster before she made a cake of herself any longer. Tonight was for fun. A large ivory sash graced the empire waist of her blue gown, and with her ivory kid slippers and matching gloves, she was positively presentable. Besides, she'd always enjoyed the theater and she was here with her closest friend in the world. Who needed men?

Frances's mother was off chatting with friends before the performance started, so the two young women sat in the Birminghams' box alone.

"Frances." Annie turned to her friend. "I've decided I shall neither think nor speak of either Arthur or Lord Ashbourne tonight. Mark my words." She gave a decisive nod.

"Ooh, speaking of Lord Ashbourne, have you managed to find anyone to tell you the story of his past?" Frances asked.

Annie sighed. "What did I just say?" She laughed. "And no, I have not, but not from lack of trying."

"Me too," Frances admitted. "I've inquired of nearly everyone who's crossed my path. I swear if they didn't think I was madly obsessed with Lord Ashbourne before, the *ton* certainly does now." She shook her head. "But it would be worth the gossip to find out that tidbit."

"Keep trying," Annie replied, squeezing her friend's hand. "This town adores gossip. Surely it's only a matter of time before we find someone who knows. All right. From now on. No more talk of either man. I mean it."

Frances bit her lip. "Um. Anne."

"Yes?"

"What if . . . Mr. Eggleston is . . . here?" Frances whispered.

Annie's head snapped up. "What? Where?" She glanced around.

Frances pointed her fan a bit to the right, indicating a box at the far end of their row. Not a particularly enviable view, but any box was better than a seat on the floor, of course. Annie strained her neck to see into Arthur's box. There he sat, a pleasant smile on his always pleasant face, his peaked-looking sister propped up in a chair by his side.

Annie pushed up her chin. "I had no idea he would be here tonight," she sniffed. "But I do not care."

Frances gave her a skeptical look. "You don't?"

"Not a bit." But Annie couldn't help glancing back over at him. "Do you think he's seen us?"

"I'm not sure he can from where's he's sitting."

"It's for the best then." She turned to look at the stage, praying the performance would begin and spare her from the uncertainty of whether Arthur knew she was there.

"I think you should go greet him," Frances said.

Annie's mouth dropped open. "Frances! No. Why should I? If he wanted to see me, he would come over here."

"But he hasn't seen you, obviously," Frances reasoned. "I'm sure he'd like to know you're here."

Annie bit her lip. Was it rude of her not to greet him? No. No. She'd already decided that she would not throw herself at him ever again. "No. I refuse to be the one—"

"I'll go with you," Frances whispered.

"Frances." Annie plunked her hands on her hips and gave her friend an exasperated look.

Frances winked at her. "I know. I know. But if you're a hopeless romantic, I'm an even more hopeless one and I've always believed Mr. Eggleston loves you. You must give him a chance to prove it."

"Why? What has he ever really done to prove it?" Annie asked, Lord Ashbourne's words echoing in her head.

"Let's see. Let's make a list."

Annie nodded. Indeed, a list. Perhaps it was just the thing she needed to decide whether Lord Ashbourne was right and she was making a fool of herself over Arthur.

"First of all," Frances began, "he told you you were beautiful. That proves his intelligence."

Annie had to smile at that.

"Secondly, he did attempt to take you to Gretna Green. And while we can all agree that wasn't the best idea, it proves he truly wanted to marry you."

Annie nodded. She couldn't deny that.

"And lastly, didn't you tell me that he told you in the Lindworths' gardens that he does indeed still intend to marry you?"

"Yes, but—"

"Yes, but nothing. Your future husband is sitting right over there, Anne, and you're refusing to go speak with him."

Well, when Frances put it like that, it did seem a bit petty of her.

"Now, do you want me to go with you or don't you?" Frances asked, settling the matter.

Annie glanced around. She supposed she could just pop over quickly and be back before the performance started. It wouldn't be so very awful, would it?

"I'll go," Annie said. "But just for a moment. You stay here."

"Good luck." Frances gave her a conspiratorial grin. "But do hurry back before Mother arrives. She'll wonder where you've gotten to."

"I'll hurry." Annie squeezed her friend's hand and stood to leave, but she bit her lip and sat back down quickly on the edge of the seat.

Annie's heart pounded. She searched Frances's face. "So you really, truly think Arthur . . . cares for me?"

Frances's eyes were wide. "Why, of course he does, Anne. Who wouldn't love you?"

"Thank you, Fran." She stood and gave Frances an encouraging smile and a wink just before she pushed the curtain aside and slipped out of the box.

Annie took a deep breath and walked the thirty or so paces down to Arthur's seat. She pressed her hand to her belly to calm her nerves just before she pushed the curtain aside. "Good evening, Mr. Eggleston, Miss Eggleston. So good to see you."

Jordan Holloway glanced across the theater and looked twice. He was sitting with Nicoletta, who was absolutely not pleased with him of late. He'd spent the last several nights noticeably absent from her life and her bed while he traipsed about the city, chasing around a certain incorrigible brunette. Tonight he was taking a long-awaited and much-needed break from doing so. Or at least he'd intended to.

Jordan had made some inquiries and discovered that Eggleston would be at the theater tonight. That suited Jordan's purposes fine. He could take Nicoletta out for a long overdue evening's entertainment and he could keep an eye on Annie's prey at the same time. After all, if she were going to appear, it would no doubt be here. But even she must have the sense not to chase the man to the theater when he obviously hadn't invited her. Or so Jordan had thought.

When he'd stopped by Devon's town house to see Annie earlier, he'd certainly been more than skeptical about the state of her health and the note she'd sent, but it was not as if he could have stalked up to her bedchamber and called her a liar. He supposed there had been a large part of him that had wanted to believe the story. Wanted to assume she'd be safely at home all night and not out roaming the streets hunting down that ridiculous Eggleston.

Jordan glanced across the theater again to the row of seats at the end of the opposite gallery. There she was. Her bright blue dress shining like a beacon in the box of none other than Arthur Eggleston.

Jordan expelled his breath. Hard. She had lied to him. She had thwarted him. But most importantly, she was making a fool of herself. Again. Did the girl have no concept of the rumors swirling about? He was worried for her reputation. Why didn't she seem to be? The entire *ton* was agog over the way she appeared to be throwing herself after Mr. Eggleston, ever since her sister left town.

And Jordan had been the one following her around like a bloody lady's maid, trying to convince her to see reason. He'd even gone so far as to deliver a deuced chivalrous speech on the matter in an attempt to convince her. And he was never chivalrous. What the hell had he become?

"Ah," said Lady Cranberry from one box over. "There goes that Miss Andrews again. If her new dowry hasn't attracted that Eggleston lad by now, she hasn't much hope, does she, poor dear?"

Jordan clenched his jaw.

"I daresay," replied Lord Cranberry. "Colton's obviously going to have to settle a bit more on the gel before Eggleston comes up to scratch." The corpulent man chuckled.

That was it!

Annie's reputation was being ripped to shreds on his watch, and while Jordan might not relish his role as a chaperone, he had absolutely no intention of failing at the task. Not to mention he'd be forced to explain the embarrassing situation when Devon and Lily returned.

But blast it, there was something else. Something that clenched in his chest every time he saw Annie throwing herself at Eggleston. It was the same helpless emotion that grabbed him every time he thought about the hapless twenty-five-year-old lad he once had been, mooning over Miss Georgiana Dalton. It was the same blend of disgust and regret he felt each time he wished he could go back and talk to that young lad, tell him to stop it, tell him what a huge mistake he was making. He already knew talking to Annie would get him nowhere. She was so sure of herself and her supposed feelings. She refused to listen to him. And she was making a blasted huge mistake.

Eggleston wasn't good enough for her and it had nothing to do with his lack of either title or fortune. Eggleston wasn't good enough for Annie simply because he didn't adore her in the way every single person deserved to be adored by the one they intended to dedicate their life to. True, he personally didn't believe in love and all of that nonsense, but Annie did. And when someone believed that strongly, they deserved a partner who believed too.

And there was another emotion there, Jordan realized, rising to the surface and blocking out all the others like a black cloud on the horizon before a thunderstorm. Anger. He was angry with Eggleston for being such a blind idiot. He was even more angry with Annie for refusing to see the obvious. But he was most angry with himself for giving a bloody damn.

Jordan surged to his feet, his jaw still tightly clenched. "Excuse me for a moment."

Nicoletta glanced at him with a wary look in her dark eyes. *"Certamente,"* she replied with a short nod.

Jordan stalked down the corridor, down the steps, through the lobby, up the opposite steps, and into the corridor on the other side of the theater, his anger eclipsing all rational thought. He ripped open the curtain to Eggleston's box and lunged inside.

The heads of the box's three occupants snapped up to look at him. Annie's eyes were moons. The engaging smile that had been on her face turned to a cold frown. Surprise briefly registered on her face. Then her hand flew to her throat.

Jordan stared her down and he spoke through clenched teeth. "Miss Andrews, it seems you've made a miraculous recovery from your previous condition this evening."

She cleared her throat, her eyes cast downward. "Yes, well, I—"

"Miraculously recovered?" he taunted.

"Something like that," she murmured.

Jordan sensed she didn't want him to embarrass her in front of the Egglestons, but he was beyond caring.

"I'm sorry to have interrupted your evening, Mr. Eggleston, Miss Eggleston." Jordan nodded briefly to the siblings before turning his attention back to Annie. "Miss Andrews, gather your things; I'm escorting you home. Now." The last word was growled through clenched teeth.

She didn't look at him, but the pink glow that spread along her cheeks indicated both her embarrassment and her anger. "Thank you for the kind offer, Lord Ashbourne, but I intend to stay."

He narrowed his eyes on her. "It was not a request."

She turned to face him head-on. Her fists clenched at her sides. "No. *You* misunderstand *me*. I'm not leaving."

His smile was tight, his voice low and dark. "Don't make me drag you out of here, because I swear I will."

Annie gasped. Miss Eggleston looked as if she might need to inhale an entire vial of smelling salts. Mr. Eggleston stood up and cleared his throat uncomfortably. "Look here, Ashbourne," he said in what was no doubt the bravest voice the man could manage. "I must admit I tended to discount it when Miss Andrews told me she thought you were following her about, but given your behavior here tonight, it seems she may not have been exaggerating in the least and it concerns me greatly."

Jordan turned to face the slightly shorter man and glared at him. "Eggleston, if I were you, I would stop talking. There's every possibility further conversation between the two of us might end over pistols at dawn, and I think we both know who the victor in such a circumstance would be."

Miss Eggleston murmured something that sounded suspiciously like a prayer. Without waiting for a response, Jordan turned back to Annie. "Are you walking out of here with me or do I have to carry you?"

"You wouldn't dare!"

Miss Eggleston reached out a small, white hand and tugged at Annie's sleeve. "Go, dear, go."

Annie, apparently aware of the scene they were causing, turned on her heel and left without saying another word. Jordan followed her into the corridor.

"I can hardly countenance the fact that you've followed Eggleston to the theater," he growled.

She glared at him. "Not that I expect you to believe me but I did not—"

Jordan held up a hand. "Spare me. This entire episode is only one old randy goat and a misdirected house-party key away from becoming a farce. You chasing Eggleston around, me chasing you around. It's ridiculous."

Annie clenched her teeth. "It's not my fault. I didn't know Mr. Eggleston would be here and—"

"Enough. Meet me outside in front in five minutes," he commanded.

She spun away from him sharply. "I must gather my cloak and tell Frances and Mrs. Birmingham I'm leaving."

Jordan turned in the opposite direction. "I suggest you make it quick. I'll have the coach brought round." He turned to face her again. "Five minutes," he repeated in a menacing voice.

She stomped down the corridor.

"Annie," he said, and she stopped short. "I promise you will not like the consequences if you're not there."

Without another word, he stalked away.

Annie rushed down the corridor, unshed tears of pure anger threatening to spill from her eyes. She'd turned away from him abruptly so he wouldn't see her cry. The absolute nerve of that man. How dare he chase her down and humiliate her. Again! She could go nowhere. Do nothing. It was as if he were employed by the war office. He seemed to know everything about her whereabouts. And of course he assumed she'd followed Arthur here tonight. He'd never believe it had been a mere coincidence. Especially not when he found her standing in his box. Blast it all.

That part had been unfortunate. But that ass refused to listen to reason.

She flew into the Birminghams' box just as the performance was beginning. Frances jumped up. "There you are, Anne. I was about to come look for you."

"I cannot stay," Annie answered in a wooden voice.

Frances's brow furrowed. "What? Whyever not?"

"Lord Ashbourne," she ground out. "Insists on taking me home."

"What?" Frances's eyes nearly popped from her skull. "Lord Ashbourne's here?"

"Yes. He's here and he's making a complete nuisance of himself. As usual."

Mrs. Birmingham stood up and patted Annie's hand. "Would you like me to speak with him, dear?"

"No. No. I'll be fine," Annie replied. No sense in dragging poor Mrs. Birmingham into her humiliation. "He just wants to prove a point. I've never seen anyone so set on being right. Well, save for Lily."

"Are you quite certain you'll be all right, dear?" Mrs. Birmingham responded.

Annie nodded.

"Can I come with you?" Frances pleaded. "Please?"

"No, Frances. Stay. Enjoy the performance." Annie grabbed up her shawl and reticule and said her good-byes, then she hurried back down the corridor, down the staircase, and into the lobby. She made her way outside and glanced about for Lord Ashbourne's coach.

The conveyance sat across the courtyard, Lord Ashbourne's magnificent matched black horses at the bit, his fancy liveried coachman and two footmen waiting attendance. Lord Ashbourne stood next to it, a decidedly angry look chiseled on his annoyingly handsome face.

When he saw her, his stance relaxed, but only a bit. She stalked over to him.

"Happy?" she asked with a false smile as she allowed him to assist her up into the coach.

"Not particularly," he replied.

He hoisted her up with one hand and she entered the coach and settled on the seat across from where he usually sat. Her chest heaving with indignation, she considered all the things she would verbally hurl at him as soon as he sat down.

She took a deep breath to prepare for her tirade.

A glint of light caught her eye.

She glanced across the seat. The candlelight in the lantern secured to the side of the coach reflected off a dazzling amethyst ring.

Curled into a perfect, sensual ball in the corner of the seat, wearing an exquisite fur wrap and a deep purple satin gown, reclined the most gorgeous and exotic-looking woman Annie had ever seen before.

Annie sucked in her breath.

Lord Ashbourne's mistress.

CHAPTER 16

Annie blinked at the beautiful woman sitting across from her. Perhaps the goddess was a figment of her imagination and would dissolve before her eyes. No one could really be that beautiful, could they? Why, she nearly made Lily look plain.

The woman uncurled from the corner and raised a lovely brow. Her hair was midnight black, her eyes were dark orbs. She had finely drawn cheekbones, a perfect point of a nose, and lips the color of dark cherries. She had a beauty mark on her cheek and she eyed Annie warily from behind long, luxurious lashes.

No. Not a figment of her imagination. Not at all.

Oh, perfect. This is all this evening calls for.

Lord Ashbourne's mistress looked like she'd just descended from Mount Olympus. Or Cleopatra. Though Cleopatra, Annie decided, had nothing on this beauty. Her heart sank when she thought of Jordan alone with this woman, kissing her.

Her own inexperienced pecks must have been laughable to him if this creature was the company he normally kept. Annie glanced down at her own bright dress. She was inadequate, like a little girl playing dress-up. She eyed the woman without saying a word before Lord Ashbourne climbed into the coach and sat next to Cleopatra.

"So, you're the *signorina* who's been occupying so much of Jordan's time lately?" Cleopatra asked.

Annie flinched at the barely concealed anger in the woman's beautiful Italian-accented English. Annie didn't like the way she called him Jordan, for one thing, and she certainly didn't like the way Cleopatra made "occupying his time" sound positively indecent.

"I'm Anne Andrews," she replied steadily, lifting her chin.

"Yes. I know. Good for you," Cleopatra replied with a tight smile.

Lord Ashbourne cleared his throat and Annie, glad for the reprieve from the woman's prying eyes, turned her attention to him. "I cannot believe you pulled me out of there like that."

His voice was flat. "I cannot believe I had to. Have you learned absolutely nothing?"

Annie crossed her arms over her chest. "I was merely talking to him. It was hardly inappropriate. His sister was there, for goodness' sake."

Lord Ashbourne clenched his jaw. "That is entirely beside the point. First, you lied to me earlier when I came to your house, and second, you need to stop chasing Eggleston around like a lovesick schoolgirl. You're making a fool of yourself. The entire *ton* is talking about it. You should have heard what Lord and Lady Cranberry said."

"Lady Cranberry is a notorious gossip," Annie replied, but tears sprang unbidden to her eyes. She fiercely bit the inside of her cheek to keep from crying. She refused to look like a baby in front of Lord Ashbourne and his goddess. But Lord Ashbourne's words rang true all of a sudden. Were people talking about her? Saying she was chasing Arthur around like a fool?

"You went to her house earlier?" Cleopatra asked Lord Ashbourne. One finely drawn eyebrow rose.

Jordan tossed his mistress an unamused look.

"Aren't you going to introduce me to your . . . friend?" Annie asked, wanting to die of shame.

Lord Ashbourne looked nothing if not completely bothered. He spoke with his jaw clenched. "By all means. Miss Annie Andrews, this is Signorina Nicoletta Monrovia."

"Cannot say it's a pleasure," Nicoletta said, her eyes narrowed to slits.

Annie just glared at her. Leave it to Ashbourne to have a mistress as rude as she was beautiful. They were well matched in that respect.

Lord Ashbourne gave Nicoletta a displeased look.

Annie glanced away, out the window. "Just take me home. This night has turned into a disaster."

"Agreed," Lord Ashbourne replied.

Annie couldn't keep her mouth shut. "I know you won't believe me, but I didn't know Arthur was going to be there tonight."

"You're right. I don't believe you," he drawled.

Annie squeezed a fistful of the velvet seat cushion. "You keep saying you're so put out, yet you insist upon following me around and interfering in my life."

"You give me too much credit. Tonight, my dear, I stumbled upon your foibles entirely by accident. Or did you forget that you told me you were ill and staying in this evening?"

Annie clenched her jaw. "I wouldn't have to invent such stories, *my lord,* if you were not such a nuisance."

Nicoletta had been glancing back and forth between them, watching their fight with glowing, dark eyes. She leaned toward Annie. "How dare you call him a nuisance? He is doing Lord Colton a favor watching you. If you were not such a burden, it would not be such a chore."

Annie closed her eyes tightly so the two of them wouldn't see the unshed tears. "I never asked to be anyone's favor," she bit out.

"No, but you are," Cleopatra answered.

"Nicoletta, enough." Jordan's voice was a thunderous command in the small confines of the coach.

Annie's eyes snapped open.

Nicoletta shot him a glare but settled back into her seat like a Persian cat, eyeing Annie through narrow slits of eyes.

Annie couldn't look at her. Signorina Monrovia was everything she was not—worldly, sophisticated, exotically beautiful. This was the woman who knew the world of men, the secrets of men. Nicoletta was not a woman who needed to chase anyone. Oh, no. Men obviously pursued her. Men as rich, charming, worldly, handsome, and dashing as Jordan Holloway. Now Annie realized that he was exactly all of those things. He was everything Frances had said he was and more. Annie had just been too blinded by his connection to Devon and Lily to see things clearly. And here she was, this silly young lady, wasting his valuable time. She was like a fly buzzing about at his elegant dinner party.

Oh, God, it was too humiliating to contemplate. All this time, she'd been fighting with him and acting like a spoiled brat while he'd wanted nothing more than to get her to behave so he could be off to his usual pursuits like taking his incomparably lovely mistress to the theater. Annie wanted to sink through the seat and disappear.

Had they been together, these two, night after night, talking about her, laughing about how foolish she was and what an idiot she was being over Arthur Eggleston? Arthur seemed like a ridiculous boy compared to Lord Ashbourne's suave sophistication. Oh, how could she have misjudged him so? She would never be able to face him after tonight. She prayed for a quick journey home.

She glanced over at Signorina Monrovia again. Why did she even care about his exotic mistress? Annie had done this to herself. If she hadn't lied and gone to the theater tonight, she wouldn't be in this hideous situation right now. She had only herself to blame.

When Lord Ashbourne next spoke, his voice was still tight but less angry. He leaned forward and braced his forearms on his knees. "Annie, listen to me, I've done all of this for your own good. Eggleston's feelings for you are not as strong as you'd . . . like them to be, and I—"

Annie lifted a hand. "Stop, just stop." If she could have swallowed an invisibility pill and escaped from the carriage at that moment, she would have. As it was, she eyed the door and briefly considered jumping. The only thing that stopped her was the mortifying thought that she might further interrupt Lord Ashbourne's evening by requiring a surgeon to treat a broken limb. She could just picture the sour expression on Signorina Monrovia's face were that to take place. And the worst part was, Lord Ashbourne was right. She'd been doing nothing but making a fool of herself over Arthur Eggleston. She'd known that but had let Frances convince her it wasn't true. But no more.

"I don't need another lecture," she said. "I'm through chasing Mr. Eggleston about."

Lord Ashbourne looked unconvinced, but his voice was still soft. "I think that's wise."

The coach pulled to a stop in front of Devon's town house. Lord Ashbourne alighted first and turned to help Annie. She didn't say good-bye to Nicoletta.

Annie walked quickly to the front door, acute embarrassment spurring every step. She unlocked the door, but could not bring herself to face him. Instead, she stood completely still, her eyes fastened on the shiny, brass door knocker.

"Lord Ashbourne, I am very sorry for your trouble tonight, and all of the other nights you've been forced to pay attendance on me."

He nodded. She saw the movement from the corner of her eye. "Don't mention it."

She pushed the door open, intending to run inside and never look back, to not stop running until she reached the safety of her bed, but his hand on her arm stopped her. It was warm. Comforting. She still couldn't look at him. "Yes?"

"Annie, it really is true, what I said in the coach. I'm not trying to make your life difficult. I truly believe it's what is best for you."

She nodded once, and swallowed the enormous lump in her throat. Now he was pitying her. Oh God. Could this night become any more humiliating?

She forced herself to jerk her head in his direction. "Thank you, Lord Ashbourne. I can honestly say I no longer intend to prove to be any trouble for you."

He nodded. Annie entered the house and shut the door behind her. She pushed her back against the wood and slid down to the marble floor until she sat in a pool of bright blue satin.

She was a fool. A complete fool. She'd been chasing Arthur around with nothing to show for it and it took the gorgeous Lord Ashbourne and his mistress to convince her how wrong she'd been. She'd been humiliated tonight. Twice. First in front of the Egglestons and then in front of Jordan's exquisite mistress. Wonderful! But was it any more than Annie deserved? If Lily had been in town, no doubt her sister would have locked her in the attic by now given her outlandish behavior.

Annie picked herself up and made her way to her room. Oh, good God, had Lord Ashbourne's mistress been beautiful. Annie's own too curly hair and too wide mouth and too blunt nose were positively plain compared to the signorina's perfect countenance. She looked like she'd been chiseled from marble as well. Perfect, both of them. A pair of sculptures.

Annie cringed when she thought of how she'd asked Lord Ashbourne to kiss her that night at the Lindworths'. Now she realized just how out of her depth she had been. Oh, she could just kick herself for being so naïve.

An unsettling sick feeling roiled in her belly. Nicoletta was Jordan's mistress and they were going home together. No doubt they intended to spend the evening naked in each other's perfect arms. Why did that thought make Annie feel like someone had hit her in the gut? Why did it make her feel melancholy and lonely and unhappy all at the same time? It didn't have anything to do with her.

She rang for Mary to help her undress and shook her head. She mustn't think any more about Lord Ashbourne. It was too awful. The man had scolded her, in front of his stunning mistress, no less. Tears of frustration and anger sprang to Annie's eyes. "I will not make a fool of myself ever again," she vowed.

And she intended to tell Arthur Eggleston exactly that. Tomorrow.

CHAPTER 17

Jordan had one hell of a time extricating himself from Nicoletta's arms after escorting her to the front door of her town house minutes later. She pouted. She pleaded. She even attempted tears. She finally accused him of being in love with Annie Andrews, which, of course, was the most absurd thing he'd heard all month. And while spending time with Annie, he'd heard a great many ludicrous things this month.

"Why won't you stay with me then?" Nicoletta stamped her foot. "You haven't been to my bed in nearly a fortnight."

Jordan ran a hand through his hair. Yes, a fortnight. Since he'd begun watching Annie. It was no coincidence. "I'm out of sorts. I need a drink."

Nicoletta ran her hand down his arm. "I have brandy here, Jordan. Come in. Have a drink. Relax." She smiled at him coyly.

"I'm meeting friends at the club," he'd finally insisted before pulling his arm from her grasp and turning on his heel. It had been a lie, of course, but how could he explain to Nicoletta that seeing Annie with tears in her eyes had made him feel all sorts of things but amorous wasn't one of them?

"You will not be welcome if you try to come back," Nicoletta hurled at him through the darkness.

Jordan didn't respond to that threat. He strode back to the coach and entered it.

"The club," he snapped in response to John's inquiring look.

John didn't say a word but Jordan was beginning to feel damned ridiculous for his choices of late. Not that it was any of his coachman's affair where he spent his evenings. "The club," he repeated. "And make it quick."

Jordan was two drinks and four hands of cards into the night when James Bancroft joined his party.

"Medford? Really? Again? Twice in one week is far too often to encounter you."

Medford quirked a brow. "I'm here nearly every night, Ashbourne. The question is why have you been frequenting the club so often?"

Jordan took a drink. "That's none of your affair."

Medford cracked a smile. "I heard you caused quite a scene at the theater tonight."

Jordan groaned. "Who told you that?"

"I have my sources. Besides, I already informed you I've been keeping an eye on Annie."

"You're still more than welcome to the position."

"Actually," Medford replied, "I came to say I think you've been doing a splendid job."

Jordan's eyebrows shot up and he cupped a hand behind his ear. "What was that?"

"I'm serious. I might have done the same thing had I been at the theater tonight. Pulling her out of there, taking her home. Well done."

Jordan raised his voice so the few gentlemen sitting in their small group could hear. "Catch that, gents? Medford here just told me 'Well done.' Record it in the book for posterity."

Medford chuckled. "Don't get too cocky, Ashbourne. My congratulatory speech comes with a warning."

Jordan rolled his eyes. "I should have expected as much. Are you going to tell me I'd best not make her angry because she's like a sister to you, et cetera? I've heard it already."

Medford rubbed his jaw. "No. Not at all."

Jordan blinked. "What's that?"

"I was going to say the exact opposite, really. You shouldn't trust her."

Jordan whistled. "Now that's a surprise. What exactly do you mean?"

"It's about now she'll try to tell you she's given up and you win. Am I right?"

Jordan cracked a smile. "She did mention that I might expect better behavior out of her from now on."

"Yes, well, don't believe it. Rubbish, all of it."

"How can you be so sure?"

"I know Lily and Annie well. It's just when they seem as if they've acquiesced that you must be the most careful."

"That begs a question, Medford. How exactly *did* you and Lily become thick as thieves?"

Medford grinned. "Let's just say we have similar senses of humor."

"Ah, yes. And your sense of humor carries over into publishing scandalous pamphlets together?"

Medford gave him an innocent look. "I don't know what you're talking about."

Jordan eyed him carefully. "I've always wondered, Medford—was it your idea or Lily's to publish *Secrets of a Wedding Night*?"

Medford's crack of laughter bounced against the wood-paneled walls in the salon. "Really, Ashbourne. That wasn't even a good try."

Jordan shrugged. "Oh, play your little games. I know you two colluded to produce the thing."

Medford leaned back in his chair and took a swig from his glass. A glass that no doubt contained water. Jordan shook his head.

"It's a shame, really, Lily marrying Colton. If I *were* the publisher of *Secrets of a Wedding Night,* I'd have to look elsewhere for a new scandalous author."

"I'm sure you'll have little trouble finding someone else willing to write your drivel."

Medford's only reply was a smirk.

"You fascinate me, Medford," Jordan continued. "How is it that a perfectionist like you turned into the most scandalous publisher in London?"

"You act as if I publish something positively indecent, Ashbourne. Everything I'm involved in is entirely legal, I assure you."

"Oh, I'm sure of it."

"I'm working on my next venture as we speak, actually."

Jordan cocked a brow. "Really? Do tell."

"You'll be one of the very first to know. I assure you,

Ashbourne." Medford straightened his shoulders. "But we're not talking about me tonight. We're talking about you . . . and Annie."

Jordan nodded. "So we are."

"I've no idea why Lily saw fit to leave a rake like you in charge of her sister. I suppose it has something to do with your saving her husband's life like a bloody knight in armor. But you'd do well to take my advice."

Jordan leaned back in his chair and crossed his own feet at the ankles. "And your advice is not to trust Annie. Is that it?"

Medford lifted his glass and smiled. "Keep a close eye on her. She's not done yet. Not by half."

CHAPTER 18

Arthur Eggleston arrived at Annie's house the next morning at ten. She'd sent him a note. And Evans informed her that Mr. Eggleston had been sitting quietly in the drawing room awaiting her presence.

Annie paused outside the drawing room door, took a deep breath, and squared her shoulders. This wasn't going to be easy, but so often important things weren't.

She pushed open the door and walked inside. Arthur immediately rose to greet her, a smile on his face.

"Mr. Eggleston." She nodded, not smiling one bit.

His smile fell. "Anne? What is it? Are you all right? I was worried about you after your encounter with Lord Ashbourne last night."

"I'm fine."

"Are you . . . angry?" He eyed her inquisitively.

"No. Not angry." She tossed her head to the side.

He looked a bit worried. "Are you embarrassed then? About what Lord Ashbourne did? Don't worry, hardly anyone noticed. My sister said Lord Ashbourne was very rude to do what he did. He should be the one to be embarrassed, not you."

"I'm not embarrassed. Not any longer," Annie replied.

"Then what is it?"

Annie took a deep breath. She'd spent the entire night thinking about the situation. Arthur's father might want him to wait and think things through a bit more before he made a decision. Arthur himself might not think anything of waiting. He'd made that clear.

But it mattered very much to Annie, and she was done. He might very well be fine with waiting, but he would not be waiting for *her*.

She stared Arthur in the eye and drew a deep breath. "Mr. Eggleston. I no longer intend to marry you."

Arthur blinked in rapid succession. "What do you mean, Anne? What has our marriage to do with last night?"

Annie folded her hands in her lap serenely. "Absolutely nothing. I just thought you should know."

Arthur smacked his head with his palm. "Where is this coming from, Anne?"

A bit of the tension eased from Annie's shoulders. "It's become clear to me that you have no intention of marrying me and I refuse to chase after you any longer."

"Chase after me? I don't understand. What's gotten into you?"

Annie tossed up her hands. "That's just it, Arthur. Nothing has gotten into me. I'm still the same young woman you intended to marry in Gretna Green six months ago. I have always wanted the same thing, to marry you. You, however, have seemingly changed your mind. Lord Ashbourne said some things to me the other night, things that were difficult to hear if I'm being honest, but I think he was perfectly right. And I've come to the conclusion that I cannot wait for you any longer."

Arthur reached out and grabbed her hand. "Lord Ashbourne said some things?" he echoed. "What sort of things?"

"Oh, Arthur, does it matter?" She sighed.

"Yes. It matters very much. I have a right to know what I'm being accused of, do I not?"

A bit of hope unfurled in Annie's chest. For the first time, ever, Arthur seemed a bit miffed—one might even say put out. Certainly it didn't compare to Lord Ashbourne's grand display of anger last night, but it was a start. It seemed Arthur did care, after all.

Annie pushed up her chin and looked back at him. "Very well. He said I was making a fool of myself chasing after you. He said you didn't appear to be particularly interested in me. He said the entire *ton* is talking about it."

Arthur dropped her hand and paced the floor in front of her chair. He ran his fingers through his hair. Ooh, Annie had never seen him with his hair disheveled. He was working his way into a high dudgeon now. Could it be that he really cared?

"Lord Ashbourne said those things, did he?" Arthur said, continuing to pace.

"Yes." She nodded and said no more.

"What else did Lord Ashbourne have to say?"

"That was the gist of it, but I had to agree with him. I've spent my days of late chasing after you at parties where you barely pay attention to me and spend your time escorting your sister about."

His jaw dropped. "Why, I've been concerned for your reputation, Anne. My sister requires an escort, and I'm able to see you at the parties as well. It's been a lovely arrangement."

"Lovely for you, perhaps. But what about the fact that I always seem to be seeking you out in the crowd? Last night I came to greet you when you could have easily done the same."

His mouth gaped like a fish. "My astonishment is beyond measure. I didn't seek you out last evening for no reason other than the mere fact that I had not seen you. I was nothing but pleased when you came by."

Annie pushed up her nose in the air. Willing herself to keep her resolve. "Be that as it may, it's still true that we appear to want different things. I want to marry, and you do not."

"Anne, don't say such things. Of course I want to marry you."

Annie expelled her breath. It felt so good to hear those words, but she wasn't finished yet. "Not so much that you're willing to tell your father you do not want to wait."

"Father merely thought it best—"

She raised her hand and looked away. "Please, Arthur, no more excuses. You have obviously been trifling with my affections, and I will not allow it any longer."

He grabbed up her hand again and squeezed it. "Anne, how can you say such a thing? I would never trifle with your affections."

She refused to look at him. "I'm afraid I cannot do this any longer."

He searched her face. "Do what, Anne?"

"Wait for you. Besides, I could not wait any longer even if I wanted to. Lily will be back in a fortnight, and she intends to take me to Colton House in Surrey. I won't be back until Christmas."

"We'll be married at Christmas then. Don't worry."

"No. Lily means to keep us from each other, I'm sure of it, and you've already seen what Lord Ashbourne has done. Your father has also made his feelings clear, and between the three of them, it seems the entire town is conspiring to keep us from being together."

Arthur had a faraway look in his eyes. He stood up and nodded. "You're right. I've been such a fool. I will not allow anyone else to dictate our future ever again. We shall marry immediately."

Joy leaped in her chest. Annie stood and squeezed his shoulder. "Oh, Arthur. Do you mean it?"

"I've never been so sure of anything in my life," he replied with a determined look in his eye.

Annie had to squelch her squeal of excitement. She'd never expected to be this successful. She should have been firm with Arthur months ago. "I've waited so long to hear you say that. Arthur, will you do something for me?"

"Yes, of course, Anne, anything."

"Kiss me," she breathed.

Arthur hesitated only for a moment before leaning down and pressing his lips to hers. Annie squeezed her eyes shut and waited for the fireworks to explode inside her brain, her belly, lower. But there was . . . nothing.

She pressed her lips to his more firmly. Perhaps they were not doing it correctly. Very well. If she were being honest, she would admit she preferred Lord Ashbourne's style of grabbing her and pulling her into his arms instead of Arthur's meek leaning motion, but her true love was kissing her and that was what was most important. The man, not the technique.

She wrapped her arms around his neck just as she'd done with Lord Ashbourne and . . . nothing. No fireworks,

no anything. His lips were cool and soft but that was all
They had none of the demand, none of the urgency, none
of the *need* . . .

And none of the tongue. Her cheeks flushed. Lord
Ashbourne certainly knew what to do with his tongue.

Arthur awkwardly pulled away, looking quite shaken.

Annie shook her head, her brow furrowed. She stared
incomprehensibly at the rug. What was wrong? Why
hadn't she felt the same things—more—that she'd felt
when she kissed Jordan Holloway? It made no sense.

She glanced at Arthur, who looked quite proud of himself. Oh, it was nothing. Nothing but the nerves and the
trouble of all this sneaking around. Caused by Lord Ashbourne himself. Once she and Arthur were married, Annie had little doubt his kisses would make her knees
positively weak.

"Thank you, Arthur," she murmured, because he
seemed to require a reply.

Arthur squared his shoulders. "I've made a decision,
Anne. I don't think becoming engaged is good enough
You've convinced me. There are too many people con-
spiring against us. Pack your things. We will go to Gretna
Green. We will leave today."

CHAPTER 19

"I will not ask again. Tell me where Miss Andrews is and tell me immediately." Jordan's voice boomed through the town house. Devon's normally staid butler had managed to summon both Evans and Mary and now all three servants stood quaking in front of him in the foyer while he asked for the third time where their mistress had gone.

Evans gulped and pulled at his neckcloth. "I told ye, milord. I haven't seen Miss Annie today."

Jordan's raking gaze settled on Mary.

"Ye must believe me, Lord Ashbourne. I'm quite sure Miss Annie told me, but I cannot remember. It's an affliction I've 'ad, ahem, had for quite some time. Ye can ask these gents." Mary gestured to Evans and the butler with her thumb.

"Aye, that I can vouch fer, milord," Evans replied. "She can't remember a thing wot happened five minutes ago."

Jordan turned his piercing gaze on the butler. "Nicholls, I'm counting on you to be the only sane member of this trio. Tell me where Miss Andrews is."

Nicholls bowed. "My lord, I assure you. I've already

related all of which I am aware. Miss Andrews had a caller around ten o'clock this morning. It was Mr. Arthur Eggleston. He left his card."

Jordan had already seen the damned card. In fact, he'd crumpled it in his fist, wanting to crush it to dust.

"Mr. Eggleston and Miss Andrews spoke in the blue salon until half eleven," Nicholls continued. "Then he took his leave."

Jordan paced. "What did they speak about?"

"That I don't know, my lord. I was not asked to bring refreshments and I pride myself on never eavesdropping." He gave Evans and Mary a stern look.

"And I might well have been eavesdropping, milord," Evans admitted with a wry smile, "had I known there was anything to hear, but I swear upon my honor I wasn't even awake at ten o'clock."

"That I can vouch fer, me lord," Mary interjected. "Saw 'im meself, upstairs dozing in a chair by the window round that time."

Oh, that *she remembered?*

Jordan paced back and forth across the fine Indian carpet that adorned Devon's foyer. "Annie did not order a coach?"

Nicholls shook his head. "No, my lord."

"She did not leave a note?" Jordan continued.

"No." Mary shook her head.

"She did not go on an errand with a friend?" Jordan ground out.

"No. I went round to Miss Birmingham's house meself and Miss Frances hadn't seen nor heard from her all day," Evans assured him.

"Has Aunt Clarissa seen her?"

"My lady has been . . . indisposed." Nicholls cleared his throat. "Most of the day, sir."

Jordan raked a hand through his hair. It was nearly ten o'clock at night and apparently Annie had been missing all day. How had this happened?

He'd wanted to discount Medford's warning. Annie had seemed so sad and so repentant last night. But some niggling sense of doubt in the back of his mind had spurred Jordan to check on her tonight. The tears in her eyes and the look on her face had convinced him that she finally understood why she should not be chasing after Eggleston. But now, standing in front of the three unwitting servants, Jordan understood that Medford had been exactly right. Annie hadn't been ready to give up at all. It had merely been the proverbial calm before the storm. She'd regrouped, ready to do her final damage. And all on Jordan's watch again. Perfect.

Jordan turned on his heel and reached to open the front door. Nicholls rushed to do it for him but got there too late. "Where are you going, my lord?" the butler asked in a strained voice.

Jordan barely turned his head. "To visit Mr. Arthur Eggleston, and if he is not there, there will be hell to pay."

Jordan left, slamming the door behind him.

Jordan's questioning of the Eggleston servants yielded much the same information. Mr. Arthur had left around ten that morning to pay a call and he hadn't returned since.

Minutes later, Jordan left the house with a growing sense of dread in his belly. Damn it. She'd done it again.

Somehow convinced that idiot Eggleston to take off to Gretna Green. Jordan knew it. Just as surely as he knew he must follow them immediately.

Less than half an hour later, he was back home packing a bag, tossing money in a pouch for the journey, and imagining what he'd do to the errant lovers when he caught up to them. How in the hell had that young woman managed to fool him? Again? And what was either one of them thinking? No doubt she would argue that Jordan had pushed her to this. He could hear the explanation now. But putting her life and reputation in danger again was serious. The last time the little fool had done this it had taken her sister and Devon's marriage to deflect the scandal. God only knew what it would take this time.

The good news was that no one seemed to know. The servants at both households knew the master and mistress were gone but didn't appear to suspect they'd gone to Gretna Green together. The servants might be persuaded to remain silent.

Jordan knew one thing for certain. He was through playing the beleaguered chaperone. As soon as he found Annie Andrews, he intended to make it clear that he was in charge. He'd tried it her way for nearly two weeks now. The next fortnight would be on his terms. And she wouldn't like his terms one bit.

Jordan hefted his bag to his shoulder. His valet, Cunningham, scurried into the room. "My lord. I didn't know you'd returned. Do you require my assistance?"

Jordan shook his head. "No. I'm just taking a few things for now. I'm going on a trip."

Cunningham nodded. "Is there anything else you require?"

Another shake of the head. "I'll stop by the kitchens before I leave to get some food for the journey."

"Will you be back soon, my lord?"

Jordan stopped for a moment in the doorway. He turned to look at the valet. "I won't be back for a fortnight."

CHAPTER 20

Jordan shook his head and smiled wryly. They hadn't even the sense to change their route. He'd caught up to them just where he thought they would be. Apparently, they'd assumed no one would know where they'd gone. The Gray Horse Inn. That's where they'd stopped for the night the last time they'd taken off for Gretna Green. Jordan shook his head again. History had *such* a way of repeating itself. The runaway bride had struck again.

A pleasant conversation with a smile and a nod to the young woman who worked there earned Jordan a description of the couple staying in the room upstairs.

"Aye, guv'na. I remember ye and yer handsome friend from the last time ye all were 'ere in the spring." She giggled.

"Yes, well," he replied. "This will be the last time. You may count on it."

"Oh, I'm sorry ta 'ear that. Very sorry indeed." She waggled her eyebrows at him. "Do ya think ya might be persuaded ta 'ave a tumble before ya interrupt 'em upstairs? No doubt that's wot they're up ta themselves."

Jordan arched a brow. "As tempting as that offer is . . ."

"Now don't turn me down, guv. I didn't get a chance ta 'ave fun wit yer 'andsome friend last time. That dark-haired lady wot was wit 'im didn't seem like the type ta take kindly ta 'is going elsewhere for 'is jollies."

Jordan coughed into his hand, thinking of Lily and hiding his smile. "You're perfectly right there, but I'm afraid I must still decline. I've come to retrieve another dark-haired lady and the sooner we're gone, the better."

The girl winked at him. "Aye. I've 'alf a mind ta tell that gel she's a nitwit wot wit taking off wit that bloke she's got upstairs when she's got ye and yer 'andsome friend chasing 'er about. Though come ta think o' it, maybe that's 'er game." The girl laughed then, a high-pitched, cackling sound.

Jordan winced. "I'll just be going up to pay them a visit."

The inn girl waved good-bye and Jordan stalked toward the staircase, taking the stairs two at a time.

Once he made it to the second story, Jordan stood outside the door to Annie and Eggleston's room. He cracked his knuckles. That fool Eggleston was about to rue the decision he'd made. Twice. And Annie, that little baggage, was soon to regret the day her sister had left town.

Jordan sucked in a deep breath and lifted his hand to knock. The last time they'd been here, Devon and Lily had found both of them fully dressed, and Arthur had been sleeping on a pallet on the floor. Devon had told Jordan as much.

Jordan steeled himself. This time there was every possibility that he might find a very different situation indeed. Annie may well have decided to give herself to

Eggleston, thinking it would ensure once and for all that they would be together. They'd be forced to marry—or so Annie might think—if Eggleston had truly compromised her. Jordan squeezed his fist poised in the air, cracking his knuckles again. If Annie had been mad enough to suggest it, Eggleston had best pray to the god of idiots that he'd had enough sense to refuse, to be a gentleman. Eggleston would leave here in a prostrate position if he'd so much as touched her.

Jordan rapped twice on the door. Hard. Scurrying and mumbled voices ensued. *They'd better not be getting dressed.*

After a few moments, Eggleston's shaky voice sounded through the wood. "Lor . . . Lord Ashbourne?"

"How *did* you know?" Jordan's voice dripped with sarcasm.

"I'll open the door, Lord Ashbourne, but I want your promise, first, as a gentleman, not to strike me."

"No."

A squeak. "N . . . no?"

That boy had best be sweating right now.

"You heard me. Now open this door immediately or I'll hit you harder than I'd planned. And what I see when it's opened will determine exactly how badly you are hurt."

The door swung open and a cowering Eggleston stood there fully dressed. He covered his face with his hands while Jordan's gaze swung into the room. A rumpled pallet lay on the floor, thank God.

Annie stood next to the bed, also fully dressed, an angry, defiant look on her face. "I cannot believe you're here."

"I assure you, the feeling is entirely mutual."

"Do you do nothing more than follow me?"

"Do you do nothing more than foolishly get yourself into bad situations? Not to mention, lie to me? Now get your things, we're leaving."

Eggleston was hiding in the corner. Jordan ran a hand through his hair and sighed. "Blast it, Eggleston, I'm not going to strike you, though God knows you deserve it. Lucky for you, I find it distasteful to strike a cowering man. But if you *ever*, and I mean *ever*, attempt to make this ill-advised journey again, I will see you at dawn. Do you understand me?"

Eggleston attempted to straighten his shoulders and speak clearly. "Yes. Ye . . . yes, my lord."

"Good. And Lord Colton will happily be my second, I've no doubt."

"Don't worry, my lord. Ev . . . everyone knows what a crack shot you are. I've no wish to be your opponent."

Annie turned to Eggleston. "Arthur. Tell him. Tell him you love me and you want to marry me. You said you'd not allow anyone else to dictate our future ever again. Remember? You cannot allow Lord Ashbourne to do this."

Jordan watched the younger man through narrowed eyes. "Do you have something to say?" He crossed his arms over his chest and waited.

Arthur bravely raised his chin. "I do love Anne, my lord. And I want the best for her."

"And do you agree the best thing is not to run off to Gretna Green and ruin her reputation?"

Arthur's gaze moved quickly to Annie and then to the floor, his head bowed. "Yes, my lord."

Annie wrung her hands. "Arthur. No. We talked about this."

He glanced up at her. "I'm sorry, Anne. But Lord Ash-bourne is right."

Jordan nodded. "Good. Now go summon your car-riage and get back to London as quickly as possible. I don't care if you tell people you've been sick or drunk or what, but I'd better never hear you mention Miss An-drews's name. Ever. Do you understand?"

"Perfectly, my lord."

"Good, now go." Jordan jerked his head toward the door.

Eggleston quickly gathered up his belongings. Obvi-ously finding a jolt of courage somewhere, he turned back to address Jordan. "Aren't you and Anne coming too, my lord?"

Jordan narrowed his eyes on the young man. "Not. With. You."

Eggleston nodded. Then his gaze moved to Annie. "I'm sorry, Anne." He gulped when Jordan took a step toward him. "Miss . . . Miss Andrews." Eggleston nod-ded once more and was gone.

"Arthur," Annie pleaded, moving toward the door and watching him leave. "No. Don't go."

The clip of Arthur's boots receded down the hallway and then the steps.

Annie turned to look at Jordan, a crestfallen look on her face. For a moment, Jordan's anger drained away and his heart wrenched.

"I can't believe he left," she whispered.

It took her a few moments to visibly recover, and when she did, her entire countenance changed. Ah, there was the little hellcat he'd come to know. She stood glaring at Jordan, her chest rising and falling; then she charged across the room, shoved her belongings into her bag, and gathered the handles. She swept past Jordan and paused in the doorway to turn back and look at him. "Aren't you coming? We might as well be on our way back to London too."

Yes, the little hellcat was back, and Jordan had already been exposed to her claws one time too many. He took two steps toward her. "We're not going back to London."

Annie's brow furrowed just before a look of sheer panic flashed across her lovely face. "What do you mean? Where else would we go?"

"You've proven yourself to be an unpredictable nuisance, Miss Andrews. I cannot keep you safe from yourself in London."

Annie's mouth dropped open. Her grip on her bag tightened. "If we're not going to London, where are we going?"

Her voice held just enough antagonism to make the delivery of his news a true pleasure. Jordan brushed past her into the corridor. "We're going to Surrey. To Ashbourne Manor."

"Your country estate? But why?" Her voice was thin.

Jordan slowly turned to face her, a triumphant smile on his lips. "I'm keeping you out of Society and away from Eggleston. He's just stupid enough to be dangerous. Until Devon and Lily return, you and I will spend our time in the country, in isolation. I will send for Aunt Clarissa and your maid. You're about to become my houseguest, Miss Andrews. For a fortnight."

CHAPTER 21

Two days later, Jordan spent the morning pacing his study at Ashbourne Manor. Annie was asleep in the suite of rooms he'd asked the housekeeper to make up for her when they'd arrived in the middle of the night. When she awoke, she'd be plotting her escape, no doubt. But Ashbourne Manor was nestled in the quiet countryside. Quite remote. In fact, the closest neighbor was Colton House, nearly an hour's ride away.

Even if Annie managed to shimmy down the side of the manor house on a vine—which he already knew was not beneath her—she'd have nowhere to go, and Jordan had already given his stable master strict instructions not to allow her any mounts whatsoever.

The woman was an escape artist. A troublemaker. And a damned nuisance. All rolled into one. She'd caused him nothing but trouble since she'd been thrust into his life. Not only were his pastimes in London and his work at Parliament cut short due to the necessity of chasing that little baggage down and carting her off to the countryside, but now he was forced to stay in seclusion with her for the next two weeks.

So be it. He could attend to some much-needed work on his estate, but that wasn't the problem. The problem would be keeping Miss Andrews adequately occupied so she didn't plot even bigger and worse things than taking off to Gretna Green with Arthur Eggleston. Jordan could hardly imagine what that might be, but he had no doubt Miss Andrews could conjure up something.

He ran his fingers through his hair. He could always write to Devon and Lily and tell them they must cut short their trip to come back and handle their ne'er-do-well sister. But such a missive would make him look like the veriest fool. If Jordan couldn't even keep a nineteen-year-old out of trouble for two weeks . . . If he couldn't handle one small, albeit determined, young woman, what the hell was wrong with him? He was an earl, for God's sake. A peer of the realm. The eldest of four brothers who had often been up to no good, and since his father had died nearly ten years ago, he'd managed to keep his brothers alive and well despite their various exploits. No, he refused to concede that a young lady making her debut was too much for him to handle.

And he knew just how to handle Annie. He'd thought about it extensively on the long road to the Gray Horse Inn and back. He'd handle her on her terms. Or at least what she thought were her terms. Foolish though they may be. Miss Andrews was a woman who was in love with love. So that's exactly what he needed to be about. Putting love in her path. Jordan would handle the affairs at his estate for the next two weeks, but he would also endeavor to put some eligible chaps in Annie's path. That way, she could fall in love with someone decent and stop her silly infatuation with Arthur Eggleston. Jordan would merely ensure anyone he introduced her to would be eligible and a better choice than Eggleston. Quite simple, really.

Once Annie realized Arthur wasn't coming to her rescue, she would choose one of them and that would be that. After all, the girl was beautiful, intelligent, and had excellent connections like the Marquis of Colton. She should aspire to much greater heights than Eggleston in the first place.

Not to mention the fact that Jordan couldn't stand seeing her make a fool of herself any longer. She should be infatuated with someone who wanted her back. God only knew what had gotten into Eggleston to spur him to make the trip to Gretna again, but the young man seemed anything but madly in love. He hadn't even put up a fight, for Christ's sake, when Jordan had arrived and ordered him to go. Instead, the sop had been more worried about Jordan hitting him. The problem with Eggleston was the man allowed whomever he was with to talk him into their point of view. Eggleston agreed with the loudest voice in any room. Annie had spent her time convincing him, but when he got around his father, he was convinced there too. And when Jordan had arrived at the inn and threatened him, he'd abandoned all of his plans to run off to Gretna. Arthur was a milksop. Couldn't Annie see that? And Annie, with her stubborn insistence, needed the opposite of a milksop for a husband or she would crush him beneath her will in a matter of months. Arthur Eggleston was the exact wrong man for her.

Yes, Annie definitely deserved better than Eggleston, and Jordan would put a better chap in her path. She wouldn't thank him now, of course, but once she was happily married and had a baby or two as she wanted, she'd see how right he'd been all along. It was a perfect plan.

Jordan rang for the housekeeper and Mrs. Phillips arrived moments later.

"Yes, my lord?"

"Good morning, Mrs. Phillips. Good to see you again."

"My lord." The housekeeper curtsied.

"Is Miss Andrews awake?"

"Yes, my lord. One of the maids was just bringing up her breakfast, in fact."

"Excellent. See to it that she has everything she needs. Her maid will be arriving this afternoon."

"Yes, my lord. So far she's asked for a quill, some ink, and parchment," Mrs. Phillips reported.

Jordan snorted. "I bet she has."

Mrs. Phillips's brow was furrowed.

Jordan shook his head. "Will you please ask Miss Andrews to join me in the study in one hour?"

"Of course, my lord. Will there be anything else?"

"No, thank you, Mrs. Phillips."

The housekeeper hurried away and Jordan strolled over to the sideboard where he popped open the nearest bottle of brandy and poured himself a glass. Then he crossed back over to his desk to peruse paperwork while he waited.

Annie was just finishing the last of her breakfast consisting of warm buttered toast, smooth, delicious hot chocolate, and delectable sweet berries when Mrs. Philips, Lord Ashbourne's housekeeper, came trotting into the room to inform her that his majesty requested her presence in his study in an hour.

Annie pushed the tray away and waited for both the maid and Mrs. Phillips to leave the room before she settled back against the pillows in the absolutely opulent bedroom Lord Ashbourne had provided for her use. She'd spent so many years being poor that her time in Lord Colton's house and now Lord Ashbourne's house seemed something like a dreamland to her. The men were rich. No, not just rich. Indecently rich. She would have lived a much simpler life as Arthur's wife.

Arthur.

The name caused a stabbing pain to her heart. Arthur wasn't the man she'd thought he was at all. Lord Ashbourne had been completely right about him though she'd die a thousand deaths before she would admit it. Arthur was a man who allowed himself to be ruled by whoever shouted at him the loudest. He had no opinions of his own. No backbone. And how she'd ever thought he was the man for her, she would never know. She'd allowed herself to believe because she'd wanted to so badly. She could see that now. But if Arthur wasn't even willing to stand up to Lord Ashbourne, he wasn't willing to stand up for her. No. She couldn't accept a husband like that.

It would be useless, trying to explain to Lord Ashbourne that he needn't keep her out here in the country for the next two weeks. He'd never believe anything she said now and she couldn't blame him. She'd acted like a fool time and time again.

It was heavy-handed of him, to be sure, dragging her off to Ashbourne Manor and dictating her life for the next fortnight, but perhaps it was for the best. Going back to London and seeing Arthur held little appeal for her. Lily and Devon wouldn't be back yet either. No, she might as well nurse her broken heart in the countryside. As long as Lord High-and-Mighty didn't intend to lecture her every day about what a fool she was. And oh

God, she was keeping him from his mistress too; that must make him unhappy. She turned and buried her face in the downy soft pillow. No doubt about it. This was going to be a humiliating two weeks.

Annie arrived precisely on time. She was wearing the same dress she'd been in the day before, her arms were crossed over her chest, and she had a resigned look on her face.

"You wanted to speak with me?" she said, walking woodenly into the room.

"Yes. Come in. Sit down." Jordan gestured to the chair in front of his desk.

Annie made her way to the seat and perched on the edge of the chair. "I'm worried about my fox. Who will take care of Dash?"

"You didn't think about that before you took off for Scotland?"

She gave him a decidedly unhappy stare.

"Don't worry," he replied. "I've already arranged for Evans to see to him and the pups."

Annie let out her breath. "Thank you for that."

Jordan steepled his fingers in front of his face. "Your maid should arrive today with some of your clothes and other things. And Aunt Clarissa, of course."

Annie nodded. "I'm glad to know in addition to abduction, you're at least giving a nod to propriety."

Jordan smirked. "The only abduction that's taken place here is you from yourself. I did you a great favor, though you fail to recognize it at present."

Annie arched a brow. "Tell me, Lord Ashbourne, is it difficult to be so very clever?"

He ignored that remark. "I don't expect you to appreciate any of this right now but—"

"I will someday. Is that it?"

"Yes."

She looked away. "I've been a fool."

Jordan eyed her profile. Her smooth skin shone like silk and the proud way she held her shoulders bespoke her frustration. "I called you in here to inform you of my plans. I intend to introduce you to some . . . gentlemen."

Annie's head snapped up to face him. "Gentlemen?"

"Yes. Starting with my brothers, in fact."

Her mouth fell open. "Your brothers?"

"Yes."

"You cannot be serious."

The look of incredulity on her face was enough to make Jordan scowl. "I daresay any one of my brothers is preferable to Eggthorpe."

Annie tossed a hand in the air. "You're mad. What? One man is just as good as another?"

"Not at all. As I said, my brothers are preferable. You need a man who won't do things like allow you to talk him into trips to Gretna Green."

She crossed her arms over her chest and glared at him. "I did no such thing."

Jordan gave her his most ironic look. "Are you honestly going to tell me that you didn't suggest the trip?"

Annie slapped her palm on the front of the desk. "I would be wasting my breath trying to convince you, but no, it was Arthur's idea."

"The dolt has bungled the job twice now. Make no mistake, a real man would have succeeded." Jordan braced both hands on the desk and leaned toward her, staring her in the eye. "Let me assure you, if *I'd* been your groom, you'd be mine by now, with or without benefit of the clergy."

Annie's face flushed a lovely shade of pink. She pushed back in her chair and cleared her throat. "*You* would never be my choice of groom," she snapped.

"Agreed," Jordan replied in a tightly controlled voice, but something about the way she'd said it with such smug assurance made him crazy. Why, London was full of ladies who would choose him for a groom. Didn't little Miss Know-it-all know *that*?

Annie glanced away, her chest rising and falling with her deep breaths. "And what will your brothers think of this? Your attempt to marry them off to a woman they've never even met?"

Jordan straightened back up and shrugged. "They're young, healthy, intelligent. They all intend to take a wife at some point; there's no reason for them not to be interested in you."

"Wonderful. Humiliating *and* a waste of time for everyone involved."

"Who says it will be a waste of time?"

"I do. You cannot just force people to fall in love. I've never even met your brothers."

"Yes, well, I intend to rectify that, starting tomorrow. My youngest brother, Michael, will be here."

Annie stood up, her arms still crossed over her chest, her eyes shooting flames at him. "Is there anything else or am I dismissed?"

Jordan raised a brow. "You're not a servant here."

"Funny. It feels as if I am."

"You're a houseguest with a penchant for trouble, is what you are."

She turned on her heel and stalked to the door. "May

I write letters to my friends in London or is that to be forbidden as well?"

Jordan grinned at her. "As long as you don't marry or leave this property for the next two weeks, you're free to do as you wish."

Annie turned back to look at him and her dark brown curls fell over her shoulder in a most fetching display. She pushed up her chin. "I shall do as I wish whether I'm *free* to or not."

Jordan narrowed his eyes on her. "Oh, I have little doubt of that. Good day, Miss Andrews. See you tomorrow when I introduce you to Michael."

CHAPTER 22

When Michael arrived the next morning, Annie was nowhere to be found. After nearly twenty minutes of searching, Jordan eventually located her in the gardens.

She was on her hands and knees next to Mr. McGivens, the gardener, planting a row of daffodil bulbs along the side of the fence. She looked like nothing so much as a pretty country milkmaid with the sun glinting off her dark hair and a radiant smile on her face.

Jordan cleared his throat. "Miss Andrews."

She glanced up and the fetching smile was replaced with a look of resignation that made Jordan inexplicably sad for a moment. "Ready?" he asked.

Annie got to her feet and brushed the dirt from her skirts. She was wearing a pretty peach-colored day dress that made her look lovely, reminding Jordan of the fact that her maid had arrived with Annie's clothing. Aunt Clarissa was there too, making inappropriate comments about his looks and asking different footmen to bring her a bit of sherry on a regular basis.

"I'm as ready as I expect to be." Annie sighed. Turning back toward Mr. McGivens, she gave him a radiant smile. "Thank you very much for allowing me to help. I do so love to plant things."

"The pleasure was entirely mine, Miss Andrews," the old gardener replied with a wide smile.

Jordan looked twice. Mr. McGivens actually blushed. He hadn't seen the old man so much as crack a smile in all his years in the family's employ. Jordan shook his head.

Annie righted her skirts and followed Jordan toward the back entrance of the house.

He shoved his hands in his pockets. "You enjoy gardening?"

Annie nodded. "Very much. I've been living in London so long, and we have no gardens there. It's quite sad, actually. The closest I've come to gardening is taking care of all of the flowers Lily's suitors used to send. Oh my, there were some lovely flowers then."

Jordan couldn't help but smile. "So what do you think of McGivens's work?"

"He has done a wonderful job. I told him so. You have absolutely beautiful flowers and trees here. But I think the sweeping entrance to the manor house would be that much more impressive if you planted some poplars along the road."

Jordan nearly choked. "What did Mr. McGivens say when you suggested that?"

"Why, he loved the idea. He said it hadn't occurred to him before."

Jordan frowned. "That doesn't sound like McGivens."

Annie's face registered her innocence. "Whatever do you mean? He's a dear man."

This time Jordan had a coughing fit in an attempt to cover his laughter. "Dear? McGivens?"

"Yes, absolutely. He listened to all my ideas and said he would make note of them. He thanked me."

"If you say so." They reached the back terrace then and Jordan opened the French doors and held one open above her head as Annie swept through before him.

Jordan hesitated. "Would you like to . . . ah, freshen up before you meet Michael?"

Her brow furrowed. "Whatever do you mean?"

"Isn't that what ladies do when they are trying to impress gentlemen?"

Annie sighed. "Most ladies, yes. But not me. Besides, with all due respect, I'm not trying to impress your brother."

He frowned. "Why not?"

She expelled her breath. "I'm afraid no amount of 'freshening up' will make me look any better. Besides, your brother is not going to want me."

Jordan scowled. What the deuce was she talking about? She looked delectable even with that streak of dirt across her lovely cheekbone. He'd be surprised if his brother didn't pounce on her and cart her off to Gretna Green himself.

"How do you know?" Jordan asked.

Annie gave him a patronizing smile. "Because this isn't the way it works."

"Nonsense." Jordan shook his head. "I've been to enough awkward Society events to know that two eligible young people meet, have an affinity for one another, and marry. Many of the *ton*'s longest-lasting unions have been based on less."

Annie shrugged. "Very well. Let's go and get this over with." She made to follow him down the corridor into the salon.

Facing her, Jordan paused. "It's just that—"

Annie stopped short. "What?"

"You've got—"

"What? What is it?"

Jordan felt like a deuced fool. How exactly did one tell a woman she had a streak of dirt on her cheek? He'd never encountered such a problem before. His mistresses were the types who would not so much as touch a speck of dust, let alone plop down in the mud next to the gardener. "You've just got—" He gestured to her cheek.

"What?"

"You've got a bit of dirt there." He pointed again.

"Oh, my." Annie frantically wiped at her cheek with the back of her hand. "Is it gone?"

Jordan smiled. She'd smudged it a bit and the resulting look was absolutely adorable. It sort of gave her the appearance of having a black eye, something he could well imagine the fiery Miss Andrews sporting. "Almost," he replied. "Here."

He pulled his handkerchief from his pocket, and using his thumb, he brushed the dirt away from her cheek. Annie gulped and glanced away, not meeting his eyes. Jordan's throat tightened. A jolt of recognition at the touch simmered through his hand. He made quick work of brushing away the dirt and pulled back his hand as if burned.

"Th . . . thank you," she murmured, her eyes still cast downward.

"You're welcome," he replied, before stepping toward the door to the salon.

"By the way," she said, with a saucy smile. "I've written to Lord Medford. I expect him to arrive and rescue me any moment now."

Jordan groaned. "Perfect."

Annie followed Lord Ashbourne into the room. A young man who looked like a shorter, younger version of Jordan stood up, a bright smile on his handsome face.

"There you are," he said, a sparkle in his gray eyes.

Annie watched him closely. He seemed exactly like Lord Ashbourne only without the air of cynicism his older brother possessed. And there was something just a bit less compelling too. But she could befriend this young man. She was sure of it.

He greeted her with a warm smile. "I didn't realize you had a guest, Jordan," Michael said, looking a bit chagrined.

Jordan pulled Annie out from behind him. "Mr. Michael Holloway, may I present Miss Anne Andrews."

Annie smiled brightly at Michael and curtsied. "A pleasure," she said.

"Miss Andrews, the pleasure is mine. It's been quite a long time since Jordan has introduced me to any of his, ah, lady friends and I—"

Jordan coughed. "No. No, Michael. I wanted *you* to meet Miss Andrews."

Michael blinked. "Me? Whatever for?"

"I thought the two of you might find something in common." He gave him a commanding stare and then motioned to Annie with his eyes.

His brow furrowed, Michael waited for Annie to sit and then sat across from her attentively. He looked a bit less comfortable than before but obviously his manners prevented him from asking his brother what the deuce he was up to presenting a woman to him like this. "Do you follow the horse races, Miss Andrews?"

Annie shook her head. "No, I'm afraid I don't know very much about them at all."

"Why, that's why I've come, Jordan. I'm off to the races tomorrow and was very much hoping you'd want to place bets too. And if you could see fit to loan me a few hundred quid, why, I'm sure to make it back ten times over."

Jordan gave his brother an unhappy stare. "This is completely inappropriate to be discussing in front of a lady, Michael. And we've talked about your gambling."

Michael's face fell. "Quite right. My apologies, Miss Andrews. I do hope I'm not offending you. But Jordan, you would not believe these horses. They're sure winners, I tell you. Sure winners."

"Not offending me at all," Annie replied with a smile. She settled into the cushions of the settee, thoroughly enjoying Lord Ashbourne's failed attempt at matchmaking.

Jordan spent the next uncomfortable hour attempting to divert the conversation away from horses and sportsmanship while Annie sat with an amused smile on her face, asking Michael all sorts of questions about his love of equines.

"Doesn't Lord Ashbourne like to gamble?" Annie asked.

Michael made a noise that sounded suspiciously like a snort. "Hardly. In fact, I've never known Jordan to gamble, not on horses at least."

Jordan gave him a cautioning glare. "I adore cards, however."

"And he never loses at them," Michael replied. "I wish I had just a bit of your luck, Jordan."

"It's not luck," Jordan replied with a wink.

Despite herself, Annie laughed. The man was unrepentantly arrogant. "Why doesn't your brother bet on horses then, Mr. Holloway?" she asked Michael, suddenly fascinated by this glimpse into Jordan's life.

"You'd have to ask him that," Michael replied, with a friendly smile. "But I swear he's the only nobleman who doesn't spend much time at Tatt's, and come to think on it, I've never known him to participate in a hunt."

This unexpected bit of news caught Annie entirely by surprise. Her gaze flew to Jordan's face.

"Awful sport." Jordan shook his head. "I've no interest in it."

Annie settled back, a half-smile resting on her face.

By the time Michael left hours later after a long and lively visit, Annie was beside herself with glee and Jordan had a deep scowl on his face.

"I told you it wouldn't work," Annie said in a singsong voice after Michael's coach drove away from the house and the two of them had waved good-bye.

Jordan turned to her, rubbing his temples. "First, I must apologize for my brother's lack of decorum. He tends to be much less formal in the country, but that is hardly an excuse for his constant talk of sport in your presence."

"I found him delightful."

Jordan smirked. "He gave me a splitting headache."

"I'm very sorry to hear that," Annie said, still smiling.

Jordan sighed. "It was my mistake. All the lad cares about is gaming and horseflesh."

Annie nodded. "If you say so. But I say it's more than that."

"I still have two more brothers, Miss Andrews, and both of them are older and wiser than Michael. And exceedingly eligible."

Annie turned toward the side of the house, intent upon resuming her work with Mr. McGivens. "Very well. If you insist upon continuing this farce, far be it from me to stop you, but at least warn your next brother that you're attempting to pair him with me."

Jordan grunted. "There's no time to warn him. Timothy will be here the day after tomorrow."

CHAPTER 23

"I hate to interrupt you, my lord, but—"

Jordan tossed the quill he'd been using to go over the ledgers to the desk. He glanced up to see Jonathan, his head groomsman, standing in the open doorway to his study. "Yes? What is it?"

Jonathan bowed. "My lord, it's Miss Andrews." The groomsman audibly gulped. "She wants to go riding, sir, and she's . . ."

Jordan quirked a brow. "Yes?"

Jonathan glanced down at his hands. "My lord. She's asked for the curricle with a team tied tandem."

Jordan leaned back in his chair and cupped his hands behind his head, a broad smile on his face. "I see. And what did you tell her?"

Jonathan pulled at his neckcloth. "I told her I'd have to check with you first. I know you said she wasn't to be given any mount. But she's very insistent. Not to mention I don't want her to break her neck, my lord. I've never seen a lady drive a tandem team."

Jordan flashed another grin. "Neither have I. Let's go."

He stood up, grabbed his gloves from the desktop, and made his way toward the door. Jonathan followed him out into the hall, dogging his heels.

"So, you plan to tell her she cannot do it, my lord?" Jonathan asked, nearly running to keep up.

Jordan didn't slow his pace. "Absolutely not." He pulled on the gloves. "I intend to watch."

Jonathan froze in his tracks momentarily, his mouth gaping, but soon was back at Jordan's heels. "My lord?"

Jordan stopped this time and Jonathan tripped and caught himself. "Yes, Jonathan?"

"My apologies, my lord, but I thought I heard you say you intend to . . ."—another gulp—"watch."

Another nod. "Precisely."

Jordan made his way out the side door and down the gravel path to the stables. The meeting with Michael yesterday hadn't gone the way he'd expected. Not at all. Bah. Michael was a fool. The fact that he hadn't scooped up Annie the minute he saw her just proved it. Where else would the lad find such a beautiful, intelligent young woman who wasn't afraid to have dirt on her face and apparently could drive a tandem team too? He refused to examine the bit of relief he'd felt when Michael had left. It was not as if Jordan wanted her for himself. No. Ludicrous notion. He shook his head, increasing his strides as he crunched along the path to the stables. He strode into the building, Jonathan still on his heels, just in time to see a clearly perturbed Annie arguing with a lesser groom.

"I'm telling you, I've driven a tandem team dozens of times." She threw up her hands. "Dozens!"

The worried look on the groom's face was mixed with a healthy dose of skepticism. He merely shook his head. "Jonathan asked me ta wait for 'is return, miss. I'm sure 'e'll be back any moment now."

Annie crossed her arms over her chest. "You do not believe me, do you?"

The groom turned a special shade of red. "I'm sure Jonathan will be back soon," he repeated.

Annie tapped her foot on the packed-earth ground. "Lord Ashbourne will hear about this," she insisted, pointing her finger at the groom.

Jordan stood several paces away, his shoulder propped against a stall door, his booted feet crossed at the ankles, the hint of a smile playing on his lips. "Indeed, Lord Ashbourne has already heard about it," he called.

Annie and the groom both swung around to face him. Annie was a bit pink herself, it seemed. She eyed him up and down and then raised her chin. "Please tell this nice young man that I am perfectly capable of driving a tandem team."

Jordan rested a knuckle under his chin and watched her. "Hmm. The fact is, I have no idea if you are capable of any such thing." The pretty pink color spread to her hairline. "But," he quickly amended, "I'm extremely curious to find out."

Annie nodded, smiled, and a bit of the color receded from her cheeks. "Very well."

"I shall order a curricle with a tandem team put to, upon one condition," Jordan said.

She rolled her eyes. "What's that?"

"I must accompany you. I wish to see this up close."

Annie smiled at him. Her lips moved into a thin, straight line. "Don't trust me, eh?"

"On the contrary. Of course I trust you, or I wouldn't risk my life by riding with you." He winked at her.

She put her hands on her hips and glared at him. "Don'
you have anything better to do with your time, my lord?"

He took two steps toward her. "Better is open to in-
terpretation, is it not?"

"Very well." She eyed him warily. "Come if you
must."

"I must." He nodded.

At Jordan's command, the two grooms hurried off to
hitch the team to the curricle. When they returned, Jordan handed Annie up into the seat and followed her. She
waited for him to sit, holding the fine leather reins in both
hands, speaking quietly to the horses. Jordan watched
her closely. She was a skilled horsewoman. That much
was clear from her use of the reins and her treatment of
the animals.

She clucked to the pair, shook out the reins, and they
trotted off at a brisk clip. "Where to?" she asked as they
cleared the stable door.

Jordan grinned at her. "What? No plan?"

She eyed him with disdain. "You know this land better than I do. You tell me. What's the best route?"

Jordan scanned the horizon and nodded toward the
right. "Through the meadow, there." He pointed. "There's
a well-worn path with an excellent view at the end."

Annie nodded. Keeping a tight hold of the reins, she
expertly maneuvered the two horses to the right.

Jordan's eyebrows rose. "Impressive, Miss Andrews,
very impressive."

She smiled and preened. "I told you I could do it. But
you don't fool me, Lord Ashbourne. I don't believe for
one moment you came with me for any other reason than
to keep me from escaping your property." She winked
at him.

Jordan tossed back his head and laughed. "If that had been my concern, I would have sent Jonathan with you."

Annie swallowed and glanced away, making a show of seeing to the horses. The lightly sprung curricle made its way through the meadow and into a copse of trees. "Just beyond here," Lord Ashbourne said, pointing, "is a lane that follows the pond."

Annie nodded. Being in Lord Ashbourne's company would be much less difficult if the man weren't so gorgeous. She cleared her throat. And if she didn't have the memory of their kiss at the Lindworths' ball swimming around in her head. Oh, and the other kiss in the Roths' library floating about as well.

Jordan pointed toward the horses. "Maggie and Martin are a fine pair, are they not?"

Annie nodded again. "They're lovely, as is this curricle."

He inclined his head. "Thank you. I just purchased it over the summer. Haven't had much of a chance to use it before now."

"It's a lovely day for a drive," Annie said, and then mentally cursed herself for saying such an idiotic thing. Specifically because it in fact was *not* a lovely day for a drive. Storm clouds had been brewing all morning.

"Where did you learn to drive a tandem team with such skill?" Jordan asked.

Annie had to bite her lip to keep from smiling at his compliment. She shrugged. "I didn't have much to do when I was a child. The grooms at our stables would take me riding with them and my governess loved to ride as well."

Jordan's brow furrowed. "You had your studies, did you not?"

"Yes. But Lily was the one who received all our parents' attention. I was always an afterthought."

Jordan remained silent for a moment. "That must have been difficult," he finally said.

She shrugged. "I was the younger daughter, not beautiful, not talented. Absolutely nothing remarkable about me."

Jordan turned to face her. His voice was soft. "You cannot believe that."

She smiled a ghost of a smile. "I know it's true, Lord Ashbourne. I was told it often enough."

Jordan's face turned to stone. "What idiot was foolish enough to tell you that?"

She clucked to the horses and chuckled a humorless chuckle. "My father," she admitted.

"Your father, may he rest in peace, was an idiot."

A surge of happiness bubbled in Annie's chest. She'd never admitted these things to anyone before. She didn't know why she was admitting them now, but she certainly hadn't expected sympathy. "Aren't all second daughters less valuable than the first? Besides, it wasn't Lily's fault that she was so much more beautiful and accomplished than I. My parents' hopes rested on her securing an excellent match."

Jordan shook his head. "You've got a great many things wrong. First of all, Lily is a beautiful woman, there's no doubt on that score, but it's not true that she's more beautiful than you. Secondly, I've lived thirty-one years and have yet to see a lady drive a tandem team with the skill you've exhibited today. Hell, I've yet to see a *man* drive a tandem team with your skill. Lastly, we've all seen the results of your father's maneuverings with Lily's match. He had her marry Lord Merrill, for God's sake, which just proves my point that the man was an idiot."

Annie's face pinkened again. "It's nice of you to defend me, Lord Ashbourne." She kept her eyes trained on the horses.

"Annie," he said quietly. "Call me Jordan. I daresay we're on a first-name basis by now."

She smiled at that and glanced away nervously. "Very well."

"I never realized how difficult it must be for younger siblings," Jordan said. "My brothers always seemed to be enjoying themselves while I was stuck with responsibility."

Annie's brow furrowed. "Stuck with responsibility? I wonder if Lily ever felt that way." She shook her head. "I always assumed she enjoyed our parents' attention. And their praise."

His voice was low. "Just because your father told you that you weren't beautiful or accomplished doesn't make it true, Annie."

Annie took a deep breath. It was very polite of Jordan to try to tell her so. Truly it was. If only she could believe him. "My father wasn't the only one who said it," she nearly whispered.

They'd come to the end of the little path that meandered around the water. Annie let the horses go slowly, walking them. She barely noticed the beauty of the secluded little pond with sparkling green water surrounded by a myriad of trees graced with the first signs of autumn's changing leaves.

Jordan looked at her. "Who else said it? Surely not your mother? Or Lily?"

She shook her head. "No, no. Not Mother. Never her
Mother had no idea that Father had ever said such things
to me. And of course Lily always adored me, and I, her."

Jordan glanced at her profile, fetching in her bonnet
"Then who?"

She shook her head. "You're not going to stop, are
you?"

"No."

"It was no one, really. Just a boy once. A long time
ago. It hardly matters now."

"Annie." He moved to touch her hand. "Who would
say such a thing to you?"

The wind kicked up then and a crack of thunder
spooked the horses. Annie clucked to them softly and
held the reins with a firm hand. She shook her head. Smiling brightly, she didn't meet Jordan's eyes. "We should
get back to the stables. It's going to rain."

Dark gray clouds were ominously gathering in the
distance and the wind had kicked up with a cold edge
to it.

Jordan glanced up at the sky. He nodded. "You're
right. We should get back. Let's see what you can do
with this team." He grinned at her.

Annie's eyes flared. "Really?"

"Really," he answered, smiling at her.

Annie refused to think about what his smile did to her
insides. She shook out the reins and urged Maggie and
Martin into a fine gallop back down the path they'd come.

"Hold on," she ordered. Jordan braced a hand against
the side of the curricle and winked at her.

They raced back to the stables, the wind kicking up
behind them, the clouds chasing them. They'd barely

pulled into the building when the sky opened up and poured.

"Just made it," Annie said, winking back at him.

The grooms rushed to take the reins from Annie and Jordan jumped from the seat. He landed in the soft hay and bowed at the waist to her. "Thanks to the skill of the driver," he said, offering her his hand.

Annie inclined her head and smiled brightly, allowing him to help her from the vehicle.

She hopped to the ground and Jordan stared down at her. "I knew Eggleston made a mistake that day."

A lump formed in her throat. "Which day?" she asked as Jonathan and the other groom pulled the curricle away. She dusted off her skirts and watched Jordan closely.

"That day I came upon you two riding in the park with your fox. You'd wanted to drive his team of four."

She tapped her cheek, remembering. "Yes. That's right. He wouldn't allow it."

Jordan nodded. "A mistake, that. He missed some fine horsemanship."

"Horse*woman*ship."

He inclined his head toward her. "Indeed. And not the only mistake Eggleston made, to be sure."

Annie glanced away self-consciously. But some devil on her shoulder prompted her. "If you think my driving is good, my lord, you should see me shoot a pistol."

CHAPTER 24

This time, when Jordan went looking for her, Annie was speaking to Mrs. Phillips, the housekeeper. "But if you change the delivery to twice a week instead of once, the greens will be fresher and—"

Jordan crossed his arms over his chest and cleared his throat. "Sorry to interrupt."

Mrs. Phillips jumped and Annie twirled around to face him.

"My lord," Mrs. Phillips said, curtsying. "Miss Andrews was just giving me some advice on the deliveries from the farmers."

"I can see that."

Annie smoothed her hands down her skirts. "I suppose it's time for my next introduction."

He smiled. "Indeed."

"I'll be back soon, Mrs. Phillips, and then we may discuss the pantries. I hope you do not mind but I took a look and I have some ideas on organization that I think you may like."

Mrs. Phillips smiled. "Oh, I should like that very much."

"How do you know so much about the pantries?" Jordan asked as he escorted Annie from the room.

"Why, back when we had little money, Mary and I used to come up with the most creative ways to stretch the stores," she admitted with a giggle. "Lily never thought I understood how bad it was, but we made a game out of it, Mary and I. It was quite enjoyable, actually."

Jordan shook his head. He was not quite sure how Annie had managed to charm both the gardener and the housekeeper in the space of three days, but it seemed she had.

He smirked at her insistence that she would be back soon. She clearly wasn't taking these little meetings with his brothers seriously. Fine, perhaps inviting Michael had been a mistake. His youngest brother was still a bit too distracted yet to settle down. But Timothy was a respectable twenty-seven, had a fine income from their mother's side of the family, and he was, thankfully, not entirely preoccupied with sports.

Jordan thought about their outing the day before with the tandem team. She was a skilled horsewoman. He'd been completely sincere about that, but he couldn't shake the thoughts about the other things she'd said. *I was the younger daughter, not beautiful, not talented. Absolutely nothing remarkable about me.* It made Jordan want to hit something. Annie was beautiful and talented and there were a great many things remarkable about her. Her father had been a complete idiot to tell her anything different.

Why, the girl had managed to elude Jordan on more than one occasion, was a gardener, obviously a skilled organizer, and a talented rider. And as for her beauty, he couldn't believe anyone, especially her own father, had ever been foolish enough to suggest she was plain. He couldn't credit the notion that anyone had said it, and he certainly couldn't understand why she seemed to refuse to believe him when he'd tried to tell her differently. It made no sense. And whoever the boy was who'd confirmed her suspicions, why, he'd like to wring the little blighter's neck.

Annie was lovely, intelligent, and talented. She'd be the perfect choice of wife for someone in the market for such a companion, and his brother Timothy would be a fool not to recognize it. Damn it.

Timothy Holloway looked like a lighter-haired version of his eldest brother. He was tall and lean whereas Jordan was a bit more solidly built, but Timothy was very handsome nonetheless.

The introductions were handled much the same way as the previous day, but this time Annie spoke up sooner.

"It's very nice to meet you, Mr. Holloway, but I think you should know, your brother is attempting to play matchmaker."

Timothy blinked nearly as many times as his younger brother had the day before.

He glanced at Jordan, his brow wrinkled. "Matchmaker?"

Jordan shrugged. "I merely thought the two of you might . . . find something in common. You know? If you got to know each other a bit."

Annie hid her smile and poor Timothy looked as if he'd just swallowed a bug.

"Oh, no. No. No," he said, backing up a bit. "And please do not be offended, Miss Andrews, because you seem quite lovely, but . . . well . . . that's one of the reasons I came out to visit today, Jordan. I wanted to tell you I've met a young lady in town, Miss Agnes Wintergale. I intend to offer for her."

Annie plopped down into a nearby chair and watched with unmitigated glee while the two brothers discussed Timothy's future bride.

"I must say I think Lord Ashbourne has taken this news quite well," Annie finally said with a grin.

"What do you mean?" Jordan asked, eyeing her warily.

She directed her words toward Timothy. "It's just that your brother doesn't seem to be a proponent of marriage and certainly not love. Yet you sound as if you are a man in love, Mr. Holloway. Congratulations to you."

Timothy nodded and smiled at her. "Thank you very much. I must admit I am that."

"I do not condemn marriage for others," Jordan replied, his eyes narrowed on her. "I am merely uninterested myself."

"And convinced you know who should marry whom," she added. "Lest we forget. Indeed, have you met Miss Wintergale? How can you be sure she meets with your rigorous approval?"

"I'm sure she's a lovely young woman," Jordan ground out, while Timothy eyed them both curiously.

"I see," she continued. "So your standards are different for your own brother than, say, for someone you barely know?" She batted her eyelashes at him sweetly.

"Jordan's been in love," Timothy finally inserted into the conversation. "It's just that Georgi—"

"Enough," Jordan snapped, a muscle ticking in his jaw.

Timothy promptly shut his mouth, and Annie raised

her eyebrows. Ah, so the mysterious woman was named Georgi-something? Interesting. Why, if she continued to meet Lord Ashbourne's brothers, she just might learn all of his secrets. It was enough to nearly make her look forward to the next matchmaking attempt.

In the end, congratulations were issued all around and Annie was left with the feeling that both of the youngest Holloway men were quite jovial and friendly compared with their older brother.

"I wish you and Miss Wintergale every happiness," she said to Timothy as he took his leave.

After Timothy's coach was on its way back to London, Jordan turned to Annie. "My apologies. I had no idea Tim had taken an interest in a young lady already or I obviously would not have introduced you."

"Obviously," she replied, inclining her head. "Don't worry. I didn't take offense at all. He seems quite nice. And he's fallen in love. What a wonderful thing." She beamed.

Jordan shook his head and then nodded resolutely. "Blast it, Charlie will be here in two days, and I *know* he doesn't fancy anyone. I just spoke with him last week."

Annie crossed her arms over her chest. "It'll be something," she assured him.

"What are you expecting?"

"I don't know. Anything. For instance, are you quite sure Charlie's interests lie with females?"

Jordan's eyes narrowed on her. "I'm *quite* sure."

"Very well, then, I look forward to meeting him, as I have all your brothers." She smiled at him. "For now, I'll just pop back into the kitchens to speak with Mrs. Phillips." Annie patted Jordan on the arm, turned, and flounced away. As she left, she tossed over her shoulder, "Don't despair. They say the third time is the charm, do they not?"

Jordan grunted.

CHAPTER 25

The next day, Jordan left off his business early on purpose. Dismissing his steward, he gathered up his ledgers and tossed his quill aside. He leaned back in his chair and stretched his arms behind his head. For the first time in . . . well, ages, he was feeling restless, bored. His time in the city was usually full of pursuits of pleasure and his time in the country more often than not full of hard work on his lands and ledgers, meeting with his solicitor and steward. It had always been more than enough to keep him occupied, but today he felt . . . agitated.

Damn that fool Michael and his silly love of betting on horses. Jordan had been convinced Michael and Annie would make a fine pair. And damn himself for not realizing Tim had taken an interest in Miss Wintergale. Fine. Jordan would take the responsibility for that mistake. But no harm done after all, and Charlie would be here tomorrow.

Charlie. His brother was whip-smart and had a knack for insight into human character. Yes, Charlie was sure to see Annie's merits right away. No doubt the two of them would be engaged before the month was out. Perhaps even married by Christmas. A Christmas wedding would be perfect. So why did the thought make Jordan uneasy? And why had he breathed a bit of a sigh of relief when Michael and Timothy had been uninterested?

Damn it. He scrubbed his hands across his face. And rolled his head on his neck. He'd been working too hard, that was all. He just needed to go outside and get some fresh air. Do something. Have a bit of sport.

Jordan pushed himself from his chair and strolled out of his study. Shoving his hands in his pockets, he made his way to the kitchens.

"Is Miss Andrews here?" he asked Mrs. Phillips, who was busily inventorying the pantry.

She glanced up at him, a surprised look on her face. "No, my lord. I haven't seen her today. But I'm busily making her changes to the pantries. She had *such* good advice."

Jordan smiled at that. Annie, it seemed, was full of surprises. Her parents must have paid her education some attention, if not the girl herself. She had obviously been raised to be the lady of a grand house. Another reason throwing herself away on Arthur Eggleston made no sense.

Jordan thanked Mrs. Phillips and wandered out into the gardens where Mr. McGivens was busy planting spring bulbs. "Have you seen Miss Andrews today?" he asked the gardener.

Mr. McGivens shook his head. "I'm sorry, my lord. I have not," he replied. "But she was perfectly right about these flowers. They'll be downright eye-catching come spring."

Jordan mumbled something in the affirmative and walked away.

He found her in the stables. She was playing with the puppies the springer spaniel had just given birth to days before.

"You shall be named Duchess," she said to one of the small bits of fur. "Because it is obvious that you are in charge here and you are a very grand lady indeed." She laughed as the puppy named Duchess pushed over another one of the puppies with her tiny, black nose.

"What would your fox think of this rival for your affections?" Jordan asked from his place several paces away, leaning against the wooden door frame.

Annie glanced up quickly. She pulled the puppy to her chest and laughed a self-conscious little laugh. "Oh, Dash isn't jealous, to be sure, but I've no doubt Evans is spoiling him right now. I've long suspected Evans loves him as much as I do, if you want to know the truth."

Jordan laughed. He made his way over to where Annie sat. Pulling one hand out of his pocket, he scooped up a puppy and cradled it to his chest. "How are they?" he asked, gesturing to the litter.

"They seem healthy and happy to me," she answered, standing up and brushing the straw from her pink skirts.

Jordan nodded and stood up, too. "I'm glad to hear it. How is Aunt Clarissa enjoying herself?"

"You just missed her, actually. She came out to visit the puppies not long ago. Then she said something about being a bit . . . thirsty."

Jordan smiled at that. "I see."

Annie kicked at the straw with her slipper and the silence drew out uncomfortably between them. "Wh . . . what brings you to the stables?" she finally managed to ask. "Your brother isn't expected until tomorrow. Has he arrived early?"

"No," Jordan replied, mirroring her action and kicking at the dirt with his top boot. "I came to . . . Would you like to go shooting?"

"Shooting?" Her eyebrows rose.

"Yes," he said, smiling. "You did boast of your skill, did you not? I've been looking forward to witnessing it."

A smile spread across Annie's face. "Then by all means, let's go shooting."

"Excellent. I'll meet you by the edge of the meadow at half past."

Annie nodded. "See you then."

By the time Annie wandered out to the meadow, a bull's-eye had been set up across the field near a willow tree and a table that held an assortment of pistols rested in the soft grass. Jordan stood next to it, looking as handsome as ever. His statement earlier that he'd been looking forward to seeing her shoot had done funny things to her insides. And when he'd walked away, she'd watched him go and tried to ignore the way his backside filled out his breeches so well.

Oh, it was ludicrous, the thoughts she was having. Completely ludicrous. And she needed to stop. Now.

Annie sauntered over to where Jordan stood and surveyed the pistols. "I must warn you, I'm very competitive," she said.

He flashed her a knee-weakening grin. "And I must warn you, I've been asked to be the second in a great many duels."

Annie's eyes went wide. "My, you must have seen some scandalous sights."

"I've seen too many fools get too angry too quickly."

It struck her memory then. Jordan had shot Gilbert

Winfrey, the head of the London underworld, as he rode off after firing at Devon. Winfrey had been riding a horse on a dark street in the middle of a foggy night and Jordan's shot had been flawless. Devon often remarked on how fine a marksman his friend was. Even Arthur had mentioned it.

Suddenly, Annie felt very foolish indeed to be challenging him. It was true she'd been a good enough shot among the groomsmen at her parents' stable. But she couldn't compare herself to Jordan, one of the *ton*'s most renowned marksmen. What had she been thinking?

"Would you like to go first?" Jordan asked, and Annie swallowed.

"No!"

"What? Why?"

"I was just now thinking how good you are at this."

"Second thoughts on challenging me?" He winked at her and Annie's insides flipped.

"Something like that." She bit her lip. "You go first."

Jordan inclined his head. "As you wish." Bracing apart his feet, he cocked the pistol and aimed his left arm at the bull's-eye.

"You shoot with your left hand?" she asked.

"Yes. I prefer it, but I can shoot with my right too." His arm was straight and strong and when he pulled the trigger, smoke and ash blew out and wafted on the breeze.

Annie glanced down at the bull's-eye. A perfect hit in the center of the thing. She gulped. Oh, perfect. How would she ever top that?

She clapped her hands and Jordan bowed. "Your turn," he said, moving back to the table full of pistols and picking one for her. "This used to be my mother's," he said, handing the smaller weapon to her.

Annie glanced down at the beautiful mother-of-pearl handle and took her place on the mark. She straightened her shoulders. She could do this. She'd been in competition with the groomsmen often enough. She would not embarrass herself. She pushed up her chin and aimed with her right arm.

She pulled the trigger and the pistol reverberated and pushed her back a pace. When the smoke cleared she eyed the mark. Just a hint off center. Blast it.

"Not bad." Jordan whistled.

Annie shrugged.

"Do you want me to show you my secret?" he asked.

Annie nodded. Slowly. Then she swallowed. Jordan was looking far too good today with his dark hair windswept, his white lawn shirt open at the neck, and wearing chocolate-brown breeches and black top boots. She glanced away.

He grabbed up a medium-sized pistol and brought it back to the mark where Annie still stood. He moved behind her and carefully placed it in her hands. Then he put his arms around her and positioned her arm with both of his own. The smell of soap and horse leather emanated off him and Annie breathed it in. He made her tremble. Oh, why did the man have to be so good-looking? It was like getting shooting lessons from Adonis. Completely intimidating.

"Do you feel that?" His breath came hot on her neck and cheek and Annie shuddered.

"Ye . . . yes." But she wasn't exactly sure what he was asking. She felt quite a lot at the moment.

"Do you feel how the pistol is like an extension of your hand when you hold it this way?" he asked.

"Uh-huh." All she could do was nod. She wanted to

turn and bury her face in his neck, but instead she swallowed and kept her eye on the target.

"Cock your thumb, like this," he breathed, and Annie closed her eyes briefly while he nudged her thumb with his forefinger. "Now stare down the target."

She nodded and bit her lip.

"Keep your eye trained along the top of the pistol. Do you see?"

She could barely get a yes from her dry throat.

"Lock your arm," he commanded, moving his strong, warm hand down to her elbow and squeezing.

Annie gulped. "All right."

"Now," he said. "Keep your eye on the pistol and the target at the same time."

Another nod.

"Fire!"

Annie squeezed the trigger, and this time when she was thrown back, it was into Jordan's arms. He wrapped an arm around her waist to steady her. The smoke blew into her face and she coughed.

"Excellent job," Jordan said, pulling his hand from around her waist. Annie looked toward the target. She'd been so distracted by Jordan's touch, she hadn't bothered to see how she'd done. She blinked. A perfect hit in the center, overlapping Jordan's previous hit.

"I did it!" she exclaimed, carefully handing him the pistol before twirling around in a circle.

"Of course you did," he replied.

"Thank you," she said, suddenly self-conscious. "For showing me your trick."

"It's not a trick, it's a secret," he replied, a sensual smile on his face.

Annie glanced away, biting her lip again. "Yes, of course."

"Seems you were telling the truth. You are an excellent shot."

Annie curtsied. "Thank you."

Jordan's answering smile made Annie wish they were alone in a secluded alcove.

"My mother was a great shot too," he said.

Annie smiled at that. "Ah, no doubt that's where you get your ability."

Jordan threw back his head and laughed. "Yes, no doubt. But you should see Charlie. He's nearly as good as I am."

Annie's smile faded at the mention of Lord Ashbourne's third brother. It reminded her that Jordan was intent on finding someone for her to marry, getting her out of his life. And here she was enjoying herself when she should have been writing another letter to Lord Medford asking him to come and retrieve her.

Annie shook her head. But there was no sense in not enjoying herself, was there? It wasn't as if she would have such an opportunity again, having London's most famous shot (and rake) give her personal shooting lessons. A smile played on her lips and a shiver traced along her spine. "Will you show me again, Jordan? I'm not quite sure I've got it yet."

CHAPTER 26

Annie was speaking with Jeffries, the butler, when Jordan rounded the corner and found her the next day. He raised a brow. Mr. McGivens and Mrs. Phillips might have been perfectly content with Annie nosing into their affairs, but Jeffries came from a long line of distinguished butlers, all of whom had been in service to the Earl of Ashbourne for generations. Jeffries would not stand for any questioning of his methods or his authority.

Jordan glanced at the butler's face. By God, the man actually wore a . . . smile. Jordan hadn't seen Jeffries smile since . . . ever.

"I'd never quite thought of it that way, Miss Andrews," the butler was saying.

"Thought of what what way?" Jordan asked before he could stop himself.

Seeing his master, Jeffries straightened to his normal regal position. "My lord." He clicked his heels together and bowed.

Annie glanced up, a slightly guilty look on her pretty face.

Jordan waved away the formalities with his hand.

"No need for that, Jeffries. What were you discussing? I'm curious."

Jeffries cleared his throat. "Why, Miss Andrews was just pointing out that were I to allow some of the footmen to oversee the less important aspects of my position, I would be free to perform the more important tasks with much more care and precision."

Jordan shook his head. Jeffries had been famously into everything for as long as Jordan could remember. The footmen detested his overly fastidious manners and the housemaids were unhappy with the way he told them how to do their work. But Jeffries was the head of the household servants and Jordan had always allowed him to handle everything as he saw fit. Now, somehow, Annie had managed to get the butler to see reason? It was nearly impossible to believe.

"I'm so pleased you agree," Annie replied to the butler with a tinkling laugh. "Mrs. Phillips has already agreed to ensure the housemaids meet their standards."

"It should be quite a relief to me, Miss Andrews," the butler said with a bow. "Not to have to worry about such things any longer. Seeing to the wine and the silver alone take half my day."

Annie beamed at him before taking Jordan's arm and allowing him to lead her away.

"I've never seen Jeffries so amenable," Jordan said as they walked toward the terrace.

Annie flashed him a bright smile. "Mrs. Phillips has just been beside herself dealing with his, ahem, attention to detail, and I thought I might convince him if I appealed to his vanity. After all, butlers are meant to be butlers."

Jordan shook his head. "I don't know what my household did before you came along."

Annie playfully slapped his sleeve.

"No, I'm quite serious," Jordan replied. "You've managed to charm the gardener, the housekeeper, and the butler in just a matter of days. In addition to your driving and shooting skills, I stand very much impressed by you, Miss Andrews."

Annie couldn't squelch her smile. She shrugged. "I've got to do something to occupy my time while I'm . . . visiting."

Jordan flashed her a grin. "I'm just glad you've stayed out of trouble."

"Who says I've stayed out of trouble?"

He winked at her and Annie swallowed.

They came to the French doors that opened onto the terrace behind the house and Jordan pushed one open and allowed Annie to precede him through it. "Charlie is here and I thought we'd meet outdoors. Perhaps the air will be good for all of us today."

Annie nodded and pasted her most enchanting smile on her face. But Jordan frowned. For some reason Jordan didn't like the idea of her meeting Charlie today after all. He didn't like it one bit.

Like his older brother, Charles Holloway was tall, dark, and handsome. Unlike his older brother, he had dark brown eyes, a cleft in his chin, and a friendly, welcoming smile. He was a beautiful man. Certainly second to Jordan himself, but she couldn't help that *that* rogue was so good-looking.

"How do you do, Mr. Holloway?" she said with her usual curtsy. "Your brother thinks we should marry."

Charlie looked twice, something that reminded Annie of a gesture she'd seen Jordan make a time or two.

"Pardon?" Charlie said.

"I've beaten you to the chase today, Annie," Jordan replied with a smug smile. "I met with Charlie before I came to find you and he is neither preoccupied with sports nor in love with another woman."

Annie opened her mouth to speak.

"He's not that either," Jordan said with a disapproving stare.

Annie shrugged.

Charlie cleared his throat. "Yes, well, now that we've established that I'm eligible, Miss Andrews, I would be honored if you would come for a walk with me in the gardens so we might have a chance to speak."

Annie nodded and gave Charlie another bright smile. "I should like that immensely. I have quite a lot of questions regarding how your older brother got to be the way he is. I suspect your mother dropped him on his head or something. Though of course I assume it was entirely accidental."

Jordan growled at her. "Oh, you'd like that, wouldn't you?"

"Immensely." She narrowed her eyes on him.

Charlie glanced back and forth between the two of them.

"I'll be back soon, my lord," she called in a singsong voice.

Charlie offered her his arm and they took off together, strolling down the path out into the meadow. Annie was suddenly nervous to be alone with him. Charlie was too good-looking. He reminded her of being alone with Jordan.

"I trust your journey here was uneventful," Annie began.

"Indeed," he answered. "I always enjoy visiting Ashbourne Manor."

Annie bit her lip. "I must warn you, if you meet Aunt Clarissa, she might well say . . . inappropriate things to you."

"If Aunt Clarissa is the older lady I met earlier carrying around a bottle of Madeira, she's already said a handful of things to me and, yes, all of them inappropriate."

Annie flushed. "I'm so sorry."

"No need to apologize. I have to admit it was . . . entertaining, actually. But tell me, how are you enjoying your time here, Miss Andrews?"

"Your brother has been an excellent host," she replied, swallowing.

Charlie looked suspiciously as if he were fighting a smile. "Ah, that's interesting, considering Jordan told me you'd probably inform me you'd been abducted by him."

Annie's eyes went wide and she clutched Charlie's sleeve. "He told you that?"

Charlie nodded. "Yes."

Annie began walking again. "I'm surprised he was so . . . forthcoming."

"So, tell me, do you consider yourself abducted?"

Annie stopped again. This time she bent to pluck a pink aster from the ground and pushed the pretty flower behind her ear. "Abducted? No. More like . . . diverted."

"A nice way to put it."

Annie expelled her breath. "I cannot blame your brother for losing his patience with me, Mr. Holloway. My sister asked a very large favor of him and he's just doing his best to keep his promise."

"You sound resigned to your fate. A very different

picture than Jordan painted. I think he expects you to bolt at any moment." Charlie chuckled.

Annie smiled at him. "I wouldn't give your brother the satisfaction of telling him I've changed my mind." She winked.

"So it's like *that* between you?"

Annie slid her arm back through his and resumed their walk. "If you mean combative, then yes. Your older brother can be quite dictatorial, or haven't you noticed?"

Charlie laughed then and Annie once again thought how handsome and friendly he was. "Yes, I've noticed, Miss Andrews, or do you forget I grew up with him? Jordan's only a year older than I am. But he's always been quite sure his way is best."

"I know how you feel," Annie replied, with a sigh. "My older sister, Lily, is the same way. She'd live my life for me if she could."

"Forgive me, but I take it your sister isn't any more fond of Arthur Eggleston than Jordan is."

Annie's face heated. She glanced up at Mr. Holloway. "He told you about Arthur?"

Charlie nodded. "Yes. I hope you don't mind. Jordan was just explaining to me why he was looking about for other—shall I say?—eligible gentlemen."

Annie expelled her breath. "I should have expected that. Once again, he's quite sure he's right."

Charlie helped her step over a log that had fallen across the trail. "And you're so sure he's wrong?"

Annie turned to face him. "The truth is, Mr. Holloway, just between you and me, of course."

"Of course," he promised, laying his hand over his heart. "On my honor."

Annie glanced back toward the house. "The truth is I do think he's right. About Arthur, that is."

Charlie nodded. "Why the change of heart, if you don't mind my asking?"

She laughed, shaking her head. "I don't know why I'm telling you all of this. I've only just met you. You're very easy to talk to. Do you know that?"

"Both a blessing and a curse, I assure you. However, in this case, it is decidedly a blessing."

Annie glanced back at the house again. The wind blew the curls around her face and she pushed them aside with the tips of her fingers. "Arthur promised me he wouldn't let anyone come between us ever again."

"And?"

"And when Jordan came to get me, Arthur just . . . left."

Charlie winced. "It doesn't sound very noble of him."

She shook her head. "I couldn't believe it. And the truth is, your brother has seemed much more concerned about my reputation than Arthur ever did."

"Jordan may be controlling, but he is full of honor. Of that I can assure you."

Annie eyed him carefully and decided to ask the question that had been lingering on the tip of her tongue ever since she'd been alone with Charlie. "Do you know what happened? With Jordan, years ago? Who he made a fool of himself over, I mean?"

Charlie's eyes went wide. "Who told you Jordan made a fool of himself?"

"He did."

"I wouldn't say he made a fool of himself. Just a bad decision. A mistake. We all make them. But Jordan tends to be extremely hard on himself when he does."

Annie searched Charlie's face. "What happened?"

"Now that, Miss Andrews, I cannot tell you. You'll have to ask Jordan himself. It's not my story to tell. But I know he likes you very much. He told me so. I'm sure he'll answer whatever questions you have."

Annie's face fell. She hitched up her skirts in her hand to avoid dragging them through a mud puddle. She wasn't about to ask Jordan to tell her the story. She sighed. "Yes. He's done everything to help me, including bringing me out here and even introducing me, to you and your brothers. I've only now realized what high regard he must have for me to do so."

Charlie gave her a conspiratorial grin. "You know what I think, Miss Andrews? Just between the two of us?"

Annie smiled. This time she placed her hand upon her heart. "Upon my honor."

"I believe my brother holds you in very, very high regard indeed."

"So what did you think of her?" Jordan asked Charlie several hours later when the two brothers were kicked back in Jordan's study enjoying a brandy.

Charlie propped his booted feet on the desk in front of him. "I think she's lovely, intelligent, funny, and quite nice."

Jordan felt a twinge of jealousy. Unexpected and entirely unwelcome. He forced himself to relax back in his leather chair and smiled a smug smile. "There. I knew at least one of my brothers would have some sense."

Charlie cleared his throat. "The more important question, however, is what do *you* think of her?"

Jordan blinked. "What do I think of her? What does that matter?"

Charlie took a long drink. "I think it matters very much."

Jordan's brow furrowed. "Why?"

"For one thing, I haven't seen you this interested in a young lady for about, oh . . . five years."

Jordan allowed a dark scowl to creep across his face. "Interested?" He snorted. "Hardly. You know Colton set me to watch after the girl. She's his sister-in-law, for God's sake."

"Yes, and did you not tell me last month you planned to check in on her once or twice and leave it at that? And now she's living here?"

Jordan rolled his eyes. "She's hardly living here. She's merely proven more difficult to manage than I'd anticipated. She'll be gone in little more than a week."

Charlie shrugged. "Proving more difficult to manage than you'd anticipated I can well believe, but it seems to me that trying to marry her off to your brother is beyond your promise. Is it not?"

Jordan tossed back his drink and shrugged this time. "I told you, the girl fancies herself in love with Arthur Eggleston of all people."

"So?"

"So, Eggleston is a twit. He's proven that time and again."

Charlie gave him a skeptical glance. "So the only reason you're interested in this girl's future is to keep her from making a match with Eggleston?"

"It's as you said—she's smart, pretty, clever. She'd make an excellent wife and mother."

"I agree."

Jordan swallowed. He'd expected this to happen. Planned it, actually, but now that the moment was here and Charlie seemed to be smitten with Annie, he couldn't help feeling a twinge of . . . regret. He cleared his throat, a dark mood suddenly coming over him. "So, you do want to offer for her?"

Charlie threw his head back and laughed, then downed the last of the amber liquid in his glass. "Absolutely not."

Jordan scowled at him. "But you just said she'd make an excellent wife and mother. She could be the mother of the future heir to the earldom."

Charlie raised his empty glass in a silent salute. "No doubt, she could, old chap. Only what if the heir was your son, not your nephew?"

CHAPTER 27

Jordan asked her to join him for dinner. They'd been dining separately, up until now. The more space he kept between them the better. But the longer Annie had stayed at Ashbourne Manor, the more he looked forward to her company. And confound it! He couldn't resist asking her what she and Charlie had spoken about this afternoon.

Charlie. Jordan growled. Charlie had always been astute, but the man had completely missed the mark on this one. Perhaps Jordan hadn't been completely right in his attempts to play matchmaker for Annie with his brothers, but Charlie's proposal that Jordan should marry her, why, it was completely absurd. Charlie knew damn well what had happened in the past and Annie Andrews couldn't change it.

It was just like Charlie to be so deliberately provocative too. But Jordan refused to allow it to ruffle him. If Annie and his brothers didn't hit it off, there were still plenty of eligible men to whom he might introduce her. It was only a matter of finding the right one.

Aunt Clarissa was already sitting at the table, eyeing Jordan in a way that made him feel positively uncomfortable, when Annie flew into the dining room in a swirl of pink satin. The color looked fetching on her. When she entered a room, it always seemed as though she'd been rushing from somewhere else, as though her life were too busy and fun for her to be precisely on time. Despite himself he liked that quality about her. He liked it a lot.

"Good evening, Jordan," she said in a breathless rush. "Aunt Clarissa." She nodded.

"Helping Mr. McGivens again? Or was it Mrs. Phillips tonight?" Jordan asked.

Annie slid into her seat to his immediate right, across from Aunt Clarissa, and pulled her napkin onto her lap. A footman rushed forth to pour her a glass of wine.

"Neither," she said with a tinkling laugh.

"The puppies again? Or was it Jeffries?" He winked at her.

"None of those," she replied, and then with an irrepressible smile, "though I do have one or two suggestions for your steward if you think he might care to listen."

Jordan watched her carefully over his wine glass. "Tell me something. How do you know so much about running an estate?"

She shrugged just one shoulder. "I did a lot of eavesdropping on Lily's lessons," she admitted. "My mother ensured she was brought up to run a great household. I was always fascinated by the things she was allowed to study."

"You're every bit as capable as Lily," Jordan replied. "Which makes me wonder why you're so determined to waste yourself on Eggleston."

Aunt Clarissa glanced up from her wine glass. "Here, here," she said, raising her glass.

Annie looked twice at the older woman. "Why, Aunt Clarissa. I'd no idea you felt that way."

"You never asked, dear. But I quite agree with Lord Ashbourne. That Eggleston chap is a boob."

Annie shook her head. "Is there no one who actually likes Arthur?" She sighed.

"No," Aunt Clarissa replied a bit too loudly before turning her attention back to her wine glass.

Annie shook her head and said to Jordan, "Regardless, I could have saved you and your brothers time and effort as well, you know?"

"How?" He didn't remove his gaze from her face.

"You shouldn't have bothered to call them here, tried to introduce them to me."

"Why? Because you're so madly in love with Eggleston?" Jordan swore if she answered yes, he'd go find that idiot and snap his neck.

"No," she replied, waiting patiently for the footman to serve her the first course of roast duck. "But the way you're going about it isn't right at all. It just isn't the way true love happens."

Aunt Clarissa vigorously shook her head. "If I were you, dear, I'd toss Eggleston on his ear and marry Charlie Holloway before the year is through."

Jordan nearly choked on his food. "Aunt Clarissa has a point." He smiled. "Besides, do you still believe you love Eggleston?" This time there was no denying it. Jordan felt the spark of . . . jealousy. Blast it, where had that unwelcome emotion come from? But there it was. He was jealous. Of that idiot Arthur Eggleston. He wished he could take back the question. Didn't want to hear the answer. But it was too late. Aunt Clarissa pushed her chair away from the table and excused herself to use the convenience. They both silently watched her go. Jordan eyed Annie closely, waiting for her to speak.

Annie glanced away and shook her head. When she spoke, her voice was soft so the footmen hovering near the sideboard would not overhear.

"Loved," Annie whispered to Jordan. "I realize now that I was a fool. But as to why I loved him, I told you. No one ever wanted me. But when I met Arthur, he told me how pretty he thought I was. Of course he must have been exaggerating, but he was the first person to ever tell me such a thing. And I thought, oh, there *is* someone for everyone."

Her face lit up then and Jordan had the insane urge to bury his fist in Eggleston's gut. Jordan set down his fork and slid his hand over hers. "Annie," he whispered.

Annie pulled her hand away and took a shaky sip of wine. "What I lack in beauty, I make up for in pluck," she declared, the smile returning to her pretty face.

Jordan had to struggle to control his anger. This time he wanted to snap her idiot father's neck. "You're wrong," he said quietly, staring her in the eye. "You're very beautiful."

Her breathing hitched and she glanced away. "You don't have to say that."

Jordan narrowed his eyes on her. "How old were you when your father died?"

"Fourteen."

"Yes, well, he never should have implied that you weren't beautiful, but you've grown into one of the loveliest young ladies I've ever seen."

She laughed a self-conscious laugh. "Now I *know* you're just being kind. I've seen your mistress."

"God, Annie. Listen to me," Jordan whispered. "You're

every bit as lovely as Nicoletta. More so, actually, because you are completely unaffected."

Annie didn't meet his gaze. She pushed her chair back and stood. "I hope you don't find this too rude, my lord. But I've suddenly lost my appetite. Please excuse me." She dashed from the room, her handkerchief pressed to her mouth, before Jordan could say a word.

He let her go, then thought better of it. He pushed his own chair aside, tossed his napkin to the table, and quickly followed Annie out the door. He saw a flash of pink enter the salon at the end of the hallway.

In several long strides, Jordan was at the door and rushed inside. Annie was pacing back and forth across the Aubusson rug, her arms wrapped across her middle.

"Are you all right?" he asked, feeling like a damned fool.

"I . . . just . . . need a moment."

"Annie, look at me," he commanded, and when her eyes met his he saw the unshed tears shining in their dark depths. She wasn't crying. He'd expected her to be crying. Didn't most females cry in circumstances like this? Nicoletta certainly would have. But then he realized the difference. Nicoletta wouldn't have told him a story like that unless she wanted something from him. A trinket or some sympathy, it didn't matter. But Annie hadn't been trying to get anything from him. She'd just told him the truth and then she'd tried to leave his company so he wouldn't see that she was upset. Nicoletta would have ensured he witnessed every moment of it.

He crossed over to Annie and took her chin firmly in his hand, forcing her to meet his eyes. "Your father was an idiot and I can't believe that Arthur Eggleston was the first man to ever tell you how beautiful you are. But trust me, he was not the first man to think it."

Annie tugged her chin away from his grasp and shook her head. "Jordan. Don't. Please."

He grasped her shoulders. "Listen to me, Annie. You must believe me. Why are you so upset?"

She wrapped her arms more tightly across her middle. "You have a mistress who looks like Cleopatra and you tell me I'm beautiful. Of course it's not true."

"Blast it, Annie. It sure as hell is true. Why would you think it's not? Because of a few careless things your idiot father told you?"

She dashed her hands across her eyes. "No. Ronald Richardson said it too."

"What? Who is Ronald Richardson?"

"A boy." She took two steps away, wringing her hands. "The first boy I ever loved. Well, thought I loved . . . I fancied him for as long as I can remember."

Jordan's voice was calm, smooth. "What happened?"

"We were alone together once, in the meadow by my father's house. It was exceedingly romantic. The wind was blowing. The sun was setting. I was *sure* he would kiss me." Her voice trailed off.

"He didn't?"

"No, he didn't. He took me into his arms. He looked into my eyes, and he said, 'Mud. Your eyes are the color of mud. Do you know that?' Then he laughed . . . and asked if I wanted to go riding."

Jordan cursed under his breath. Another person who needed his neck snapped. "He's an idiot too. How old were you?"

She turned back to face him and shrugged. "Fifteen,

perhaps. Sixteen. I thought he fancied me as much as I fancied him. But I realized that day, I wasn't like the other girls. Not like Lily with her beautiful violet-blue eyes and tinkling laughter. I'm just Annie. The girl with the mud-colored eyes who's everyone's friend. The girl you go riding with. The girl you go shooting with. The girl who can drive a tandem team. Never the girl you take into your arms and kiss."

Jordan reached her in one long stride and he pulled her to him, clutching her upper arms and searching her face. "Annie, listen to me, you're much more than that."

"No. I'm—"

"Damn it, you've been driving me mad for days now."

"Wh . . . what?" Her eyes were wide.

"All I can think about is this." Jordan's mouth swooped down to capture hers. Annie's head tilted back. Her hands went around his neck. Jordan's hot mouth ravaged hers. His tongue pushed her lips apart and she melted against him. He scooped her up into his arms and in two long strides was at the settee. He sat down with her, never letting his mouth leave hers. Annie pressed herself against him. Her reaction to him was driving him even more insane. She tasted like honey, sweet and languorous. She smelled like lilacs and soap and happiness.

Jordan couldn't remember the last time he was this on fire for a woman. His mistresses had all been worldly and wise, experienced enough to know exactly how to touch a man. But Annie's innocent tongue was making him crazy. He pulled the pins from the top of her hair and the mass spilled down around her neck and shoulders. He buried his face in it. He knew it would be beautiful, as beautiful as she was. Then his mouth was back on hers and her hands were plowing through his hair, making him want to rip all the clothing from her body and make her his, right here on the settee in the middle of the salon. He briefly considered the odds of being interrupted by Aunt Clarissa. But that lady could barely find her way to her own room. He doubted she'd discover them. A poor, poor choice for a chaperone, he thought with a wry smile. He'd have to speak to Lily and Devon about it when they returned.

He kissed Annie's cheek, her mouth, her neck, her earlobe. The little sounds she was making in the back of her throat made him rock hard. His mouth moved to her neck and he sucked there as if he were a very young man again, unable to go further with this woman. God, yes, Annie made him feel things he hadn't felt in an age. But mostly she made him feel overwhelming, all-consuming *lust*.

His mouth went to her neck again, down, down, and he nuzzled at her décolletage. And she had *such* perfect breasts. Annie sucked in her breath sharply. He couldn't do this. Couldn't do more. Annie was innocent and she was Devon's sister-in-law. His mind kept repeating the warnings, but his hand moved to brush against her nipple. Annie gasped. His thumb flicked back and forth against her underneath her dress. Her breast wasn't even bared to him but Jordan was so hard he hurt. He clenched his jaw and moved his mouth back up to hers. He kissed her until his lips were numb, kissed her until he couldn't think straight anymore, kissed her until Annie pulled away from him slightly, looked at him with those soul-searching dark brown eyes, and whispered, "Jordan?"

Jordan drew a shaky breath. She was using his name. And she was asking him what was next. Jordan knew it deep down just like he knew that nothing could be next. It took every single modicum of strength he possessed—he would ever possess—to push her from his lap. He set her gently on the settee, took a deep breath, willing his overheated body back to normalcy, and stood. But he couldn't face her. Not only would she see the stark evidence of his arousal, but there was every chance if he looked at her again, he would kiss her again, and next time he wouldn't stop.

Jordan clenched his eyes shut and opened them again before making his way toward the door. He didn't look back.

"My apologies, Annie." He cursed under his breath and left without saying another word.

CHAPTER 28

Annie hurried into her room and closed the door behind her. She leaned back against it, expelled her breath, and closed her eyes. What in the devil's name had *that* been about? How had the night begun with her telling Jordan about her past and ended with them locked in a torrid embrace upon the settee?

And, oh, God, what a torrid embrace it had been. Annie went hot and cold again just thinking about it. He'd touched her breast. No man had ever done that before. He'd touched her breast and made her feel things deep down she couldn't explain. All she'd known was that she never wanted him to stop. She wanted to kiss him until she died. And she hadn't even cared if they'd been discovered by a servant or Aunt Clarissa. Though Aunt Clarissa would probably pat her on the shoulder and say, "Well done," she thought with a wry smile.

Annie crossed over to her bed and sat on the edge, contemplating her slippers and trying to make sense of what had just happened. It hadn't been out of pity, had it? His kisses? Oh God, she couldn't bear it if it had. But

he hadn't been dissembling, she knew that much. She
felt the evidence of his arousal when she'd been sittin
on his lap. Felt his hardness. She'd wanted to reach dow
and touch it, but she'd been too hesitant.

Instead, she'd wrapped her arms around his neck an
kissed him until her head was spinning. It felt so good
And his kisses were so unlike Arthur's one inept a
tempt had been. When she kissed Jordan it was lik
drowning in a sea of molten honey. So sweet and ric
and wonderful.

Annie shook her head. But what did all of it mean
Jordan had dragged her out to his estate, trotted h
three brothers in front of her unsuccessfully, and now h
was kissing her? Was the man such a rake he simpl
couldn't keep his hands off any woman in his company
Was that it?

Oh, what did it matter? Regardless of his intention
no good could come from her kissing him. She needed t
get away from here. She needed to get back to Londo
She desperately wished for Lily. She missed her sister s

Lily wasn't there, but surely going back to Londo
was the best choice. Oh God, she wasn't even sure any
more exactly what she should do, but staying out here i
the country being tempted by the most handsome ma
in the kingdom was not a good idea. Not a good idea a
all. Oh, where the deuce was Lord Medford when yo
needed him?

She pressed her fingers to her aching temples. Sh
needed some sleep, then she would make a plan. Ye
tomorrow she would pool her resources and ensure tha
she and Mary and Aunt Clarissa somehow made it bac
to London. Tonight, tonight she would rest.

And she just might replay the last half hour in the salon with Lord Ashbourne in her head while she drifted to sleep.

Jordan stalked into his bedchamber and slammed the door behind him. Damn it. What had that been about? He didn't have any right doing that. Any of that. It made no sense. It must be his self-imposed celibacy that was getting the best of him. What the hell was he thinking? There was something about Annie's vulnerability and simple beauty that had drawn him in, and her story about her father and that idiot boy who'd told her she had mud-colored eyes had tugged at his heart.

Of course Eggleston said she was pretty. She was bloody gorgeous and she didn't even know it. And *that* was the reason she'd thought she was in love with Eggleston? A tragedy.

Jordan paced the floor. His sojourn into the country with Annie was not progressing in the way he'd hoped. Not at all. Fine, he was willing to concede that his plan to introduce her to his brothers hadn't been the best idea he'd ever concocted, but how could he know that Michael, Timothy, and Charlie wouldn't want her? She was the perfect candidate for a wife. Yes, she caused trouble now and then, but once she settled down into marriage, he had no doubt she'd be a devoted wife and mother.

And what the hell had Charlie been talking about, telling Jordan he should marry her? That was insanity as well. He was attracted to her. He had to admit that to himself. But this couldn't go on. He couldn't keep her in his house for the remainder of the fortnight with just the two of them. No, damn it. He would find her a husband.

His own brothers were fools, but there must be some man of breeding, good looks, fortune, and good taste who would know a perfectly fine choice of wife when he saw her. He would find that man.

Jordan stalked to the window and stared out into the blackness.

A ball.

He would host a ball. One intended solely to find Annie a husband. He'd invite every eligible bachelor from London and call in all his favors to ensure they attended. Yes. That's what he would do. Next week. That way, by the time Devon and Lily returned, all that would be left to do would be to gain their blessing of the union and the contract could be signed. Perfect. He'd be solving Annie's problem and his own simultaneously.

Get her off his hands and help his two friends.

Yes. A ball was in order. A selfless act. It had absolutely nothing to do with the fact that he was lusting after Annie himself. Though he did need to get her safely off the market and out of his reach. He didn't trust himself anymore where she was concerned.

He would host a marriage ball for Annie.

CHAPTER 29

When Medford was escorted into Jordan's study two days later, all Jordan could do was offer the man a drink.

"By all means," Medford said. "Make it a double."

"I didn't think you knew what a double was," Jordan replied with a tight smile. "Besides, shouldn't you be in London, Medford, publishing some scandalworthy literature?"

Medford ignored that barb. "I assume you know why I've come."

Jordan sighed. "Annie wrote to you and told you I was torturing her, no doubt."

"Annie wrote me and told me you'd abducted her."

"Ah, even better." Jordan flashed a grin.

"Is that true?"

Jordan handed Medford his drink. "Yes."

Medford cracked a smile. "And the torture?"

"To commence any moment now."

Medford leaned back in his chair and kicked up his booted feet on the top of the desk. "I assume you removed her from London because she'd caused even more trouble."

Jordan leaned his head back against his leather chair and stared at the ceiling momentarily. "If you must know, I chased her down on the way to Gretna Green again with that fool Eggleston. I brought her here so she'd have no access to the sop for the next fortnight." He leveled his eyes on Medford, his drink resting in his hand.

"Ah, waiting out the time it will take Lily and Devon to return, no?"

Jordan lifted his glass in a silent salute. "That's exactly what I'm doing. You're still welcome to take over if you see fit, Medford. Bring her back to London, watch her yourself."

Medford took a sip of his drink. "What? And miss all this fun?"

"Fun or not, I'm planning to host a ball to find Annie a husband."

Medford's eyebrow arched. "Really? Now *that* is an interesting turn of events."

Jordan opened his mouth to reply but a sharp knock sounded on the door and Annie rushed into the room. She took one look at Medford and relief swept across her face.

"Lord Medford, finally. Where have you been?" She flew to him like a delicate bird. She was wearing a soft blue day dress, and Jordan tried to ignore how good she smelled. And looked. He'd studiously avoided her for the last two days.

Medford pushed his drink aside and stood to take Annie's hand. "If it isn't our runaway bride."

"Oh no. You're not calling me that too, are you?" Annie allowed him to bow over her hand and then she crossed her arms over her middle and tapped her foot, glaring at him.

Medford flashed a smile. "You must admit, you have a penchant for running off in search of marriage."

Annie ignored that. "Why has it taken you so long to come to take me back to London?"

Medford flashed her a smile and gestured to the chair next to him. "Sit down. Sit down. I assume we can all discuss this like rational adults."

Annie grudgingly settled into the chair next to Medford, her arms still crossed. "Don't worry, Jordan," she said, not looking at him. "I've no doubt Lord Medford will take over the responsibility of me."

Jordan cracked a smile. "I wouldn't be so sure about that."

Annie's gaze flew to Medford's face. "Tell me that's not so. Tell me you're here to take me back with you."

Medford glanced back and forth between the two of them, wearing an open smile. "First of all, I see you're on a first-name basis with each other now. And secondly, if I didn't know any better, I'd think the two of you are doing your level best to avoid looking at one another."

Annie bit her lip and glanced down at her slippers. Jordan narrowed his eyes on Medford.

"And thirdly," Medford continued, "I've yet to decide if you need me to rescue you, Anne. Aunt Clarissa's with you so it's entirely proper and you appear fit enough to me." He winked at her.

Annie nearly came out of her seat. "Did he tell you he tried to pair me with his brothers?"

Medford raised his brows. "His brothers?" He glanced at Jordan. "All of them?"

Jordan grunted. "Yes, I had some damn fool notion."

Medford settled into his chair. "None of them offered for her, I take it."

Another grunt from Jordan. "No. The fools. Not one."

Annie's eyes widened slightly at that.

"And now you're planning a ball?" Medford asked.

Jordan nodded. "Partly to keep Annie occupied and partly to find a decent bloke for her to marry. Anyone I invite shall be a sight better than Arthur Eggleston."

Annie clutched the arms of her chair. "A ball? What are you talking about?"

Jordan nodded. "Yes. I was just telling Medford about it. I'm planning it for Thursday."

"The night before Devon and Lily return?" Annie murmured.

"Yes."

Medford took a sip of his drink. "It's not my imagination. The two of you are definitely having a conversation without looking at one another. Hmm."

Annie made a show of smoothing her skirts, while Jordan cursed under his breath, stood and walked to a window to stare out across the lawns.

Annie cleared her throat. "A ball to find me a husband? You see?" she asked Medford imploringly. "You see what I have to deal with? He's mad."

Medford glanced at her. "I don't see what's so very wrong with a ball. People have them all the time in London."

"Yes, but he's expecting me to marry as a result of it."

"Tell me, Anne, will you invite Eggleston to this ball?" Medford asked.

"Oh, by all means, let's invite Arthur to this farce." She tossed her hands in the air.

"That fool won't show his face here if he knows what's good for him," Jordan snapped.

Medford's eyebrows shot up. "You intend to keep him away, Ashbourne?"

Jordan shoved his hands in his pockets. "No, he's welcome to come. I'd relish the excuse to beat him to a pulp. The last time I saw him, I threatened just that."

Annie shook her head. "You wouldn't dare."

"Wouldn't I?" Jordan replied.

Medford laughed. "Well. Well. Well. This promises to be quite the fete. I'm only sorry I cannot make it myself. But not to worry. I'm hardly eligible, and now that I've seen that Annie is not damaged or bruised, I can return to London in good conscience."

This time Annie shot out of her chair. "Lord Medford! You cannot be serious. You do not intend to leave me here."

"My dear, your sister left you in Ashbourne's care, and I must say you look as if you're perfectly healthy and safe to me. I've seen enough to convince me."

Jordan turned to face him. "You really came all the way out here thinking she'd been hurt?"

"Absolutely not, but I could hardly ignore Anne's pleas. She'd written me so many letters I was beginning to fear the cost of ink would beggar you, Ashbourne."

Annie gave both of them a condemning glare. "I cannot believe this. You're both mad, as far as I'm concerned. I'm going back to my room." She swiveled on her heel, made her way to the door, pushed it open, and sailed through it.

Medford watched her go with a wry smile on his face. Jordan snorted. "She's not going to take kindly to your leaving her here. I believe you are persona non grata of a sudden."

Medford downed the rest of his drink, set the glass on the table, and stood to leave. "Be that as it may, I do believe she's in good hands."

"Would you please tell her that on your way out?" Jordan asked.

"Not a chance, my good man, what fun would there be in that? Half of the excitement here is Anne believing you've trussed her up and carted her off. And frankly, that girl could use a good trussing. Just remember, she may seem brave and tough, but she's really very sweet and well-meaning."

Jordan gave him a tight smile. "Sure you won't reconsider and take her with you?"

"What? And deny you the fun of hosting a ball? I wouldn't dream of it, Ashbourne."

Jordan accompanied him to the door. "Very well, I'm sure Annie will keep you informed of her torture."

"Make sure you find a good chap for her, Ashbourne. Someone honorable, kindhearted, wealthy, handsome, and noble."

"Oh yes, quite an easy order. It shall prove no trouble at all, I'm sure."

Medford winked at him. "Think hard, Ashbourne. I'm sure you know *someone* who fits the bill."

CHAPTER 30

shbourne Manor was ablaze with the light of thousands
twinkling beeswax candles. A steady stream of fine
aches lined the drive, depositing their elegant occu-
nts upon the steps of the grand house. Everyone who
as anyone in London had arrived in the country. When
e Earl of Ashbourne hosted a ball at his country estate,
e drive to Surrey was a minor inconvenience, it seemed.

Mary had spent hours putting up Annie's hair in a
gnon, letting a few soft, fat curls dance along her
oulders. She had a bit of pink rouge on the balls of her
eeks, a hint of fine powder on her nose, and she was
earing her most dazzling ball gown of soft, ice-blue
tin with tiny flowers around the empire waist and her
ng white kid gloves and matching ice-blue slippers.
e felt like a fairy princess and a glance in the mirror
d her she looked halfway presentable.

"You're a vision as usual, Miss Annie," Mary said,
anding back and surveying her handiwork.

"A dream," said Aunt Clarissa, who sat on the side of
e bed, watching the proceedings with great interest.

Annie blushed. "Thank you very much, both of you."

She pressed her hand to her middle. "I fear I'm a bit nervous. I've no idea why but I haven't been this anxious since the night of my debut."

Mary squeezed her hand. "Ye'll be perfect."

Annie blinked into the looking glass. Her eyelashes were long and lovely. She could admit at least that much. They were, perhaps, her finest feature.

Oh, why was she so filled with nerves? It wasn't as she hadn't attended a dozen balls before and those London, which were much more formal.

She hadn't invited Arthur. He would not be here tonight. Did he even wonder what had happened to her since he'd left her at the inn? Probably not. But she was through with him anyway, so what did she care?

She sighed. Oh, she knew exactly why this ball was setting her on edge. It was because Jordan had planned in her honor, because it was meant to catch her an eligible gentleman. Very well, and if she were being honest facing Jordan again made her knees shake. Ever since their kiss the other night and Lord Medford's visit, she studiously avoided Jordan, unsure how to think or feel. She'd decided he'd obviously kissed her because he felt sorry for her and her sad little tale about being so plain. The man had taken pity on her. And she couldn't bear to think of it, but the fact was that his kiss had made her go all melty inside. She couldn't stop her body's reaction to him. The man was simply gorgeous. And the best thing to do when faced with a gorgeous man who had penchant for kissing you every now and then was to stay scarce. Obviously.

Annie turned to face Mary and squared her shoulders. One large curl fell over her shoulder and caressed her décolletage. "Am I presentable then?"

"Ye're a vision, Miss Annie," Mary breathed.

"Might I suggest you make your way toward Charles Holloway and stay there?" Aunt Clarissa suggested with a wink and a hiccup.

Annie laughed. "You know, Aunt Clarissa, I just may take that advice." Gathering up her skirts in her hands, Annie left the room. The ball was already well under way. She'd purposely intended to make a late entrance. Perhaps then she wouldn't feel so self-conscious. But now as she made her way to the grand ballroom on shaky legs, she realized it didn't matter when she made her entrance; self-conscious she would be. She paused to press her gloved hand to her middle and still her nerves. She took a deep breath.

When Jeffries saw her approaching, his face lit up.

"Miss Anne Andrews," his loud voice intoned as he announced her arrival to the other guests.

Annie immediately felt the hundreds of pairs of eyes on her as she entered Jordan's magnificent ballroom. She pushed up her chin and pretended she was Lily. Her sister would never be nervous in such a situation. Lily was born to be the center of attention. Oh, how did she make it look so effortless? Annie was having awful visions of tripping on her slippers and sliding across the floor in front of London's most fashionable set.

Annie made her way into the room with as much confidence as she could muster. Suddenly, Jordan was there at her side, taking her arm.

"You look ravishing tonight," he said, and gooseflesh popped out on Annie's skin where his warm breath had touched.

"Th . . . thank you," she managed. "You're very kind."

"I'm serious. You're a vision."

Annie swallowed. "Mary brought this dress with he from London."

"Dance with me," he breathed. "I insist on claimin your first dance."

Annie laughed. "But what of the other gentleme who have come to meet me—won't they be severely dis appointed with you keeping me all to yourself?"

"They'll just have to wait," he said, sweeping Anni into his arms.

They danced and danced and danced. Jordan was a exquisite partner. She remembered dancing with hir one other time, last spring at the Atkinsons' estate. Ap parently Lord Colton had put him up to it, but she barel remembered any details. Most likely they'd discusse the weather, the house party, the refreshments. All ver bland, she was sure. That night she'd been entirely pre occupied with Arthur.

Arthur!

Annie glanced around. She hadn't even looked fo Arthur yet. So unlike her. Even knowing he wouldn't b there, she'd danced an entire dance with Jordan and Ar thur hadn't even so much as crossed her mind.

When the dance ended, Jordan thanked her and sh curtsied to him. "I think I see my friend Frances," sh said. "Won't you excuse me?"

"Frances? Why, I feel as if Frances and I are ol friends. Introduce me," Jordan replied.

It was on the tip of Annie's tongue to laugh it off, bu then she remembered Frances's infatuation with the mar Meeting Jordan would be the highlight of her friend whole night, whole month; perhaps. Yes, she would brin Jordan with her. "Thank you. I believe she'd like tha very much." She struggled to hide her smile.

Annie led Jordan over to the side of the ballroom where Frances stood with her mother. Her eyes were wide as teacup saucers watching Annie and Jordan approach. Annie prayed Frances didn't cast up her accounts on Jordan's expensive Hessians or swoon in front of him.

Annie made the proper introductions and Jordan bowed elegantly to both ladies while they stammered and stamped about. He took Frances's hand and bent over it. "My pleasure," he said in his smoothest voice, and Annie guessed that Frances's knees were knocking together.

"Oh, Lord Ashbourne, the pleasure is mine," Frances said. "I mean ours. I mean mine." Behind Jordan, Annie bit her lip, and gave her friend a silent plea to contain herself.

"I must see to my other guests," Jordan said at length after they'd discussed a variety of perfectly respectable topics, "but I do hope you will honor me with a dance later, Miss Birmingham."

Frances looked as if she'd swallowed moonlight and Mrs. Birmingham looked positively charmed too.

"Why, yes. Yes. Yes!" Frances replied. "Yes."

Jordan chuckled, bowed, and strode away into the crowd while Frances frantically clutched at Annie's sleeves. "Oh my goodness. I've made such a ninny of myself that that gorgeous man is sure never to return."

Annie laughed. "Don't worry. He's quite unpretentious, actually."

"I cannot believe that," Frances replied. "I don't want to believe that. Now, tell me, what on earth have the two of you been doing out here in the country together? I nearly fell over when I received the invitation to this ball."

Mrs. Birmingham excused herself to greet some friends and Annie pulled Frances into the corner. "As you know from my letters, Jordan decided to *invite* me out here to keep me from trouble in the city."

Frances pressed her hand against her chest. "You're calling him Jordan now? Never mind. Go on."

"He brought his brothers out here one by one to meet me, thinking they might take a fancy to me."

"My goodness, that man is a dream."

Annie shook her head. "Suffice it to say not a one of them offered for me, so Jordan decided to host this ball."

"And what of Arthur?" Frances asked. "I haven't seen him tonight. Is he here?"

"He wasn't invited," Annie replied, lifting her chin. "Though I suspect Jordan's threat to beat him last time they met might have kept him from coming even if I had invited him."

"Lord Ashbourne threatened to beat Arthur?" Frances's eyes were wide. "Oh my goodness, don't just stand there, tell me more."

Annie laughed and explained the meeting with Lord Medford and the plans for the ball. By the time she finished, Frances looked as if she might swoon.

"Oh my goodness. I can hardly believe it. Oh, Anne, all the best things happen to you. I've spent the last fortnight trying to get my little brother to give me back one of the feathers he plucked from my favorite bonnet. He's been using it to play pirate in the library. And here you are being abducted by the most handsome man in London and having a ball hosted in your honor. It's completely unfair, I tell you. By the by, I've also spent the last two weeks trying to learn the story of what happened to Lord Ashbourne years ago with very little success. I'm convinced I'm just not asking the right people. It's most disconcerting."

Annie tapped her cheek with a finger. "Hmm. I've had little success on that score as well. We'll just have to keep looking. There must be someone who was around at the time and would be willing to share the scandal."

Frances clutched Annie's sleeve and nodded to the entryway of the ballroom. "Annie," she murmured. "I believe we've just found her."

CHAPTER 31

When Catherine Woodbury, Lady Eversly, strode into the ballroom, half the male population turned to stare. Annie and Frances were still huddled in the corner discussing Arthur's defection when Catherine made her way directly over to them.

"Good evening, Miss Andrews. I hear you are to thank for this little party. Jordan hasn't had guests out to Ashbourne Manor in an age. Fancy that an innocent could get him to open his doors once again."

Annie gave the woman a guarded smile. She remembered how Lily had described the beautiful blond woman's casual repartee with Jordan at the Atkinsons' house party last spring. Lady Eversly was married, but it obviously didn't stop her from outrageously flirting with Devon, Jordan, or any other good-looking man who crossed her path.

"It was exceedingly kind of Lord Ashbourne to hold this ball," Annie replied.

"I see the rumors are false," Lady Catherine continued, her sky-blue eyes narrowing to slits. "All of London's been whispering about how you and Arthur Eggleston are about to declare your engagement, but I don't even see Arthur here tonight."

Annie pushed up her chin and shrugged. "I've no idea where Arthur Eggleston is and, frankly, I don't care."

"Excellent attitude, my dear," Lady Catherine said with a catlike smile.

Frances seemed in awe of the woman. She stared at her gorgeous white-blond hair and crystal-blue eyes.

Catherine arched a brow. "Miss Birmingham, may I help you with something?"

"You're just so . . . pretty," Frances breathed.

Lady Catherine touched her hair and an eyebrow with one long elegant finger. "Yes, dear, but to be honest it's often a burden."

Annie elbowed Frances, who responded with an "oomph."

"You and Jordan make a beautiful pair," Lady Catherine continued, directing her gaze at Annie.

Annie sucked in her breath. "Lord Ashbourne has been very kind to me," she managed to reply.

"Yes, well, Jordan and I go so far back. I just wanted to stop by and tell you what a feat it is for you to have persuaded him to throw a ball."

Annie's spine tightened every time that woman called him Jordan. Lady Catherine turned to leave.

"How far back?" The words flew from Annie's mouth before she had a chance to stop them.

Catherine turned around again. "Pardon?"

This time Frances elbowed Annie. But Annie ignored her friend. "Exactly how far back do you and Lord Ashbourne go?" She couldn't lose her chance at finally finding out the truth about her enigmatic host.

Catherine arched a finely drawn brow. "What exactly

are you asking, dear?" she said with a sly smile on her face.

"Yes . . . Anne . . . what exactly *are* you asking?" Frances whispered between her clenched teeth.

Annie swallowed and clutched her fan. She took a deep breath. She'd started down this path and she would see it through. She lowered her voice to a whisper and took a step closer to Lady Catherine. "I heard that Lord Ashbourne once lost his heart many years ago. Do you know anything about that?"

Annie braced herself. For an awful moment she wondered if it was Lady Catherine herself whom Jordan had loved. But Timothy had said "Georgi," hadn't he? She eyed Lady Catherine. No, she didn't believe Jordan had once been enamored of this haughty beauty.

Frances stood completely still with a horrified look on her face, staring at Lady Catherine's regal form.

Lady Catherine's smile widened and she glanced back and forth over her shoulders to see if she could be overheard. "Oh my dear," she said in a low, sultry voice. "I happen to know *everything* about that."

Annie sucked in her breath. Now or never. She looked Lady Catherine in the eye. "Will you tell me?"

Lady Catherine straightened up and pushed a nonexistent errant hair back into her elegant coiffure. "Not that we should be gossiping about our host, of course." She winked at them. "But meet me in the gardens at half past and I'll tell you the whole sordid story."

"We should not go gossip about Lord Ashbourne in the gardens," Frances said, wringing her hands. "I'm getting hives just thinking about it."

Annie clapped her hand to her forehead. "Of course we shouldn't, Frances, but that's not about to stop me."

"You'll just have to go without me. That's all there is to it." Frances stuck her nose in the air and looked away.

Annie shrugged. "Very well, but I'm not going to tell you what she says."

Frances clutched her chest. "Oh, you wouldn't be so cruel?"

Annie laughed and grabbed her friend's hand. She pulled her down the corridor. "Come along. Stop pretending you don't want to know."

They made their way out of the French doors onto the terrace. The early October air was cold on their skin. Rubbing their bare arms, they hurried along the crushed rock path that led out into the gardens. "What's that?" Frances asked, blinking. "Coming from behind the topiary."

They both skidded to a halt. "Why, I believe it's . . . puffs of smoke," Annie replied, lowering her voice.

"Oh no, someone's there," Frances whispered. "Whoever he is, we must wait for him to leave."

"Is that you, darlings?" Lady Catherine's sultry voice floated out from behind the sculptured hedge.

"Lady Catherine?" Annie blinked.

The puffs of smoke temporarily stopped. "Yes. It's me. Come back here."

Exchanging hesitant glances, Annie and Frances made their way behind the topiary to find Lady Catherine lounging on an outdoor settee nestled behind a wall of flowering hedges, a cheroot clamped between her sparkling white teeth. Annie smiled. Despite herself, she liked Lady Catherine. Now here was a woman who had no problem at all breaking rules.

"I cannot believe you're smoking," Frances blurted before clamping her hand over her mouth.

Lady Catherine only smiled. "Believe me, I've done worse." She tossed her head back and laughed. "Much worse."

Lady Catherine pulled the cheroot from between her lips. She unwound herself lithely like a cat waking up and stretching. She stood up and gestured to the settee. "Sit down, ladies. I daresay you should be sitting when you hear this particular tale."

Annie gulped. For the first time she wondered if she was doing the right thing by listening. But it was too late now. Besides, God only knew when such an opportunity would present itself again.

Frances dropped like a stone to the bench and pulled Annie down with her.

Catherine laughed. "My, my, my, you two are eager, are you not?"

"Please tell us," Annie prompted, half afraid they'd be interrupted at any moment.

Lady Eversly paced back and forth in front of them seemingly without a care, her gorgeous ruby-colored gown sweeping along the gravel. "Ah, the story of the young Jordan Holloway. It's a sad tale to be sure."

Annie and Frances both leaned closer.

"Back when I made my debut, darlings, it was nearly . . ." She smiled. "Well, nearly an age ago. I was eighteen and Jordan was twenty-six. My goodness but he was handsome and dashing. He and Lord Colton were the most sought-after bachelors of the Season. But Jordan, Jordan was actually eligible. You see at the time, Colton's father had gambled away his estate. Many mamas steered their beloved daughters away from Colton.

But Jordan was the perfect catch: titled, handsome, *and* rich. Every young lady sought to draw his attention. Alas, I was no different."

Annie's stomach tightened. Was Lady Catherine the one Jordan had loved after all? If so, what had happened? How did she become married to Lord Eversly instead?

Lady Catherine took another drag from the cheroot and blew the smoke into the chilly breeze. "It soon became apparent that Season that regardless of his lack of fortune, Colton had fallen for a young lady named Lily Andrews. You may have heard of her, dears."

Catherine smiled at Annie and Annie returned the smile.

"And the rest of that particular story, of course, is history. Though those two did take their time getting to the business of marriage. But that is another story, one I'm sure you're already intimately aware of." She winked.

"Yes, yes," Annie said, glancing down the path to see if anyone was coming. Thankfully, the path was clear.

Catherine sighed. "Ah yes, I do digress. Nasty storytelling habit of mine. At any rate, once Colton was essentially off the market, Jordan became twice as sought after. Oh my goodness, that dark hair, those smoky eyes, deliciously square shoulders, perfectly molded lips . . ." She shuddered. "There I go again, and, I might add, the man has only improved with age."

Looking a bit woozy, Frances nodded. "You're perfectly right." She fumbled in her reticule for her fan and, whipping it out, fanned herself rapidly. "Is it hot out here?"

Annie scowled at her friend. "No, it's freezing."

Catherine continued. "In the end, ladies, it came down to two of us. Myself and Lady Georgiana Dalton."

Annie clenched her jaw. *Georgi*. The name Timothy had almost said. And Dalton? Georgiana Dalton? Annie was sure she'd heard that name before.

Catherine sighed. "I suppose it was a fair fight, but Jordan fell deeply for the girl. This was when he was young and starry-eyed, if you can imagine it. He very much fancied himself in love with her."

"I cannot imagine it," Annie breathed.

"I can assure you it happened," Catherine continued. "And Georgiana was lovely. Blond hair, blue eyes, perfect figure. Oh, how many times I wished she would fall off a horse or something."

Frances wrinkled her brow.

Catherine shrugged. "Jordan offered for her, she accepted, and they made all the rounds."

"Jordan offered for her?" Annie breathed, nearly toppling off the bench because she'd leaned so far forward. "Then what happened?"

Lady Catherine examined her tapered fingernails in the moonlight. "Georgiana cried off, the ignorant chit. Seems she'd had her heart set on a marquis who hadn't offered for her quite yet. She'd accepted Jordan's proposal only after she thought her marquis was betrothed to his cousin."

"She just cried off?" Frances asked, blinking.

"Yes. The nitwit," Lady Catherine replied. "A marquis trumps an earl after all."

Annie's hand flew to her throat. "She chose the other man only because of his more prestigious title?"

"That's right." Lady Catherine sighed. "Though Lord knows why. The man wasn't half as handsome and Jordan's fortune was equally as great. Just demonstrates how ignorant some young ladies can be."

"Wasn't there a scandal?" Annie asked.

Lady Catherine sighed. "A brief stir, to be sure, but nothing Jordan's reputation couldn't survive. His heart, however, was a different matter entirely."

"What happened to Miss Dalton?" Frances asked breathlessly.

Lady Catherine shrugged. "She had the good sense to marry quickly and leave for the Continent to escape the gossip. She and her husband have been gone for years now. Only smart thing she ever did, if you ask me."

"And Lord Ashbourne just never found anyone else he wanted to offer for?" Frances asked.

Lady Catherine smiled her famous smile again. "Lord knows I came flying to his side. I offered my comfort and hoped against hope he'd offer for me." Lady Catherine sighed. "But Jordan was never the same again. I think he actually believed in love, poor bloke, one of the few men I've ever known to do so. It's quite tragic, actually. He swore off marriage after that, was sure he could never trust a woman. So unfortunate. As for me, I chose Eversly. Stewart was the third most handsome titled bachelor that Season, hence he's my husband." She winked at them.

"So that's it?" Frances asked. "Lord Ashbourne just swore off marriage forever?"

Lady Catherine nodded. "Precisely. After Georgiana left, he vowed to make his first nephew his heir and announced he would never marry. Easy enough, I suppose, since Colton remained unattached all these years too. Oh my, they've been quite a pair, the two of them, but I've been wondering, now that Colton's settled down, if Jordan won't change his mind. And that, my dear, is why I've been so intrigued by *you*." She pointed to Annie.

Annie sat up straight and blinked. "Me?"

"Yes. You. I haven't seen Jordan take such an interest in an innocent making her debut since . . . well, since Georgiana."

Annie expelled her breath. Easily explained. "Lily and Devon asked him to watch out for me. He's just doing a favor for his friends. Nothing more."

Lady Catherine shook her head. "You can tell yourself that all you like, dear, but I saw the way he looked at you earlier. Trust me, the man is interested."

Annie and Frances turned their heads simultaneously to stare at one another. "Are my eyes as wide as yours?" Frances asked.

Annie nodded. "Uh-huh."

Lady Catherine clamped the cheroot in her mouth again and sucked in. She breathed out and puffed some impressive smoke rings into the cold night sky.

"And now, darlings, I shall leave you to your thoughts. I'm due back inside the ballroom for my obligatory dance with my husband." She laughed then, her deep voice filling the little clearing.

After Lady Catherine swept away, Frances and Annie sat looking at each other.

"You don't truly believe Jordan is interested in me, do you?" Annie asked.

Frances slowly nodded. "Something tells me that Lady Catherine knows when a man is interested."

CHAPTER 32

Annie wandered through Jordan's lovely conservatory, the strains of the music from the ball still echoing from afar. It was half two. Aunt Clarissa had long since retired. Many of the guests, including Frances and her mother, had already left to return to London, but several were still dancing, mingling, and making merry. Annie had had to escape it all. She couldn't stay in that ballroom with a false smile plastered on her face, not when she was so confused. So she'd wandered into the conservatory and breathed in the fragrance of the sweet lovely flowers.

What had happened to her? Four short weeks ago, she'd been quite sure of how her life would be. She would marry Arthur, they would raise a family, and they would be in love forever. Now she was here, the guest of honor at the Earl of Ashbourne's country house, and nothing made sense anymore. Thank goodness Lily and Devon would be arriving tomorrow and she'd be traveling to London to meet them. She never imagined she'd think it, but she needed her sister's guidance. More than ever.

She wasn't going to marry Arthur. That had been

nothing more than a foolish dream. After declaring that he would never allow anyone to come between the two of them again, he'd run away when Jordan had arrived at the Gray Horse Inn. What was she left to think? Arthur hadn't ever really loved her. Perhaps he'd never ever been infatuated. She'd been the one controlling the entire relationship. She could see that now.

And Jordan, whom she'd always been angry with, was the only man who'd truly been good to her. Well except for Lord Medford and Devon, of course. But Jordan had rescued her from her own foolish self on more than one occasion and done everything in his power to save her reputation and get her to see reason. She'd been nothing but a churl to him at every turn. She wrapped her arms around her middle and shuddered. Oh, she couldn't even face him again. She'd been such a fool.

And that story Lady Catherine had told about Georgiana Dalton. It made Annie's heart wrench. She'd always seen Jordan as a statue, a perfect male specimen. She'd always thought of him as if he had no soul, no heart. But he did. Even perfect-looking people could have their hearts broken, it seemed.

But Annie couldn't imagine him in love. He laughed often, but the lighthearted twinkle never quite reached his eyes. He was always seemingly looking for a good time, but one always questioned whether he actually found it.

But now that Lady Catherine had told her what had happened, suddenly Jordan seemed . . . human. He seemed real to her for the first time.

"I thought I'd find you here."

Annie's heart thumped fast. She turned to see Jordan

tanding in the doorway, the light from the hallway il-
luminating his fine black evening attire. He looked, as
always, like a statue come to life. Her stomach did a little
ip.

"How did you know I'd be here?" She trailed a finger-
p across the soft petals of a hydrangea bush.

"You're usually in here when you want to be alone."

She smiled at that. He was right. Over the last two
weeks she'd made the conservatory her special place in
he house. She adored strolling through the lush foliage
nd breathing in the sweet scents of the lilies and the
range blossoms. But she'd had no idea he'd noticed. "I
o love it here," she murmured.

"Did you enjoy the party?" Jordan asked, shoving his
ands in his pockets as he stepped toward her down one
f the humid little mulched paths.

"I, yes, well, I—" She swallowed and looked down at
he tips of her ice-blue slippers.

Jordan caught up with her then and he reached out a
and and tipped her chin up to look him in the eyes.
Annie, what is it?"

She set her jaw and fought against the unwelcome
onslaught of tears that burned the backs of her eyes. "It's
ust that . . . I don't know what I shall do now and I . . ."
he struggled to meet his eyes. "Oh, listen to me. You
ust think I'm an awful whiner. And I truly don't mean
o be. I'm usually quite cheery." She took a deep breath.
Jordan . . . I . . ."

His hand fell away from her chin but he watched her
arefully. "Yes?"

She gulped. "I wanted to apologize to you."

His brow furrowed. "For what?"

"For being so . . ." She glanced away. "Awful."

He blinked. "Awful?"

"I've acted so abominably . . ." She twisted her fingers in a circle around her opposite wrist. "I've been so foolish. I wouldn't listen to you and all you've ever done was try to help me. I'm sorry." She glanced down. "Thank you for everything."

He tipped up her chin with his thumb and forefinger again. "Annie, you don't owe me an apology."

She pulled away, trembling. "Jordan, I—"

"Yes?"

She placed a hand on his sleeve. "I'm sorry about what happened to you. With Miss Dalton."

His jaw went tight. "Who told you?"

"Lady Catherine."

Jordan raked his fingers through his hair and groaned. "I suppose I shouldn't be surprised."

"Don't be angry with her. I asked her to tell me."

He narrowed his eyes on her. "Why?"

She swallowed and glanced away. "Because I wanted to know . . . whom you'd fallen in love with. Once upon a time."

Jordan's jaw remained taut. His eyes gleamed silver in the moonlight filtering in from the windows high above. He reached out a hand and rubbed his fingers against her cheek. "You want to know about me, Annie? My past?"

She nodded, her eyes never leaving his face. "Yes."

"You have only to ask."

She pressed her lips together tightly. "Is what happened . . . with Georgiana, I mean . . . is that the reason why you never want to marry?"

He pushed a curl behind her ear and Annie shivered.

Then he dropped his hands from her face and paced away from her. "Annie, so young, so beautiful. I was like you once. I believed in things like true love, one and only love. I hate to admit it but I did. I believed in all of it. My life just happened to take a different course. And there were signs I should have seen. Things that indicated that Georgiana didn't feel the same way I thought I felt for her."

Annie swallowed past the lump that had grown in her throat. "Is that why you've been so set against my match with Arthur?"

Jordan turned to face her. "Believe me, if I thought he loved you the way you deserve to be loved, I'd wish you nothing but happiness with Eggleston."

Annie glanced down at her gloved hands. Jordan was telling the truth. She knew it. Felt it in the tone of his voice, the way his intelligent eyes searched her face. It hurt to hear it, but Jordan had always been convinced that Arthur didn't love her. And now she was convinced too. She nodded. All she could do was nod.

"Annie, listen to me. It has nothing to do with you. Eggleston just isn't . . . capable of giving you what you want. Find someone who can, who will."

She smiled a humorless smile. "You don't truly think I can though, do you? You don't think true love exists."

He groaned again and raked his hands through his hair once more. "Don't listen to me. What do I know? Besides, your sister and Colton are certainly a love match. It's possible. It is."

Annie gave him a skeptical look. "You're doing your best to be positive in front of me. To not completely dash my naïve hopes."

"No, I—"

"Don't worry." She moved over to him, placed a col hand over his warm one and squeezed. "It wasn't you But you needn't have bothered. My hopes were alread dashed." She gave a small smile and turned to leave.

"Annie." His voice stopped her. "You're beautiful intelligent, funny. And I could beat your bloody father t a pulp for ever making you feel any differently."

Her chin trembled. She took a deep breath. "Did you father ever say anything awful to you, Jordan?"

Jordan clenched his teeth and closed his eyes and An nie was suddenly struck. He had. His father had. She' been so sure Jordan would say no.

She laid a hand on his sleeve. "It's all right. You don have to—"

He opened his eyes and looked down at her. "I'v never told anyone this before . . ."

She shook her head. "Jordan, don't—"

"No. I want you to know."

She nodded faintly, her arms crossed tightly over he middle.

"My father raised all of his sons to be strong, inde pendent, to need no one. He was convinced a real ma should be entirely self-sufficient."

"And you are, Jordan, you're so strong," Anni breathed.

"Yes, but I disagreed with my father when it came t marriage. I was convinced I'd find someone who love me. For me."

"Don't tell me . . ." Annie looked away, her heart ach ing for the young man who Jordan had once been.

" 'Your title and your fortune,' my father said, 'are wha will attract a wife. A marriage is a business arrangement Nothing more. And you'd do well to remember that.' "

Annie expelled her breath, tears filling her eyes. "I'm so sorry, Jordan."

"It was the one thing I didn't listen to my father about. The only thing. And the biggest mistake I ever made."

"No, Jordan, no." She reached out and grabbed his arms just above the elbows. "You were open, honest, loving. You didn't make a mistake. She did." And Annie realized in that moment how truly loving and caring Jordan was, even though he didn't want anyone to know it.

Jordan shook his head then and the faraway look left his eyes. He was done discussing the past. "You deserve someone who sees and appreciates you," he said. "Someone much better than Eggleston."

She lifted her chin and let her hands drop away from him. "You're right."

"But you don't believe that man exists now, do you?"

Annie shook her head. "I don't know what I believe anymore." She took a shaky breath. "What's wrong with me, Jordan?"

The skin around his eyes crinkled into a frown. "Wrong with you?"

Annie clenched her eyes shut. "Arthur doesn't want me. None of your brothers even want me. And I—"

Jordan squeezed her shoulders. "Nothing, do you hear me? There is absolutely nothing wrong with you. Eggleston is an idiot and so are all of my brothers."

Annie reopened her eyes and smiled a wan smile. "It's nice of you to say so." She pulled away from him and stepped toward the door. "Good night."

She'd only taken two steps when Jordan swung her round and pulled her into his arms. "Annie," he breathed, just before he grabbed the back of her head and pulled her mouth to his.

* * *

For Jordan, the feel of Annie's mouth on his was lik inviting a starving man to a banquet. For a horrible mo ment, he thought she would push him away. He wouldn blame her. What in the hell did he think he was doing Breaking every single rule of friendship, common sens and chaperonage, that was what. But for the life of him he could not stop. And then there was her response. He slight hands had climbed up into his hair. She'd threade one set of fingers across the back of his neck.

He pushed her lips apart and slipped his tongue insid and Annie moaned. He ran his hands up and over he arms and she pushed herself up against his chest. Goo her soft body pressed to him was his undoing. He wa already rock hard, pulling her against him. Her so mouth, her pink lips, her porcelain skin. He'd never bee so damned aroused. How was this young innocent woma making him feel like he was eighteen years old agair Her sweet smell and soft hands were torturing him. Wha he wouldn't give to pick her up, wrap her legs around hi waist, carry her up to his bedchamber, and make love her right now.

Jordan forced himself to pull his mouth away. Breath ing heavily, he rested his forehead to hers. "Annie, w can't—"

"Shut up." She pulled his mouth back to hers.

Jordan groaned.

He wanted to explode. That was all he needed t hear. He wasn't about to make love to Annie in th middle of the conservatory, but he sure as hell was goin to do more than kiss her. He had to.

He picked her up easily and pulled her against hin

pressing his hardness against her softness. She wrapped her arms around his neck. Hard. Their tongues tangled. He took two large steps over to the low stone wall that bordered the orange trees and set her there. Her head fell back. He kissed her throat. His hands deftly pulled up her blue satin skirts. His fingers skimmed her legs, moved quickly up the sides of her thighs. He swallowed hard, never letting his mouth leave hers. She smelled like soap and flowers and that, combined with the sweet scent of the orange trees, made his head spin.

"Jordan," she whispered against his hair.

She'd said his name. He'd thought he couldn't get any harder. He was wrong. He wrapped an arm around her back and pulled her against him. Hard. She cried out. His mouth dropped to her décolletage and his hand deftly unbuttoned the back of her dress. Her dress fell away. He ripped at the straps of her chemise and it too disappeared.

His eyes were riveted to her breasts. They were full and round. Perfect. Just like he knew they would be when he'd imagined them. And God, yes, he had imagined them. A shudder racked his body.

Annie squeezed her eyes shut. Jordan's mouth came down to scorch her skin. She couldn't stand it. She'd never felt like this before. Like fiery wet heat was seeping through every pore. Like she was melting into a creamy puddle. His hot hand branded her knee, her hip. God. This was shameful . . . a shame he wasn't ripping off her dress entirely. Where was the nearest bed? Most unfortunate that they hadn't picked a more comfortable location to have this discussion.

When Arthur had kissed her, nothing like this had happened. This burning heat, these sparks, this intense . . . desire. It burned her. It swept through her. It made her weak. Made her want more.

Annie moaned against Jordan's mouth. She shuddered when his deft hands moved up the outsides of her thighs. She had no idea what he was going to do next, but she desperately wanted to find out. She'd kicked off her slippers, letting them fall to the soft ground beneath them. Jordan's hand had skimmed past her stockings. Now they were underneath her chemise and her head was buzzing.

He was touching her . . . skin. The outside of her thighs. It was wrong for half a dozen reasons, but it felt so good. She wasn't just breaking the rules right now, she was beating them to death with her riding crop. Her head fell back as Jordan's mouth traveled to her earlobe. He nipped her and let his tongue trace the sensitive skin inside. She trembled, her hips moved of their own volition.

He placed his hands on her hips and settled her back down. "Easy, Annie. Don't be frightened. I would never hurt you," he whispered into her ear.

Annie knew it. He would never hurt her. Physically, at least. Emotionally, well, that was a different matter altogether, but at present she didn't care.

"I know," she whispered back.

Jordan's mouth moved down to her neck, then he pushed her back, anchoring her with his body. She looped her arms around his neck and he touched his mouth to her nipple. Tentatively at first, slowly. Then, when Annie moaned deep in her throat and clutched his head, he drew her nipple into his mouth and pulled on it. Flicked his tongue back and forth on it, nibbled it.

Annie closed her eyes and let the riotous emotions icochet through her entire body. She was drowning in a ainbow. Bright lights, strong colors, heady smells. She :ouldn't have fathomed having a man's mouth on her >reast would elicit such emotions from her, but she vanted to sob, wanted to tangle her fingers in his dark air and never let go. Jordan tugged on her nipple with is mouth and she whimpered. Oh God, what was she loing? How long could she let this go on?

Very well, the truth was . . . she didn't care. When ordan's fire-hot wet mouth scorched her other nipple, he ceased thinking at all. Instead, she luxuriated in the eel of his tongue on her, his hands kneading her breasts, naking them feel full, heavy, hot.

He nuzzled in between her breasts and dragged his nouth back to hers. Annie knew a moment of regret. She hadn't wanted him to stop. But then his hands noved up her thighs and she didn't have another coher-nt thought. Jordan grabbed her hips and pulled her to im, forcing their bodies together in an intimate maneu-er. Only he was still wearing his breeches. But under-eath her chemise, Annie was entirely bare. The heat of his erection burned her through the fabric and she obbed against his cheek.

"Jordan . . . please."

ordan took a long deep breath, letting the shudders that acked his body subside. What was he doing? What was e doing? What was he doing? Annie probably didn't ven know what she was asking for, but Jordan did. And lamn it, he was going to give it to her. He'd already gone his far. He pulled one hand down the outside of her thigh and slowly allowed it to ascend again, only this time, on the inside. The strong muscles in her thigh twitched. He steadied her. He moved his hand slowly. So slowly. Careful lest he scare her. His tongue still tangled with hers. He couldn't get enough of her. But when his fingertips gently brushed against the most private part of her, Annie's sharp intake of breath signaled her surprise.

Slowly. Slowly. A sheen of sweat broke out on Jordan's forehead. He was vaguely aware that he was trembling. He'd never felt like this before. So out of control. So mad with desire. He wanted to shed his breeches and bury himself in her. Instead, he parted the soft, springy hair between her thighs and stroked her. Oh God, he knew it. She felt like hot silk. Just like hot, wet silk.

Annie's head had fallen back on her neck. She was no longer kissing him. Just moaning incomprehensible things that he wished to hell he knew the words to. Jordan closed his eyes too. It was going to take every bit of strength he had to survive this. All he wanted to do was take her swiftly, here and now.

But he couldn't. He couldn't.

But he could do this . . .

He slipped one finger inside of her and Annie's entire body jerked. She lifted her head and looked at him with eyes wide with surprise. Jordan had expected that. He pressed his forehead to hers. "Don't be afraid."

Then he moved his finger and Annie forgot to think at all. The slow glide of Jordan's finger inside her, in and out, in and out, made Annie want to die. She'd never felt anything approaching it in her entire life. She was wet and hot, and wanting him. She grabbed his head and

issed him, kissed him with all the pent-up desire she
elt for him. If this man was a rake, she never wanted to
e without the company of a rake. She was swimming in
haze of heat and desire.

He moved his hand a bit, flicked back and forth, and
nnie sobbed against his mouth. "Jordan."

Jordan kissed her again, deeply, then, "Wait, Annie.
Wait for it."

He brushed his thumb against the little nub of her
leasure between her legs and Annie cried out. Her hips
ere moving in an unconsciously seductive rhythm
hat was driving him mad. The way she responded to
im, with such heat, such passion, such abandon. His
ock had never been so hard.

Jordan moved his thumb in a steady circle. Slowly.
lowly. She was on the pinnacle and he'd do anything to
ive her the prize.

"Jordan, I . . ." Her head moved fitfully back and forth.
le brought up his other hand to cup the back of her head.
le kissed her again. Drank her in like a fine wine.

"Shh," he whispered. "Just let it happen. Feel."

"Let what . . ." But her voice trailed off and her hips
ncreased their pace along with his thumb. She clutched
is shoulders. "Jordan!" she cried, her breathing hitch-
ng and then coming in fast little spurts. "Jordan."

Annie didn't know what was happening inside of her
ut the agonizing building tension and the crescendo
hat followed left her breathless, panting, and clinging to
ordan. He was completely still with his eyes clamped
hut and an almost pained expression on his face.

"Jordan?" she finally managed to breathe against his
eck. "Are you all right?"

He answered through clenched teeth. "I'll be . . . fine

Annie could still feel his erection through his breeche
She must have caused that. And it was causing him pai
She reached down to touch it.

"Annie. No." His voice was a too harsh command b
Annie knew the second she wrapped her hand around i
he was going to let her touch him.

"Oh God," he groaned, and Annie pressed her bar
breasts to his chest and held him. God, he was big, wid
and long. She could tell that much through his breeche
Despite having never read her sister's scandalous pam
phlet, Annie was somewhat aware of what went on be
tween a man and woman in bed . . . *not* necessarily o
their wedding night. And from Jordan's reaction, sh
had just found the source of his pleasure.

"Can I touch you, Jordan?"

His eyes clenched shut, his jaw tight, he shook his head

"Please?" she asked, slowly, carefully unbuttoning hi
breeches with one hand.

"Annie," he breathed, trying to tell her to stop. H
couldn't be held responsible if she touched his bare coc
with her perfect little hand.

"Please," she whispered. "Let me."

The last button came undone and Jordan sprang fre
Annie wrapped her bare hand around his silken warmt
He was like firm velvet. Long and lean and . . . har
She shuddered. Somehow, instinctively, she knew how t
touch him. She rubbed him up and down, making Jorda
groan and shudder.

"Annie, no." He kissed her lips fiercely, but Anni
didn't move her hand away.

Jordan braced himself against the unholy torture o
having Annie touch him. Anything he'd done to th

irl, ruining her chances with Eggleston, abducting her, aking her suffer through his matchmaking attempts, ey all paled in comparison to the torture she was in-icting upon him at the moment.

Without a doubt, after tonight, their score would be ven. She nipped his earlobe and rubbed him up and own. Jordan's cock jerked. Oh God, if he allowed her keep doing that, he'd spill his seed, right here on e bloody stone wall in the conservatory. Such. Bad. orm.

It took every ounce of strength he had to reach down nd pull Annie's torturous hand away. Her eyes were still haze of lust and confusion. He kissed her forehead. The p of her nose. Her lips.

"Why?" she asked.

His breathing was heavy, unsteady. "Let's just say if ou had continued to touch me like that, I would have ade a fool of myself."

She shook her head, confused.

He kissed her again and again until she felt like her ps would never be the same.

After what seemed like only moments but was prob-bly the better part of an hour, Jordan pulled his mouth way. "We must stop."

Annie nodded.

He refastened his breeches before buttoning the back f her gown. He escorted her through the house, up the tairs, and to her room without saying a word. She pened the door and turned back to face him, tentative, hy.

"Good night, Annie," he said, bowing. His rumpled lothing and disheveled hair were the most attractive hings she'd ever seen.

"What happened?" she managed to ask in a shak
voice.

His voice was firm, confident. He had a determine
gleam in his eye. "Something that can never happen be
tween us again."

CHAPTER 33

...e next morning, Jordan watched the coach that would ...ke Annie back to London from an upstairs window. He ...dn't dare say good-bye in person, didn't dare get too ...ose. He didn't trust himself not to turn into a complete ...adman again and ravish her in the blasted foyer.

Instead, he put his coach and four at her disposal and ...nt Aunt Clarissa, Mary, and a gaggle of footmen, all ... whom already adored Annie, off to London. She was ...ing back. Back to the safety of Devon's house. Back to ...r sister's care.

Jordan squeezed his eyes shut. He hoped she didn't ...e fit to mention their little interlude last night to her ...w brother-in-law. The thought made him smile a wry ...nile. Devon coming at him and beating him senseless ...ight be just what Jordan needed, however, to jostle ...me sense back into him.

He scrubbed a hand through his hair, leaned his arm ...ainst the windowpane, and rested his forehead against ... watching his coach recede into the distance. What the ...ell had happened to him over the last four weeks? A ...onth ago, he'd been enjoying an entirely pleasant

existence of debauchery in London, and now he was d
ing his damnedest to get an innocent out of his head.

They'd nearly gone too far last night, and it sho
him. But Annie had looked up at him with those beau
ful brown eyes and asked, *What's wrong with me?* It h
been his undoing. There was absolutely nothing wro
with her. Nothing. And it made his stomach churn
know she might think so.

If he ever saw that fool Arthur Eggleston again, he
do the lad a favor and snap his idiot neck. And Annie
father had best be glad he was dead because he was
the list too. Anyone who'd ever been mean to her was.

But where had this protective streak come from?
made no sense. He'd never made it his business to pr
tect anyone. Why was he starting now? He could te
himself repeatedly it was because he'd promised h
friends he'd take care of Annie while they were gon
but there was more to it than that and he knew it. Bla
it. He knew it. He'd protected her from her own fool n
tions, it was true, but he could have carted her out he
and left her alone, gone back to London himself. H
didn't have to watch over her the entire time.

So why did he?

And when did the chaperone become the worst po
sible person to be in her presence? God, he couldn't kee
his hands off her last night. He'd tried. Screamed
himself in his head to stop. But touching her soft ski
moving his hands along her taut thighs, he just couldn
help himself. Some madness had overtaken him and h
just had to touch her.

Jordan expelled his breath and turned from the wi
dow. Yes, they'd nearly gone too far last night. *Had* go
too far. It scared the hell out of him to know it. He

ologize to her the next time he saw her. In private, of
urse. But he couldn't see her again for a long, long
hile. Perhaps not until she was engaged, or even mar-
ed. Lily would take her into hand now and ensure her
ster made a fine match. Thank God for that. But Jordan,
, he had no business being anywhere near Annie An-
ews for the next several months if he could help it.

And that was an end to it.

nnie traced the pattern of the coach's curtains with a
ngertip. She glanced up at the manor house, wondering
here Jordan was inside the cavernous home. Was he
ven aware that she was leaving now?

"I've never been woken up so early and sent packing
suddenly." Mary mumbled the words from across the
at.

Annie bit her lip. "I'm sorry, Mary. I thought you knew
evon and Lily were expected back today. I do hope
ey make it."

"I, for one, am quite happy to be going back. The
untry is lovely but a dreadful bore," Aunt Clarissa
lded from her spot in the corner.

Mary settled into her own seat and shook her head at
nnie. "I knew Miss Lily and Lord Colton are expected
ack. I just didn't realize Lord Ashbourne was in such a
rry ta be rid o' ye."

Unexpected tears stung the back of Annie's eyes. It
adn't been Jordan who'd ordered her to leave so quickly.
he'd been unable to sleep last night after their encoun-
r. She'd been up with the sun and asked the servants to
elp her prepare to leave. They'd been such dears and
ssisted her. Apparently Jordan had offered her the use
f his coach, but he hadn't come to say good-bye and she

couldn't blame him. After all that had happened b[e]tween them over the last two weeks, and then last nigh[t] what would they say to each other? She'd been blissful[ly] relieved to know he intended to let her go without ha[v]ing to face him. Hadn't she?

Annie shook her head. She did her best to affect [a] convincing laugh. "Where have you been, Mary? Lo[rd] Ashbourne's been in a hurry to get rid of me since Li[ly] and Devon left town."

Mary rolled her eyes. "That man certainly thinks 'e['s] the king the way 'e ordered ye about and dragged ye o[ut] 'ere to begin wit. And why we need ta travel all the wa[y] back ta London to meet Miss Lily and Lord Colton ju[st] to come right back down 'ere to Surrey this week, I'[ll] never understand."

Annie's voice was quiet. "I'm anxious to see my si[s]ter. I cannot wait to get to London."

Aunt Clarissa cleared her throat. "Yes, and pleas[e] don't take this the wrong way, dear, as it's been an abso[-] lute pleasure serving as your chaperone for the la[st] month, but I cannot wait to get back to my own tow[n] house. I miss my own bed dreadfully."

Annie reached over and patted the older woman['s] hand. "You've been such a dear to stay with me, Au[nt] Clarissa."

Annie glanced back at Mary. "Besides, Lord Ash[-] bourne was only doing what he was asked."

Mary quirked a brow. "Only doing wot 'e was asked[?] My, isn't that a change o' tune from a few days ago[.] Weren't ye the one wot nearly 'ad a conniption when th[at] man tracked ye down? Abduction, ye called it, if I re[-] member."

Annie pulled at the strings to her reticule. She glance[d]

at the window and stared across the foggy landscape, the demesne of Jordan's vast property. Mary was obviously miffed if she wasn't making any attempt to pronounce her words more formally.

But Mary was right. Annie had been completely changed over the last two weeks. Not only had she finally come to realize that Arthur wasn't the man she thought he was, but she'd also seen Lord Ashbourne . . . Jordan . . . in a completely different way.

The truth was, she'd spent the last month acting like a spoiled child while Jordan had done everything in his power to save her from herself and her own idiotic notions of love. Arthur didn't love her. Perhaps he thought he did and he certainly said he did, but true love didn't run from adversity. His promise had been worth nothing. Arthur clearly wasn't committed to her. Not the way he truly should be. And the truth was, she wasn't as committed to him as she should be either. If she truly loved Arthur, after all, how could she have done the wanton things she'd done with Jordan last night? How could she have enjoyed them so much? Her cheeks flamed.

Oh God, what had she done? Jordan was Devon's best friend. He was a rakehell and better looking than he had any right to be. He couldn't seriously be interested in her. Could he? On the other hand, the man consorted with beauties like Nicoletta. He wouldn't waste his time with Annie if he didn't find her somewhat pretty . . . could he?

Her mind raced back to the day they went for a ride on his property when he'd allowed her to drive the coach tandem. Arthur had refused to allow her to do such a thing, but Jordan had seemed nothing but confident in her skills. He'd saved her reputation on two occasions

now and had put himself to considerable trouble on h
account. He'd even attempted to introduce her to h
handsome brothers. Surely that act alone proved he w
doing more than just fulfilling a simple promise to Devo

Annie shook her head. She needed to be alone for
few days, away from men. All of them. All they'd do
in the past month was serve to confuse her. "Let's g
some sleep, Mary," she whispered to the maid.

Yes. She needed to rest, rest and see Lily. She long
to be in her sister's comforting arms.

Mary nodded and Annie leaned her head against th
coach's wall. She squeezed her eyes shut, but she couldn
sleep.

She wanted marriage and children and love mo
than anything in this world. Those had been her dream
for as long as she could remember. She'd thought Arth
was the man for her, but now, when she closed her eye
Arthur's image was not the one that filled her vision.
was Jordan Holloway's image that danced across h
mind.

And there was only one problem with Jordan Ho
loway.

The man had sworn an oath never to marry.

CHAPTER 34

Annie ran straight into her sister's outstretched arms. "Lily," she breathed, inhaling the familiar scent of her sister's jasmine perfume. "Lily, I missed you so."

Lily hugged Annie tightly. "And I missed you." The two pulled apart and stared at each other, bright smiles upon each of their faces.

Lily looked perfect as always. Her black hair piled high atop her head, her violet eyes sparkling. Her sister had never appeared better. She had a rosy glow in her cheeks, a jaunty step, and a true smile that Annie hadn't seen in years. Not since before Lily's marriage to the old Earl of Merrill. The man had subsequently died, and, despite their marriage contract, had left Lily nearly penniless.

And Lily had gained a bit of weight now that she didn't have the worries of supporting a household including Annie, Mary, Evans, and the two dogs on practically no income. Her sister glowed with another radiance too, that of being completely in love with her new husband, Lord Colton.

The footmen were hurriedly unloading the trunks from Devon's coach. The conveyance had pulled to a

stop in front of the grand town house. Lily and Devo
had just swept through the front doors.

Annie stayed in Lily's arms and nodded to Devo
"Very good to see you, my lord." She smiled throug
her tears of joy.

"Good to see you, Anne," Devon replied with a wir
and a nod.

Aunt Clarissa, bags packed, kissed her nephew and h
new wife. "I do hope you'll forgive my rudeness, dear
but I'm in an awfully large hurry to be home."

"Not to worry, Aunt Clarissa," Devon replied. "I'\
already given the coachman orders."

Lily nodded to the older lady. "Thank you so much fe
serving as chaperone while I was away, Aunt Clarissa.

Annie prayed the woman didn't mention anythir
about a stay at a certain country house or anything els
to do with Jordan Holloway for that matter. "Good-by
Aunt Clarissa. And thank you," she said, waving.

"Remember my recommendation, dear," Aunt Claris:
said, winking at Annie. Annie hid her smile, and than!
fully, the older woman was gone without another wor
The next thing Annie knew, the dogs, Leopold and Ba
dit, were rushing around Lily's feet, distracting her sist
from asking what in the world Aunt Clarissa had mea
by that last remark.

"I see these two missed you, my dear," Devon saic
gesturing to the dogs and squeezing his wife's hand. H
so obviously adored Lily.

Lily bent down and scooped up both squirming pup
into her arms. "My Bandit and my Leo," she said, bury
ing her face in their fur and letting Bandit, who wa
known to be a shameless licker, scour her face with littl
dog kisses.

Annie cleared her throat. She'd decided to wait a bit before introducing her sister to the newest member of their household, Dash.

Evans and Nicholls were beside themselves with glee, obviously pleased to have their master and mistress back in town and enjoying every moment of seeing that their trunks were put to rights by ordering the footmen about.

"Oh, how I've missed a good English tea," Lily breathed.

Devon kissed her on the head. "I must attend to some business right away, but I'll see you both tonight for dinner," he said. "Besides, I'm sure you two have quite a lot to talk about."

Devon winked at Lily and excused himself. He strode off toward his study and Lily watched him go with a wistful smile on her face.

"Tea shall be served momentarily, my lady," Evans intoned in his most formal butlerlike voice.

Lily nodded. "Thank you, Evans. Very good to see you again. I trust you have been well."

"Very well, thank you, my lady." Evans couldn't suppress the smug smile he tossed at Nicholls.

"Come, come," Annie said, pulling her sister into the salon. "You must tell me absolutely everything about your holiday."

While Evans served tea, the sisters settled onto the settee in the salon. Leo and Bandit curled into balls at their feet. Lily pushed her hands down her skirts and smiled. "What would you like to hear about first?"

Annie clapped her hands. "Oh, everything. Which was your favorite city? What food did you enjoy the most? How did you find Paris?"

Lily put up her hands as if to ward off her sister's

barrage of questions. "Just a moment." She laughed. "One question at a time. Let's see. I believe Venice was my very favorite."

Annie snapped her mouth shut. Venice? The city where Jordan met his mistress. Oh, why did she have to remember such a detail at a time like this? She shook her head and focused her attention back on Lily. Her sister had been gone for weeks. She deserved Annie's full devotion. This had nothing to do with Jordan Holloway.

"What was Venice like?" Annie closed her eyes trying to picture the grandeur of the famous floating Italian city.

One hour later, full of tea and biscuits, Annie had learned to her complete dismay that *everything* apparently had to do with Jordan. The stories of the food in Paris reminded her of the delectable meals at Jordan's house in the country. They had been prepared by the French chef he employed. The story of a ride through the valleys of Tuscany reminded Annie of their romantic ride to the lake on Jordan's property. The stories of the fashions in Paris reminded Annie of what a dashing figure Jordan always cut whether he was wearing riding attire or evening attire.

Blast it. The man was in her head. She'd so been hoping that a bit of time and distance, seeing Lily and returning to her old routine, would make everything all right again, but as Lily chattered on about her wedding expedition, all Annie could think about was Jordan Holloway.

"Aren't you going to answer me?"

Annie turned to meet her sister's gaze. "What was that?"

Apparently, her tales had come to an end and Lily had discovered Annie daydreaming. "I asked what happened here while I was away?"

Annie gulped. "Oh, not so very much," she demurred, occupying herself with refilling her teacup. "More tea?"

Lily narrowed her eyes on her sister, but she nodded at the mention of the tea. "Come now, we've been gone for a month, surely *something* interesting happened here during that time."

Annie tapped her finger against her cheek for a moment. "Yes, why yes, it did."

Lily leaned in closer. "Tell me."

"I rescued a fox."

Lily scrunched up her nose and tilted her head to the side. "A fox?"

"Yes. His name is Dash and he had a wounded paw. I found him in Hyde Park of all places. Can you believe it?"

"And you brought him home?"

"He's just a kit, Lily. I couldn't leave him there to limp around the park. Now, I've every reason to suspect *you* shall allow me to keep him, but we must concoct a plan to convince Devon that he can stay."

Lily smiled. "Hmm." This time she tapped her finger against her cheek. "Let me think on it, but in the meantime, go get Dash. I must see him."

Annie rang for Evans. "Evans, be a dear and ask Mary to come. She'll want to see Lily. Ask her to bring Dash with her."

Evans nodded and hurried off to do Annie's bidding.

Lily turned her attention back to her sister. "Now, tell me, Anne. How did *you* get on while we were away?"

Uh-oh. She should have been the one to go get Dash. Annie put the back of her hand to her forehead in a feigned expression of long suffering. "Oh, it was difficult, to be sure, but somehow I managed."

Lily pushed Annie's shoulder lightly. "Did you allow

Aunt Clarissa and Mary to escort you when you left the house?"

"Sometimes."

Lily gave her a disapproving look. "And did Jordan pay you a visit every now and then to see how you were getting on? He promised me he would, you know," she said with a sly smile.

Annie pulled at the throat of her day dress. Was it hot in the salon of a sudden? "I . . . why . . . yes . . . I . . . encountered Lord Ashbourne . . . from time to time." She took a shaky sip of tea.

Lily nodded. "Glad to hear it."

Annie breathed a sigh of relief. Thank God her sister appeared to be finished with the topic. But Lily's next question nearly stopped Annie's heart. "And no more mischief with Mr. Eggleston?"

Annie's teacup clattered to the saucer. "Mischief? What *are* you implying?"

Lily folded her hands in her lap. Anyone other than Annie wouldn't have noticed the small gesture. But their mother had always folded her hands in her lap when she was displeased yet wanted to remain in perfect control.

Here it came.

"I think you know what I mean, Anne." Lily arched her brow in that older-sister way of hers.

Annie bit her lip. "I did see Mr. Eggleston upon occasion, if that's what you're asking, but it's not as if I married him."

Annie fought against the urge to jump away from her spot on the settee, afraid lightning might strike her. She'd deserve it.

"Besides, I'm quite through with my infatuation with Mr. Eggleston."

"You are?"

"Yes."

"I must say, I'm glad to hear it." Her older sister's eyebrow settled back into place. And guilt flooded Annie. She remembered the discussion that day at Jordan's house about the responsibility thrust upon the oldest sibling. Lily had more responsibility than most. She'd been forced to take in Annie five years ago, after their parents had died. Recently widowed, Lily had had to be an older sister and a mother, putting her own needs behind Annie's. Why, Lily had nearly spent her last shilling ensuring that Annie had a proper debut and this was how Annie repaid her sister's kindness? With disobedience and mischief? Oh, she was the worst younger sister in the kingdom. The worst.

"Oh, Lily, I'm so sorry." She set down her teacup and pulled her sister into her embrace.

Lily hugged her and patted her back. "Why? Whatever for?"

"For being a fool for so long." She let go of Lily and her sister's wide-eyed look restored a bit of Annie's sanity. Lily obviously didn't know what Annie meant.

"You're not a fool, Anne," Lily said, squeezing her hand. "Far from it."

"Yes I am. And I'm sorry." She took a deep breath. "May I ask you a question, Lily?"

"Of course."

Annie took another deep breath. "Did you feel very burdened when you were young? I mean, did you feel as if you had all the responsibility and I had none?"

Lily's brow furrowed. "No. No, of course not, Anne. I love you. I always wanted you to be happy, carefree."

Annie smiled and glanced down at her hands. "Thank

you, Lily, for being the oldest, for doing all the things I didn't have to."

Lily laughed and shook her head. "Like what?"

"Like marrying the Earl of Merrill." Annie's voice was quiet.

The smile vanished from Lily's face and she squeezed Annie's hand even tighter. "I'd do anything for you," she said softly. "I hope you know that, Anne."

Another wave of guilt crashed over her. Yes, Lily would do anything for her and she'd repaid her sister's generosity by being churlish and foolish. What a charming combination.

"Now." Lily shook her head and pasted a bright smile on her face. "Let's talk of more pleasant things, shall we?"

The door to the salon opened just then and Mary came hurtling through it with an orange ball of fur in her arms. She squealed as soon as she saw Lily and rushed over to the settee. She deposited Dash upon Annie's lap and grabbed Lily into her arms.

"Oh, me lady, I'm so glad ta see ye back. Lord, if Miss Annie told me ye were coming today, I surely forgot."

The two sisters exchanged knowing glances.

Annie snuggled Dash under her chin.

Lily laughed. "I was just telling Anne about my honeymoon, Mary. And I very much wanted to meet the newest member of our household."

She held out her arms and Annie handed Dash to her. Lily lifted up the little fox and looked him in the eye. "My, but you are a cute one, aren't you?" she cooed, before wrapping the baby in her arms and cuddling him against her chest. "Don't worry. Now that I've seen him I couldn't possibly let him go. Just let me handle ex-

plaining him to Devon." Lily winked at Annie and Annie winked back.

"He's quite taken to living in a town house, really,"
Annie explained. "We feed him bits from the cupboard
and warm milk. I'm convinced he thinks he's one of the
dogs."

"'E's a rascal, that Dash," Mary said, settling on the
settee next to the two sisters. "Now, Miss Lily, do tell all
about yer 'oneymoon journey. I've been waiting and
waiting ta 'ear." She cleared her throat. "Hear."

Lily laughed. "What do you want to know?"

Annie waggled her eyebrows. "I want to know exactly what happens on a honeymoon. Behind closed
doors. Tell me, Lily, what were the secrets of your wedding night?"

Mary giggled with wide eyes and Lily leaned over
and play-slapped her sister's leg. "I will tell you no such
thing, miss."

Annie pointed a triumphant finger in the air. "I've got
it. You should write a pamphlet about it. I shall alert
Lord Medford."

"Ooh, yes, it's sure ta be a top seller, me lady," Mary
agreed with a smile.

Lily shook her head. "You two think you're quite
funny, don't you?" She delivered Dash back into Annie's
outstretched arms. Then she stood and brushed out her
skirts.

"Where are you off to?" Annie asked, snuggling
Dash under her chin again.

Lily's face wore a sly smile. "It's been far too long
since I've seen my husband. I'm just going to pop into
his study for a bit."

This time, Mary and Annie exchanged knowing glances. "Ummm-hmmm."

Lily crossed over to the door, Bandit and Leo close on her heels. "Oh, before I forget. Anne, you and Mary will need to pack your bags tonight. We're leaving for Colton House in the morning."

Annie nodded. "Yes, I thought as much. I'm sure Lord Colton is eager to see Justin."

Lily opened the door and glanced back over her shoulder. "Yes, very eager. And we're having a house party next week and inviting all our friends so we can tell them about our holiday. I must prepare. Thank goodness Mrs. Applebee will be there to help, but I'll need you two as well."

Annie nearly dropped Dash into her lap. "House party?" she squeaked. "For all of your friends?" She clutched the little ball of fur to her chest.

Lily stopped and turned back around. Leo and Bandit stopped too. "Yes. It will be such fun. I cannot wait to see everyone. Don't worry. It won't be a huge crush. Just our closest friends."

Annie gulped. That's what she'd been afraid of. Closest friends. Like Devon's closest friend, Jordan Holloway.

Lily swept from the room, the dogs trotting after her. Annie and Mary sat staring at each other. Thank goodness the maid didn't recall her exploit with Jordan coming to demand her whereabouts when she'd left for Gretna Green again. Annie had sworn Evans to secrecy and Nicholls was far too staid to gossip about his master's sister-in-law. No, she was safe. Unless of course Jordan himself decided to tell Lily. But he wouldn't do that, would he?

Mary cleared her throat. "Ye didn't tell Miss Lily

about our trip ta Surrey and yer stay wit Lord Ashbourne, did ye?"

Annie gasped. "How did you—"

"I don't forget *everything*, Miss Annie. Besides, I wrote meself a note about all o' that. 'Ave it right 'ere." She pulled a piece of paper from her apron pocket and proudly displayed it.

Annie gently set Dash on the carpet. "What are you doing? Destroy it," she ordered. "If Lily finds it, I won't be allowed outside of the house until I'm sixty."

Mary shook her head. "Miss Lily wod never read me personal notes. Ye know better than that."

Annie expelled her breath. "You're right. But please promise me you won't tell her, Mary. I've never seen her as happy as she is now and I swear I have no intention of making a fool of myself over Mr. Eggleston ever again. There's no need for Lily to know any of that."

Mary shoved the note back into her pocket and plunked her hands on her hips. "What? Do ye think I 'ave no loyalty? I would never betray yer confidence. It's Lord Ashbourne ye'd best be worried about, not me."

Annie slumped against the pillows and bit her lip. "Believe me, Mary, I am."

The maid patted her hair into place. "Don't worry too much about all o' it, miss. 'E'll come around."

Annie looked twice. How and when had Mary become so intuitive? How did she know Annie had feelings for Jordan? "Oh, Mary, tell me, please. What is the secret to making a man who doesn't seem interested in marriage want to marry you?"

Mary giggled. "Want ta, miss? Or *'ave* ta? Because if it's 'ave ta, yer very best bet wod be ta get the gentleman in question ta compromise ye."

Annie sat up straight and grabbed the arms of the chair. "Compromise me?" She blinked.

Mary nodded. "Yes . . . but ye said yerself ye wouldn' make a fool o' yerself over Mr. Eggleston again, and 'ave ta say, if 'e didn't compromise ye by now, it doesn' seem ta me that man's the compromising sort."

Annie allowed a slow smile to spread across her face. Ah, so Mary didn't know she had feelings for Jordan after all. That was a relief. But the maid was perfectly right. Arthur Eggleston was not the compromising sort.

But Jordan Holloway was.

CHAPTER 35

So, how've things been in London while I've been gone, old chap?" Devon clapped Jordan on the back. "I tell you it's nice to have a proper brandy again."

The two were sitting at the club, enjoying their favorite beverage.

Jordan took a sip and shrugged. For some reason, he'd returned to town today too. He told himself he was just getting back to normal, and it was good to see Colton again, but Jordan was acutely aware that Annie was in town. He downed a larger swallow of his drink. Thank God Devon had agreed to meet him at the club. Could have been deuced awkward if he'd asked him to stop by the town house. It was better this way. Much better.

"There's not much to say, really," Jordan answered. He'd already decided less was more when answering any questions about what had happened over the last month. Especially where Annie was concerned. Devon hadn't taken a swing at him yet, so that boded well. Obviously, Annie hadn't mentioned to her new brother-in-law that his best friend had abducted her and taken liberties with her in his conservatory . . . ahem . . . an his salon.

"So, really? Nothing new?" Devon asked again. "N new bets here at the club? No new scandalbroths? Noth ing?"

Jordan shrugged.

Devon eyed him carefully. "Been keeping busy wit Nicoletta?"

Jordan kept his face blank. "Actually, I . . . ende things with Nicoletta a fortnight ago."

Devon's eyebrows shot up. "The devil you say! Why?"

Jordan cleared his throat. "We had a . . . falling-out."

"Bored with her so soon, were you? I must say I didn see that coming."

Another shrug.

"And you say you had a country ball?" Devon con tinued.

"Yes, Annie was there." Jordan glanced away, na rowing his eyes into the distance. He'd decided to giv Devon just enough information to keep him informe without adding a great many details. He'd had to tel him. Surely someone would inform Devon and Lily tha Jordan had hosted a ball. No doubt it would come up i conversation eventually.

"So I *did* miss a thing or two while I was out of th country," Devon said. "Does Anne still have her cap se for that Eggleston fool?"

Jordan expelled his breath. Now there was a question One he'd very much like to know the answer to as wel "I believe so," he answered lamely. "She fancies hersel in love."

Devon grunted. "Yes, well, we'll see about that." The he snapped his fingers, "That reminds me, Lily woul

ever forgive me if I forgot to mention that we're having
house party. At Colton House."

"A house party?" Jordan replied, taking another sip
brandy. "When?"

"Next week. To announce our arrival back in the
ountry and to greet our friends."

Jordan swallowed hard. "Splendid."

The inevitable invitation was coming. Why shouldn't
? He was always invited to Devon's parties. It would be
dd if he were not. The only thing odd this time was
ordan knowing without a doubt he could not accept. He
ould not attend and keep his sanity. He could not, *could
ot*, see Annie again. Not so soon. Perhaps not ever. His
ind raced, hastily attempting to invent some excuse as
why he could not attend.

"And between you and me . . ." Devon continued,
ulling Jordan from his thoughts, "Lily hopes to invite
many eligible chaps as possible in the hope that Anne
ill choose one and forget about Eggleston."

Jordan expelled his breath in a rush. "Excellent," he
id, perhaps too emphatically. "I mean, that sounds like
excellent plan, but unfortunately, I cannot attend."

Devon's brow furrowed. "Cannot attend? Why not?"

"I have . . . er . . . plans next week."

"What plans? Cancel them. You can't take care of
em the week after?"

"No, I . . . There's a great deal happening at Ashbourne
Ianor, and I must see to it." As excuses go, it was partic-
larly weak but Jordan couldn't think of anything else.
e'd never declined an invitation to a good friend's party
efore. In fact, he was usually the one bringing the extra
ottles of brandy and the stacks of playing cards.

"Ashbourne Manor? Why, it's only an hour away

from Colton House. You can come to the party and ste
off to do your business if you must. But you cannot sa
no. I'm inviting Charlie, Tim, and Michael as well. Yo
must come. Justin will want to see his uncle, and Li
will be beside herself. She wanted to especially thar
you for watching out for Anne while we were gone."

Jordan choked on his brandy. Wiping his mouth wi
the back of his hand, he eyed Devon cautiously. "I d
serve no thanks." It was the truest statement he'd mad
since he'd sat down with his friend.

Devon quirked a brow. "As to that, how did it g
while we were gone? Did Anne cause you any trouble'

Jordan tugged at his cravat. The thing was stranglin
him today. "She, uh . . ."

"I know it was a lot to ask you to watch out for he
Ashbourne. I do appreciate it."

"No trouble whatsoever," Jordan replied.

"Glad to hear it." Devon laughed. "I joked to Li
while we were in Italy that Anne might even get it in
her head to return to Gretna Green. She's so set on th
blasted Eggleston chap."

Jordan narrowed his eyes and silently made a show
staring out the window.

"I'm glad to see she's thought better of it," Devo
continued. "And we can only hope she takes a fancy
someone else at the house party."

"A solid plan," Jordan replied noncommittally.

"So you'll be there?" Devon took a long last swallo
from his brandy glass, emptying it.

Jordan clenched his jaw. His excuse had been pitif
and surely Devon would suspect something was amiss
he continued to decline.

Jordan nodded once. "I'll be there."

CHAPTER 36

nnie walked right into it. Well, cantered really. Just give
r the championship prize for largest fool of the day.

She'd been out on the grounds of Colton House riding
e new mount Devon had purchased for her use. As
ng as she stayed away from the house all morning she
as sure to miss Jordan's arrival, she'd reasoned.

No. Such. Luck.

In fact, she'd managed to jaunt up the drive at the pre-
se moment his familiar dark blue coach was pulling up
front of the manor house. In a panic, she tried to turn
r mount to ride away but Lily emerged from the front
ors just then, Justin at her side, and waved to her.

"Anne, look. It's Jordan."

Annie sighed. She couldn't very well gallop off now.
My hair must look a fright," she mumbled to Annabelle
e horse. She didn't miss the irony of the fact that she'd
ver before cared how her hair looked. Straightening
r shoulders, she patted her coiffure into place under
r hat as best she could with one hand holding the crop,
d she nudged Annabelle's flank to move toward the
ive. Sweat beaded on her brow. She held her breath.

Jordan emerged from the coach looking as handsor and dashing as ever, wearing skintight buckskin breech a dark green waistcoat, and a snowy-white cravat. hair was slightly mussed and his gray eyes shone li silver in the morning light.

Lily held out both hands to him. "Jordan, there y are. I'm so glad you've come. Devon told me you tried decline our invitation. I never would have forgiven you

Annie reluctantly moved closer but she was sure hadn't seen her yet. So, he'd tried to decline the invitatio

Jordan smiled at her sister. "Thank you for havi me, Lily. It's good to see you."

"Uncle Jordan," Justin cried, running up and jumpi into Jordan's arms.

Very well, Annie had to admit, that was adorab The child obviously loved him.

Lily glanced up. "Anne, look. It's Jordan."

Annie nudged her mount forward but couldn't bri herself to meet his eyes. "Lord Ash . . . Ashbourne." H name barely slipped past the lump in her throat.

Setting Justin down on the gravel drive, Jordan bowe "Miss Andrews. Good to see you again."

Was it her imagination or did his voice hold no em tion?

Lily glanced between them. "Funny. I'd have thoug the two of you would be on a first-name basis by now.

Annie tugged at the tight neck of her midnight-bl riding habit.

Jordan shifted on his feet. He kicked at the dirt wi his top boot. "Yes, well . . ."

Justin tugged on Lily's skirts. "May I go get my b and arrow, please?" he asked. "Uncle Jordan promis he'd continue our lessons when he came."

Lily glanced up at Jordan to confirm the appointment. "That's absolutely right," he said with a wide grin. And I expect that you've been practicing, lad."

"Every day," Justin replied with a devilish look on his young face. "I intend to be better than you one day, Uncle Jordan."

"Go ahead, darling," Lily said to the boy, nodding toward the door. After Justin had scampered off, she shook her head. "Watch out, Jordan. That look on his face is just like his father's when he gets something in his head."

Jordan laughed. "He's already twice as good at arithmetic than I'll ever be; I refuse to give up my claim to being the best shot."

Lily laughed too before turning back to Annie. "So, tell me, Anne didn't cause you much trouble, did she, Jordan?" Lily laughed again. But she soon stopped, glancing back and forth between both of them. "Neither of you has a smile on your face."

"No trouble at all," Jordan replied in a flat voice.

Annie tried to laugh but the sound that came out was short and dry.

Lily folded her arms over her chest and narrowed her eyes on Annie. "You *did* act properly, didn't you, Anne?"

All Annie could do was nod. And gulp.

"Jordan?" Lily's voice held a warning tone. "Is she telling the truth?"

Jordan glanced at Annie. "The entire time was almost entirely uneventful."

Annie bit the inside of her cheek. Lightning would strike him if he kept telling fibs like that. The last four weeks flashed through her mind like a shocking play. The night she'd climbed up the vine, the ride in the park, the Lindworths' ball and their first kiss, the Roths'

library, the scene in the theater, the Gray Horse Inn, an
then their last two weeks together, culminating in th
final night she'd spent at his house. Lily wanted to kno
if she'd acted properly. The truth was she'd done ever
thing *but* act properly.

She glanced at Jordan, praying he would keep h
secrets.

Lily continued to look back and forth between th
two of them, her arms folded over her chest. "Are yo
quite sure there isn't something I should know?"

Jordan's voice was smooth. "Nothing at all, Lad
Colton."

Annie expelled her breath in a long rush. He wasn
going to betray her. Thank goodness. He would keep h
secrets and she would keep his, it seemed.

A smile spread across Lily's face. "Oh, I know it
serious if you're calling me Lady Colton now. Do con
in the house." She offered her arm to Jordan and glance
up at Annie. "We'll see you after your ride, Anne."

Annie nodded and nudged Annabelle with her kne
to start the horse back into a trot and leave as quickly a
possible.

One last bit of conversation floated on the breeze be
fore Jordan and Lily slipped inside the house togethe
"So, Devon tells me you're no longer keeping compan
with Signorina Monrovia. I cannot tell you how glad
am to hear it," Lily said.

Annie's breath caught in her dry throat. Jordan ha
ended his affair with his mistress? A smile broke o
across her face. Ooh, she couldn't tell him how glad sh
was to hear it either.

CHAPTER 37

omehow, the house party meant for Lily and Devon's
ery closest friends had turned into a grand affair. Every-
ne, it seemed, had arrived, eager to hear how the Mar-
uis and Marchioness of Colton were settling into their
ew life after their honeymoon holiday.

The ballroom at Colton House was filled with candle-
ght, music, and dancing, as lovely ladies and dashing
entlemen enjoyed themselves.

"I'm sorry I didn't invite Arthur Eggleston, Anne, but
ou know how I feel about him."

Lily was taking a break from her duties as hostess to
peak with Annie, who was standing with Frances on
e sidelines of the dancing.

Annie turned to face her sister. She hadn't so much as
ought about Arthur Eggleston in days, let alone won-
ered why he wasn't at the house party. "Wh . . . what's
at?"

Lily tugged on her gloves. "I can see you scouring the
om, and I want to save you the trouble. Mr. Eggleston
ill not be here."

Frances pursed her lips and Annie nodded. It was

true, she'd been scouring the room, but she hadn't bee
looking for Arthur. Though she could hardly tell he
sister her affections had recently turned to her husband
closest friend, a confirmed bachelor, and a known rake

Thankfully, Lily didn't appear to notice. "I must b
getting back to the guests." She squeezed Annie's hand
"But don't worry, someone will ask you to dance an
moment now. There are scores of eligible gentlemen here

Frances cleared her throat. "Yes. As to that, Lad
Colton, where is Lord Ashbourne? I've yet to see hir
this evening."

Lily smiled a surprised smile and gave Frances a co
look. "Why, Miss Birmingham, I had forgotten yo
fancy Jordan." She sighed. "I can see why you'd be er
amored of him. He's handsome, dashing, wealthy, an
kind, but a word to the wise, dear, Jordan's not ma
riageable material. Much less trouble to set your sigh
on a man who is actually looking for a bride."

"Oh, I've no notion of marrying him, Lady Colton
Frances assured her with a wink. "I merely want to loc
at him."

Lily laughed and Annie swallowed against the lum
in her throat that seemed to grow larger with each pas
ing moment.

Lily winked back. "Now, *that* is fair game, my dear
Lily glanced around. "There is Mr. Holloway, Jordan
brother Charlie. Now, he is exceedingly eligible." Lil
nodded toward the man.

Annie glanced across the room to see Charlie leanir
against a pillar, smiling and laughing with a large group o
people. As if he knew he were being watched, he looke
up, then inclined his head toward them. Annie quickl
blushed and inclined her head in an answering gesture

"Oh, he is very handsome," Frances breathed. "But 'd have to see him right next to Lord Ashbourne to truly ompare."

Annie elbowed her friend and Lily laughed.

"Speaking of Jordan, there they are now." Lily nod-ed across the room.

Annie's heart fluttered in her chest. Jordan and Devon vere just entering the room. She sucked in her breath.

Jordan looked more heart-stoppingly handsome than sual. Light gray breeches, black evening coat, starched vhite cravat, tousled dark hair, and those piercing gray yes. Annie smoothed her hands down her light green kirts to still their trembling.

Lily moved away. "I'll send them over to dance." She vinked at Frances again and was gone off into the crowd efore either young woman could say a word.

"Oh dear!" Frances's hands flew to her cheeks. "She's ot really sending them over, is she?"

Annie shrugged. "It surely looks that way." She glanced ver to see Lily speaking with Devon and Jordan and ointing to where she and Frances stood. "I thought you *vanted* to dance with Jor . . . Lord Ashbourne." She oughed.

Frances's hands and face were bright red. "No, no. I vant to *look* at Lord Ashbourne. I cannot actually dance vith him. The last time we danced, I nearly tripped him. made a complete fool of myself."

Another glance informed Annie the two men were ndeed making their way over to them. They were extri-ating themselves from the hordes of women who tried o stop them to talk.

"Oh, Frances, Lord Ashbourne doesn't mind one bit. Ie's quite reasonable. Don't be so anxious." And wasn't

she the pot calling the kettle black? Her own stomac
was doing flips at the moment. But for some reason
Frances's sheer panic helped Annie remain calm.

"Oh my goodness, no," Frances was saying. "I'm
hideous dancer and I turn red when I'm nervous and I'r
clumsy. I fear I will cast up my accounts on the poor man

The men were upon them then and Frances made
noise that sounded something close to a squeak and ur
ceremoniously pushed Annie in front of her.

Devon bowed. "Good evening, ladies."

Annie curtsied in response, keeping her eyes dowr
cast. "Gentlemen." She tugged Frances forward and th
girl made a quick bob before quickly retreating behin
Annie again.

Devon eyed both of them expectantly. "My lovel
wife informs me that you two are in need of dancin
partners. Ashbourne and I have come to offer our se
vices."

Jordan bowed then and another squeak came fro
the vicinity of Frances.

Annie opened her mouth to speak, but was saved b
Devon taking charge of the situation. "Miss Birmin
ham," he said, flashing Frances his most devastatin
grin. "Would you do me the honor?" He held out hi
black-clad arm to Frances.

Frances, looking as if she'd just received a last-minut
pardon from the hangman's noose, bobbed anothe
quick curtsy, exclaimed vehemently that she would b
delighted, grabbed Devon's sleeve, and nearly pulled th
poor man to the dance floor without a backward glanc

Silence fell between Annie and Jordan. She bit her li
and dared to glance up at him. Oh, how could she hav

orgotten in the span of one short week just how hand-
ome he was up close? He straightened his shoulders.
Miss Andrews," he intoned, and the sound of his voice
noved along Annie's nerves like warmed honey.

She nodded. "Lord Ashbourne." Her voice sounded
ollow to her own ears.

He held out his arm, clad in pristine black superfine.
Would you care to dance?"

Simple acquiescence seemed to be the more appro-
riate answer than "I am madly in love with you, of
ourse I would care to dance." So, Annie took a deep
reath and then exhaled. "Yes," she answered in a too
uiet voice. Then she concentrated on placing her gloved
and on his muscled arm.

He led her to the floor while Annie racked her brain.
Vhat would they talk about? What a complete imbecile
he'd been for the last four weeks? Their passionate in-
erlude after the ball at his house? The ball he threw for
er to find her another man? Or perhaps the fact that she
vas inappropriately, madly in love with him? No. Not
he most promising of choices.

She shook her head. The music started. A waltz. Of
ourse it was a waltz. Fate's sense of humor was spot-on
f late. And a tad on the sarcastic side.

Jordan pulled her into his arms and the smell of him,
tinge of expensive cologne and something a bit spicy,
nade Annie close her eyes briefly.

"How have you been enjoying the party?" he asked in
flat voice.

Annie's brow wrinkled. "The party? I . . . oh, it's quite
ovely."

"Excellent. The weather's held too, has it not?"

She nodded woodenly. Oh God, he was treating her as if he barely knew her. As if she were some acquaintance he'd just met. She couldn't stand that.

"Jordan . . . I . . ."

He cleared his throat. "Do you intend to ride to the hunt tomorrow, Miss Andrews?"

He wasn't even going to allow her to be familiar. She pressed her lips together. "Considering I have a fox as a pet, no, I do not."

He inclined his head. "Ah, that's right. How could I forget? We have that in common. Devon and Justin are going fishing. I intend to go for a ride."

Hope surged in Annie's chest. "Perhaps we can ride togeth—"

"By myself," he finished.

Annie stared at the shoulder of his jacket. Willing her riotous thoughts back in order. He was making his intentions quite clear. They were to pretend nothing had happened between them. He was Lord Ashbourne, closest friend to her brother-in-law. And she was Miss Andrews, his closest friend's sister-in-law, and the entire last month had not occurred as far as he was concerned.

Fine. If that was the way he wanted it. Two could play at such a sport.

"Yes," she said, her voice calm and still. "I also enjoy a solitary ride."

He nodded, apparently pleased to see her playing along, accepting his rules. Pain clenched her heart. His armor was on. He was pushing her away, keeping her at arm's length. And it hurt to know it.

But there was something about the way he refused to look at her, the bead of sweat on his forehead. As if he were trying too hard. Hope surged in her chest again.

as he trying too hard? Was that what she sensed? Did
care somewhere underneath his supposed noncha-
nce?

Annie drew in a deep breath. She had just one chance,
is one opportunity at the house party to try to crack that
ell of his, to find out if there was a future for them, or
nether she'd just gone and made a fool of herself again.

Annie glanced to the right and saw Lily march past
her way to fulfill some hostesslike duty, no doubt.
er sister's words from minutes earlier clamored in An-
e's brain.

Jordan's not marriageable material, she had warned.
*uch less trouble to set your sights on a man actually
oking for a bride.*

Annie squared her shoulders and took a deep breath.
e'd never shied away from trouble a day in her life.

CHAPTER 38

Annie sidled up to Lord Medford. The viscount stoo
against a pillar surveying the crowd with a bored e
pression. "Good to see you, my lord."

Medford inclined his head toward her. "Ah, the ru
away bride," he said in a tone that couldn't be overhea
by others.

Annie gave him an exasperated look. She didn't li
that nickname one bit, but Medford was so charming,
was impossible to be cross with him.

"You look as if you're up to something," he added.

She smiled at that. Medford was one to get directly
the point. She liked that about him. Liked it immense
"That is because I am," she replied. "And you look as
you're about to die from boredom. Don't any of the I
dies here tonight catch your fancy?"

"They never do," Medford replied with a sigh. "B
you have captured my attention. Tell me. What are yo
up to tonight?"

She grinned and motioned for him to follow her in
the corner.

"I have a question for you," she said, once they'd hidden from the crowd. "Strictly hypothetical of course."

"Of course." He covered his mouth, obviously to keep from laughing, and then shoved a hand in his pocket. "By all means, ask your question."

She glanced about. "What if a young lady—we shall mention no names—were inclined to lure a gentleman into her . . . bedchamber?"

Medford's eyebrows shot up. "Miss Andrews, *please* assure me that this is indeed hypothetical."

Annie shrugged. "But of course. Now how would such a young woman accomplish such a feat?"

"Not," Medford replied, "with the assistance or blessing of her friend the viscount." He plucked his hand from his pocket, crossed his arms over his chest, and gave her a stern stare.

Annie rolled her eyes. "Of all people, Medford, I assumed you wouldn't judge me. You're responsible for publishing *Secrets of a Wedding Night,* for heaven's sake."

A muscle ticked in Medford's jaw. "Keep talking, miss, and I'll march over to Lily myself and tell her what you're up to. She disapproves of Arthur Eggleston more than I do and I hardly thought that possible. Yes, I might as well be out with it, I never liked the bloke, and—"

Annie's mouth fell open. "Eggleston? Oh no, no, no. Not Arthur. Why, he isn't even here. No, I'm . . . I mean, this young lady"—she cleared her throat—"is speaking of another gentleman entirely."

Medford narrowed his eyes at her and cocked his head to the side. "Not Eggleston?"

She shook her head. "Not at all."

"Then exactly *whom* are we speaking of?"

"Hypothetically?" she asked, leaning forward.

"Absolutely."

"What if, hypothetically, the man in question was . . the Earl of Ashbourne?"

A slow smile broke across Medford's face and l shook his head slowly back and forth. "Ah, Miss A drews, you never cease to amaze me."

Annie shrugged and flashed him a grin. "So you help me?"

"It depends," Medford replied. "On whether or n the young lady in question might agree to write a pan phlet for her friend—anonymously of course—entitle shall we say, *Secrets of a Runaway Bride*?"

Annie's eyes widened. "Why, Lord Medford. You nev cease to amaze *me*." She contemplated the matter for moment. "I have always wanted to write," she replie giving him a wicked grin. "Very well. She'll do it."

"Excellent," Medford replied. "I guarantee it shall t a top seller. The young ladies of the *ton* will be thrille to vicariously experience a clandestine trip to Gretr Green."

"So, again, hypothetically, Lord Medford, tell m Would this young lady's friend, the viscount, assist he in her plot to lure a certain earl to her bedchamber?"

Medford glanced around before he lowered his voi to a whisper. "Hypothetically," he said, "the viscou would tell her *exactly* what she should do."

CHAPTER 39

Devon's study was a sea of cravats and Hessians. A significant number of the male guests had come there seeking refuge from the ball. Jordan stood in a corner drinking a brandy and talking politics with Lord Cornwall when James Bancroft sauntered up.

"Lord Perfect." Jordan nodded. "Seems as if I've seen far too much of you recently."

Medford nodded to both men. "Ah, never without your infamous charm, I see, Ashbourne."

Lord Cornwall said good night and excused himself while Jordan eyed Medford warily.

"Tonight I've come with a purpose," Medford announced.

Jordan took a sip and swallowed. He leaned one shoulder against the wall and eyed Medford up and down. "Of course you have. You always come with a purpose."

Medford arched a brow. "Aren't you the least curious?"

"I expect you'll tell me, regardless, so out with it."

Medford flashed a grin. "Ah, you do know me well, don't you, Ashbourne?"

"We weren't the greatest rivals at Eton and Cambridg for nothing."

"What rivals? I beat you and Colton at every subjec except arithmetic. And that's only because Colton is bloody genius at arithmetic."

Jordan threw back his head and laughed. "Hardl every subject. Now you're just embellishing the truth We beat you at every sport and you could *never* best u at heavy drinking."

Medford nodded. "Ah, yes, I could never best the tw of you in that quarter. Being degenerates, you did have leg up. That much I'll allow."

Jordan flashed a grin. "It's much more difficult to b dissolute than to be perfect, Medford. You should try sometime. You might find a deeper respect for it."

Medford shook his head. "Where's the fun in that? much prefer to be unconventional without anyone know ing."

Jordan shook his head. "You don't fool me, Medford I've long believed that deep down you're harboring secret much more deep and dark than printing illici pamphlets, even."

A footman walked by just then and Medford tappe him on the shoulder. "Might I trouble you for a glass o gin? And please bring one for my friend here too."

If the footman was surprised that a gentleman ha just ordered gin, the opiate of the masses, he didn't al low his opinion to show on his face. Gentlemen rarel drank gin. But the servant merely nodded and hurrie off to the sideboard.

"Blue ruin, eh?" Jordan raised a brow. "I'm impressed.

"It's a blue ruin sort of evening, I'm afraid." Medfor shook his head. "Now as for what I came to tell you." He eached into his fob pocket and pulled out a brass key. He flipped it over in his palm and held it out to Jordan. "Here is the key to your room."

Jordan furrowed his brow. "I already have the key to my room. Thank you." He fished in his own fob pocket and retrieved another brass key.

Medford plucked the key from Jordan's fingers. "No. That is the key to *my* room." He tossed the key he'd been holding into the air and Jordan caught it in his palm.

At Jordan's questioning look, Medford continued, "I saw Lily earlier, and she told me she'd put us in the wrong rooms."

Jordan expelled his breath. "I always stay in the same room when I visit Colton's estate."

Medford's grin covered his entire face. "Stayed, my good man. Past tense now. You always *stayed* in the same room. There is a new lady of the manor at Colton House and methinks she has her own ideas about who stays where."

Jordan rolled his eyes. "Every once in a while I forget Colton's gone and got himself leg-shackled. But no matter. I don't much care where I stay. One room is as good as another 'round here." He slipped the new key into his pocket.

The footman returned with a tray holding the two drinks. Jordan traded his brandy glass for the gin glass and Medford plucked his drink from the tray with a smile on his face. The footman bowed and disappeared into the crowd once more.

Medford turned to Jordan and hefted his glass. "To a blue ruin kind of an evening."

Jordan laughed and shook his head. "Very well, to a blue ruin kind of an evening. Whatever that means."

Medford smirked at him. "Tell me something, Ashbourne. I wonder if you're still able to outdrink me. Like you could in our days at university."

Jordan's brows shot up and he nearly spat out his drink. "Are you serious, Medford? Do you honestly intend to challenge *me* to a drinking contest?"

Medford nodded to the glass in Jordan's hand. "You know, I think I do. Now, do you intend to talk all night, man, or get started?"

CHAPTER 40

Jordan made his way up the stairs, a bit unsteady on his feet. Damn that Medford. The bloke had put up a good show, but he'd been a deuced fool to think he of the barely-a-drink-with-dinner set could outimbibe Jordan. It had been absurd, actually, his challenge, and in the end, Jordan had handily defeated him. But he didn't gloat . . . much.

He'd had about three glasses of the stuff before Medford had acknowledged his defeat, and as a result, Jordan was feeling little pain, yet not completely obliterated the way he'd spent many of his evenings with Colton at Cambridge. Yes, in fact, he'd barely gotten a good drunk, really. Just went to show how wrong Medford had been to test him.

Jordan climbed to the second floor and glanced around the darkened landing before heading toward his room. He dug in his pocket for his key before snapping his fingers. Ah, yes, he'd been assigned a different room and Medford had given him the new key. He pulled the key out, and followed the directions Medford had given him.

Apparently, the new room was at the end of the opposite hall. He turned on his heel and headed that way.

Blasted wives and blasted ladies of the manor changing the blasted rooms. That's what leg-shackled got Colton. Women were always wanting to change things. They didn't know when to leave well enough alone. He shook his head and kept walking.

He'd stayed up, talking to Devon in his study after Medford had retired, and now he was headed to his room to escape the last vestiges of the ball. God forbid he return to the ballroom and encounter Annie. Again.

It had taken nearly everything he had to pretend they were merely acquaintances earlier. To forget what had happened at his house. To forget that her skin felt like satin and her hair like silk. Her exuberant laugh was like a balm to his ragged nerves and her outrageous antics often reminded him of, well, himself. A younger version of himself, at least. Annie had the kind of passion for living he'd had once. The kind of excitement and faith and belief in things that he'd long since forgotten. He growled. Annie reminded him of things he was better off forgetting. Things that made him wish for something indefinable and almost heartbreaking.

Yes, Annie had that knack, didn't she? Of making him forget all his promises and vows to himself, all his intentions and well-meaning strictures. Annie had the ability to make him feel like the young man he'd been before . . . Georgiana.

Jordan shook his head to clear it of such destructive thoughts. He hadn't allowed himself to so much as think her name in five years. And now here he was, unable to push the past to the dark recesses of his memory. Damn it. And Annie was to blame. He knew it. He hadn't felt

ny of these mixed emotions before his little stint as her
haperone came about.

He made his way to the door at the far end of the hall
nd fumbled with the key in the lock for a few seconds
efore turning the brass doorknob. He pushed open the
olid oak door with his boot.

Jordan stumbled into the barely lit room and closed
he door behind him. Something was off. Why hadn't
is valet waited up?

He squinted into the darkness. Only two candlesticks
urned on either side of the wide bed. Jordan glanced up
nd looked twice. A canopy over the bed cast a shadow,
ut through the gossamer fabric he recognized the out-
ine of a dark-haired woman sitting with her back against
he pillows. He rubbed his eyes with the balls of his
ands and started forward. Nicoletta? No. It couldn't be.

He took two steps toward the bed and stopped, suck-
ng in his breath. No. Not Nicoletta.

"Annie," he breathed.

She reclined on the bed wearing a diaphanous che-
nise and the décolletage alone was enough to pop Jor-
lan's eyes from his head.

She nodded almost imperceptibly. "Good evening,
ny lord," she said with what he could only describe as a
ensuous smile.

He closed his eyes briefly and groaned. "I don't want
o ask what you're doing here, do I?"

This time Annie shook her head. "Probably not."

He made his way over to the bed and stared down at
er. "You're up to no good, aren't you?"

She reached up and pulled his neck down to her face
nd breathed into his ear. "No good at all."

Jordan couldn't take his eyes off her. He lowered

himself to the bed, the entire time watching her full we lips. "Oh God. This is your room, isn't it?" he asked.

"Uh-huh."

He let his head drop into his hands. For a moment h considered staying. Perhaps he had had too much blu ruin. "I need to go. Now."

She reached out a hand and stroked his cheek. A shudder passed through him.

"Why would you leave?" she asked in a husky whisper

Jordan groaned. "Because this is an exceedingl bad idea."

"Is it?" she asked, tracing a fingertip along his earlobe

He caught her hand. "Yes."

"Why?"

He let go of her hand. "Because it goes against ever rule of decorum and comportment I've had drilled int my head since I was a boy."

Annie smiled at that. She moved up to her knees an knelt beside him. "Rules are made to be broken." Sh wound her fingers into the starched folds of his cravat. " thought you knew that."

His warm hand captured her fingers again. "What ar you doing, Annie?"

She smiled into his eyes. "Breaking the rules. Don look so worried, Jordan. Let's see if you really are jus like Lily. Would you ever actually *break* a rule?"

That was it. Jordan pulled her into his arms an kissed her with all the pent-up passion he felt for her.

She gasped. "What are you doing?"

"You're sorely mistaken, Annie. My ilk and I invente rule breaking. I'm just showing you how it's done."

He kissed her, long, deep, slow. He caressed her neck ran his fingers over her arms, let his mouth move to he

arlobe, her chin, her décolletage. Something dormant
ad awakened in Jordan, the young man he used to be,
arefree, fun-loving. Annie moaned and Jordan's brain
napped back to reality momentarily. He couldn't be
arefree with Devon's sister-in-law.

Could he? No. No!

Jordan pulled his mouth from hers, let go of her, and
astily moved toward the door. "I can't do this. God
nows I want to, but I can't."

Annie scrambled from the bed and hurried to the
loor. She got there first, and slipping the lock into place,
he turned and pressed her back to the door. Eyeing Jor-
lan with a challenge in her dark eyes.

Jordan closed his eyes. He braced his hand on the
loor above her head. "Annie, step aside."

"Not only will I not step aside, but I'm about to do this."

Jordan opened his eyes to see her chemise fall away
rom her breasts. She was standing there half naked and
ovely. Jordan clenched his jaw.

"Please . . ." he murmured.

"Jordan, just kiss me once more. And if you still want
o leave you can go."

She wrapped her arms around his neck and tugged
is head down to meet hers.

Jordan lost the battle then. He pulled her lush body
gainst his and kissed her deeply. He swung her up into
is arms and carried her back to the bed.

The next sound Annie heard was the tear of fabric as
e ripped her chemise from her body. Annie's hands
lew to the top of the garment to hold it in place, to tease
im. The ghost of a smile played on her lips. They were
oth breathing heavily. Staring into each other's eyes.

"Untie your cravat," she whispered.

Without taking his eyes from hers, Jordan pulled a
the fabric at his neck and unwound the cloth. He pulle
it away and tossed it onto the chair next to the bed.

"Your turn," he challenged.

Annie saw the hint of chest hair beneath Jordan's ope
shirt and the challenge that lurked in his silver eyes. H
was testing her. Taunting her. "Well?"

"Well, by all means, Lord Ashbourne, show me more.

The compromising sort, indeed.

He slowly removed his shirt, pulling it over his hea
from behind with both arms. He tossed the garment int
the corner. Annie glanced at his chest and gasped. Th
firelight played over his bare skin, highlighting the mus
cles and planes. If she'd thought he'd looked like Mi
chelangelo's David before, he did even more so now. Hi
skin was like velvet, firm, wonderful velvet. The fire
light glinted over his hard abdomen and the six muscle
there that stood out in sharp relief. Oh God, her nipple
ached. She wanted to fling herself against his chest an
rub herself against him.

Annie still clutched the chemise to her chest to shiel
her nakedness. But she watched Jordan undress in th
firelight with unadulterated enjoyment. First, he shucke
his boots, then he unbuttoned his breeches. His eye
never left hers.

Annie shuddered. He was calling her bluff. Than
God. They were really going to do this. She'd planne
this tonight, half expecting him to order her from th
bed or to stomp off himself. But now that he was here
looking into her eyes, making her want to run her fin
gers along his perfect body and pull him on top of he
there was no way she wanted to stop.

She'd made her peace with this decision and now she had no intention of doing anything other than enjoying herself. She'd decided to lure Jordan to her bed and the devil may care about the consequences. But she was not doing this to trap him. No, never that. She had too much pride to ever attempt anything so foolish or calculating. Besides, she didn't want a husband who was forced to the altar. She was doing this for one reason and one reason only. To spend the night—with Jordan. She knew full well he might not ever marry her. She was doing this because she had to know what it felt like to be with him. Even if only for one night. She would love him, truly love him, forever, and regardless of the consequences, she had to spend at least one night with the man she loved.

Jordan squared his shoulders. He pulled off his breeches and slipped under the covers with Annie. He took a deep breath. What in God's name was he doing? Apparently it *was* a blue ruin kind of an evening. But something about seeing her lush and nearly naked waiting in the bed made him so hard he ached . . . He had no thought other than losing himself in Annie's sweet innocence.

But he must prepare himself. It was true that Annie had been clothed and decent both times she and Eggleston had been interrupted in the middle of the night on the way to Gretna Green, but that was not a foolproof method of assessing her innocence. She and Eggleston had been alone together for hours, and Jordan knew from personal experience how tempting she could be. It was entirely possible that Annie was not a virgin. She didn't seem to prize innocence that much, and damn it, he couldn't blame her. But on the other hand, slightly inebriated or not, he had to be prepared for the possibility that she was a virgin. That would be a different story altogether. But there was something about tonight, the way she looked at him and challenged him. It made him wonder.

He pulled her into his arms. "Annie," he whispered. "Are you . . . ?"

"Innocent?" she asked, blinking at him with those beautiful brown eyes.

He nodded.

She bit her lip and pressed herself against him. Her body aligning with his, she touched her hand to his cheek. "I suppose I should be offended by that question. But what do you think?" she whispered. She glanced down to his chest. "I've been to the Gray Horse Inn with Arthur twice."

Jordan's head spun. There it was, her admission, the truth. He'd be a hypocrite if he blamed her, but a bigger hypocrite if he didn't admit to himself that his emotions were torn upon learning the truth. One part of him felt overjoyed that he could do this, make love to Annie without worrying that he'd be ruining her; the other part regretted that he wouldn't be the one to initiate her in the act of lovemaking.

Annie swallowed and kept her eyes downcast. Very well, so she hadn't been completely honest with Jordan. She'd deliberately made him think she wasn't a virgin, but the actual words hadn't exactly left her mouth. She hadn't lied . . . precisely. But this was part of it. Jordan was too decent to make love to her if he thought she was a virgin. She had to imply that she was not. He would forgive her, wouldn't he?

He would be surprised, no doubt, and perhaps even
gry, but she'd already decided that even if she and
rdan never saw each other again, she wanted him to
 her lover. She was counting on his not stopping in
e middle of the act itself—oh God, she hoped he
ouldn't—and she would have time later to explain
erything to him, make it clear to him that she would
ver expect him to marry her. He would never have to
orry about being trapped by her. This was something
ey both wanted, without promises or regrets.

Besides, it wasn't as if she could merely announce that
e was still a virgin. Jordan wouldn't touch her then.
e was Devon's sister-in-law and the unspoken male
de would dictate that he not take her innocence. It was
tter this way. He'd understand once she explained it to
m. Yes. It was better this way and it was about to get
en better. Jordan's hot mouth was on her earlobe driv-
g her mad.

"It's all right, Annie," he whispered. "There's nothing
 be ashamed of."

Guilt tugged at her conscience again. But all she
uld do was tilt up her head and offer her kiss-swollen
outh to him.

Jordan ran his fingers over her shoulders, her wrists,
r perfect breasts. He was half mad with wanting her
ready, and he had barely even started. He softly pushed
r back and leaned over her, bracing his elbows on ei-
er side of her head. He shifted his weight on top of her.

Instinctively, Annie clamped her legs together.

"Shh, darling. I won't hurt you," he murmured. His
outh dipped to her breasts, kissing them, nuzzling them,
aying with her nipples.

Annie head moved fitfully on the pillow and s[...]
threaded her fingers through his dark hair. The things th[...]
man made her feel. She was hot and wet and wanti[...]
him. Ready to do anything to have him. Even lie. S[...]
shook her head to dispel it of that unwelcome thought

But then his hand found her, and she ceased thinki[...]
altogether.

Jordan's sure fingers moved inside of her and Ann[...]
moaned. One finger, that's all it took. He had her be[...]
ging him, whimpering in his ear, pleading with him. A[...]
thoughts of being frightened evaporated, and Ann[...]
spread her legs, willing to allow him to do anything, e[...]
erything he wanted.

She brought her hand down to touch his hard sha[...]
wanting to feel his smooth velvet again, but he mov[...]
his hips away, obviously intending to retain control.

He slowly moved his finger up to the little nub [...]
pleasure between her legs. Annie kissed him fierce[...]
while he nudged her in perfect little circles until her hi[...]
were writhing against him in unreleased pleasure.

Jordan moved fully atop her then and Annie shu[...]
dered at the weight of him. He felt so good. So right. S[...]
wrapped her arms around his neck and kissed him wi[...]
all the pent-up longing she felt for him.

"Annie, look at me," Jordan commanded, his voi[...]
harsh, his breathing ragged. "I want you." His face w[...]
sharp in relief against the candlelight. "So much."

Annie nodded, her eyes half closed.

"Do you want me, Annie?"

Annie could have wept. Here was this man, this pe[...]
fectly attractive man, asking her in the most humble wa[...]
possible if she wanted him. Of course she wanted hi[...]

e was mad for him, had to have him. But he was giv-
g her this moment, this one moment before they did
mething they could never undo, to tell him no if she
nted to. He would stop if she said so.

She pushed her fingers through his hair and stared
ep into his dark gray eyes. "I want you, Jordan. I do."

His hot velvet slid against her thigh then, and he
dged between her legs. Annie braced herself. Another
de and a push and he was fully inside of her.

"Damn it."

The moment he breached her maidenhead, Jordan
ew.

Annie let out a soft whimper. He stopped moving im-
ediately and dragged his thumbs across her silken
eekbones, steadying her face to look into her eyes.
nnie. No. Why?" He kissed her forehead and rested
s own against hers. He was completely still.

Annie let the tiny bit of pain subside. Her nose was
runched up and she couldn't help but gasp. She wrapped
r arms around his muscular shoulders. "It's all right,
rdan," she whispered against his lips. "This is what I
nt."

The struggle played out across his face. He looked
e a tortured man. "But . . . why?"

"I want you, Jordan, please. Don't you want me too?"

A pained look flashed across his face. "God. Yes," he
oaned.

"Then make love to me, Jordan. Please make love
me."

"Oh God, Annie. I don't think I could stop." Jordan
oaned again. He wrapped his arms around her and
ntly pulled back a little.

Realizing she'd won, Annie smiled and wrapped h
arms around his shoulders even more tightly. He push
back inside of her gently, so gently, and Annie forgot
about the momentary flash of discomfort.

Oh, now this was going to be fun.

Jordan maneuvered his hips and Annie shudder
Good God, the man knew exactly what he was doir
Annie had never even dreamed about such things. I
toyed with her, he played with her, he tortured her. H
finger found her again and he brought her to the pinr
cle of release twice, making her cling to him and b
him not to stop.

But he did.

He was wicked in bed, Lord Ashbourne. And Ann
enjoyed every single moment of it.

Finally, he was through with playing games. Ann
could see the taut line of his jaw when he'd decided th
both couldn't take it anymore. He slid into her again a
again, making her feel things she'd never felt. His breat
ing was hard and his forehead slicked with sweat. H
finger found her one more time and he nudged her in ti
perfect circles, again and again, over and over while s
clung to him.

"Jordan. Yes," she called out, shivering on the pinn
cle of pleasure. She sucked in her breath and shuddere
unable to stop her intense reaction to the pleasure he
given her. While Jordan plowed into her again ar
again until he grabbed her hips tightly and whisper
her name in her ear and then shuddered himself into h
wet warmth.

Jordan pulled himself away from her, then wrapp
his arms around her, hugging her to his chest.

Minutes passed. They lay together for what seem

ke an eternity, their breathing matching, their hearts
ating in unison, until Annie fell asleep, wrapped in
e warm comfort of his strong arms.

nnie awoke to sunlight pouring through the window.
e smiled to herself, suddenly remembering the kaleido-
ope of events from the previous night. Oh, she had
en . . . *bad*. And so had Jordan. So bad, but so, so good.
  She glanced over to the opposite side of the bed, ex-
cting to see him sleeping. Instead, Jordan was propped
against the pillows. He clutched his dark head in his
nds. He'd never looked so disheveled and so . . . won-
rful. The man was an Adonis even first thing in the
orning. Completely unfair.

"Are you all right?" she asked.

He cracked a smile. "A bit of a headache but nothing
lon't deserve."

"Can I get you anything?"

Lifting his head, he glanced over at her. "Annie, we
ust talk."

She rolled over, leaned up on one elbow, and kissed
m on the cheek. "No."

He looked twice. "No? What do you mean, no?"

"I mean I refuse to talk to you." She sat up and wrapped
r arms around his neck. "Let's do what we did last
ght again."

He gently pulled her arms from around his neck and
shed away from her. "I need to keep you at arm's
ngth. Look, last night was—"

"No!" She nearly shouted this time.

He winced and pressed his fingers to his temples.

"I'm sorry," she whispered, biting her lip. "I didn't
ean to be so loud."

He groaned. "Will you please tell me why you refu
to talk to me?"

She rolled her eyes. "I know exactly what you're g
ing to say."

"Really?" He arched a brow. "That's interesting, giv
that *I* don't know exactly what I intend to say."

"You're going to say something insane like you mu
do the right thing and marry me now, et cetera."

"I—"

"And you'll go to Devon right now and offer for me
He smiled at her. "Anything else?"

"Yes. You won't go to Devon and you won't go
Lily."

"How can you be so sure?"

"Because if you go to Lily and Devon, I will tell the
that you ravished me last night. Right here, in their ov
home."

Jordan crossed his arms over his chest. "And yo
think Devon will disagree with my offer of marria;
then?"

"Not at all. I merely think he'll be too preoccupie
with loading his pistol to ask any questions about th
nuptials."

Jordan's face turned a shade paler. He narrowed h
eyes at her. "You wouldn't dare."

"I would dare. If you dare." She propped herself u
against her pillows, pulling up the sheet over her breast
and crossed her arms over her chest. "So you and I a
going to make a pact. You won't say a word about any
this to Lily and Devon and neither will I."

"It's that simple, is it?"

"Yes," she answered with a bright smile. "Now, yo
must go."

His eyes widened. "Kicking me out already?"

"No, not at all. It's just that . . ." She bit her lip again. ow that I realize what time it is, Mary will be here in s than five minutes."

Jordan tossed the covers aside, grabbed his clothing l boots, and raced for the door.

CHAPTER 41

Annie awoke later in the morning with a huge smile [on] her face. She rolled over, hugged her pillow, and squeal[ed,] kicking her feet rapidly against the mattress.

"What has got into you, miss?" Mary asked.

Gasping, Annie rolled to her side to eye the maid, w[ho] sat in a chair by the window darning a pair of stockin[gs.] "I didn't know you were still here, Mary."

"Been 'ere all morning waiting fer ye ta wake[.] Ye've slept 'alf the day away. I came at my usual time a[nd] ye told me to come back, ye needed more sleep. 'Ow i[s] that I remember it and ye don't?" She shook her head.

Annie hid her smile behind the sheets. "Oh, I reme[m-] ber," she said in a singsong voice.

"'Ere I am, back again, and this time I'm determin[ed] to 'elp ye wit yer bath and dressing."

Annie stretched her arms over her head. The ac[hes] were a bit unfamiliar but *so* delicious. "By all mea[ns,] let's get started." She tossed off the covers and spra[ng] out of bed.

Mary shook her head again. "I swear I don't rec[-]

e last time I saw ye so happy. And Mr. Eggleston isn't
en here. What's got into ye?"

Annie pulled her chemise over her head. She'd tossed
a new one just before Mary arrived this morning.
e'd already changed the sheets and hidden her ripped
emise. She'd do away with that incriminating evidence
ter.

"Oh, I'm just expecting to have a very good day to-
y, that is all." She winked at Mary.

The bath had already been prepared in her adjoining
amber and she waltzed over there humming to herself
d performing a couple of dance steps she'd particu-
rly enjoyed from the night before.

Annie poked one toe into the bath to test its tempera-
re, then slid into the hot water and let it cover her
ad. Mary crossed her arms over her chest. When An-
e's head resurfaced, the maid wore a suspicious look on
r face. "What is it exactly you plan to do today?"

Annie closed her eyes and slipped beneath the water
ain. She wasn't about to say it out loud. What she
anned to do today was simply scandalous.

She pursed her lips under the water and let the bubbles
at to the surface. What she planned to do today was
nvince Jordan Holloway to make love to her again.

CHAPTER 42

After dipping into the breakfast room for a scone and cup of tea, Annie found her sister sitting in the gold s lon with several of the other female guests. Annie swu into the room biting her lips to hide her smile. It w such a pleasure to see her sister as the gracious Socie hostess she was born to be. Lily, who had once be whispered about due to her scandalous pamphlet, w now the toast of Society, it seemed. The same wom who had questioned Lily's honor were now vying f invitations to her house party.

Now that Lily and Devon were married, they we entirely respectable. Lily was a marchioness, after a and to everyone's amazement, it had turned out that Lo Colton was wealthy, after having spent years trying convince everyone he was not. Yes, Lily and Devon we welcomed back into the fold with open arms, even if t *ton* did believe the two of them had run off to Gret Green to marry on a whim.

It wasn't even true, of course, but Lily and Devon h been entirely forgiven. They'd waited five long years, a ter all, or so the ladies who discussed it behind their te

ps said. They'd waited five long years and they couldn't
ait as much as one more day to be together. And who
uld blame them? They were so very much in love.

And so, when Annie entered the salon wearing a soft
nk day dress and saw Lily chatting with Lady Fox-
wn and Lady Hathaway, she smiled to herself. Lily
oked smart in her amethyst-colored day dress. The
ters, who had been completely destitute just months
o, were now dressed in the latest fashions. Stylish, the
n called them in fact.

Annie shook her head. It was comical, really, how
ickly Society changed its fickle collective mind.

Lily glanced up from both her sewing and her con-
rsation. "There you are, Anne. I'd begun to worry
out you."

Annie flashed her sister a wide smile and spun in a
rcle. "Yes, it seems I was a bit tired after all the . . .
ncing last night. I slept in this morning."

Lily glanced at the clock on the nearby mantelpiece.
can see that."

"Good morning, Miss Andrews," Lady Foxdown said
ith a wide, approving smile. "I do hope you'll join us."

Annie plucked a Michaelmas daisy from a vase on the
de table and inhaled its sweet scent. There was no way
e could sit still and embroider today. The sun was shin-
g, the air was crisp, and she felt better than she had in
age. "I'm going for a walk, actually," she announced.

Lily barely glanced up this time. "Devon and Justin
ave gone fishing, but the rest of the men have all gone
f to ride not long ago. If you stay to the road past the
eadow you might see them."

Annie's stomach dropped a bit. She was suddenly
y, nervous. The thought of seeing Jordan again after

their night together made her hands tremble. Wh
would it be like between them today? How would
treat her? Would he give her that sensuous smile he ga
her last night just before he—

"Anne, did you hear me?"

With a start, Annie dropped the daisy and bent ov
quickly to scoop it from the rug. "Yes . . . uh . . . pardon

"I asked if you'd be back in time for tea."

"Oh well, yes. Yes, of course." Would Jordan be
tea? "I'll just be off then. See you this afternoon." S
waved as she left.

Grabbing up a small satchel one of the maids had pr
pared for her, Annie made her way out the back doors
the terrace and along the gravel path into the garder
Instead of taking the lane near the meadow, she opt
instead for the one that led through the forest. She walk
briskly, allowing the wind to whip her face and the sm
to touch her cheeks despite her bonnet. Oh, she had th
odd sore spot and twinge from the night before, but th
made her smile.

"I still can't believe I did it," she whispered to herse
bending to scoop up a small pile of leaves and breathe
their autumnal scent.

Feeling decidedly saucy, she pushed her bonnet fro
her head and let it hang down her back. The sun c
ressed her cheeks. Ah, who cared if she got a bit of col
on her face? Today was the first day in her entire li
where she felt free, truly free. Somehow, making th
choice to be with Jordan last night had changed her.
was true that she'd never given a snap for rules, b
somehow performing the definitive scandalous act wi
the definitive scandalous man had given her a glimp
of a freedom she never knew existed. She could do an

ng. Anything. Marry or not marry, have children or
t have children, fall in love or . . . well, there wasn't
ich of a choice there. But still, there were endless pos-
ilities now and they all awaited her.

She sobered for a moment. She knew perfectly well
it making the decision to be with Jordan last night
is no guarantee for her future. If she was going to be
th the man she loved, she might very well have to give
her dream of marriage. Jordan had been perfectly
·ar on that score. He had no intention of marrying. She
aightened her shoulders. So be it. She'd made her de-
ion, and she would face the consequences, whatever
·y might be.

Annie slowed her pace once she entered the forest.
e made her way through the trees and eventually
me to a small pond. She exhaled. Like paradise. She'd
en here to this lovely peaceful spot before. It had
ickly become her favorite place at Colton House.

She pulled a quilt from her satchel and made her way
er to the soft grass by the pond. The ground was
rinkled with fallen leaves and Annie fluffed out the
ilt and let it drift softly to the ground. She settled her-
·lf on top of the blanket and pulled the pins from her
ir. She shook out the long, brown mass and stretched
t on the quilt, squinting against the sunlight that fil-
·ed through the trees. She closed her eyes and breathed
the leafy scent that surrounded her. Then she lay back
the blanket and spread out her arms and legs.

Freedom. Ah. Wonderful feeling.

Annie lay there for several minutes listening to the
uirrels chattering in the trees and the soft swoosh of
: leaves falling to the earth in the woods around her.
e'd always been partial to summer. But autumn, autumn

was a lovely time of year. Why had she never quite re
ized how crisp and fresh and beautiful the season wa:

It took a few more moments before Annie becar
aware that the sounds of the forest were being replac
by the sound of . . . thunder? She rose up to her elbov
Was it thunder? She cocked her head and listened fo
few more moments. And then she saw him, a lone ri
on horseback galloping full pelt toward her. Whoever
was, he must know that a path to the manor house l
through the woods. And what was he doing ridi
through an untouched part of Devon's property? Was
a poacher? Or did she know him?

She squinted. No, she couldn't make out his identi
Perhaps it was Devon. But Devon had gone fishing w
Justin. And if it were Devon, why would he be comi
back from this direction? And alone?

Annie shielded her eyes from the sun with one ha
and watched intently as the rider drew closer. When
was still many paces away, he called out a command
his horse and Annie sucked in her breath.

She knew that voice.

Jordan.

But what was he doing? Where was he coming fro
Crazily, she thought she might grab up her blanket and r
away, but he was close enough now that he would see l
no matter what. Not to mention, a part of her—the p
that had butterflies winging through it at the moment
wanted to see him. What would he say? She held l
breath and pressed a shaking hand to her stomach.

He must have seen her because he changed his cou
slightly, slowed his mount and maneuvered the stalli
right up to Annie's blanket. Jordan tipped his hat. An

haled and looked up into his shadowed face. He
iiled at her. Oh yes. It was her new favorite smile.

"What are you doing out here alone?" he asked.

She sat up straight, her palms braced behind her on
e quilt, her hair tumbling down her back. She squinted
at him. "Funny. I planned to ask you the same ques-
n."

"Why is your hair down?" His brow was wrinkled.

"Why not?" she answered with a smile she felt all
e way to her toes. She'd already tossed her bonnet to
e corner of the quilt and now she sat up straight and
ve him a saucy smile.

Jordan didn't say a word. He dismounted from his
rse and tied him to a nearby tree. "I was just coming
ck from Ashbourne Manor, actually. I went there this
orning to see to some business."

"Eager to get back, I see." She dropped her gaze to
e quilt. Until she'd said those words aloud, she hadn't
ondered if he'd been galloping back to see her. Now
at was *exactly* what she wondered. Her heart pounded.
). No. She would not think such things. She would not.

He braced a shoulder against the tree and contemplated
r. "I told you why I was out here. What about you?"

She inclined her head toward him. "I . . . needed
me fresh air."

"And your hair?" He gestured toward the top of her
ad.

A shrug. "For fun."

"Ah, I see."

Oh, it was good to see him. He looked so handsome.
ie said a quick prayer of thanks that she happened to
 seated. If she'd been standing, surely her knees

would've buckled by now. She shook her head and
her hair ripple over one shoulder. Then she gave him
coquettish look and fluttered her eyelashes.

Good heavens, the man had her fluttering her ey
lashes. She'd never been flirtatious before. Jordan ma
her feel beautiful just by being in his presence. He'd
ways made her feel that way. "I've come to love tl
spot. It's very pretty in autumn."

Jordan nodded. A large orange oak leaf floated fro
the branches above his head. He caught it in one ha
and twirled it between his fingers by its stem. "I've
ways been partial to autumn myself."

Annie grabbed a leaf from the ground beside h
quilt and twirled it between her fingers too. "Yes. I
lovely." She squeezed her eyes closed. *Idiotic, asini
thing to say!*

His top boots crunched through the leaves as he a
proached her. He cleared his throat. "May I escort y
back to the house?"

"No!" The word flew from her lips much more forc
fully than she'd meant it to. "That is to say, I don't inte
to go back . . . just yet."

Jordan frowned. "I see." He swiveled on his heel
return to his mount. "Will I see you back there later then

Was that regret she heard in his voice? No. No. S
would not be sad. This whatever-it-was with Jordan w
just for fun. "No. I mean, yes. I . . ." She forced herse
to inhale a deep, cool breath. "Would you care to jo
me? On the blanket, I mean."

Jordan swiveled fully around. His eyes narrowed
her.

"Or . . . not," she quickly amended, her face heati
despite the chill in the air.

He stared at her. The longer the silence continued, the
re desperately she wished she could disappear like a
od sprite. Yes. Just like a wood sprite. Wouldn't that
convenient?

'Annie, I . . ." He took a step toward her and then
pped. He pulled off his hat and shoved his hand
ough his thick, dark hair.

'It's all right. You don't have to explain." She glanced
vn at the blanket and traced the quilt's pattern with
tip of the leaf. She bit her lip and glanced up at him.

"No, it's just that . . ." He stood there looking hand-
ne and perfect and almost . . . vulnerable. One knee
s bent, he'd discarded his leaf, and now he was turn-
his hat over and over in his hands.

He met her gaze. "It's not a good idea for us to . . ."

She turned her face to the side sharply, as if struck by
words. Other words he'd said, the night he'd found
in the Roths' library, pounded through her brain.
n aren't that complicated. If they're interested, they
w their interest.

And Jordan wasn't interested. The words might be un-
ken, but it didn't matter. She clenched her teeth and
d to breathe through the pain in her chest. When
uld she ever learn? When would she stop doing this to
self? Throwing herself at men who didn't want her?

Jordan tossed the hat to the ground. "Damn it, Annie,
at I mean to say is, if I sit down next to you there's
ry chance I won't be able to keep my hands off you."

Her head snapped back around to face him. Her eyes
le, a slow smile spreading across her face. Well, wasn't
t the cutest thing anyone had ever said? She scrunched
her nose and looked up at him. "Then, by all means,
down." She grinned and patted the spot next to her.

He shook his head and smiled back, biting his lo⋯ lip in a way that made Annie's heart skip a beat. Oh, he was a beautiful man.

Jordan let go of his lower lip and she knew a mom⋯ of regret.

"Do you really think that's wise?" he asked.

She shook her head. "No. Not at all."

He scrubbed his hand through his hair again. "An⋯ listen, what happened between us last night was . . . credible, but we cannot let it happen again. I must—"

"Why not?" she demanded, sitting up and cross⋯ her arms over her chest.

Jordan turned to stare at her with eyes that looke⋯ if they might pop from his skull. *"Why not?"*

"Yes. Why can't it happen again?" Tossing the ⋯ aside, Annie drew her knees to her chest and wrapp⋯ her arms around them.

Jordan paced back and forth under the large oak tr⋯ leaves drifting down around him. "For one thing, ⋯ *only* one. If Colton found out, he'd have me drawn ⋯ quartered."

Annie contemplated that argument for a mome⋯ "Agreed. But the fact is that the damage is done, so w⋯ does it matter?"

His eyes went wide. *"The damage is done?* I can⋯ believe you said that."

"It's true, isn't it?"

"Despite your nonchalance about all of this, this⋯ not something we can simply dismiss. There are con⋯ quences and—"

"Oh, Jordan, please just sit down. I'd feel much m⋯ comfortable discussing this with you if you weren't p⋯

like that. Especially if we're going to talk about un-
asant things like consequences." She smiled at him.

He stopped and expelled his breath. "Very well." He
de his way over to the blanket and lowered himself to
 ground. Sitting, he pulled up his knees and rested his
arms on them.

Now I've got you.

"Thank you," she said, unbending her knees and
tching out on her side next to him.

"We must talk about this—" he began.

"No, we mustn't." She pulled herself up beside him
 blew into his ear. Then she nibbled his earlobe.

"What do you think you're doing?" His voice shook
it.

Perfect.

"What do you think I think I'm doing?" she asked
athily.

"Seriously, we must talk."

"No, we mustn't. Talking is much overrated. Besides,
 just going to repeat what I told you this morning. I
 l deny everything if you try to tell Lily or Devon about
 s. I mean it. This is nothing more than a little flirtation
 ween you and me, no consequences involved."

"Annie, be serious. You cannot mean—"

She slid her lips to his jaw and Jordan closed his eyes
 l groaned.

"Yes I can," she murmured.

Jordan turned to her then and pulled her into his
ns. He kissed her deeply and Annie's fingers eagerly
an to unravel his cravat.

"Damn it. Why can't I keep my hands off you?" he
wled.

Annie giggled. "I don't know, but I'm *so* glad."

"No!" Jordan pulled away from her then and quic[k]
stood. "Gather your things, I'm taking you home."

Annie frowned. "But I don't want to—"

"It was not a request."

Glaring at him, Annie hastily retrieved her bon[net]
and pushed it back onto her head. She stuffed the q[uill]
into her satchel and Jordan pulled her by the hand o[ver]
to his mount and unceremoniously hoisted her up. T[hen]
he swung up behind her. The horse took off at a br[isk]
pace toward the house.

"I don't see why we can't—"

"Which is precisely why I'm taking you home,"
replied.

He wrapped one arm around her waist and An[nie]
smiled a smile he couldn't see. Oh, it felt so good to ha[ve]
him behind her, solid and strong, touching her. [His]
blasted morals were keeping him from doing more. S[he]
sighed. The man might be a rake, but unfortunately, [he]
was a rake with honor.

She turned her head and rubbed her cheek against [his]
shirtfront, breathing in the familiar welcome scent [of]
him. "Tell me. Why do you want to spoil all the fun?"

He groaned. "Annie. You tell me. Exactly how do y[ou]
think this will play out? You won't allow me to [tell]
Devon and Lily but you want to continue this . . . this—"

"Affair," she offered helpfully.

"No. Not an affair." His voice was sharp.

"Very well." She faced forward again. "What do y[ou]
suggest we call it?"

"Madness?"

Annie laughed. "How about a liaison?"

"Not that either." Jordan pulled her closer against hi[s]

"Rendezvous?"

"What? Have you been reading a book of scandalous nch words?"

She clutched at his strong arm. "No, but if you have I should very much like to borrow it."

Jordan sighed.

"Jordan, I told you. I'm perfectly content with this be- nothing more than a . . . tryst."

He glanced down at her. "Annie, you don't really an that."

"Yes I do. What happened last night was my choice. I ew what I was doing. I remember your speech from t night in the Roths' library. You were right. I'm not ing to throw myself at a man ever again. If you don't nt me, you don't want me."

His arm tightened. "Don't want you? Are you mad? l I do is want you."

Her heart flipped. "That's not what I meant."

"Promise me something, Annie."

She forced her voice to be nonchalant. "Depends on what it is."

"You are an unholy temptation and I've no desire to murdered by my own closest friend. Promise me u'll stay away from me, far away, until we make some cisions."

Annie sighed. Jordan didn't know it, but she wasn't out to make any such promise.

They galloped up to the back of the house then. Dev- 's housekeeper, Mrs. Applebee, was standing on the race. No doubt seeing to the tea that was to be served re later.

Jordan dismounted quickly and pulled Annie down. e quickly dragged her over to Mrs. Applebee and foisted her off to the housekeeper's arms. "Get her ▊ stairs before someone sees her with her hair down," ▊ said.

Mrs. Applebee's eyes were wide as moons but ▊ quickly curtsied. "Yes, my lord." She dragged An▊ into the house quick as could be.

Annie gave Jordan one final parting glance. He di▊ know it, but he'd just sealed his fate. Unholy temptati▊ he'd called her. And that's exactly what she intended to ▊

CHAPTER 43

nner the next evening was excruciating. Annie was
ated several chairs away from Jordan but she couldn't
ep her eyes off him. The tone of his voice, the melody
his laughter. Pictures of their night together kept flash-
g through her mind. Images of his hands on her thighs,
s mouth on her neck.

He'd managed to avoid her all night last night just as
'd warned. Tonight she was having none of it.

Retiring to the salon with the other ladies may have
en more excruciating than the dinner, simply because
rdan wasn't there to see, hear, smell. She smiled through
 of the endless chitchat and tepid tea and finally re-
rned to her room with a sigh of relief.

Mary helped her off with her evening dress and An-
 tossed on a flimsy white chemise. She crawled into
d and attempted to read a book. A book. Did Jordan
ally have a book of scandalous French words? Where
s Jordan? What was he doing? He was determined to
nore her, and fine, she'd *seemingly* promised not to fling
rself at him anymore. She snapped her book shut. And
 would not.

Just as soon as the house party was over.

She counted to one hundred to ensure Mary had h
time to retire and then she tiptoed to the door of I
room. This time, she was going to Jordan's bedchamb
She slipped out the door and down the hall, keeping
the shadows. Medford and Jordan had switched roo
after all. His new room was five doors down from he
She'd already stopped by Devon's study before she'd
tired to ensure Jordan and Devon weren't staying up l
drinking. The study had been empty. Apparently, Dev
had retired already too. Best not to think about what
and Lily were up to.

Annie raced down the shadowed corridor until s
came to a stop in front of Jordan's room. She drew
deep breath before she knocked. What if he'd gone hor
tonight? It was possible. He'd already been there on
today. Lily and Devon had planned another ball for t
following evening as the final event of the house par
but perhaps Jordan had left and planned to return tom
row. Or worse, perhaps he'd left for good. Annie's stor
ach dropped. He wouldn't leave without saying good-by
would he?

She closed her eyes and took another deep breath. I
had seemed eager to escape her yesterday after th
encounter in the woods. She raised her chin. There w
only one way to find out, wasn't there? She turned t
knob and nudged open the heavy wooden door.

She moved quietly into the darkened room. Only tv
candles were lit, one by the bed and one by a washsta
in the corner. She shut the door with a soft click, lock
the bolt behind her, and leaned back against it. She e
pelled her breath. Her eyes adjusted to the dim light a
soon she heard the swish of . . . water.

Jordan was taking a bath? Yes, he was. She focused on the copper tub that rested near the washstand. Jordan sat in the tub, his back toward her. He obviously hadn't heard her enter the room. Thank goodness. She smiled to herself. She had the upper hand at the moment and she wanted to keep it that way. She slipped her chemise over her head and tossed it in the corner. Then, completely nude, and feeling oh-so-bad, she tiptoed over to the tub.

"Enjoying yourself?" she asked in the most seductive voice she could muster.

Jordan's head swiveled around. He nearly leaped from the tub.

"No. No," she said. "Relax." She wrapped her naked arms around his shoulders.

His voice shook. "Annie, what are you doing here and . . . why are you naked?"

She laughed softly at that. "Do I really need to explain it?"

She entwined her arms around his neck and bit his earlobe. Jordan shuddered.

She kissed his jaw, his cheekbone, the side of his mouth.

"Annie, you shouldn't—" He made a move as if to get up. Annie slipped her hand down into the steamy water and let her fist close around him. He was already hard.

He clenched his eyes shut and slid back into the tub. "Don't do this to me," he begged. "You promised to stay away."

She stroked her hand up and down and he kept his eyes closed, a pained look on his face.

"I didn't really promise," she whispered huskily against his rough cheek. "I just let you think I did. Besides, this is more fun. Isn't it?"

Without letting go of him, she slid around the side of the tub and slipped into the water on top of him.

Jordan groaned. "Annie, why?"

She rubbed him up and down and he stopped talking. "I want you, Jordan," she whispered.

Jordan's jaw was clenched, sweat broke out across his brow, his eyes were tightly closed. "You must stop." He pushed himself up in the tub to try to move away from her but it only served to push their bodies closer in contact in all the right places. She wrapped her other arm around his neck.

"Kiss me, Jordan," she whispered.

"God, Annie, I can only ask you one more time. Please get out of this tub and go. For your own good."

"I can't do that."

He shuddered.

She shifted atop him and guided him into her. Jordan grabbed at her hips, trying to pull her away but failing. "Oh God," he groaned. "Please."

"That's what I was just about to say to you," she murmured.

She slid her hips up and down and Jordan's head fell back against the rim of the tub. "Damn it, Annie," he ground out between clenched teeth.

He grabbed her then and pulled her to him, kissing her fiercely and moving his hips under her to take control. Annie moaned with delight. His hands braced on her hips, he pushed into her again and again before he finally murmured against her neck, "Not here, I want you on the bed."

"By all means, my lord."

He pushed himself from the tub and carried her to the

ed in his arms. He laid her down there, water dripping
ll around them, and braced himself atop her. He was
st about to enter her again when a knock sounded at
e door. Jordan fell to his side and rolled over; Annie
uickly moved atop him. Her eyes were wide.

"Ashbourne?" Devon's voice filtered through the door.

"Don't say a word," Jordan warned in a harsh whis-
er, and Annie nodded rapidly.

"Yes," Jordan called back in a thunderous tone.

"Ashbourne, I came by to see if you were interested
a drink. Meet me in the study?"

Annie squelched her giggle against Jordan's chest.
Now this was an interesting turn of events. Oh, what
vould her big, strong brother-in-law do if he knew his
nnocent little sister was lying naked atop his best friend
n the other side of the locked door? It was downright
candalous. Would make for an interesting pamphlet,
eally. She bit her lip to keep from laughing again.

"I . . . um . . ." Jordan's breath caught in his throat,
or Annie hadn't kept still. Instead she was wiggling her
vay down his chest and her mouth was perilously close
o his cock. He couldn't breathe, couldn't think straight,
ure as hell couldn't talk to his friend who would cas-
rate him if he knew what was going on at the moment.

"I—" Jordan repeated, sweat popping out on his brow.

Annie's hands were braced on either side of his hips
nd when she brushed her mouth against his tip, his hips
ucked. "Oh God. Don't," he warned in a whispered
alf growl, half plea. "Not now."

She glanced up at him with dark mischievous eyes and
vhispered, "I think now is the perfect time, actually."

Jordan squeezed his eyes shut.

"What's going on in there, Ashbourne?" came Devon voice just as Annie clamped her soft pink lips arour Jordan.

He *could not* stop his groan.

"Ashbourne, are you all right?"

"Yes. Yes. I'm . . . so . . . good," Jordan manage through tightly clenched teeth. "I'm bloody perfect, a tually," he whispered for only Annie to hear. His hane moved through her luxurious dark hair, and lookin down at her tiny pink tongue darting across his cock, 1 got even harder.

She looked up at him through half-lidded eyes ar removed her mouth from him momentarily. "Aren't yc going to answer him, my lord?" she whispered just bt fore sliding her lips back down him again, making hi: insane.

"If I live through this, I swear I'm going to tortur you endlessly," he ground out in a harsh whisper.

Annie fluttered her eyelashes at him and pulled hii from her mouth. "Promise?" Her mouth descended agai:

Jordan clutched at the bedsheets on either side of h hips. "I'll meet you down there in say, fifteen"—he mouth moved again—"uh, half an hour," he called.

"Good, see you then," Devon replied, and the clip (his boots on the marble floors signaled his retreat.

The minute Devon was gone, Jordan snatched Ann up into his arms. He rolled over on top of her and pulle her hands down so they were pinned on either side (her hips, then he started his own slow descent. "Tha was unfair," he said.

Annie shuddered with delight. "So?"

"So, now it's my turn. And when I said torture, meant it."

He moved slowly, steadily down her body. Annie closed her eyes and moaned the moment his tongue found her. Oh God, she'd never felt anything like it. It hadn't even occurred to her that Jordan might use his mouth on her. Only sheer instinct had led her to do it to him. But oh my, had it been fun.

She looked down at his perfect countenance and his tongue brushing against her, licking her, owning her. His tongue boldly stroked, controlled, and Annie moaned again, burying her face in the pillow to the side so no one could hear. She tried to pull her hands from his grasp, to tangle them in his hair and hold him to her, but he held them fast.

"No, no, love," he whispered against her thigh.

"Why won't you let go of my hands?" she asked, a sly smile on her face.

"Because," he answered, his mouth hovering near her trembling thigh. "You're about to discover how good being bad can feel."

CHAPTER 44

Annie hurried to Jordan's room the next day, intent o saying good morning to him and ensuring that he no lor ger had those silly concerns about them avoiding eac other. After last night, how could he want to avoid her They'd done things that were not only indecent, the were probably against the law. And oh, but how she love to do them all again. The place between her leg ached just thinking about it.

She raised her fist to knock on the door, but her han remained frozen in the air at the sound of two ma voices drifting from the room.

"We've been over this before, Charlie."

"Yes, and I just want to be clear about your answer."

Annie's brow wrinkled. What were they talkin about?

"My answer remains the same," Jordan replied.

Charlie's voice was harsh. "You're sure you have i intention of marrying her."

"Absolutely none," Jordan replied. "Whatever her far tasies about marriage are, they will not include me."

Annie sucked in her breath. Her chest pounded, ache

"And you intend to tell her so?" Charlie asked.

"Absolutely. At the first opportunity."

Annie had heard enough. Tears clogged her throat. She hirled around. Picking up her skirts, she just ran. Her ippers slapped against the marble floors and she didn't op until she reached the safety of her bedchamber and er bed. There, she sobbed, sobbed as if her heart would reak. Oh, how had she been such a fool? She hadn't anted to speak of marriage with Jordan because deep own she hoped he'd fall in love with her. She'd been de-rmined to make him fall in love with her.

But she'd been a complete idiot. When he'd tried to roach the subject on the blanket in the woods, she'd put im off because she didn't want him to think she'd tried ▸ trap him into marriage. She would never do that. he'd given herself to him because she loved him, des-erately, madly. She'd known it was a possibility that he light not reciprocate her love, and she'd told herself she as all right with that. Repeated it over and over again ┐ her head, but she'd known it was a lie the minute she eard Jordan say he had no intention of marrying her.

And it wasn't Jordan's fault. He had never pretended ▸ be anything other than what he was: a bachelor and a ke. She'd been the one to invent an entire other future ▸r both of them. One that existed only in her stupid lit-e mind. She'd been the one to tempt him, seduce him.

She doubled over in the fetal position. Oh God, it urt. He obviously didn't feel anything special for her ven after all they'd shared. She was a fool to believe er affair with him was anything serious.

She sat up on the bed and hugged a pillow to her hest. The scent of lavender filled her nose, and she ulled her handkerchief off the nightstand and buried

her face in it. She had gambled. Gambled and lost. Th[...]
was her fault.

But she refused to chase him around as she'd do[...]
with Arthur. No, she was finished with chasing me[...]
Now she mustn't allow anyone to know about her shan[...]
or her sorrow.

CHAPTER 45

The ball that night marking the end of the house party was a blur to Annie. The refreshments, the dancing, the faces. She didn't remember a bit of it. She'd searched the crowd for Jordan, but he was nowhere to be found. She wouldn't go speak to him, of course, but she couldn't stop herself from looking. She had the sinking feeling that he'd already left for his estate. She had no idea when she'd see him again. She couldn't bear the thought of not seeing him again. And she hated herself for it. Besides, how would it be between them when she did? He would just tell her he had no intention of marrying her, and she would do her best to pretend not to care. No, she must forget all about him. Entirely.

But the loud music and laughter in the ballroom had given her an ungodly headache. Finally, unable to breathe, she excused herself from the group she'd been standing in and rushed into the cool, unpopulated corridor.

"Miss Andrews, *what* are you doing here?" Lady Catherine Eversly's silky voice was unmistakable.

Annie turned to face Lady Catherine, her brow wrinkling into a frown. "Good evening, Lady Catherine. I

didn't realize you were here. I haven't seen you at [
house party before tonight, have I?"

Lady Catherine flashed a catlike smile. "Oh, darli[
I came down from London just now with the most int[
esting assortment of people."

Odd for Lady Catherine to appear here like this a[
say such strange things, but then again, Lady Catheri[
had always been a bit eccentric.

Annie tried to give the woman a polite smile. "[
nice to see you. I do hope you enjoy yourself." S[
turned away, intending to excuse herself from the oth[
woman's company.

Lady Catherine slinked forward and slid a hand alo[
Annie's sleeve and wrapped her arm around hers. "Y[
didn't answer, m'dear. Why are you here? You *rea*[
should be on the terrace"—she raised her brows—"rig[
now."

Annie looked at her out of the corners of her ey[
"The terrace?"

Lady Catherine sighed. "London's been a bore t[
last few weeks, and I was at a perfectly dreadful dinn[
party when the most intriguing guest appeared. T[
dowager Marchioness of Blakely."

Annie searched her memory for the title. She did[
recall meeting any such person during her come-out, bu[
was certainly possible she'd overlooked an elderly wid[
She merely nodded to be polite. "That's very nice," s[
said, slowly extricating herself from Lady Eversl[
clutches. "I expect you enjoyed your visit with her."

Lady Catherine rolled her eyes. "You're not going [
tell me you don't know, are you?"

Annie's brow wrinkled. "Know what?"

Lady Catherine watched her through narrowed ey[

here were just a few interesting people at this entirely
interesting dinner party and the marchioness was one
them. She sat right next to me. It took her less than five
ire minutes to ask, 'How is the Earl of Ashbourne? I
hope he's in good health.' "

Annie fought her sigh. So some old widow was ac-
ainted with Jordan. He knew nearly everyone in Soci-
. Why should it be of any concern to Annie?

"That's very nice . . ."

This time Lady Catherine stamped her foot. "Listen,
ir. I told the marchioness that Jordan and a significant
mber of Society's finest were resting at Colton House
s week. The marchioness insisted we travel out here."
dy Catherine shrugged. "She may have gotten the idea
m me. I told her Lily and Devon would love to have
So we all piled into a few coaches and here we are."

The pounding intensified behind Annie's temples.
hatever it was that Lady Catherine wanted her to care
out, she was failing miserably. "I hope your entire
rty enjoys themselves and that the virtues of Colton
use make it worth your trip. Good evening." She
ned away.

"Miss Andrews, *must* I spell everything out for you?"
Annie turned back around and plunked her hands
her hips. "What is it you want me to know, Lady
therine?"

Lady Catherine tossed up her hands. "As we speak,
Marchioness of Blakely is out on the terrace with
dan. *Alone*."

Annie felt a bit of relief knowing Jordan hadn't left,
she was quickly tiring of Lady Catherine's innu-
do. "I do hope they enjoy their visit," Annie ground
between clenched teeth.

Catherine's ubiquitous catlike smile spread across her face like jelly on a biscuit. "Miss Andrews," she said with a sigh. "The dowager Marchioness of Blakely's first name is *Georgiana*."

CHAPTER 46

nie froze like a fox in a trap. She couldn't move,
uldn't breathe. The corridor turned into a nauseating
r of color and noise.

'Georgiana?" she repeated in a thick voice.

'Yes, and may I suggest you get out there immedi-
ly. The marchioness is a widow now, and unless I
stake my guess, she's come looking for her second
band."

Annie's stomach dropped. *Second husband? Jordan?*
No. It couldn't be. "But she . . . she rejected him
rs ago."

Catherine shrugged. "She rejected him when she got
offer for a more esteemed title. But now that she's
lowed, I suspect she's trying her luck at becoming a
ntess."

Bile rose in Annie's throat. "No," she whispered. She
rled around and made her way to the terrace. She
nced through the windows out the French doors.

There Jordan stood, his hair touched by moonlight,
broad shoulders accentuated by the perfect cut of his
ning coat. His face was inscrutable, blank. It gave no

hint of his emotion. She touched her hand to the glass movement to the right caught her eye.

That's when she saw her.

The blond woman stood about ten paces away, a pla tive look etched upon her ethereal face. Annie coul tell from such a distance, but she guessed Georgiana eyes the color of bluebells. She looked like a siren cc to life. And she was obviously pleading with Jord Begging him.

What was she saying? Oh, it was wrong for Anni be watching them, let alone listening. After her little s eavesdropping on Jordan and Charlie earlier she sho know much better, shouldn't repeat the behavio detestable as it was—but she stood rooted to the sp unable to move. Unable to leave or look away.

Lady Catherine sauntered up behind her then a Annie jumped. She clutched at her chest. "Lady Cat rine, you gave me such a fright."

Lady Catherine folded her arms across her chest a nodded toward the terrace. "Aren't you going to go there?"

Annie turned her face away from the doors. P welled in her chest. "Why would I do that? They're viously having a private conversation."

Lady Catherine's eyebrows shot up. "Yes. A priv conversation you desperately need to interrupt."

Annie squeezed her eyes shut. Lady Catherine v like the devil on her shoulder. "It's not my place to in rupt them. It's none of my affair."

"Unless I mistake my guess, Miss Andrews, you madly in love with the Earl of Ashbourne, and wl you may not be inclined to eavesdrop, I have no s

lms. For all you know she could be declaring herself
im right now. Begging him for a second chance."

ears sprang to Annie's eyes. "Why are you doing
? Do you enjoy torturing me?"

ady Catherine took two steps forward and grabbed
iie's upper arms. She stared her straight in the eye, a
l look on her face. "No, my dear. I'm trying to con-
e you to fight for him."

Annie wrenched herself from Lady Catherine's grip.
glanced out the window where Georgiana contin-
to speak to a stone-faced Jordan. The marchioness
beautiful. She'd been the only woman Jordan had
r loved. Annie couldn't compare with Georgiana's
owy grace. Annie was short and silly and had mud-
red eyes.

3ut she would hate herself forever if she didn't at
st try. Annie took a deep breath.

'Yes," she whispered, touching the glass with her
ertips. "But I won't eavesdrop. I'll simply go out
e and tell Jordan how I feel."

ady Catherine nodded. "I'll come with you. For
port, dear."

Annie didn't care anymore who heard or who knew.
conversation she'd overheard between Charlie and
lan didn't matter anymore. She loved Jordan, and she
n't told him so, and if he was going to choose that
ghty blond beauty over her, he'd do it knowing he
tossing away her love. She might not look like a
dess, but she had heart, and spirit, and sincerity, by
l, and that counted for something.

She straightened her shoulders and placed a trem-
ig hand on the cool brass door handle. She pushed it

open. She stepped outside into the cold night air, L
Catherine close behind her. Annie took about ten s
and stopped. Wringing her hands, she opened her mo
to declare her presence.

Georgiana's words floated to her on a breeze. "
Jordan, I was a fool. I made a horrible mistake choo
Blakely. My life's been miserable. Just miserable.
were never happy. Not like I was with you. I want
back, Jordan. I know now what a love we shared."

Lady Catherine squeezed Annie's cold hand. Her
gers were numb. It was as if she'd turned to ice. She
frozen. She couldn't move. The ache in her lungs
her she'd been holding her breath, waiting for Jord
reaction, his response. She *had* to hear it. Had to.

Jordan shook his head. It was as if time suspen
while Annie watched his reply fall from his perfe
molded lips. "Blast it, Georgiana. Do you know I
long I've waited to hear you say those words?"

Annie watched from the shadows in horror as G
giana flew into Jordan's arms. Annie clamped her h
over her mouth, afraid she would retch. She spun arou
heedless of Lady Eversly's attempt to put her hand
her shoulder, to comfort her, or stop her, she didn't k
which. Annie flung off her touch and ran, fled, bacl
the house, through the French doors, down the ma
corridor, past the ballroom, the guests, into the fo
And straight into the arms of Arthur Eggleston.

CHAPTER 47

dan caught Georgiana in his arms. She'd come at him
 a bullet from a pistol, but he firmly pushed her back,
ping her a good length away.

'No, Georgiana."

Jordan stared down at her. The moonlight glinted off
 blond hair. The years hadn't been particularly kind
 er. Worry lines creased her eyes and mouth and she
s far too thin. She'd always been a bit dramatic too.
 remembered that now. Always wanted what she
ldn't have. Always had a bit of the martyr in her.
se things had all been easily forgivable when they
re young. Her beauty and her love for him—or what
 mistook for her love for him—had caused him to
rlook her many flaws. She cried when she didn't get
 way, just like she was crying now.

Jordan's mind turned to Annie.

After all Annie had been through, she'd never once
d tears to try to manipulate him. Even that night at his
ntry house after the ball, when she'd been so sad about
gleston's defection, she still hadn't resorted to feeling
ry for herself. She fought her tears. When Annie was

confronted with a problem, she came at it from a dif[f]
[er]ent direction until she solved it, and he loved that a[bout]
her.

Annie had an indomitable spirit, one that had [her]
driving a coach and four, shooting a pistol with a s[teady]
hand, and defying anyone who stood in her way. H[ell,]
she'd even eloped to Gretna Green with the man [she]
thought she loved, not once, but *twice*. Jordan had [al]
ways believed she'd done it out of foolishness, beca[use]
she was so young, but now he realized it was beca[use]
her heart was pure, full of love, devotion. Annie [was]
nothing but sincere and brave. Very brave. She was w[ill]
ing to marry Eggleston even though he was a mere r[ec]
ter and not particularly wealthy because she thought [she]
loved him and that was all that had mattered to her.

In the last month, Jordan had realized that Annie [was]
the opposite of Georgiana. Fickle Georgiana, who [had]
chosen the man with the most prestigious title, scorn[ed]
Jordan's love. Annie would never toss someone over [for]
a better title. It wasn't in her.

Georgiana looked up at him with wet cornflower-b[lue]
eyes, eyes that had once lingered in his dreams and [tor]
tured him. She shook her head. "No? I don't understa[nd."]

Jordan clenched his jaw. "No," he repeated, his v[oice]
harsh.

She reached for him, but he stepped back. "But di[d]
you hear me, Jordan? I made a mistake. An awful m[is]
take. Blakely never loved me. Not like you did. I ne[ver]
forgot you all these years."

She attempted to take another step toward him bu[t he]
held up a hand. "Perhaps that's true." His face w[as]
grim. "But I forgot you."

She pressed her handkerchief to her eyes. "Jor[dan,]

lan. You cannot mean that. I cannot believe that."
ling the cloth away, she batted her wet eyelashes and
e him her most innocent look.

ordan cursed under his breath. Damn it. He'd been a
ger fool than he even realized. He'd vowed to stay
narried because of *this* woman, the one standing in
nt of him now. The one who he now realized had
er been worthy of his love to begin with. Georgiana
sn't his mate, she wasn't his equal. She'd just been a
tty girl out to nab the most eligible bachelor of the
son five years ago, and he, like a complete fool, had
ned off his emotions, his future, for *that*? For *her*? If
asn't so sad he could almost laugh.

Blast it. Annie had been right all along. He'd lived his
being too controlling, too controlled. What had it
r gotten him? Nothing. Staring at Georgiana, realiz-
she was offering him everything he'd thought he'd
ays wanted, he finally understood he didn't want it at
What he wanted was a love and a mess and a life
h someone who had always truly loved him.

Annie.

Georgiana blinked at him. "Please, Jordan, won't you
e me a second chance?"

ordan shook his head, eyeing her with no emotion. "I
er should have given you a first chance. You made
r choice five years ago, Georgiana," he ground out.
d now I'm making mine."

Ignoring her look of shocked outrage, he turned on
heel and strode away.

CHAPTER 48

Jordan marched back into the house, but he wanted run. Not to get away from Georgiana, but to find An He had to find Annie, must find her right now.

A quick scan of the ballroom yielded no results soon he was scouring the salons and corridors, sear ing for her. Nothing. Finally, he entered the ballro again and questioned Lily, Devon, Frances. No one seen her.

There was no help for it. Proprieties be damned, have to check her bedchamber. He started up the gr staircase in the foyer, taking the marble stairs two time, when a sultry voice floated out of the shado stopping him.

"She's not there."

Jordan froze, his hand on the cherry balustrade. turned to see Catherine Eversly slink out from a sh owy corner of the foyer.

"Who's not there?" he asked, eyeing her warily.

"Why, Miss Andrews. That is who you're search for, is it not?"

Jordan turned around, his brow furrowed. "How did
I know?"

Catherine shrugged. "Ah, let's say I've found it exceed-
ly dull to be a matron and your little exploits of late
e kept me entertained. Yours and Miss Andrews's.
e really is a very sweet young lady, you know?"

Jordan narrowed his eyes on her. "How do you know
nie is not upstairs?"

Catherine crossed her arms over her chest and sighed.
know because I saw her leave."

He vaulted down the stairs and came to stand directly
front of Catherine. "Where? Where did she go?" His
ce was harsh.

Catherine's eyes grew wide. "Don't get angry at me,
hbourne. I assure you, I did my best to try to stop her."

He searched Catherine's face, resisting the over-
elming urge to shake the woman until she told him
at had happened to Annie. "Stop her from what?" His
est was in a vise.

"From leaving." She shrugged. "But it was deuced dif-
lt to convince her that what she'd overheard on the
cony was nothing more than Georgiana's latest histri-
cs. Never did understand what you saw in that chit."

Jordan clamped his hands on the top of Catherine's
ns and stared her directly in the eye. "What did An-
hear?"

Catherine smiled slowly. "Oh, my dear, until this very
ment, I wasn't entirely sure."

"Sure of what?" Jordan growled.

"Why, that you're in love, Ashbourne."

Jordan released her arms immediately, as if he'd been
rned. His voice was quiet. "What did Annie hear?"

Catherine tossed a hand in the air. "She heard t
fool Georgiana say she wanted you back and then :
heard you say you'd waited for years to hear it. Not
best timing, I must admit. It made me wince."

"You were out there too?"

"Yes, but again, only with your best interests at hea
dear. I'd nearly convinced the girl to tell you how ma
in love with you she is. I assumed you'd either send I
away or say the same yourself, but either way you'd b
be out of your misery. It's been quite difficult to wat
actually." She tugged absently at one of her gloves.

Jordan stalked past Catherine toward the back of
house. "Where did she go, Catherine? Tell me."

Catherine fluttered her hand in the air. "I'm not si
how much good it will do. The girl is convinced t
time."

Jordan gritted his teeth. "Convinced of what?"
shook his head. "Tell. Me."

Catherine sighed. "If you must know, that fool Eg
leston came with us from London. He insisted upon :
companying us, followed in his coach. He found M
Andrews and promised her he had a vicar in town an
special license. Apparently the lad has finally grow
backbone. Took him long enough, I daresay. They've
nearly an hour on you, I'd say. Annie's on her way ba
to London to marry Arthur Eggleston tonight."

CHAPTER 49

...nie sat back hard against the cushions in Arthur's
...ach. A dead weight settled in her stomach. Arthur sat
...ross from her, a smile on his face and a determined
...k in his eye.

"I'm so pleased you agreed to accompany me, Anne.
...was half afraid you wouldn't, what with the way I
...ngled things the last time I saw you."

"I must admit I was surprised to see you, Arthur."
...e watched him closely. She'd been convinced that the
...k feeling in her stomach would be alleviated the
...ser they got to London and the vicar, but it had been
...arly half an hour and she still felt like she might retch.
...Jordan was back at the house, talking to Georgiana.
...ere they kissing by now? Were they announcing their
...gagement? Oh, how she wished she could stop her
...ain from thinking. Stop the awful thoughts from in-
...ding her mind.

Arthur scrubbed his hand through his hair. "I know. I
...ow. I'm so sorry for what happened at the inn. I was
...st so . . ." He straightened his shoulders. "I've finally
...alized that I've let other people dictate to me my entire

life. I am a man now, graduated from university, and
life is my own to do with as I will." He nodded resolute
but Annie was left with the feeling that he was still tryi
to convince himself.

Annie watched him carefully. "What made your fat
change his mind?" All her words seemed to wooder
fall from her numb lips.

Arthur puffed up his chest. "I convinced him, tha
what happened. I was so miserable without you. It v
like living with a bear with a sore paw, or so Theodo
said. Father finally realized how intent I was upon kee
ing my promise to you."

Annie stared at Arthur as if seeing him for the ve
first time. Oh, she knew why she'd come away with hi
When she'd nearly flown into his arms, it felt like suc
safe refuge from the awfulness of knowing Jordan v
out on the terrace declaring himself to the dowag
Marchioness of Blakely.

She'd refused to listen to Lady Eversly too. Catheri
had pleaded with her not to leave, but Arthur had a
peared and this time he'd been the one to demand s
marry him and it had all seemed so romantic and rig
for a few moments. It had been an escape, an esca
from that house, and Jordan, and the knowledge t
she'd never be good enough for him.

But now that she was sitting across from Arthur, st
ing at him, she knew without a doubt that she could
marry him. No, Arthur might be willing to offer l
love and marriage and children, but she could no long
offer him her love back. She didn't love Arthur. She kn
that now for sure. Perhaps she had once, she couldn't
certain, but she didn't now. And Arthur had never lov
her. Arthur was weak. Jordan had tried to tell her th

hadn't wanted to listen. She'd accused Jordan of be-
that way. But now she realized, Jordan had simply
n right, not controlling.

And the awful truth was that even if Jordan married
rgiana, even if Annie never saw him again, she loved
. She couldn't help it, and even if it meant spending
e alone without children, she would do it before she
ried Arthur, whom she didn't love, or before she mar-
Jordan, who didn't really want those same things.

Arthur smiled at her. "Oh, Anne, just think. We'll be
ried before the night is through if all goes well. It's
t we've always dreamed of."

Annie reached over and squeezed his hand. "Oh, Ar-
r, it's what I used to dream of, not you. And the truth
t's not my dream any longer."

Nothing she'd thought was her dream was really her
am any longer. She'd been chasing what she'd thought
should want for so long, she hadn't even questioned
o be an adult, make her own decisions, be respected
Lily and Devon and now . . . Jordan. But she hadn't
ned their respect. She realized that now. She'd be-
ed like a child and had been treated accordingly. It
 nothing more than she deserved.

And she'd even gone so far as to try to turn herself
o a different person, calling herself Anne instead of
nie. Annie was her name. It always had been. It was
 and fun and felt right. She didn't need to prove her-
 to her sister, or Jordan, or Arthur. She was who she
 and could finally accept that. The people who truly
ed her would love her for who she really was.

And her looks were perfectly acceptable. Jordan had
wn her that. When he looked at her, she actually
ieved she was beautiful. But even that didn't matter.

Being herself, accepting herself, those were the thi
that mattered. And she liked who she was, or who
intended to be from now on. She liked her very muc

Arthur searched her face. "Anne, I don't understai

"Arthur, you can't honestly say you ever really wai
me that much. I thought I was in love with you and
were kind to me. I'd never had a beau before and it
thrilling for me. But we've tried to marry what feels
half a dozen times and it has never worked." Jord
words came back to haunt her. "If you really wanted
Arthur, you would have made me yours long ago."

Arthur shook his head. "But . . . I'm doing the r
thing. I promised to marry you."

She nodded. "And that is part of the problem. I d
want a husband who is only marrying me because
promise, because he's *doing the right thing*. I wai
man who loves me desperately and cannot live witl
me. You cannot honestly say you feel that way about
can you, Arthur?"

His brow was furrowed. He bowed his head. "I d
understand, Anne. I thought we were supposed to mar

Annie smiled and squeezed his hand again. "I ki
you don't understand. I'll try to explain. But first,
must turn the coach around. I must get back home
mediately."

CHAPTER 50

dan raced into Devon's stables. "Find me your stron-
t, fastest mount, posthaste, boy." He clapped his hands
he startled groom who rushed off to do his bidding.

Jordan turned to follow the lad, to help him himself if
vould get him on his way faster, when he nearly ran
o Lord Medford, who was holding up a wooden stable
st with his shoulder, his legs crossed casually at the
les, a cheroot firmly in his mouth.

Jordan stopped short. "Good God, Medford. I didn't
you there. I swear you've turned into a bloody ghost.
ms you appear everywhere lately."

Medford pulled the cheroot from his lips and smiled.
atherine told me you'd be out here. It was only a mat-
of time."

Jordan shook his head. "Between you and Catherine,
a appear to know everything lately. It's a wonder you
ve time to manage your own affairs what with the
ount of time you spend attempting to manage mine."

Medford pushed his back off the column and strode
ward. "You really don't know the half of it and I

should very much like to go back to managing my ᴏ
affairs, but since you keep bungling yours, I'm st
with you."

"What the bloody hell are you talking about?" Jorᴅ
glanced down the corridor. "Where did that blasted grᴏ
get to?"

Medford paced behind him and took a pull on ᴛ
cheroot. "I nearly handed Annie over to you on a siᴎ
platter the other night and now I find you chasing ᴛ
down to fetch her from that clod Eggleston yet again.
amazing, truly mind-boggling."

Jordan looked twice. "Handed her to me on a whaᴛ

"The night we had our little drinking contest. ᴅ
member?"

Jordan slapped his hand to his forehead. "What ᴅ
you mean?"

"You're really going to pretend you don't rememb
The gin, the room keys? Coming back to you now?"

Jordan shook his head. "You set me up?"

"Of course I set you up. You really didn't thinᴋ
would seriously challenge you to a drinking contest,
you? You're a drunkard."

Jordan clenched his fist. "Why? Why would you ᴅ
that?"

"For someone so intelligent, Ashbourne, you can
extremely dense. It was clear to me from the momeᴨ
first saw you and Annie together that you were perfeᴄ
matched. If only the two of you weren't so stubborn, y
might have enjoyed a nice, normal little courtship mon
ago and spared all of us this infernal drama."

Jordan shook his head and eyed Medford. "Noᴡ
know you've gone mad."

"Nothing of the sort. I always believed you woulᴅ

;ood man for Annie. That's why I left the two of you
one together more than I should."

The groom returned then with a large chestnut stal-
n. "He's our fastest rider, my lord," the young man
id, gesturing to the horse.

Jordan tossed the lad a guinea and thanked him. He
ilked over and took the reins, then swung himself up
the large horse's back and glanced down at Medford.

"I'll never understand you, Medford. I've long since
ven up trying, but I'm not about to argue with you to-
ght. I'm going after Annie." He whirled the stallion
ward the open stable door.

Medford's voice followed him. "That's right. Go fetch
ir little runaway bride, and do me a favor, don't come
ck with her until after you've asked for her hand."

Jordan stopped and looked back over his shoulder at
edford. He shook his head. "Annie's said time and
ne again she doesn't want that."

Medford shook his head. "When in the hell has that
er stopped a fool in love from proposing?"

Jordan blinked. Medford's words echoed in his brain.
fool in love . . . *In love.*

Bloody hell, he was in love. That was this blasted
eling in the pit of his stomach. Love. Love and the sure
nowledge that if he didn't find her, didn't stop her in
ne, he'd regret it for the rest of his days. And if she
ily believed she was still in love with that damned
;gleston, he'd just have to kill the bloke.

Jordan tipped his hat to Medford but growled slightly
ider his breath. "God help you, Medford, when this hap-
ns to you. I cannot wait to watch you suffer."

Medford's laughter followed him out into the chilly
ght.

CHAPTER 51

When the coach pulled to a stop, Annie glanced arou
anxiously. They were still a good half hour away fro
Colton House. She leaned her head out the window b
could see nothing in the darkness.

Seemingly oblivious, Arthur sat pouting on the se
across from her. When he didn't seem inclined to a
the coachman why they were stopping, Annie decid
to take things in hand. Not only did she need to return
Colton House to ensure Lily wasn't worried about h
she also intended to kick Georgiana, the dowager Ma
chioness of Blakely, out of her brother-in-law's hor
and declare herself to Jordan. Many things to do. T
sooner she got started, the better.

She rapped upon the door that separated them fro
the coachman. "What's happening? Why are we sto
ping?" she asked in a near frantic voice.

The coachman cleared his throat. "A man on horseba
has flagged down the coach, miss."

The air rushed from Annie's lungs. A highwayma
Really? Now she'd be forced to dispatch a blasted hig

yman before she could tell the man she truly loved
at she truly loved him?

Perfect!

"Hand me your pistol," she demanded of the coach-
an.

"I don't have a pistol," the coachman replied.

She turned around to face an oblivious Arthur. She
ook his arm. "Arthur, a highwayman's stopped the
ach. Do you have a pistol?"

Arthur's eyebrows shot up. "A pistol? What are you
king about?"

She rolled her eyes. "You know, a pistol? Meant for
ooting someone who's trying to steal your belongings
d keep you from your journey."

Arthur shook his head slowly but a look of stark ter-
r sparked in his eyes. "No. I don't carry a pistol."

Annie tossed up her hands. "A coach with two men
d no pistol? Ridiculous."

Surely someone had had the good sense to hide a pis-
l in this coach. Arthur's father, perhaps. Annie hopped
f the seat and pulled up the cushion she'd been sitting
. Nothing. Drat.

"Move. Move," she demanded, motioning for Arthur
get up. Shaking a bit, he slid to the opposite side of
e coach so Annie could look under his seat.

She ripped the cushion away. A small silver pistol
y on its side wedged between the seat cushions. She
eathed a sigh of relief. Thank heavens. Annie snatched
the weapon, ensured it was primed and loaded,
inted it out the window, and pulled back the hammer.

She could hear the stamp of the highwayman's horse's
oves not ten paces away. She swallowed hard and

squared her shoulders. "Sir highwayman," she shoute[d]
"I regret to inform you that we have little money, [no]
jewels, and I am a crack shot. Furthermore, you're kee[p]
ing me from something I desperately need to do [at]
Colton House. If you don't desist in your mischief a[nd]
allow us to continue on our journey right away, I shall [be]
forced to shoot you, which is something I have no wi[sh]
to do. I am actually a very nice person. I have a fox fo[r a]
pet and everything."

A loud, hearty laugh met her ears. "Is the fox wi[th]
you?"

The voice sounded strangely familiar, but it was de[ep]
and raspy, almost as if it were a trifle disguised. [He]
needn't have bothered. It's not as if she'd know the ide[n]
tity of a highwayman, after all.

Her hand shook on the trigger. "Yes. And it's a rab[id]
fox. I shall let him loose on you if you don't go away."

Another laugh. "What is your business at Colt[on]
House? That which you desperately need to do?"

"I fail to see how it is any of your affair," she answere[d]

The highwayman's voice thundered through the chil[ly]
night sky. "I must insist you come out of the coach, m[y]
lady. My pistol is trained on your driver. I do not want [to]
shoot him, but I will if I must."

Annie cursed under her breath.

"Don't go," Arthur begged in a whisper, and Ann[ie]
got the distinct impression that he was more concerne[d]
about being left alone than about her going out into th[e]
night to confront a highwayman.

"Don't worry, I'm taking the pistol," she whispere[d]
back. Though a shiver of doubt and fear hurried dow[n]
her spine.

"Very well, I'm coming out. Don't shoot," she a[dded]

unced, kicking open the door to the coach and hop-
ng out, the pistol still trained into the darkness.

"You are very beautiful, my lady," the highwayman
id once she stood facing him. He, however, was still
oaked in darkness.

Annie narrowed her eyes. "How can you tell? It's
rk as sin out here," she replied. "Besides, flattery
ems a bit much for someone threatening to shoot me,
n't you think? Let's get on with it. What do you want,
actly? I've already told you, I have no jewels."

"What is your business at Colton House?" the high-
yman asked again.

Annie pursed her lips. "If you must know, I need to
l the man I love that I love him and no one is going to
op me."

"Is that so?" The highwayman slid from his horse.
e could hear his maneuverings in the darkness. "Hasn't
yone ever told you that love was invented by poets and
ols?"

A vague memory triggered in her brain.

"You don't have a rabid fox with you, do you?" the
ghwayman asked.

She narrowed her eyes. "How do you know?"

"Because you bit your lip and glanced away, and
ose are your tells."

He took a step forward then and a shaft of moonlight
uminated his face. Annie's breath caught.

Jordan.

He had come for her. Come after her. She tossed her
stol aside, expelling her breath in a rush. She couldn't
op her smile, nor the tears that flooded her eyes.

She shook her head. "So I've been told, my lord. But
ever believed it."

"So you plan to tell the man you love that you lo him, eh?"

"Yes," she managed through her tears. "And I c mand that he tells me he loves me too."

Jordan held out his arms and Annie rushed into the He scooped her up and kissed her, swinging her arou

Annie wrapped her arms around his neck and clu to him. "Oh, Jordan, I overheard you telling Charlie th you have no intention of marrying me," Annie sa "But I love you, and I know you love me whether you admit it or not."

Jordan stopped then and stared her straight in the e "Love, what you overheard was me telling Charlie I h no intention of marrying *Georgiana*."

Annie's eyes went wide. "Oh. And what did you t Georgiana on the terrace?"

"That she was far too late to win me back. Seems I hopelessly in love with an adorable brunette. I love yo he whispered against her ear. "Very, very much."

He set her gently back down on the ground and fell one knee in the soft grass in front of her.

"Annie Andrews, will you marry me?"

CHAPTER 52

dan and Annie came galloping up to the front of
lton House on the chestnut stallion.

The front door of the manor house flew open and
cked against the side of the door frame. Devon came
rreling out, Lily close on his heels. An entire group of
ests and servants filed out behind them, including those
torious gossips Lord and Lady Cranberry, and Aunt
arissa, who had arrived specifically for the ball tonight.

Devon raced up to the horse. "Where is that fool Egg-
ton? He'll be lucky if I don't snap his neck."

"Eggleston's on his way back to London," Jordan re-
ed, helping Annie down from the stallion with Dev-
's assistance. "And you can rest assured he won't
her Annie again."

Lily came scurrying up, her hand at her throat. She
gged her sister. "Are you all right, Anne? I don't know
at made Mr. Eggleston think he was welcome here.
e Marchioness of Blakely has left, thank heavens. I
s busy or I would never have allowed either her or Mr.
gleston through the door." She pushed Annie to arm's
gth and searched her face. "Oh, Anne, I can only

imagine what you've been through. What nerve he h
coming into our home and abducting you."

Annie hung her head. "He didn't abduct me, Lil
went with him."

Jordan nodded. He swung himself off the horse a
tossed the reins to a nearby groom. "And she came ba
by her own choice as well."

Lily squeezed Annie's hand. "Oh dear. I was so w
ried."

Annie nodded. "I know and I'm sorry. I'll ne
worry you again, Lily. I've acted like a child but tha
all over now." She stepped over to Jordan and wrapp
her arms around his waist.

Devon's eyebrows shot up and he gave Jordan a me
acing glare. "Ashbourne? What is the meaning of th
Tell me you didn't do anything improper with Anne."

Annie's hands dropped. She looked away. F
clutching her chest, she bit her lip.

Jordan pulled Annie back into his arms and hugg
her close. Annie turned in Jordan's arms and leaned
to kiss him. Jordan's mouth came down to meet hers.

Devon leaped forward, pulled Annie out of Jorda
arms, and pushed him into the dirt. Devon jumped
him, throwing punches that Jordan deflected as
struggled to shove his friend away.

The two men fought, delivering blows in the du
gravel, while Annie pressed her hands to her chee
"This isn't necessary," she called out. But it was app
ent neither man was listening.

"I'm afraid they're just going to have to have it ou
Lily said, patting Annie's shoulder. "Don't wor
they're quite equally matched. This isn't the first ti
they've done this."

Annie turned wide eyes to her sister, before glancing
ck anxiously to the fight.

Devon growled. "I demand you give up your stupid
w of not marrying, Ashbourne. Because you're damn
ll going to marry Anne after kissing her like that in
nt of the entire houseful of guests."

Devon hauled back his fist to deliver another punch.

"I have every intention of marrying her," Jordan an-
ered, smiling despite a split lip.

Devon's fist remained suspended in midair. He looked
ice. "What did you say?"

"I want to marry her, Devon," Jordan replied.

Devon's fist fell harmlessly to his side.

Jordan shoved Devon off him and scrambled to his
t. "I plan to marry her, but not because you said so.
 marrying her because I love her and because I've al-
dy asked for the honor of her hand and she accepted."

Devon stood there with a stunned expression on his
e. "What are you talking about? Has the entire world
ne mad?"

Lily clutched her chest. "Oh, thank heavens!"

Devon turned to stare at his wife. "Thank heavens?
e entire world has gone mad."

Lily shook her head, tears filling her eyes. "No. No.
is is perfect. I'd been hoping for weeks this would hap-
n. It's the reason I chose Aunt Clarissa to be Annie's
aperone. Aunt Clarissa is sweet, of course, but hardly
apt companion. I knew Annie would be a handful and
rdan would be forced to chase her around."

At that moment, Aunt Clarissa toddled up with a half-
pty bottle in her hand. "You're welcome," she said to
nie, winking at her, hiccupping, and then blending
ck into the crowd.

They all watched her go with looks of incredulity
their faces. Then Devon blinked and glanced back a
forth between Jordan and Annie. "I can scarcely belie
what I'm hearing. Any of it."

"Believe it, old chap," Jordan said, tugging his han
kerchief from his coat pocket and pressing it to I
bloody lip. With his other hand, he pulled Annie clo
and wrapped his arm around her.

Devon made another move toward him and Lily leap
forward, stopping her husband with a hand to his che
"Think about it, Devon. We didn't want her to marry th
fool Eggleston, did we? How can you be angry? I lo
Jordan. You love Jordan. He saved your life once. If
and Anne marry, he will really, truly be your brother."

Jordan gave Devon an innocent look and a shrug.

"I thought you didn't want to marry?" Devon aske
his eyes narrowed on Jordan.

Jordan shrugged again. "You of all people shou
know that sometimes love can play havoc with the ve
best of intentions."

Devon still eyed him suspiciously. "And you've nev
wanted any children. Anne wants a score of them."

Jordan leaned his head back and laughed. "Chang
my mind. Now I want a house full of them." He looke
at Annie and his face shone with love and wonder. "A
with their mother's shiny dark hair and beautiful brow
eyes, of course."

Lily sighed and put her hand over her heart.

A wide smile spread across Devon's face. He shoc
his head. "By God, you're right. You will really and tru
be my brother now."

The two men shook hands and slapped each other c

back while Annie and Lily let out matching sighs of
ief.

Annie jumped into Jordan's arms.

"Excellent. We must begin planning the wedding im-
diately, Anne," Lily squealed. "It will be such fun."

Annie let her arms fall away from Jordan's neck and
turned around to face her sister. "Call me Annie,
ase. That's always been my name and I realize what a
ol I've been, trying to change it."

The front door opened then and Frances came run-
ng out. She glanced around at the group of people on
e drive. "Lady Catherine told me this would happen,
t I must say I didn't believe it."

Annie crossed over the gravel to her friend. "Frances,
ere's something I must tell you. Lord Ashbourne and I
e to be married. Please tell me you're all right with that."

A slow smile spread across Frances's face. Finally,
e was grinning from ear to ear. "You are? Truly?" She
anced between the two of them and they both nodded.

Frances shrugged. "I suppose I shall be constantly
stracted by how handsome your new husband is." She
ghed. "But I'm quite willing to attempt to accept it. Be-
les—" She winked. "I've seen Lord Ashbourne's brother
harlie and he remains quite eligible, does he not?"

They all laughed. "Oh, Frances," Annie said, laugh-
g through the tears that were now streaming down her
ce. "Thank you for being happy for me." She squeezed
r friend's hand. "And I shall arrange an introduction
Mr. Charles Holloway at your earliest convenience."

"It shall be a beautiful wedding." Lily sighed. "And
ances, you must help us plan it."

Frances nodded happily. "I daresay it will be the only

wedding in London history to include a dog, a raccoon and a fox."

"And the most beautiful bride in the world," Jordan said, running a hand over Annie's hair.

"I daresay the most beautiful groom," Annie replied and the two of them stared longingly into each other eyes.

Devon cleared his throat. "Yes, well, seems the wedding cannot happen soon enough."

"Agreed," both Jordan and Annie said simultaneously.

"We must marry as soon as possible," Jordan said squeezing Annie's hand in his.

"Why is that, my lord?" Annie replied with a smile

"Because, my love, I'm not about to give you the chance to run away again."

Annie leaned up on tiptoes and pressed a kiss to his cheek. "I am going to be the author of a top-selling pamphlet on the subject." She winked at him. "But I would never run from you, my lord. Never run from you."

d on for an excerpt from Valerie Bowman's next book

ecrets of a Scandalous Marriage

Coming soon from St. Martin's Paperbacks

Tower of London, December 1816

e large metal door to her cell scraped open and Kate
sed her eyes. Then she stepped forward, summoned
m one cold dank room into another. She had a visitor.
first since she'd been taken to the gaol.

She opened her eyes. The harsh winter light filtered
ough the only window in the antechamber. The yeo-
n warder wore a blank expression on his face. He and
other guards always gave her the benefit of respect
her title. Whether they liked it or not.

The guard stepped aside, revealing the room's other
cupant. Interesting. Her visitor was a man. She nar-
ved her eyes on him. Who was he and what did he
nt with her? He stood with his straight back to her. He
s tall, that much she could discern. Tall and cloaked in
dows.

The smell of mold and decay, rife in the Tower, made
stomach clench. The unforgiving winter wind whipped
ough the eaves, raising gooseflesh across her arms.
e shivered and clutched her shawl more tightly around
shoulders.

"Ye 'ave ten minutes an' not a moment more," [
gaoler announced before wrenching open the door
clanging it shut behind him as he left. The loud sc
and subsequent clank sealed Kate and the stranger in
small room together. She took a step back. A small ric
table rested between them. She was glad for that b
separation at least. Whoever the man was, his cloth
marked him a gentleman. He had better behave as o

The tall man turned to greet her. He doffed his
but she still couldn't make out his face. He wore a
gray wool overcoat of considerable expense. A s
beam of sunlight floated through the dirty air, let in
the one small window nestled in the stone wall ac
from them.

He executed a perfect bow. "Your Grace?"

Kate cringed. She detested that title. "Bowing
prisoner?" she asked in a voice containing a bit of ir
"Aren't you a gentleman?"

He smiled and a set of perfectly white teeth flashe
the darkness. "You're still a duchess, Your Grace."

She pushed the hood from her head and took a te
tive step forward. The stranger's eyes flared for a mom
and he sucked in his breath.

Kate's stomach clenched. No doubt she looked a fri
She hadn't bathed in days and could only imagine
own smell. Her hair, normally piled properly atop
head, was a mass of tangled red curls around her sho
ders. She might be grimy and in trouble, but she wa:
broken. And she refused to let the stranger see that
reaction affected her. She pushed up her chin and e
him warily.

He stepped forward then, into the light, and Kate n
rowed her eyes on his face, rapidly assessing every det

didn't know him. But whoever he was, the man was
dsome. Devastatingly so. Perhaps in his early thirties,
ad dark-brown cropped hair, a perfectly straight nose,
uare jaw. But his eyes were what truly captivated.
el in color, nearly green, assessing, knowing, intel-
nt eyes. They stole her breath. Lower, the faintest hint
smile rested upon expertly molded male lips.

Do you know who I am?" His voice splintered the
t cold like a hammer hitting ice.

he regarded him with a steady stare. "Are you a bar-
r? Come for my defense?"

he man furrowed his brow. "You haven't yet been
n access to a barrister?"

he straightened her shoulders. "I've been . . . waiting."

he stranger's captivating eyes narrowed on her.
m what I understand, you've been in gaol for at least
rtnight. I find it difficult to believe a lady of your sta-
has not yet met with a barrister."

he lifted her chin. "Be that as it may, I have not."

I'm sorry to disappoint, Your Grace, but no, I am no
rister."

Not a barrister? Then who are you and why have
come to visit me? Please don't tell me it's just to see
spectacle of a duchess accused of murder."

His gaze remained pinned to her face, his eyes still
ssing, wary. "I am here to assist you, Your Grace."

Assist me?" she scoffed, stepping forward to get a
er look at the man. "I rather doubt that. Assist your-
perhaps. Tell me, how much did you bribe the gaoler
et you see the infamous duchess who shot her hus-
d?"

The stranger arched a brow. "Did you? Murder your
band?"

She clenched her jaw. Then she laughed. "Oh, b[u] course. Didn't you know? My husband, the Duk[e] Markingham, made it public that he intended to se[e] divorce. Being divorced would have caused a hor[r] scandal. I couldn't allow that. So, naturally . . ." squeezed her fists against the fabric of her shawl, tw[ist]ing it so tightly that her fingers ached. "Naturally, I [de]cided to shoot him, causing an even worse scandal. Ma[kes] perfect sense. Don't you agree?"

The corner of the stranger's mouth quirked up. "[My] apologies, Your Grace. It was not my intention to off[end] I assure you, I'm not a common gossipmonger com[e to] witness your degradation. I intend to assist you. [And] yes, in return, there is something I want."

She lifted both brows. "So, tell me then. What is [it]

He swept another bow. "I've come to make you [an] offer, Your Grace. One that can benefit us both."

Pulling her shawl over her shoulders more tigh[tly] Kate crossed her arms over her chest. "Forgive me [I] am a bit doubtful, sir. I've seen enough deception in [my] twenty-eight years to be highly skeptical of the prom[ises] of men."

His head quirked to the side and he regarded her w[ith] an inquisitive look. Her statement had obviously surpr[ised] him. "I understand, Your Grace. And I fully inten[d to] explain. But first, I must ask for your discretion. If [we] are to help each other, I cannot reveal my identity un[til] you promise to keep what I am about to tell you enti[rely] secret."

She pursed her lips and narrowed her eyes on h[im] "Secret? Are you a spy?"

His brow rose, and tension seemed to radiate thro[ugh] his body. "Would you aid me if I were?"

he pointed toward the door. "Get out," she said
ugh clenched teeth.

Pardon?"

Her nails dug so hard into her shawl she was certain
would rip the fabric. "I may be accused of a murder
I not commit, but being called a traitor to my home-
I is not an insult I will bear. If you are seeking my
in that manner, you most certainly have come to the
ng person. I am not, and never will be, that desper-
" She turned toward the door to call for the gaoler.

The stranger quickly held up a hand. "I assure you,
r Grace. I am no spy."

Kate snapped her mouth closed and turned back to
, still eyeing him warily. "Then what exactly do you
t from me?"

He nodded slowly. "Your promise, first?"

She watched him, assessing him from the top of his
dsome head to the tips of his precisely polished—
obviously expensive—top boots. Apparently, this
n was willing or desperate enough to trust an accused
rderess, too. Interesting. She had absolutely no rea-
to trust him, however. Every reason not to, actually.
conversing with a handsome stranger about whatever
t idea he had was preferable to counting the cracks in
walls of her cell or writing letters to . . . nobody.
ry well, you have my promise. Now tell me, who are
and why are you here?"

The stranger clicked his heels together and bowed
in. "James Bancroft, Viscount Medford, at your ser-
e."

She couldn't help the tiny gasp that escaped her lips.
aristocrat. The man was a peer. Why on earth would
eer pay her a visit? "Why are you here, my lord?"

Brushing back his coat, he pulled papers from ar
side pocket and tossed them on the wooden table.

Her eyes still trained on him, Kate stepped forw
and picked up the papers. She scanned the first pag
was a pamphlet. She shuffled through the stack. But
pages were blank.

She gestured to the papers with her chin. "Wha
this?"

His mouth quirked again. Distracting, that. "You m
say I have a bit of a hobby on the side. A printing pre

Her gaze snapped to his face and she stepped ba
clutching the pamphlet, genuinely surprised. And a li
bit intrigued. "A viscount in trade?"

He grinned. "That's the secret." His grin faded
he strode forward. Bracing his hands apart, he lea
across the table. "I offer women in scandalous situati
a unique opportunity. This, Your Grace, is a chance
tell your side of the story. . . ."

"What do you mean . . . exactly?"

His eyes blazed at her. His jaw tightened. "Writ
pamphlet for me. It will be a top seller, I assure you."

She shook her head. "A pamphlet? Telling my sto
What do I stand to gain from it?"

His eyes, dark green now, captured hers. "What
you want?"

Kate spun around, pacing across the small room
chance to tell her story? A frisson of hope skittered do
her spine. Yes. An opportunity to inform the entire c
what a hideous husband George had been. To tell
truth. Lord Medford didn't know it, but he'd just offe
her what she truly wanted. She must handle this ca
fully, however. There was something else she want
Well, two things actually. She turned back toward hi

d what exactly will the pamphlet be named, my
?"

is jaw relaxed and his eyes lost some of their inten-
He stood up again to his full height and regarded
down the length of his nose. "*Secrets of a Scandalous
riage.*"

APACK